PRINCESS CANDY

THE COMPLETE COMICS COLLECTION

WRITTEN BY
MICHAEL DAHL & SCOTT NICKEL

ILLUSTRATED BY
JEFF CROWTHER

STONE ARCH BOOKS
a capstone imprint

WRITTEN BY
MICHAEL DAHL & SCOTT NICKEL
ILLUSTRATED BY
JEFF CROWTHER

DESIGNER: **HILARY WACHOLZ**
EDITOR: **CHRISTOPHER HARBO**

Stone Arch Graphic Novels are published
by Stone Arch Books, an imprint of Capstone.
1710 Roe Crest Drive, North Mankato, Minnesota 56003
www.capstonepub.com

Library of Congress Cataloging-in-Publication Data is available on the Library of Congress website.
ISBN: 978-1-4965-8731-2 (library binding)
ISBN: 978-1-4965-9320-7 (paperback)
ISBN: 978-1-4965-8735-0 (eBook PDF)

Summary: On Halo Nightly's eleventh birthday, her Aunt Pandora gives her a collection of jars filled with
brightly colored candies. Soon she learns that the candies give her the incredible powers of nature. Halo
uses the powers to combat the evil Doozie Hiss and other sour-villains at Midnight Elementary School.

Printed and bound in China.
2493

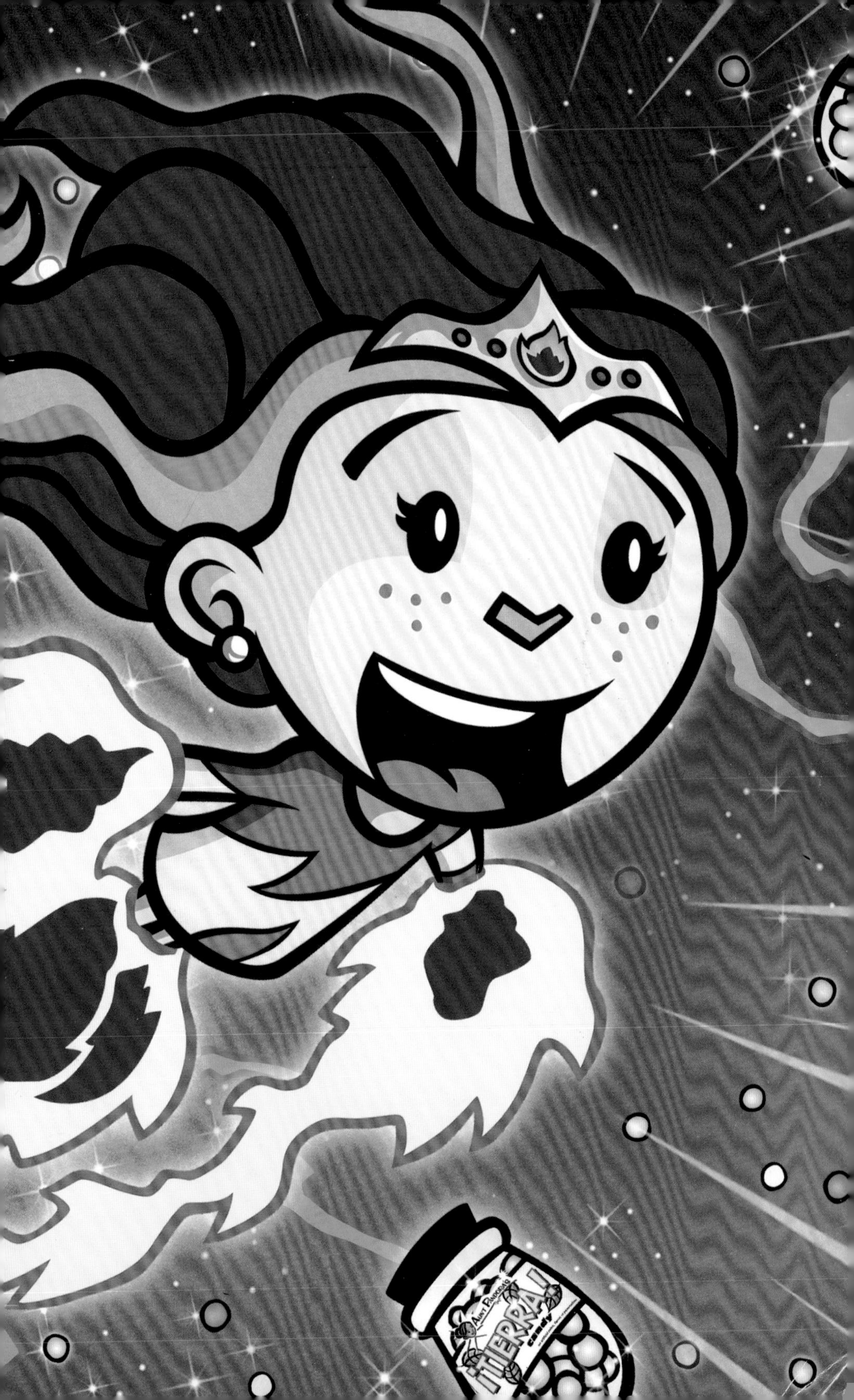
AUNT PANDORA'S
¡TIERRA!
candy

CONTENTS

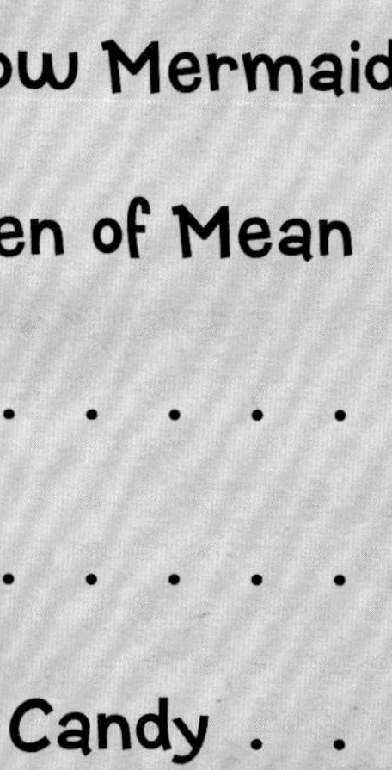

¡AGUA!
candy

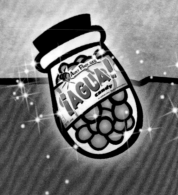

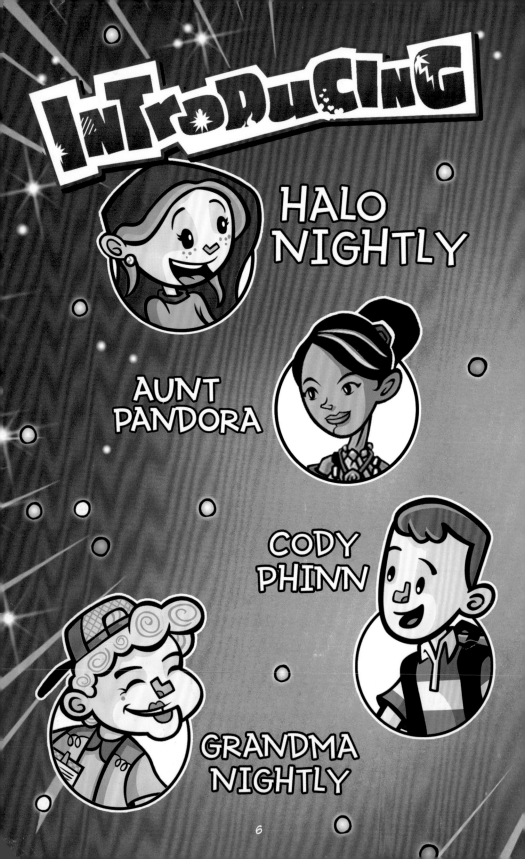

INTRODUCING

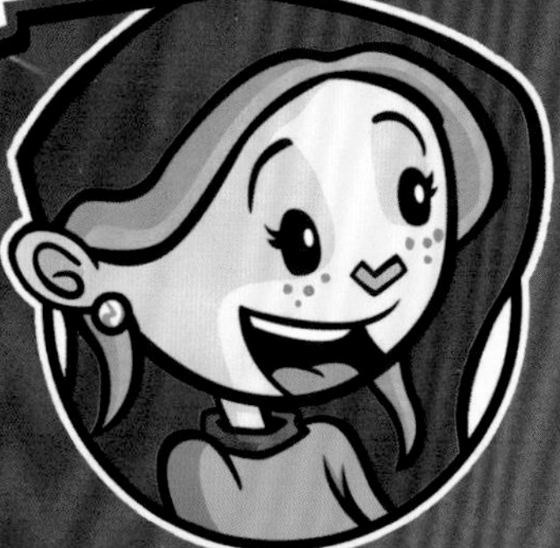

HALO NIGHTLY

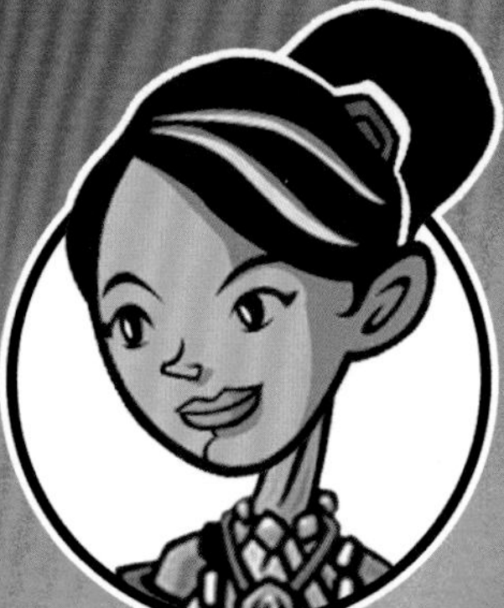

AUNT PANDORA

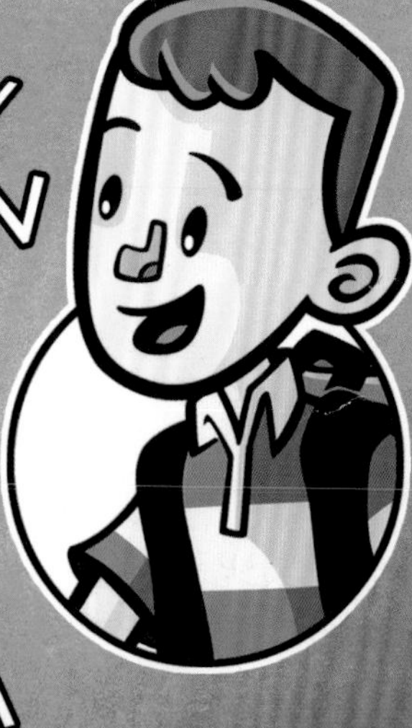

CODY PHINN

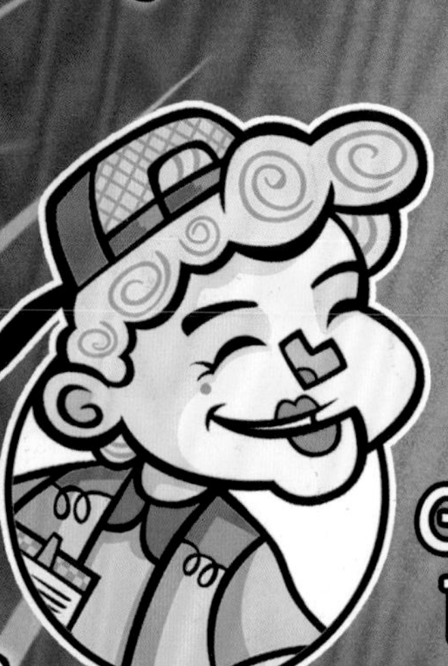

GRANDMA NIGHTLY

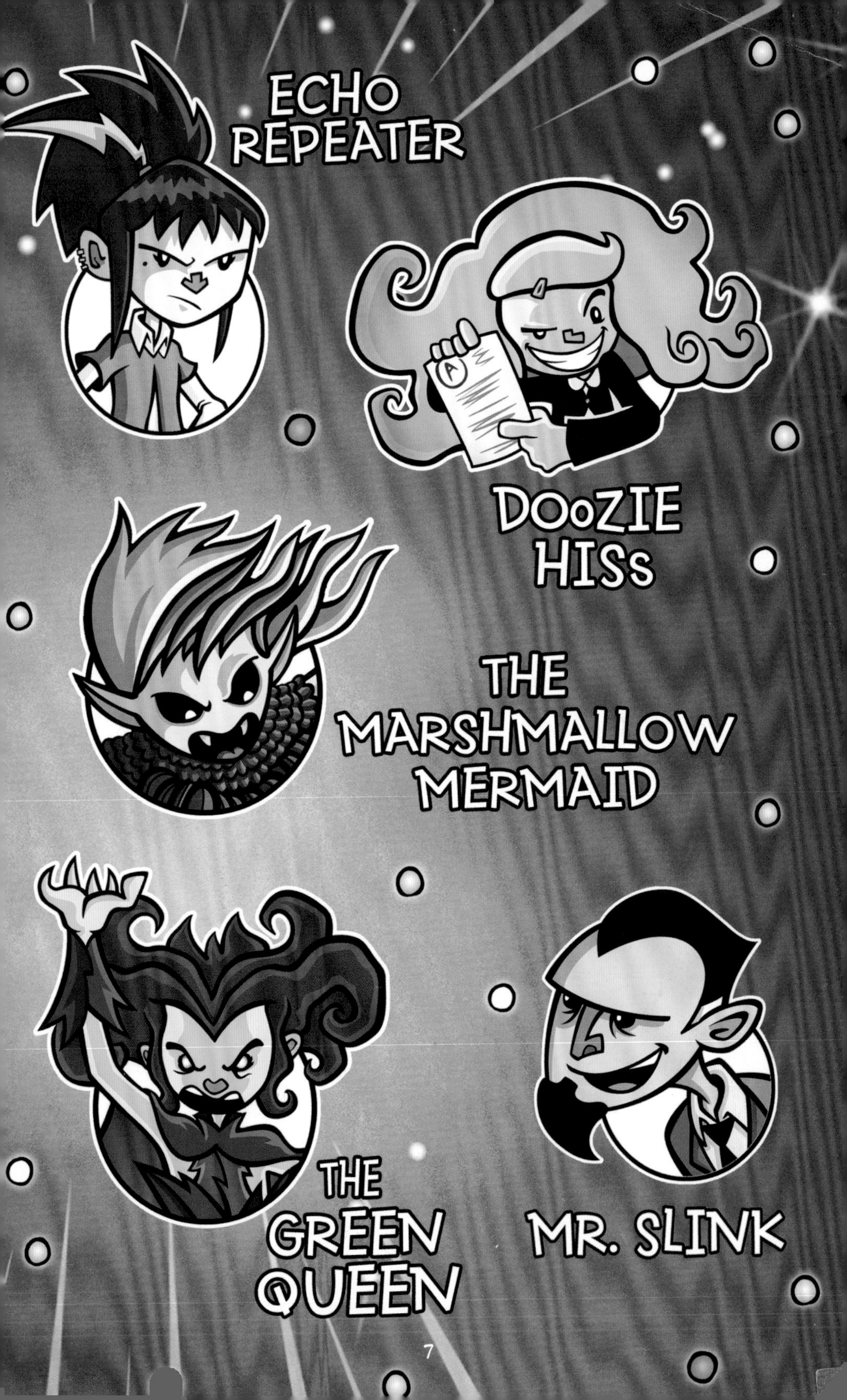
ECHO REPEATER
DOoZIE HISs
THE MARSHMALLOW MERMAID
THE GREEN QUEEN
MR. SLINK

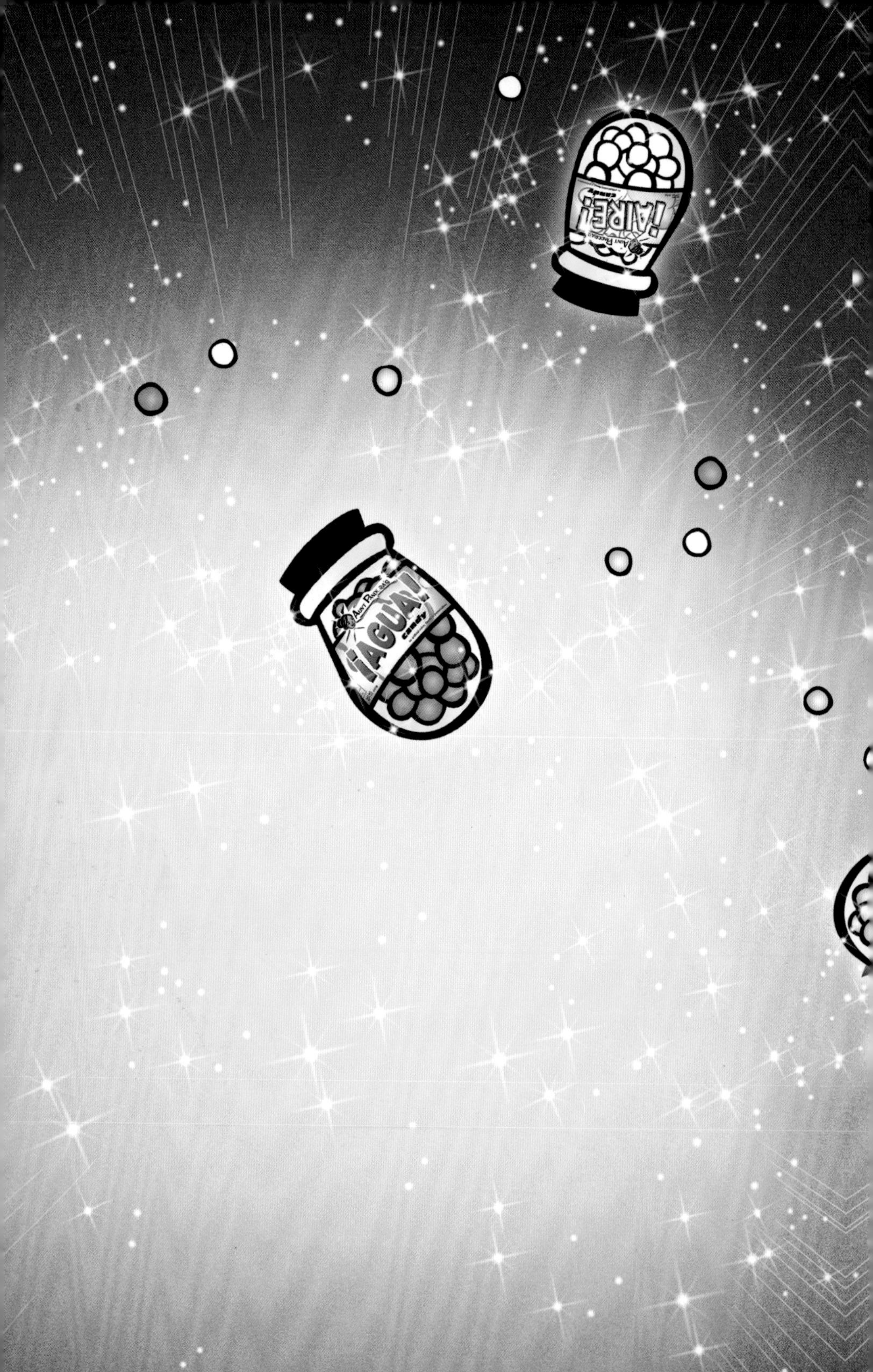
¡AIRE!
candy
¡AGUA!
candy

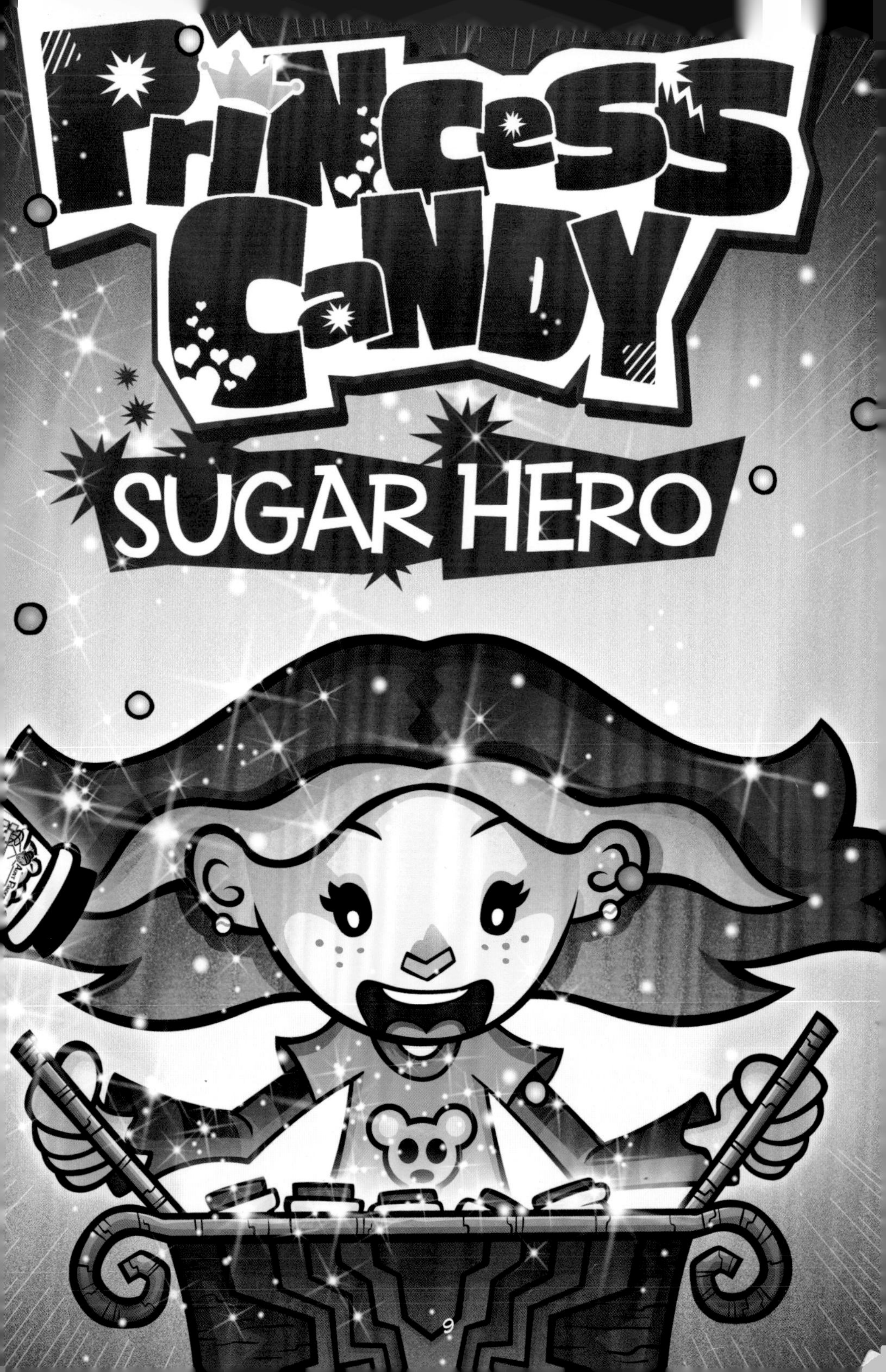
PRINCESS CANDY
SUGAR HERO

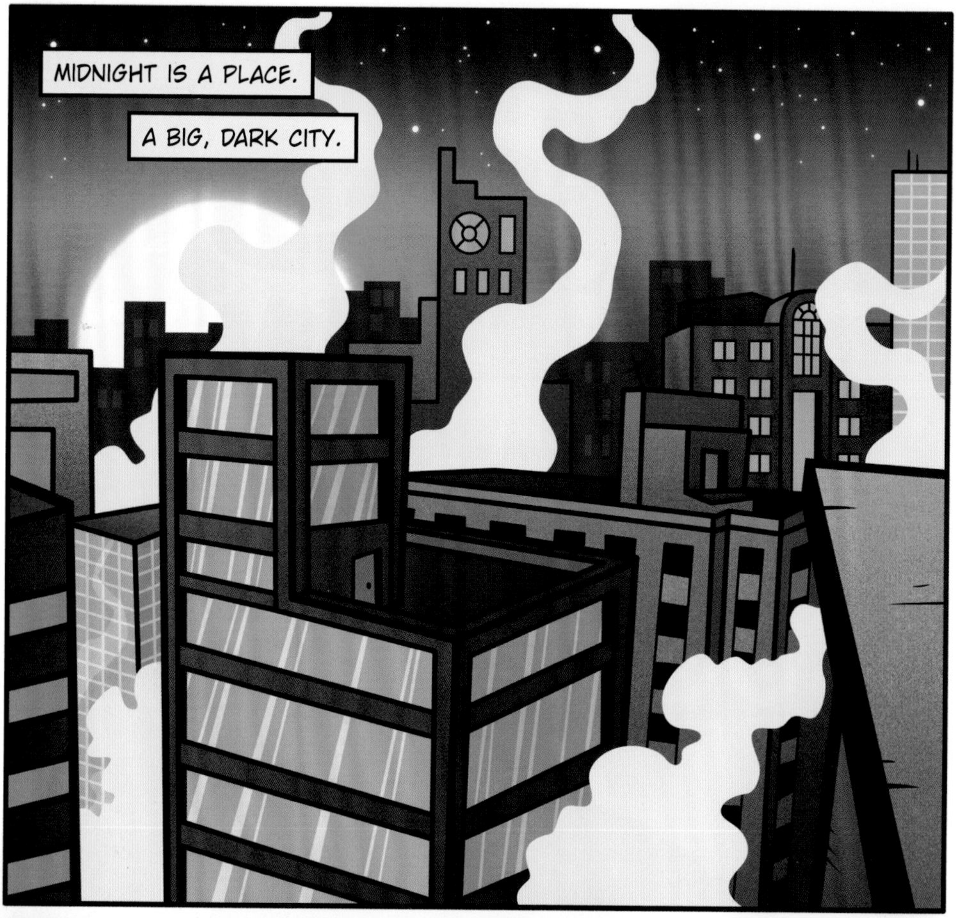
MIDNIGHT IS A PLACE.
A BIG, DARK CITY.

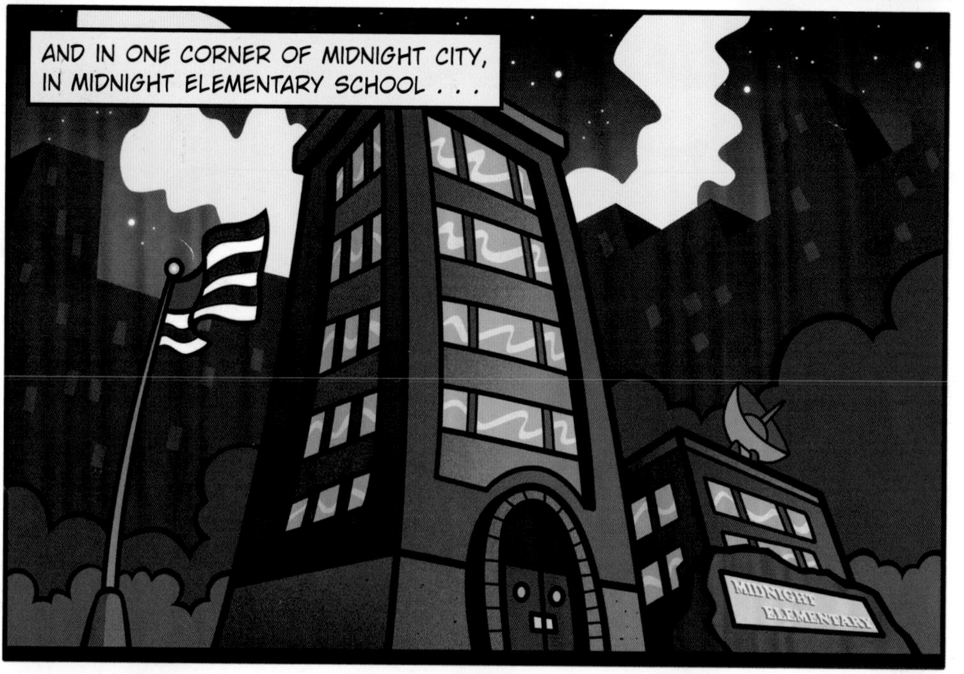
AND IN ONE CORNER OF MIDNIGHT CITY, IN MIDNIGHT ELEMENTARY SCHOOL . . .
MIDNIGHT ELEMENTARY

SOMETHING WEIRD IS GOING ON.

SOMETHING SO SCARY . . .

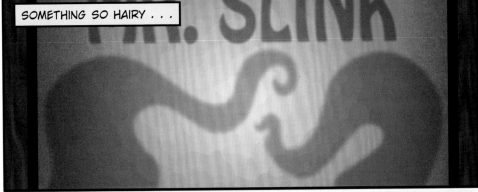

SOMETHING SO HAIRY . . .

THAT WE CAN'T EVEN LOOK!

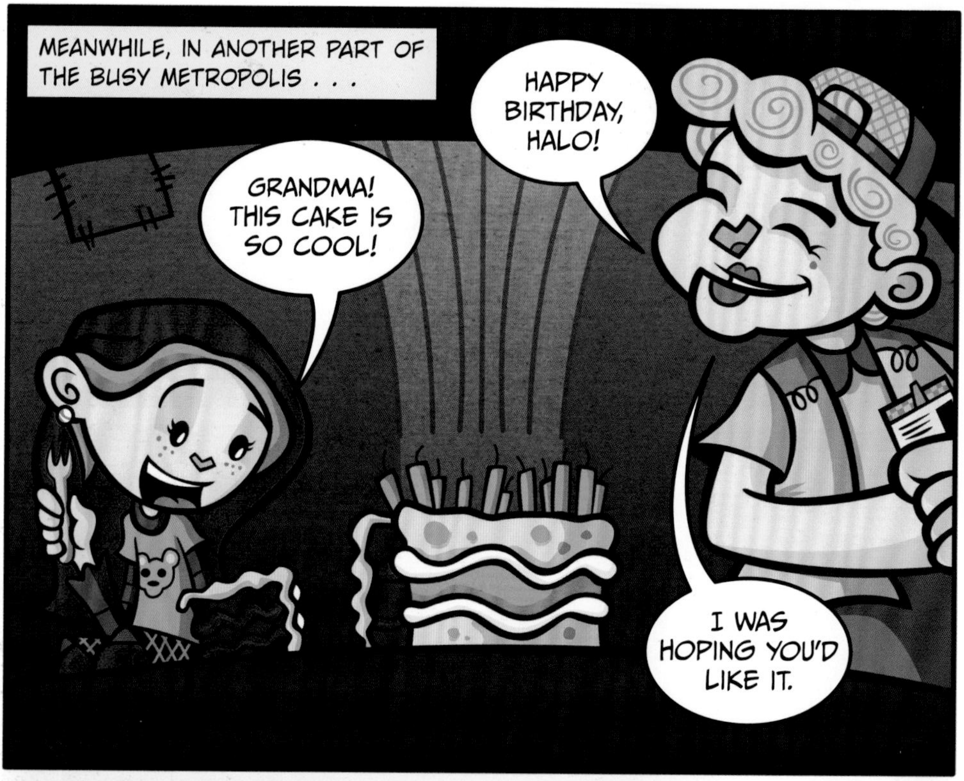
MEANWHILE, IN ANOTHER PART OF THE BUSY METROPOLIS . . .
HAPPY BIRTHDAY, HALO!
GRANDMA! THIS CAKE IS SO COOL!
I WAS HOPING YOU'D LIKE IT.

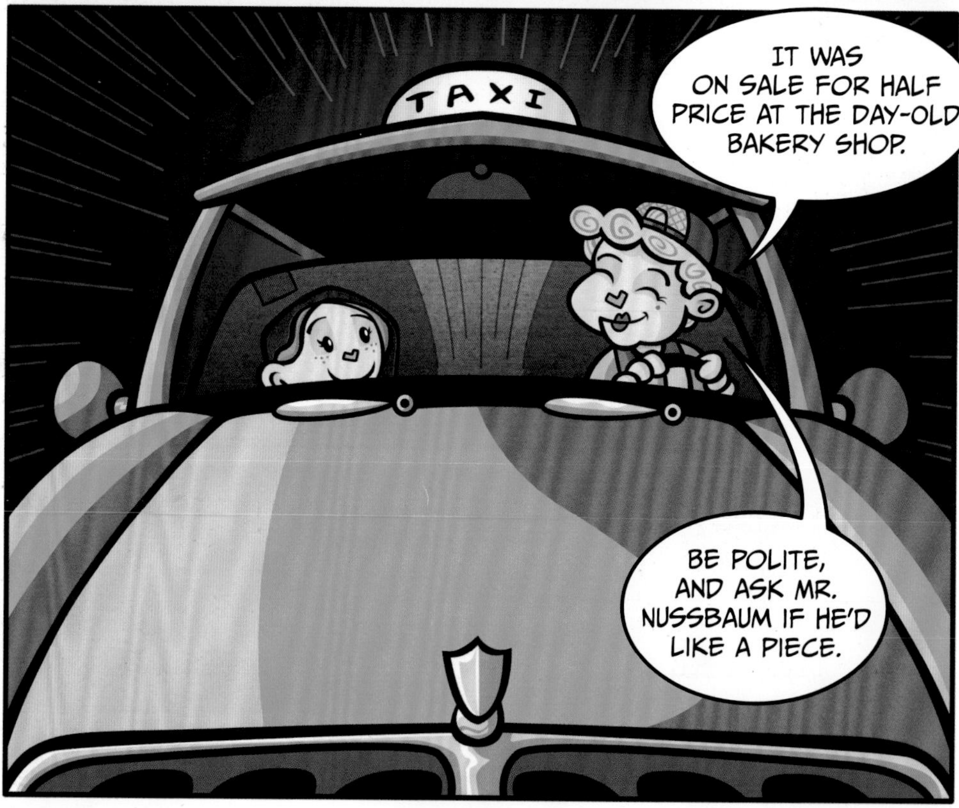
TAXI
IT WAS ON SALE FOR HALF PRICE AT THE DAY-OLD BAKERY SHOP.
BE POLITE, AND ASK MR. NUSSBAUM IF HE'D LIKE A PIECE.

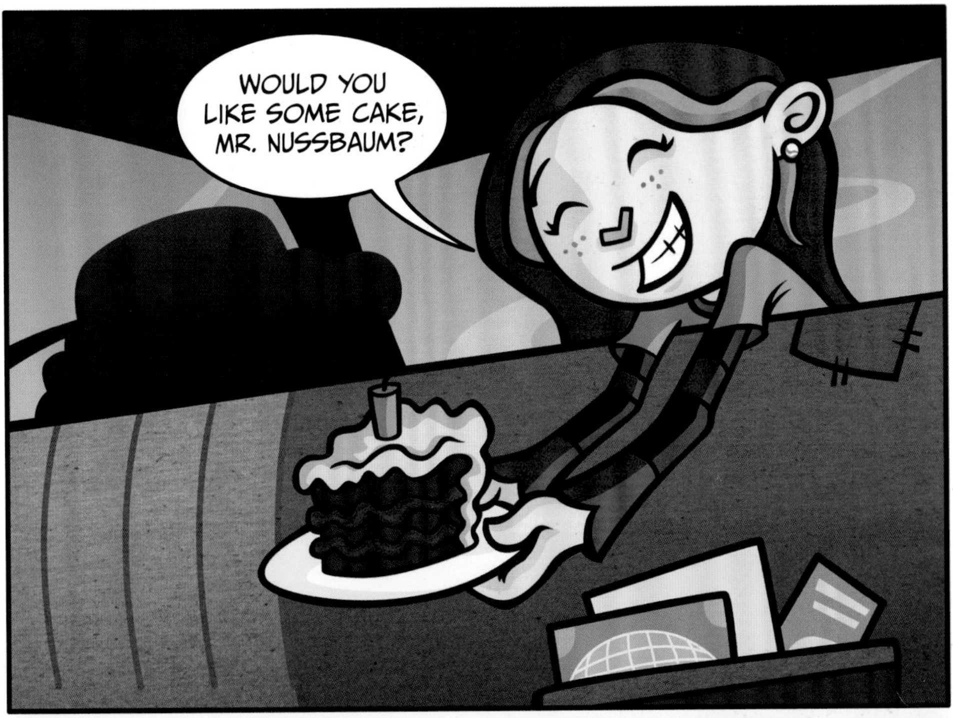
WOULD YOU LIKE SOME CAKE, MR. NUSSBAUM?

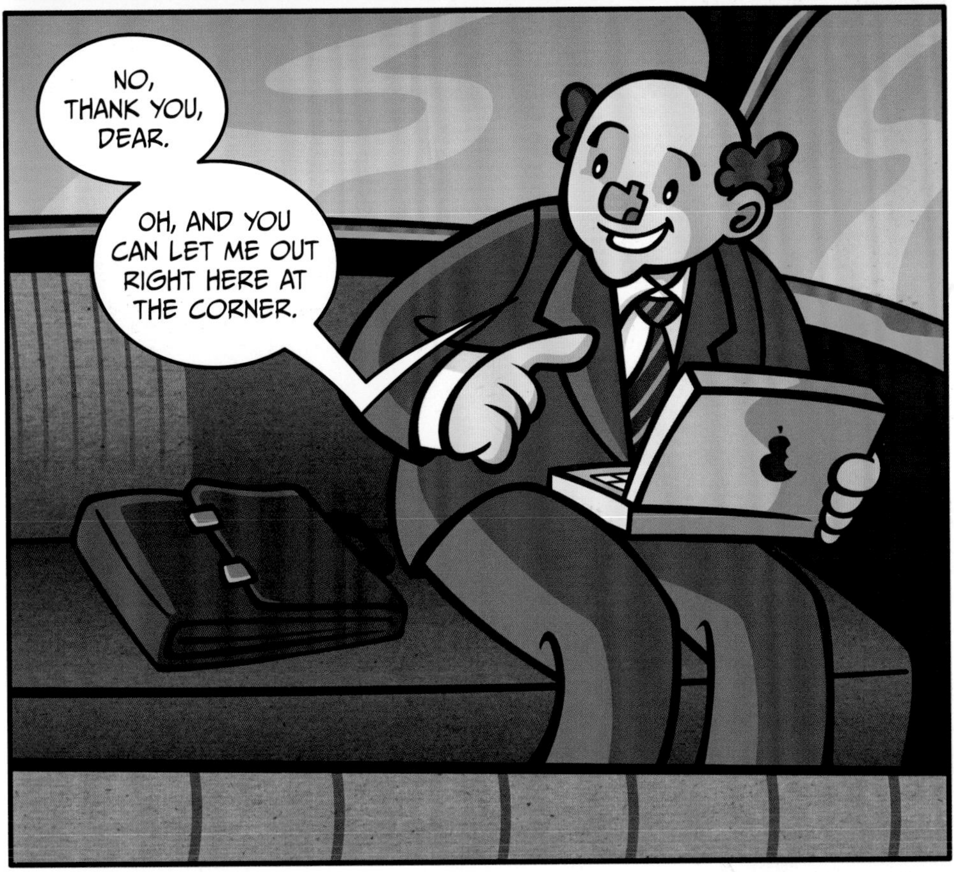
NO, THANK YOU, DEAR.
OH, AND YOU CAN LET ME OUT RIGHT HERE AT THE CORNER.

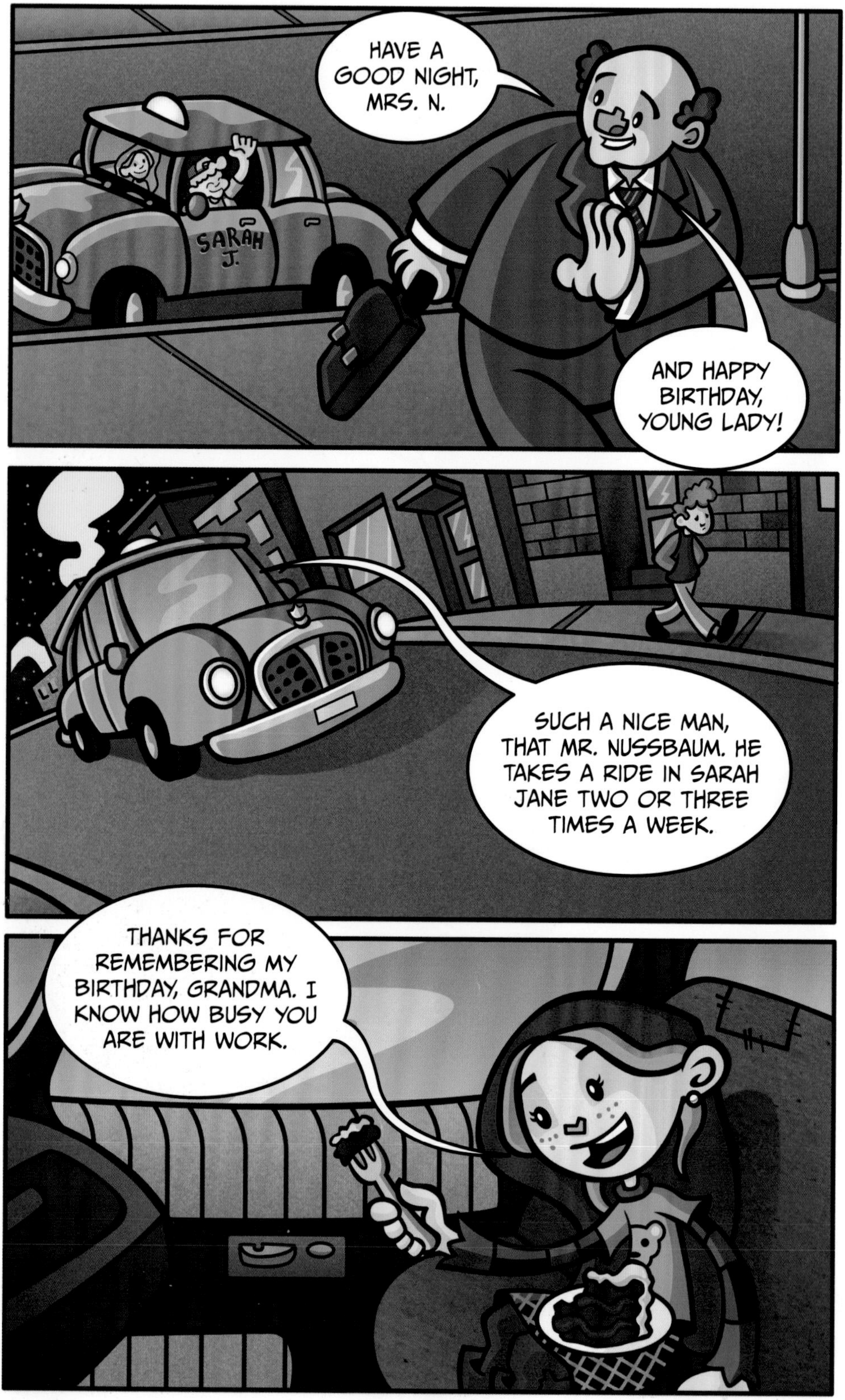
HAVE A GOOD NIGHT, MRS. N.
SARAH J.
AND HAPPY BIRTHDAY, YOUNG LADY!
SUCH A NICE MAN, THAT MR. NUSSBAUM. HE TAKES A RIDE IN SARAH JANE TWO OR THREE TIMES A WEEK.
THANKS FOR REMEMBERING MY BIRTHDAY, GRANDMA. I KNOW HOW BUSY YOU ARE WITH WORK.

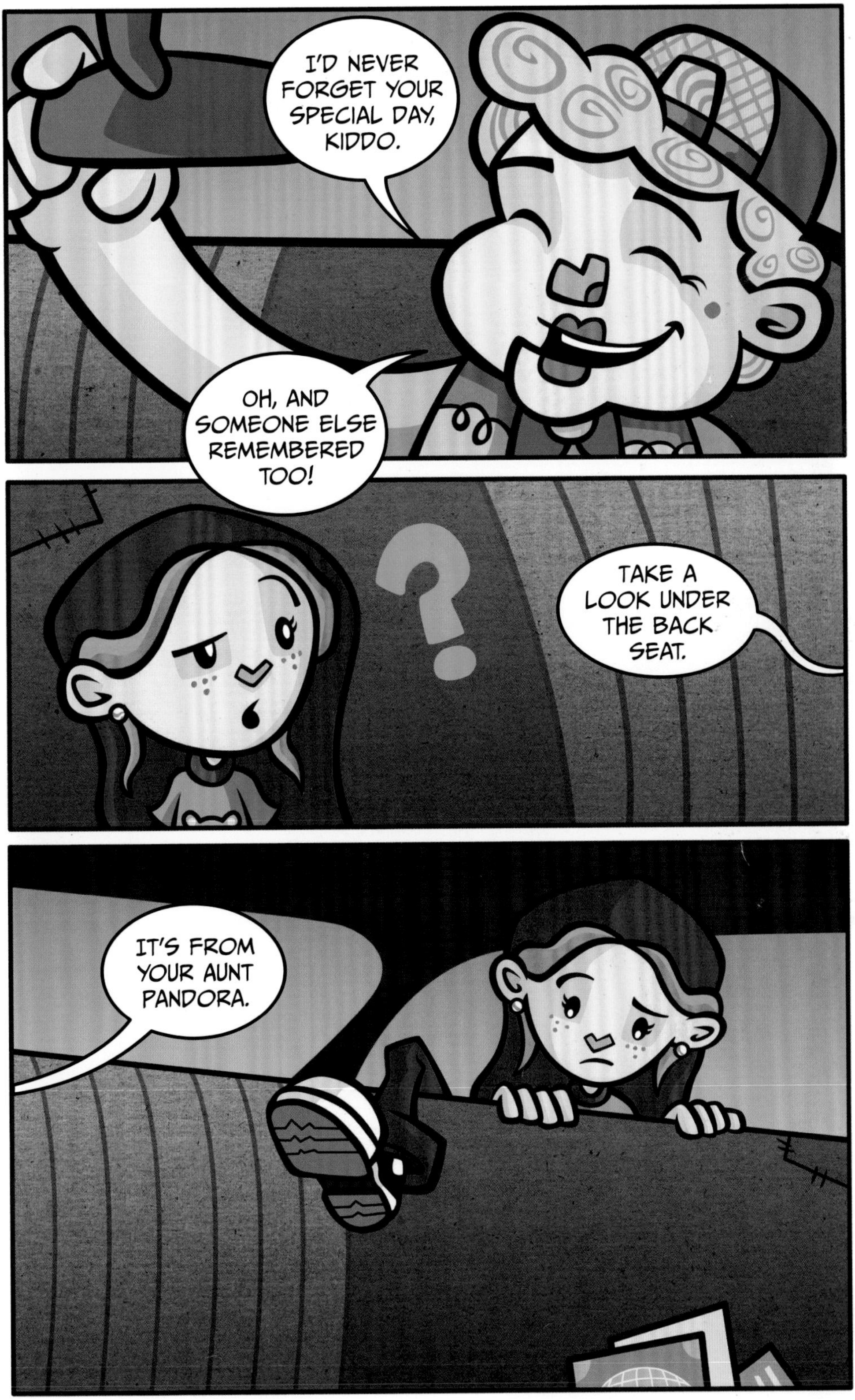
I'D NEVER FORGET YOUR SPECIAL DAY, KIDDO.
OH, AND SOMEONE ELSE REMEMBERED TOO!
TAKE A LOOK UNDER THE BACK SEAT.
IT'S FROM YOUR AUNT PANDORA.

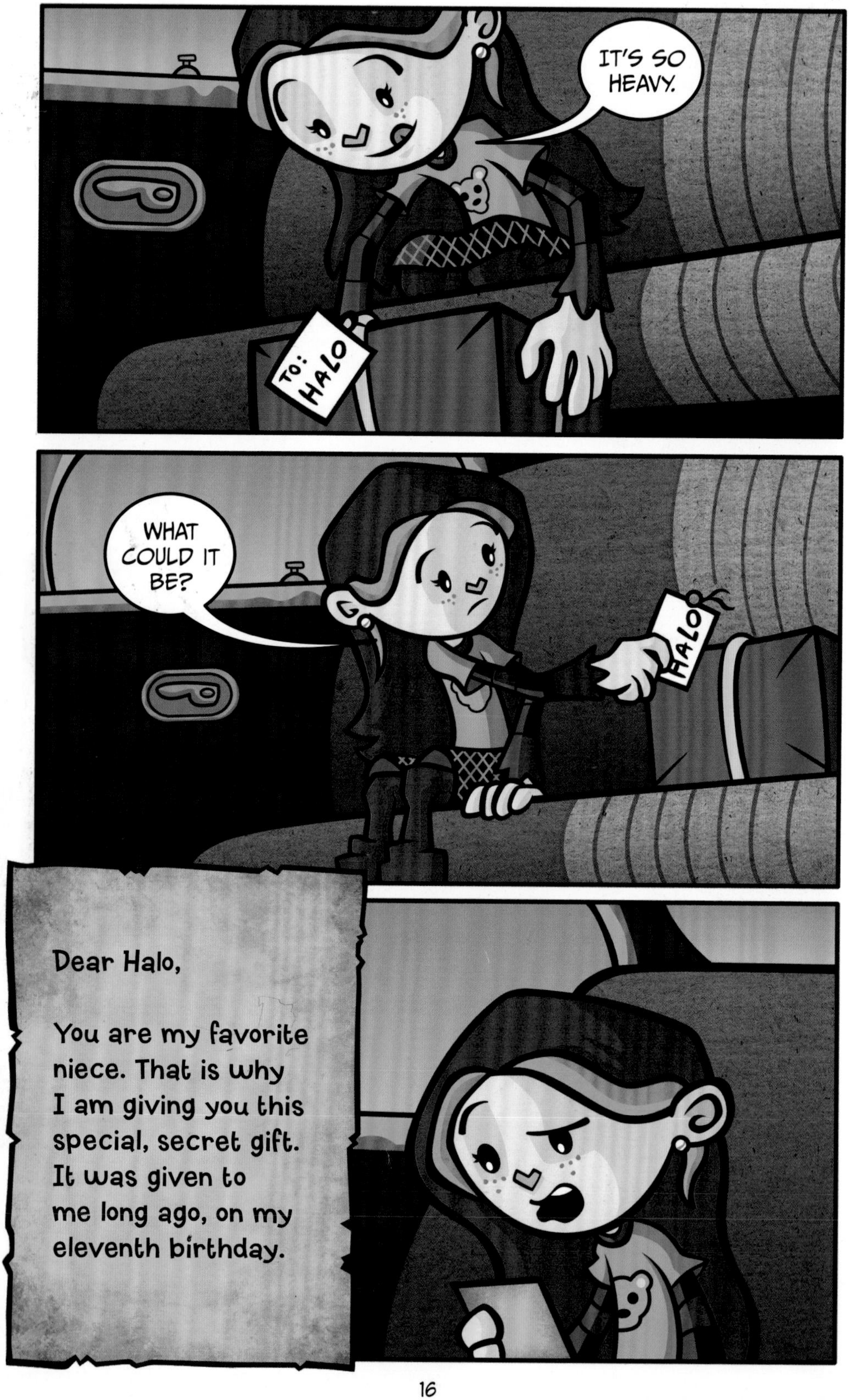
IT'S SO HEAVY.
TO: HALO
WHAT COULD IT BE?
HALO
Dear Halo,
You are my favorite niece. That is why I am giving you this special, secret gift. It was given to me long ago, on my eleventh birthday.

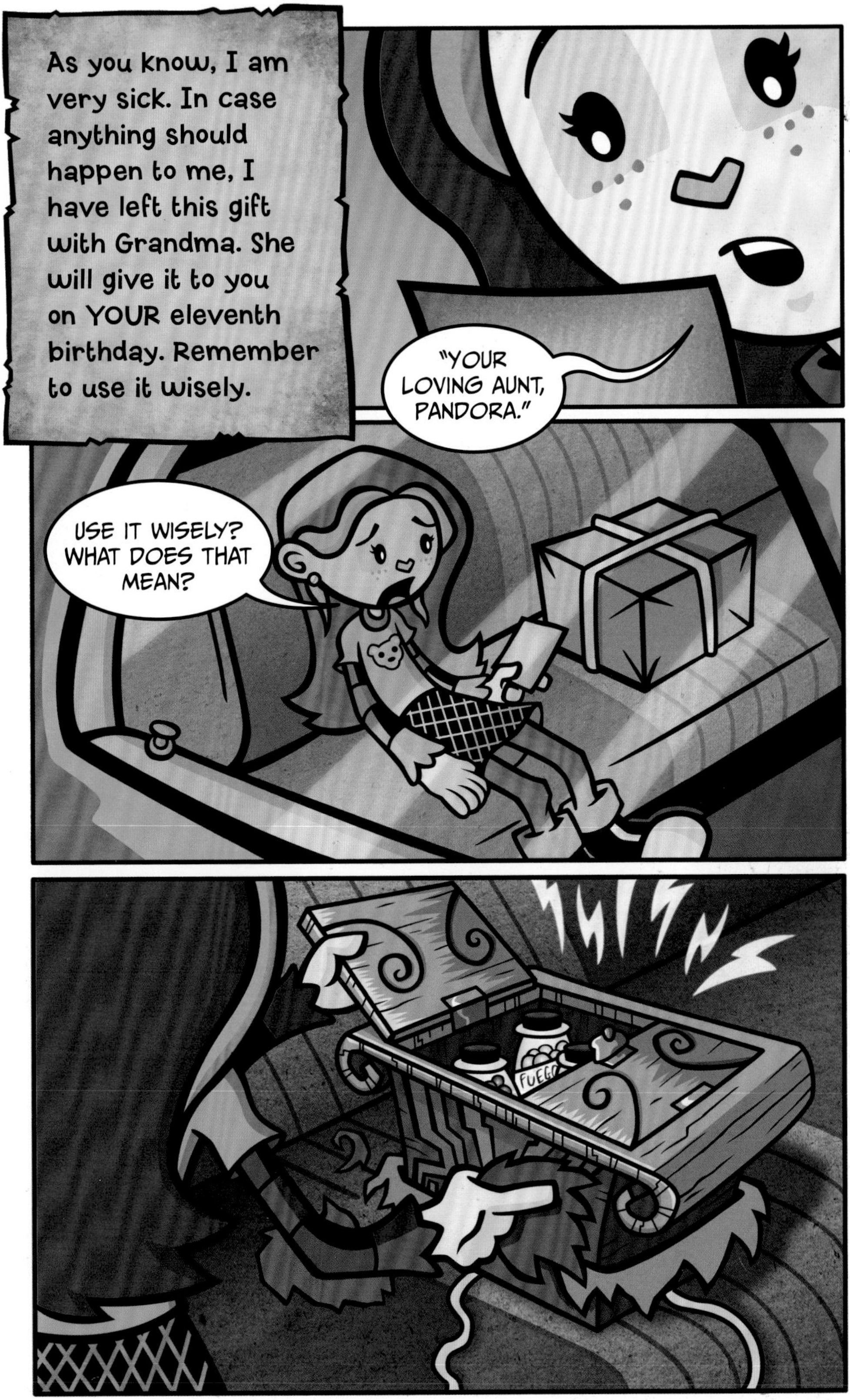
As you know, I am very sick. In case anything should happen to me, I have left this gift with Grandma. She will give it to you on YOUR eleventh birthday. Remember to use it wisely.
"YOUR LOVING AUNT, PANDORA."
USE IT WISELY? WHAT DOES THAT MEAN?

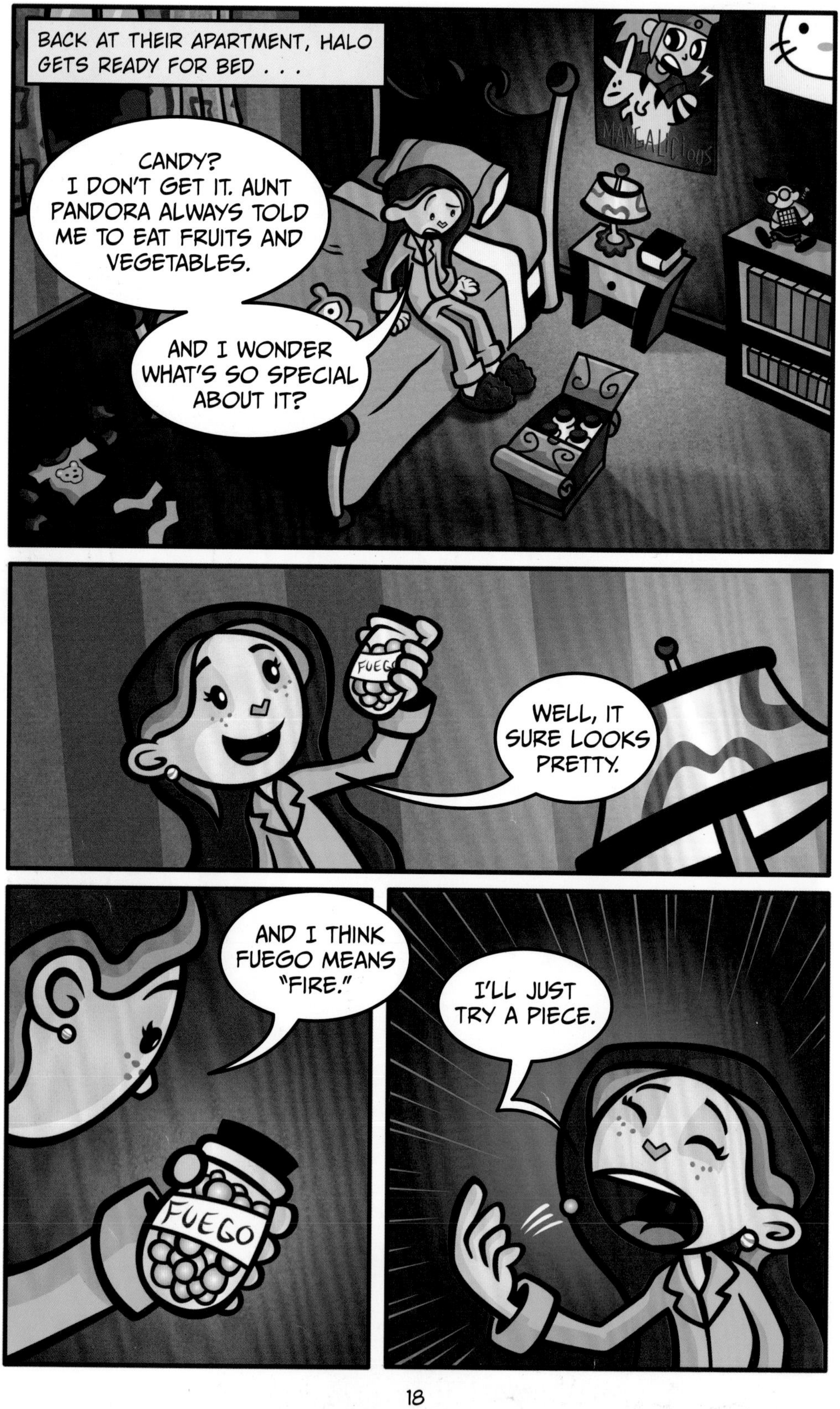
BACK AT THEIR APARTMENT, HALO GETS READY FOR BED . . .
CANDY? I DON'T GET IT. AUNT PANDORA ALWAYS TOLD ME TO EAT FRUITS AND VEGETABLES.
AND I WONDER WHAT'S SO SPECIAL ABOUT IT?
FUEGO
WELL, IT SURE LOOKS PRETTY.
AND I THINK FUEGO MEANS "FIRE."
FUEGO
I'LL JUST TRY A PIECE.

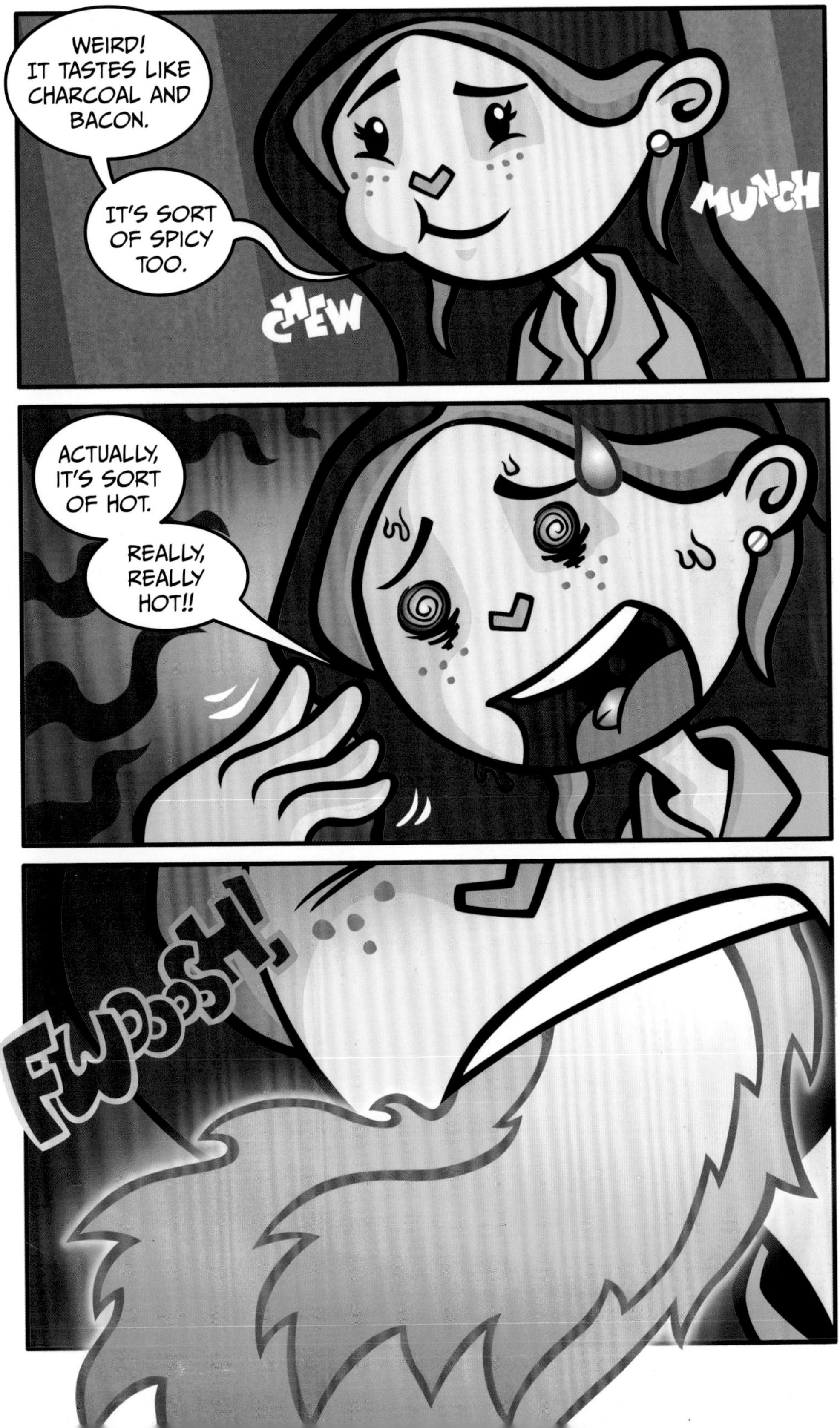
WEIRD! IT TASTES LIKE CHARCOAL AND BACON.
IT'S SORT OF SPICY TOO.
MUNCH
CHEW
ACTUALLY, IT'S SORT OF HOT.
REALLY, REALLY HOT!!
FWOOSH!

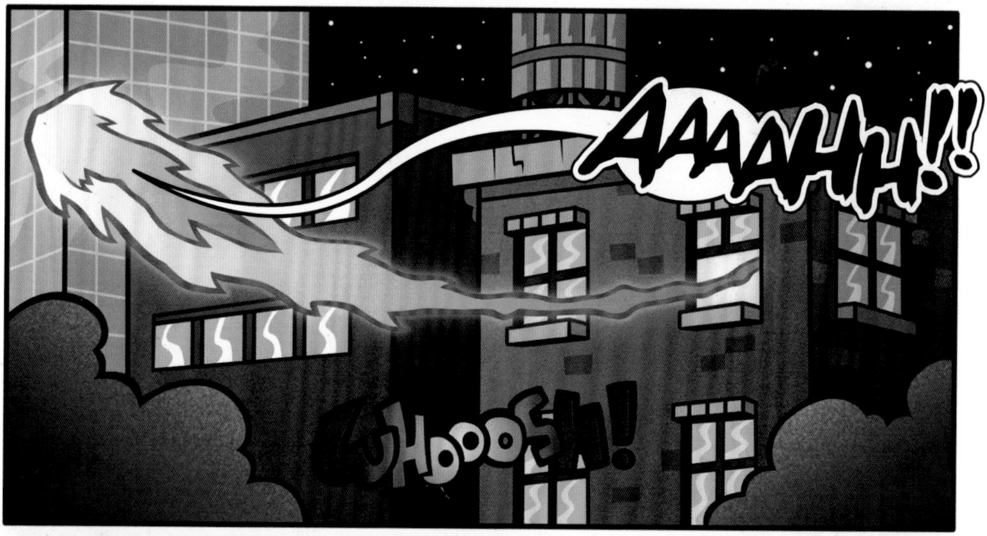
AAAAHHH!!
WHOOOSH!

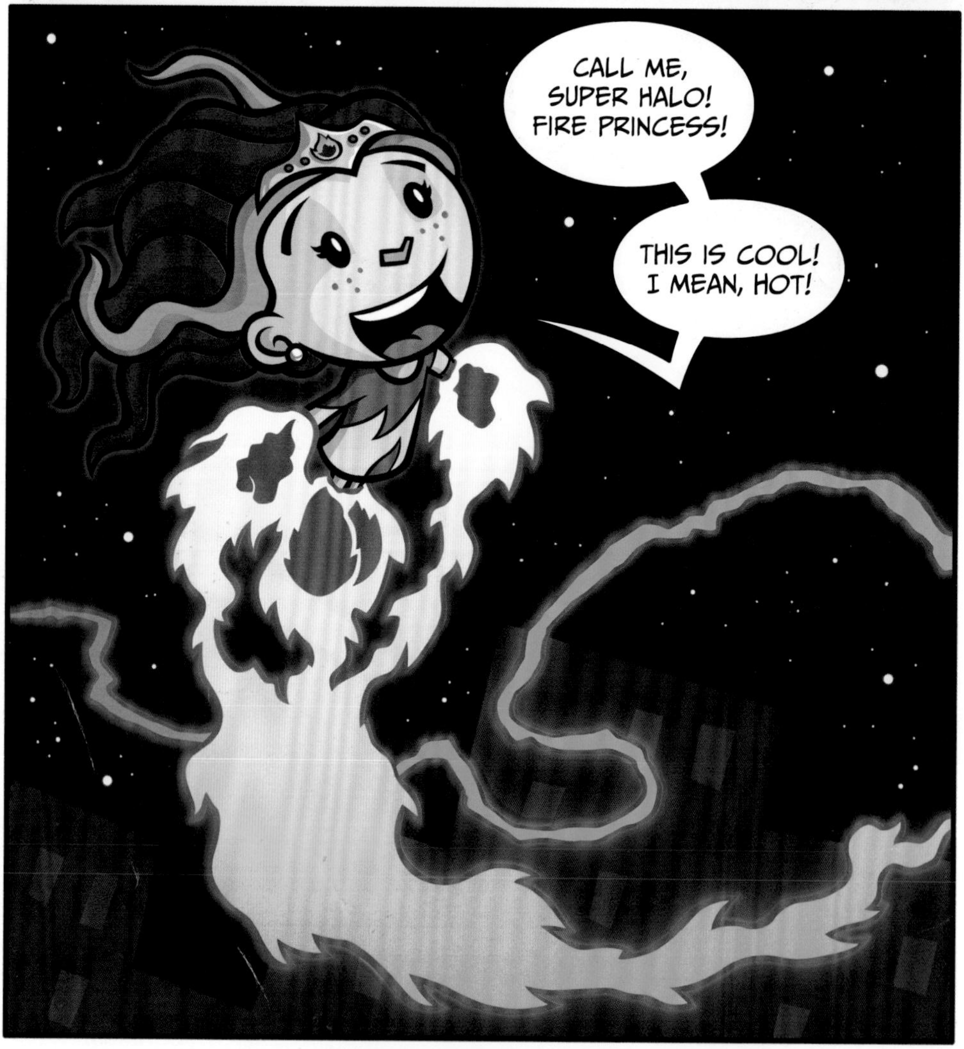
CALL ME, SUPER HALO! FIRE PRINCESS!
THIS IS COOL! I MEAN, HOT!

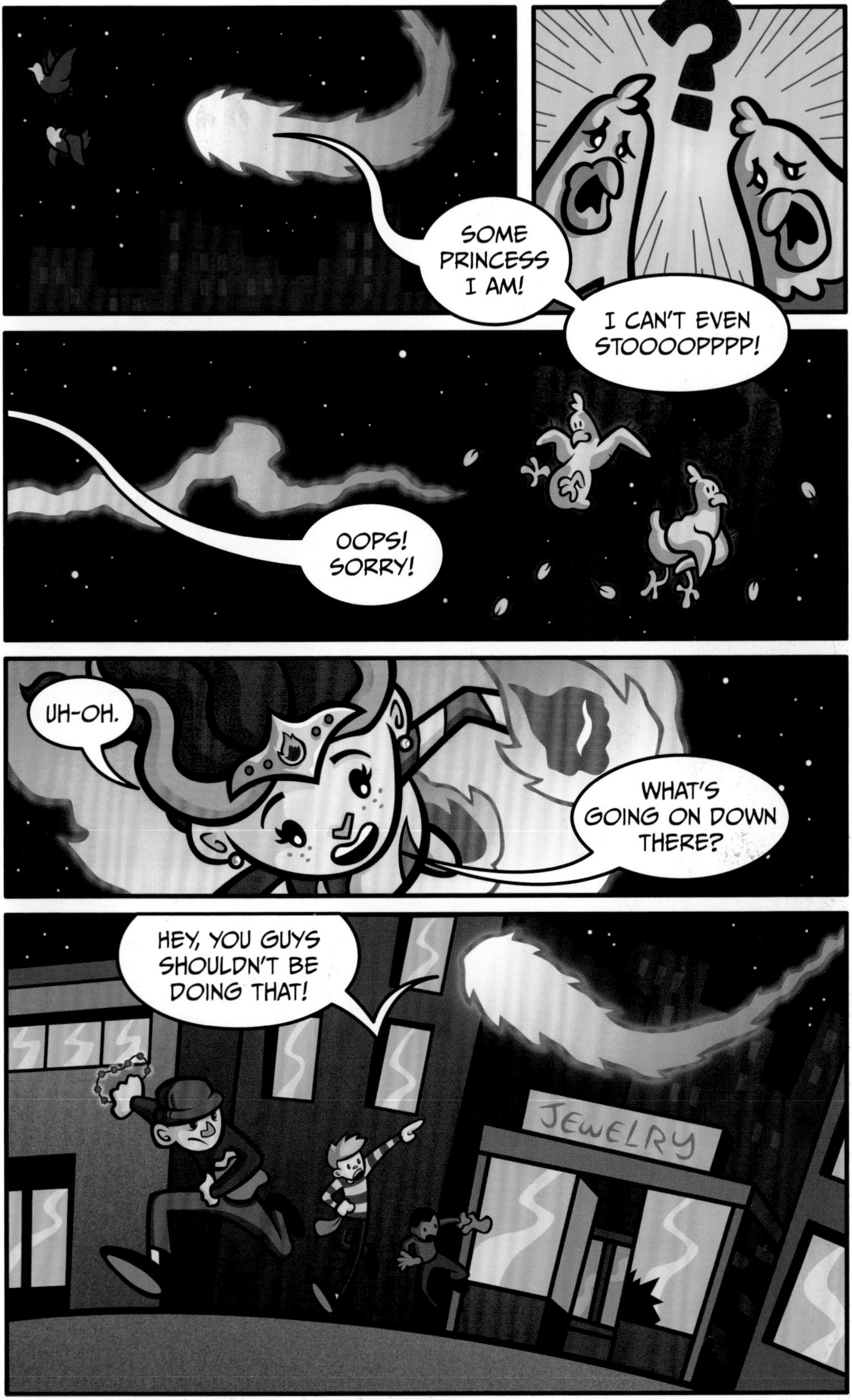
SOME PRINCESS I AM!
I CAN'T EVEN STOOOOPPPP!
OOPS! SORRY!
UH-OH.
WHAT'S GOING ON DOWN THERE?
HEY, YOU GUYS SHOULDN'T BE DOING THAT!
JEWELRY

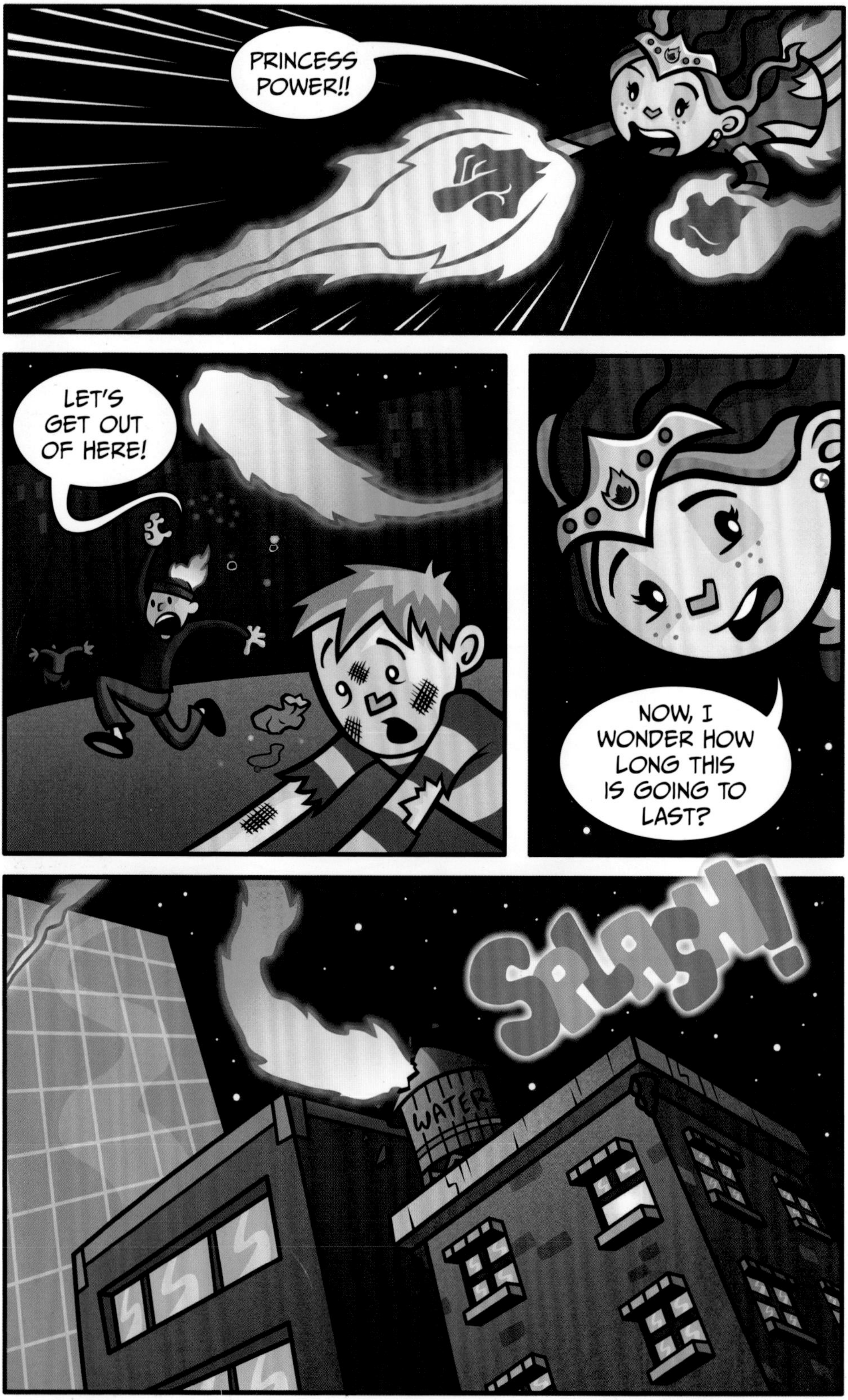
PRINCESS POWER!!
LET'S GET OUT OF HERE!
NOW, I WONDER HOW LONG THIS IS GOING TO LAST?
SPLASH!
WATER

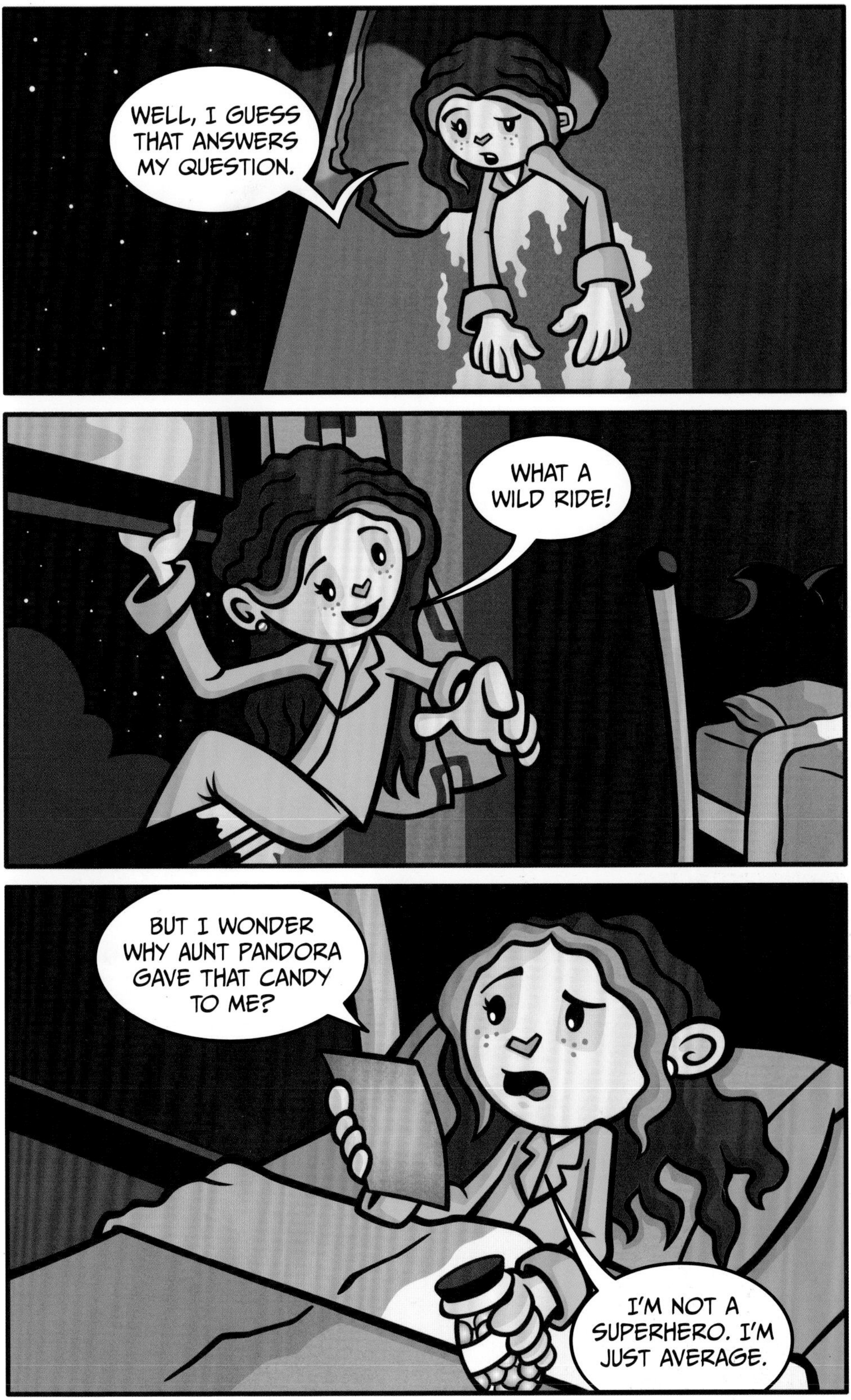
WELL, I GUESS THAT ANSWERS MY QUESTION.
WHAT A WILD RIDE!
BUT I WONDER WHY AUNT PANDORA GAVE THAT CANDY TO ME?
I'M NOT A SUPERHERO. I'M JUST AVERAGE.

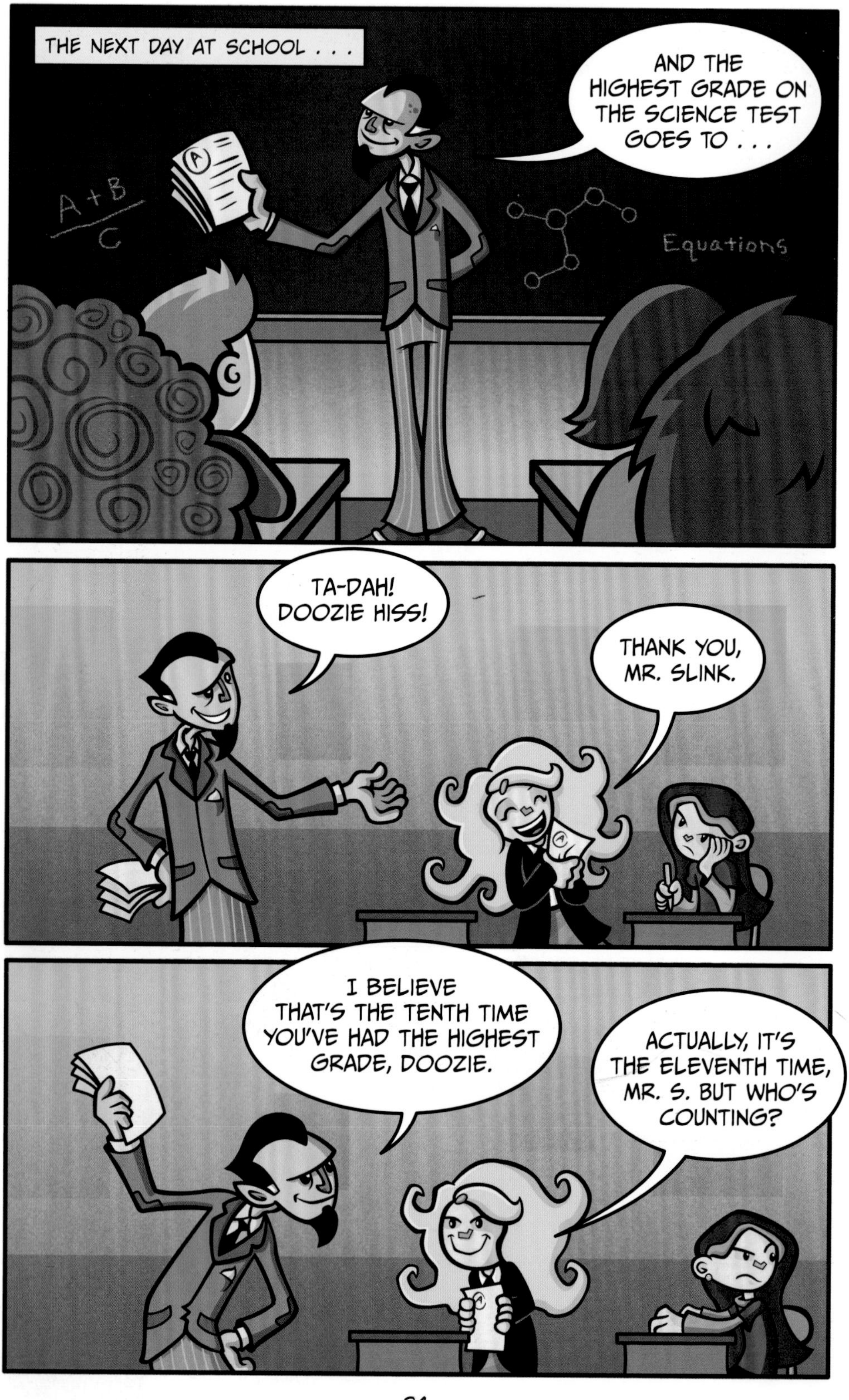
THE NEXT DAY AT SCHOOL . . .
AND THE HIGHEST GRADE ON THE SCIENCE TEST GOES TO . . .
A+B
C
Equations
TA-DAH! DOOZIE HISS!
THANK YOU, MR. SLINK.
I BELIEVE THAT'S THE TENTH TIME YOU'VE HAD THE HIGHEST GRADE, DOOZIE.
ACTUALLY, IT'S THE ELEVENTH TIME, MR. S. BUT WHO'S COUNTING?

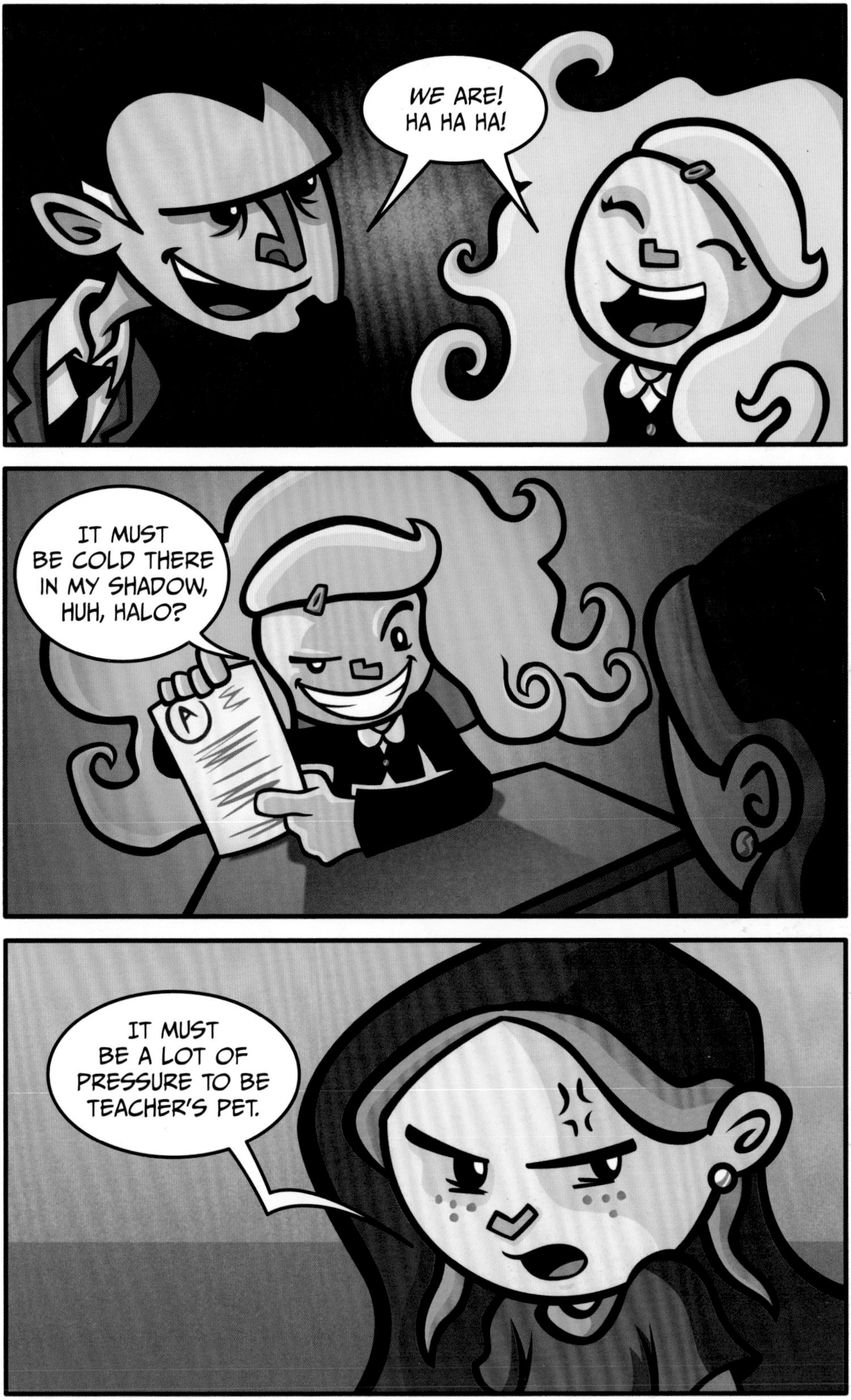
WE ARE!
HA HA HA!
IT MUST BE COLD THERE IN MY SHADOW, HUH, HALO?
A
IT MUST BE A LOT OF PRESSURE TO BE TEACHER'S PET.

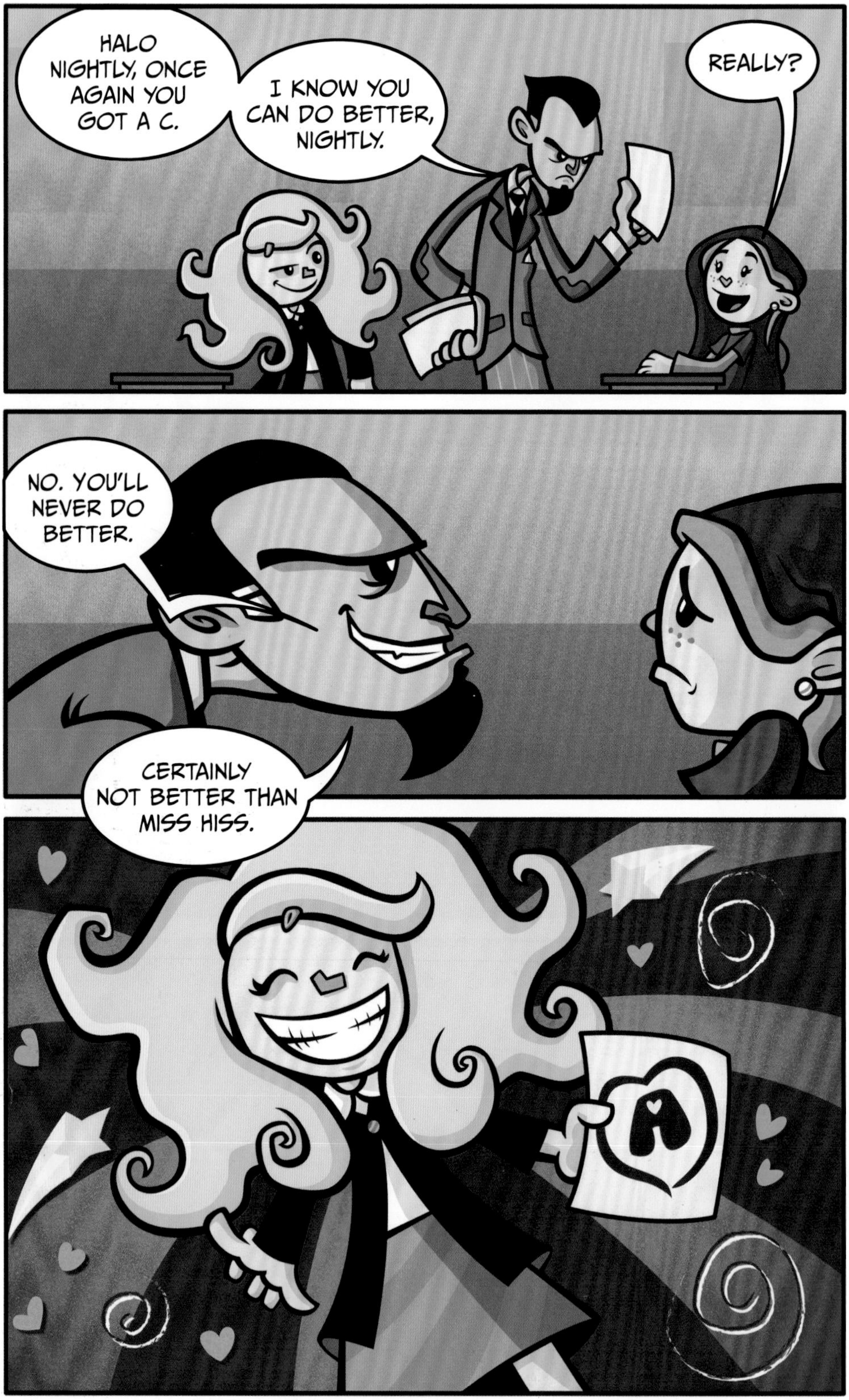
HALO NIGHTLY, ONCE AGAIN YOU GOT A C.
I KNOW YOU CAN DO BETTER, NIGHTLY.
REALLY?
NO. YOU'LL NEVER DO BETTER.
CERTAINLY NOT BETTER THAN MISS HISS.

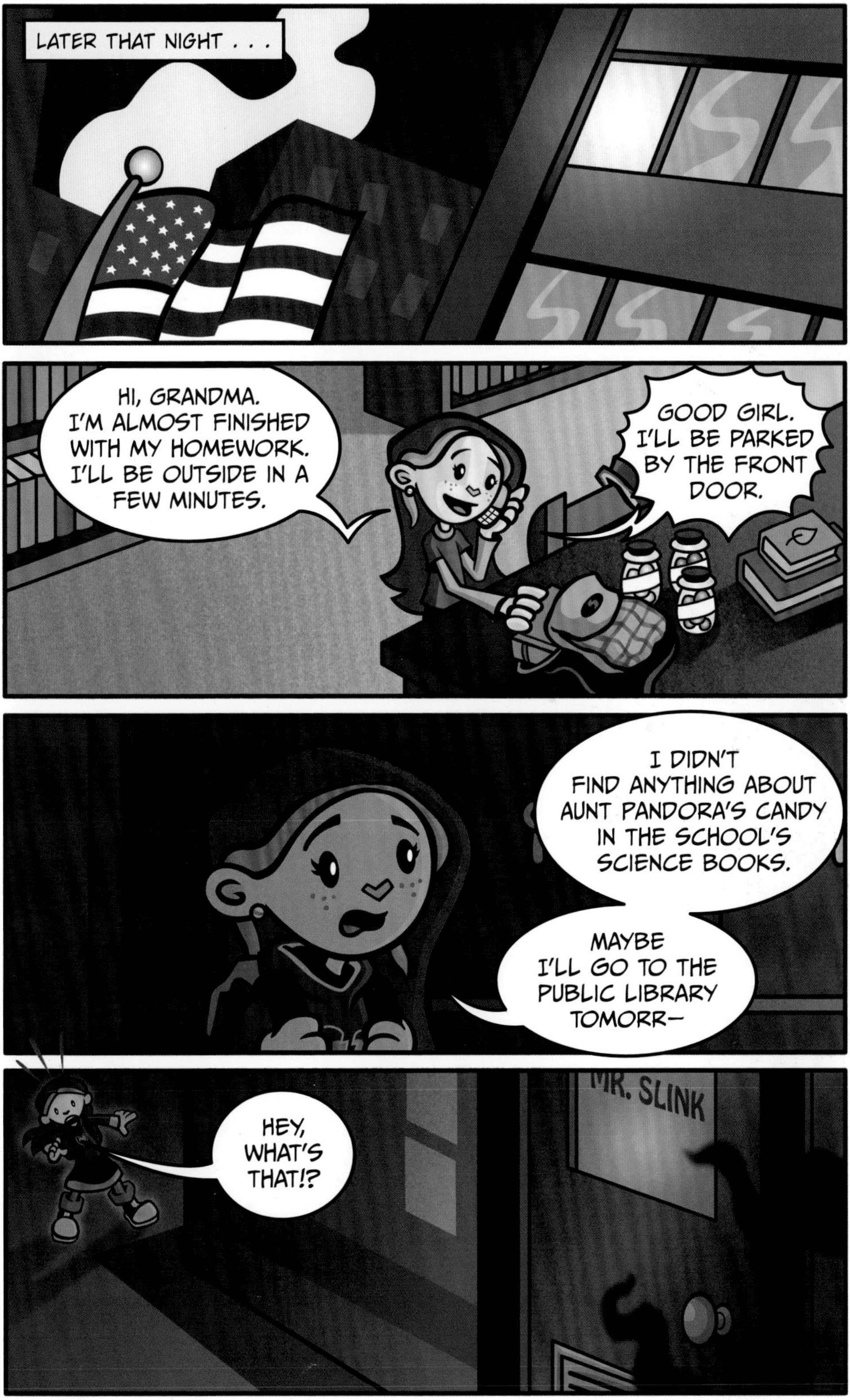
LATER THAT NIGHT . . .
HI, GRANDMA. I'M ALMOST FINISHED WITH MY HOMEWORK. I'LL BE OUTSIDE IN A FEW MINUTES.
GOOD GIRL. I'LL BE PARKED BY THE FRONT DOOR.
I DIDN'T FIND ANYTHING ABOUT AUNT PANDORA'S CANDY IN THE SCHOOL'S SCIENCE BOOKS.
MAYBE I'LL GO TO THE PUBLIC LIBRARY TOMORR—
MR. SLINK
HEY, WHAT'S THAT!?

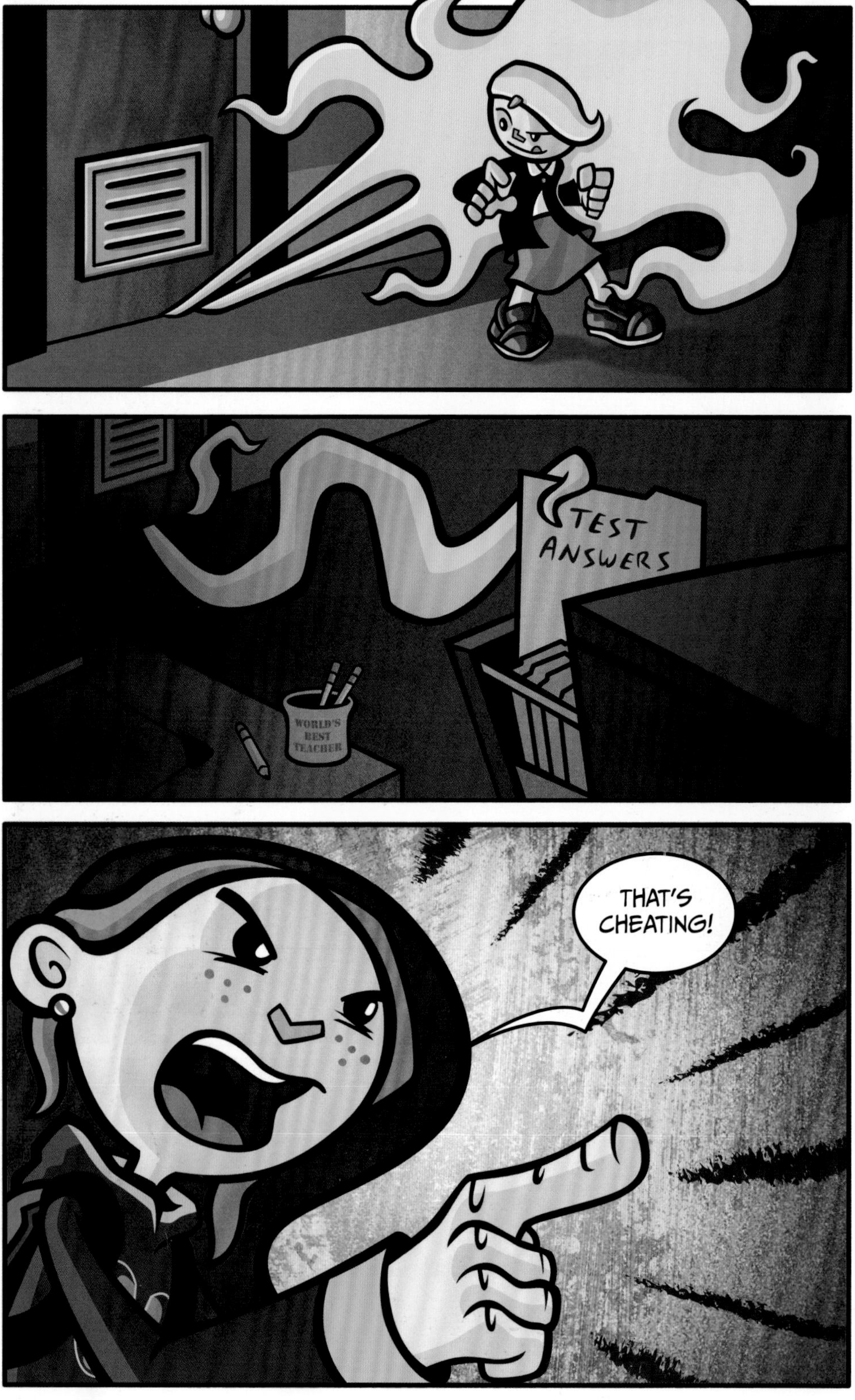
TEST ANSWERS
WORLD'S BEST TEACHER
THAT'S CHEATING!

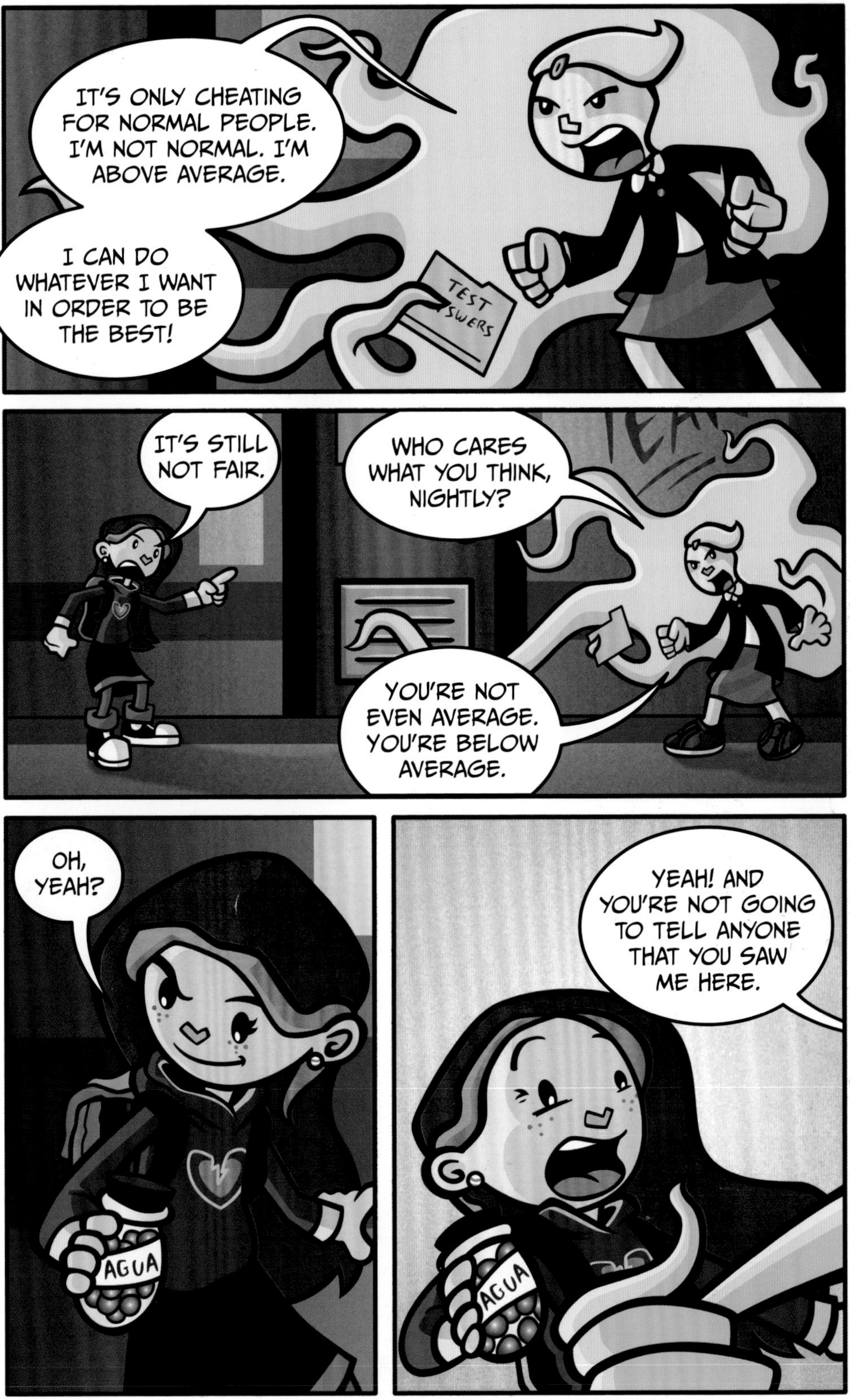
IT'S ONLY CHEATING FOR NORMAL PEOPLE. I'M NOT NORMAL. I'M ABOVE AVERAGE.
I CAN DO WHATEVER I WANT IN ORDER TO BE THE BEST!
TEST
SWERS
IT'S STILL NOT FAIR.
WHO CARES WHAT YOU THINK, NIGHTLY?
YOU'RE NOT EVEN AVERAGE. YOU'RE BELOW AVERAGE.
OH, YEAH?
AGUA
YEAH! AND YOU'RE NOT GOING TO TELL ANYONE THAT YOU SAW ME HERE.
AGUA

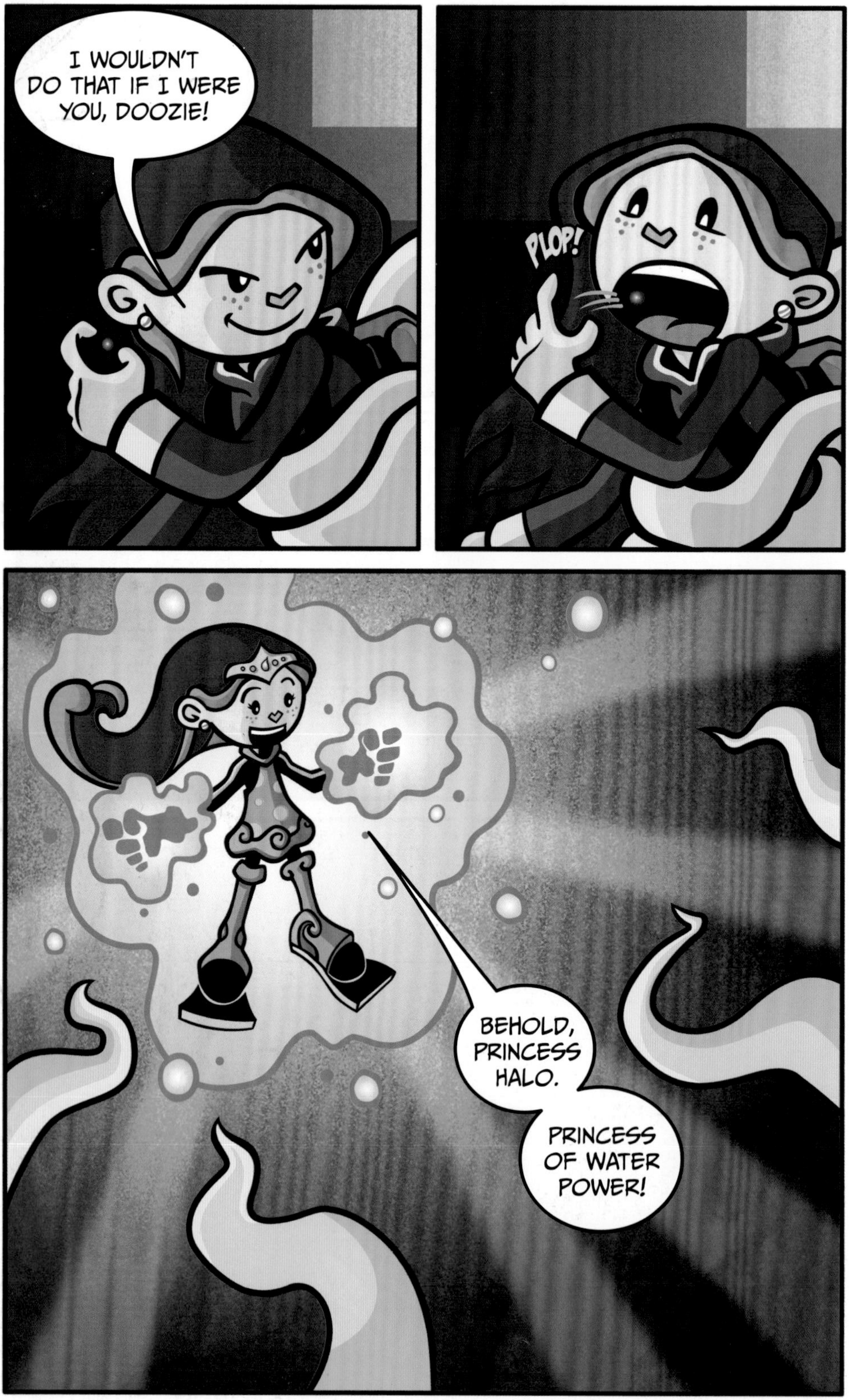
I WOULDN'T DO THAT IF I WERE YOU, DOOZIE!
PLOP!
BEHOLD, PRINCESS HALO.
PRINCESS OF WATER POWER!

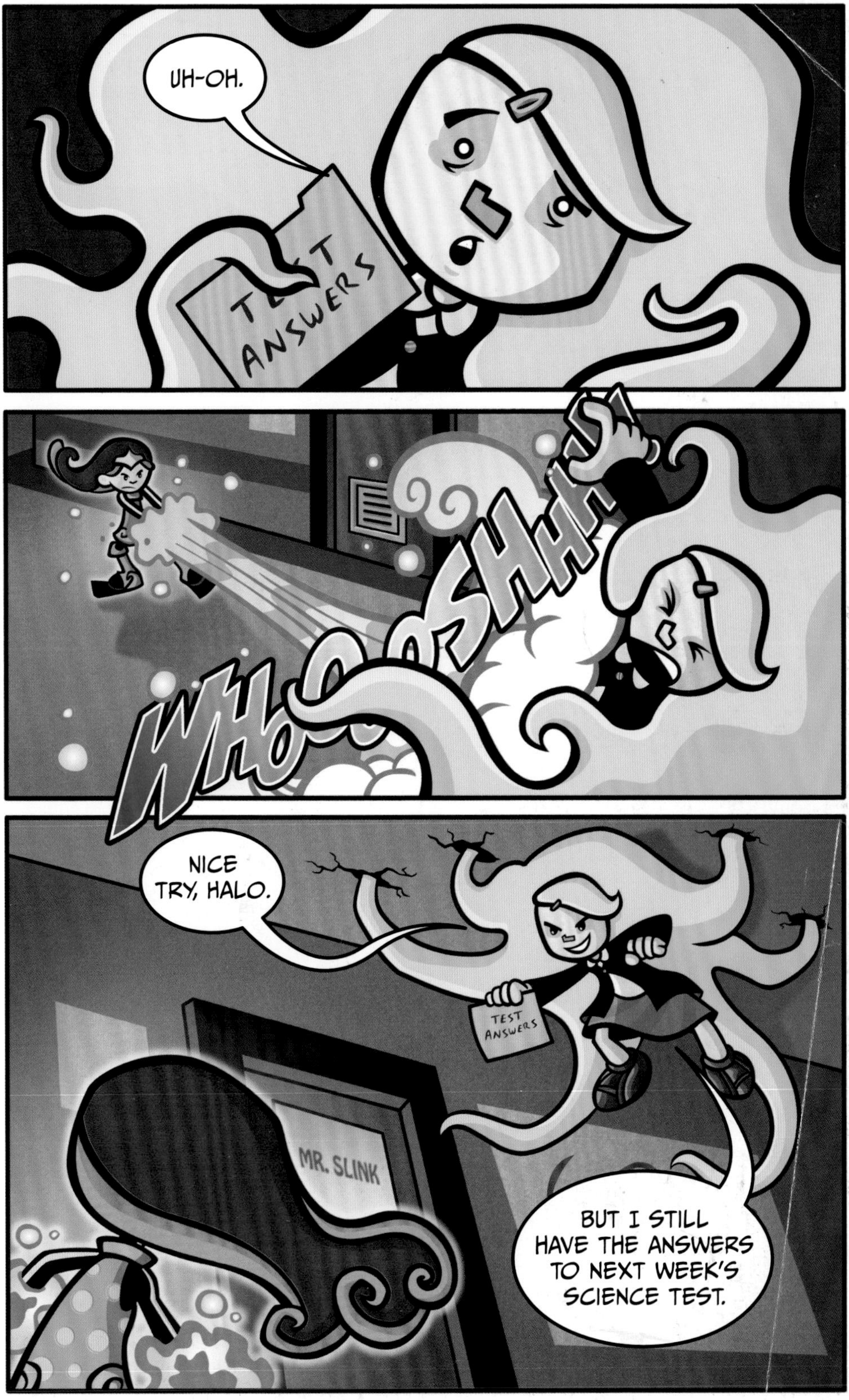
UH-OH.
TEST ANSWERS
WHOOOSHHH!
NICE TRY, HALO.
TEST ANSWERS
MR. SLINK
BUT I STILL HAVE THE ANSWERS TO NEXT WEEK'S SCIENCE TEST.

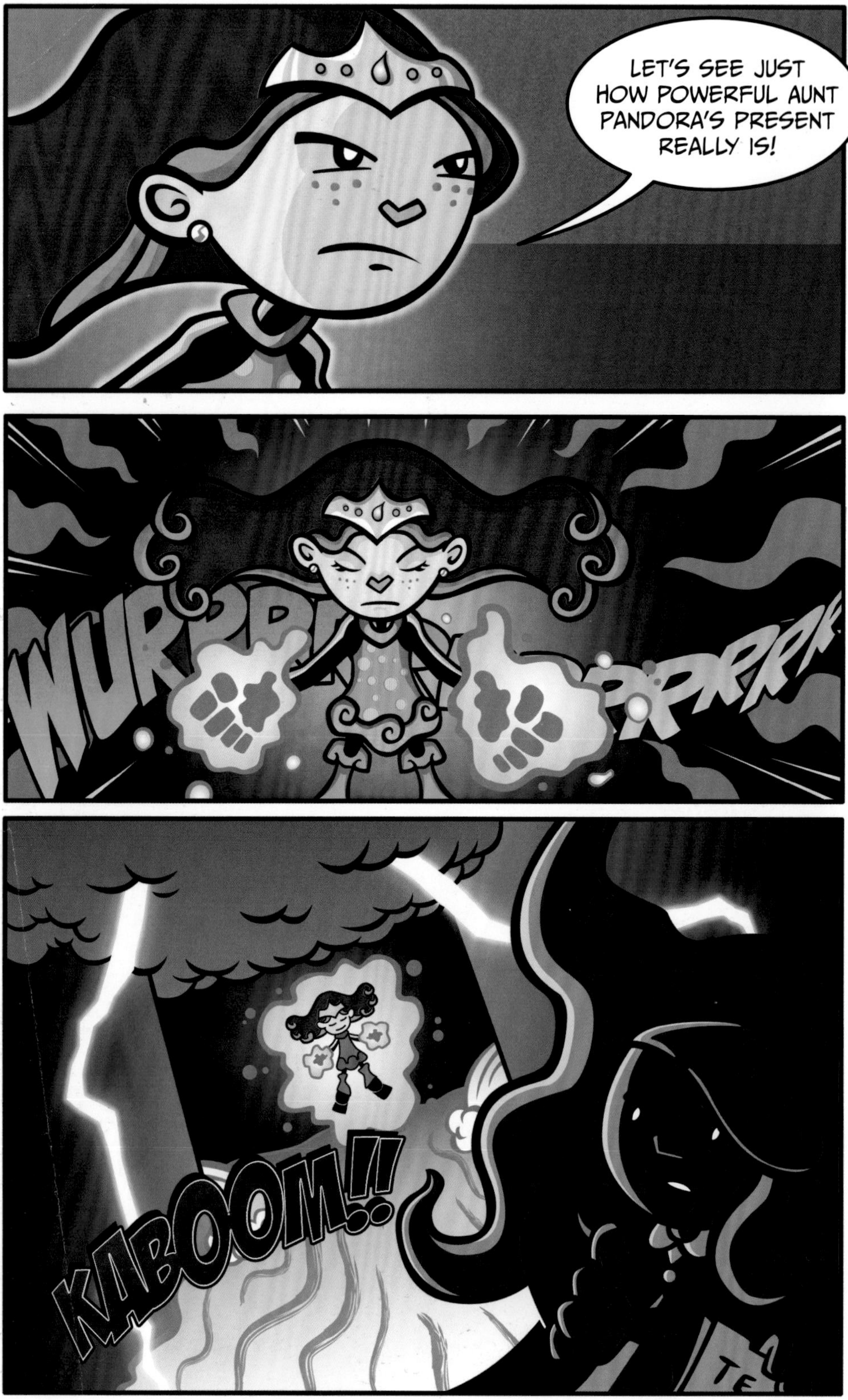
LET'S SEE JUST HOW POWERFUL AUNT PANDORA'S PRESENT REALLY IS!
WURRR PRRRR
KABOOM!!

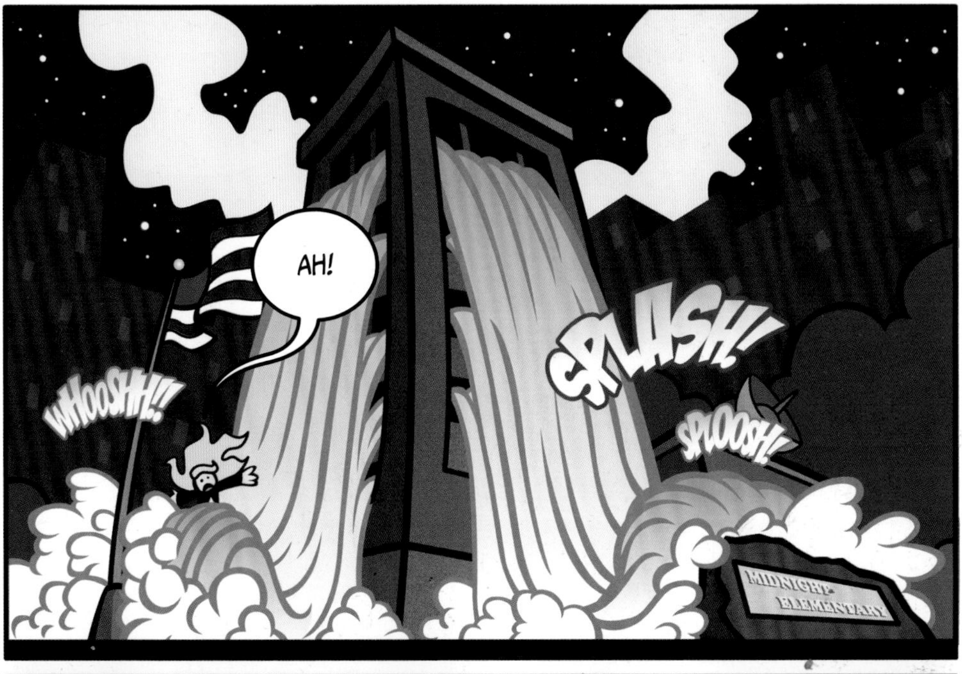
AH!
WHOOSHH!!!
SPLASH!
SPLOOSH!
MIDNIGHT ELEMENTARY

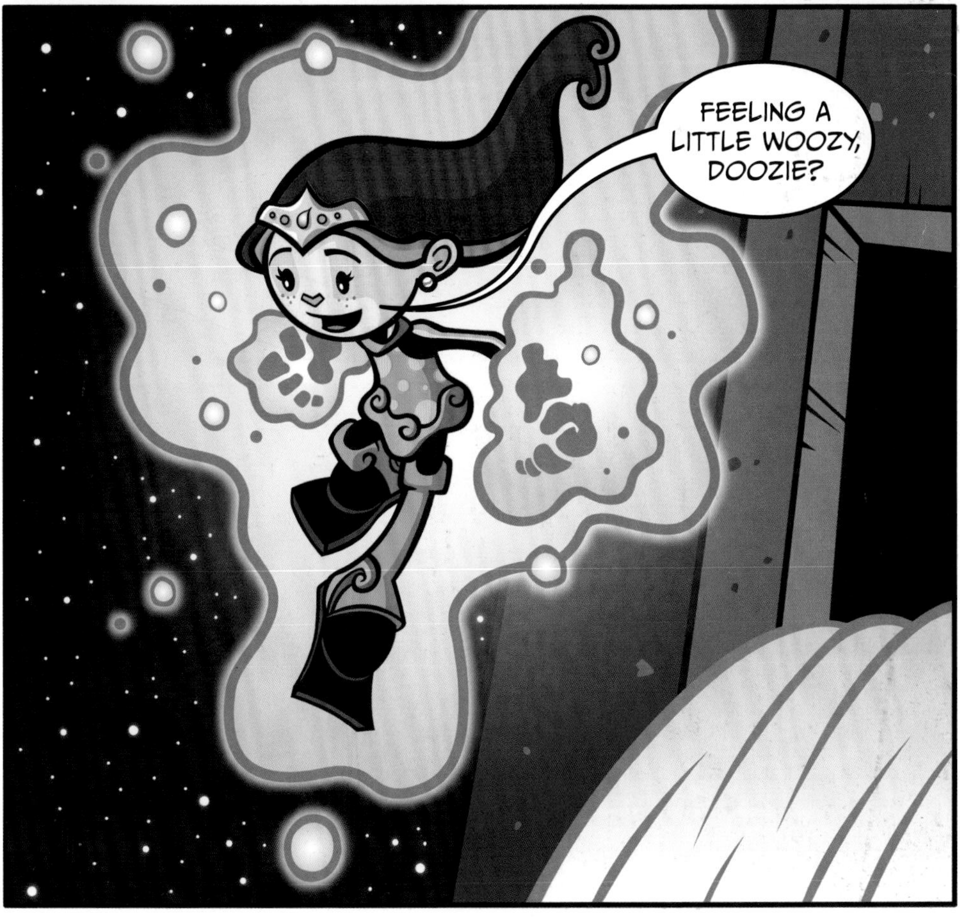
FEELING A LITTLE WOOZY, DOOZIE?

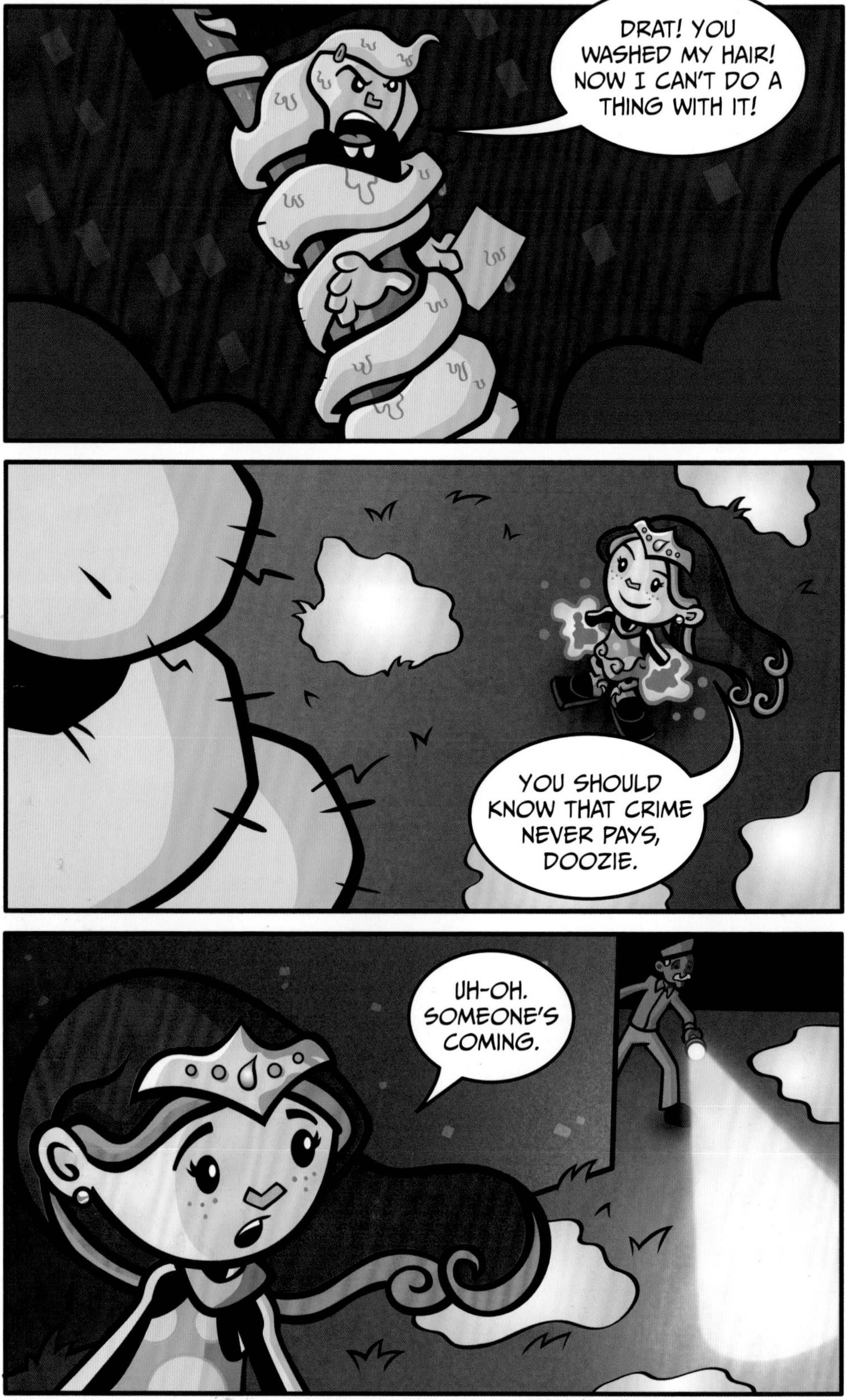
DRAT! YOU WASHED MY HAIR! NOW I CAN'T DO A THING WITH IT!
YOU SHOULD KNOW THAT CRIME NEVER PAYS, DOOZIE.
UH-OH. SOMEONE'S COMING.

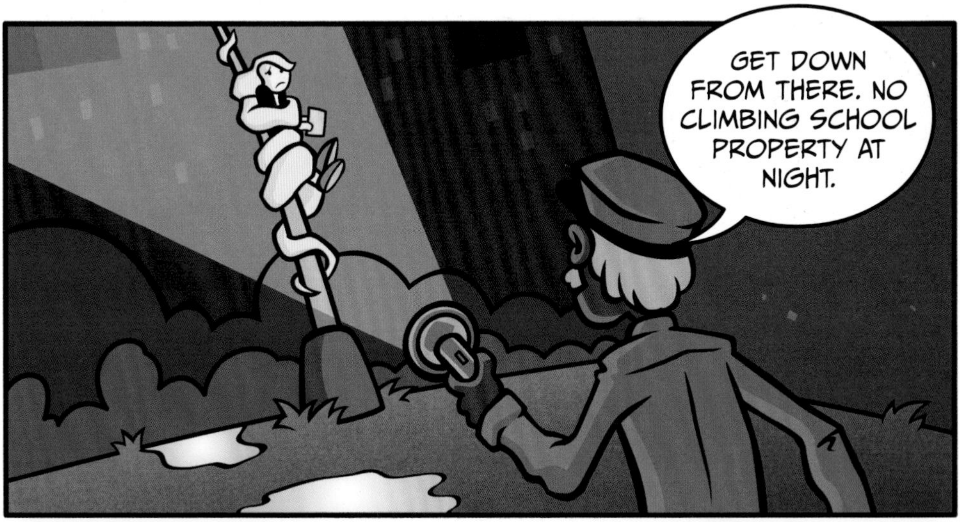
GET DOWN FROM THERE. NO CLIMBING SCHOOL PROPERTY AT NIGHT.

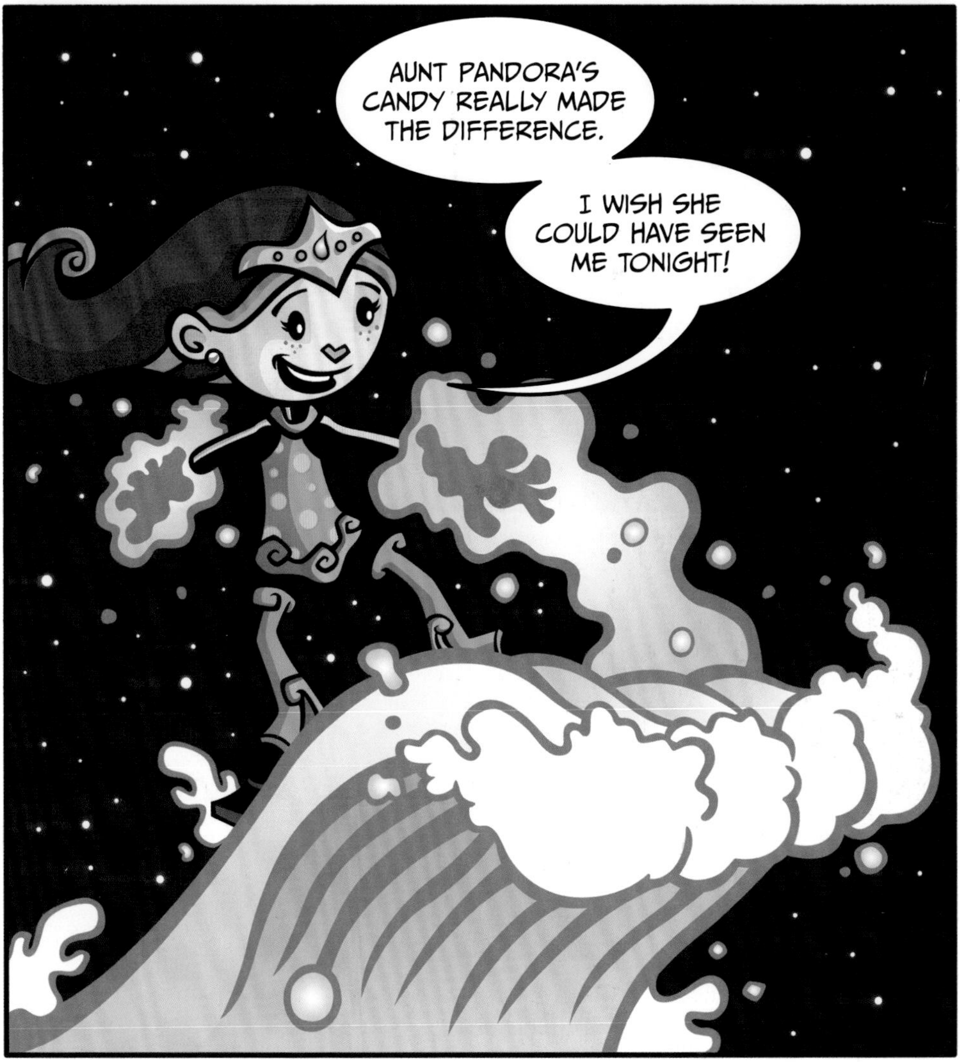
AUNT PANDORA'S CANDY REALLY MADE THE DIFFERENCE.
I WISH SHE COULD HAVE SEEN ME TONIGHT!

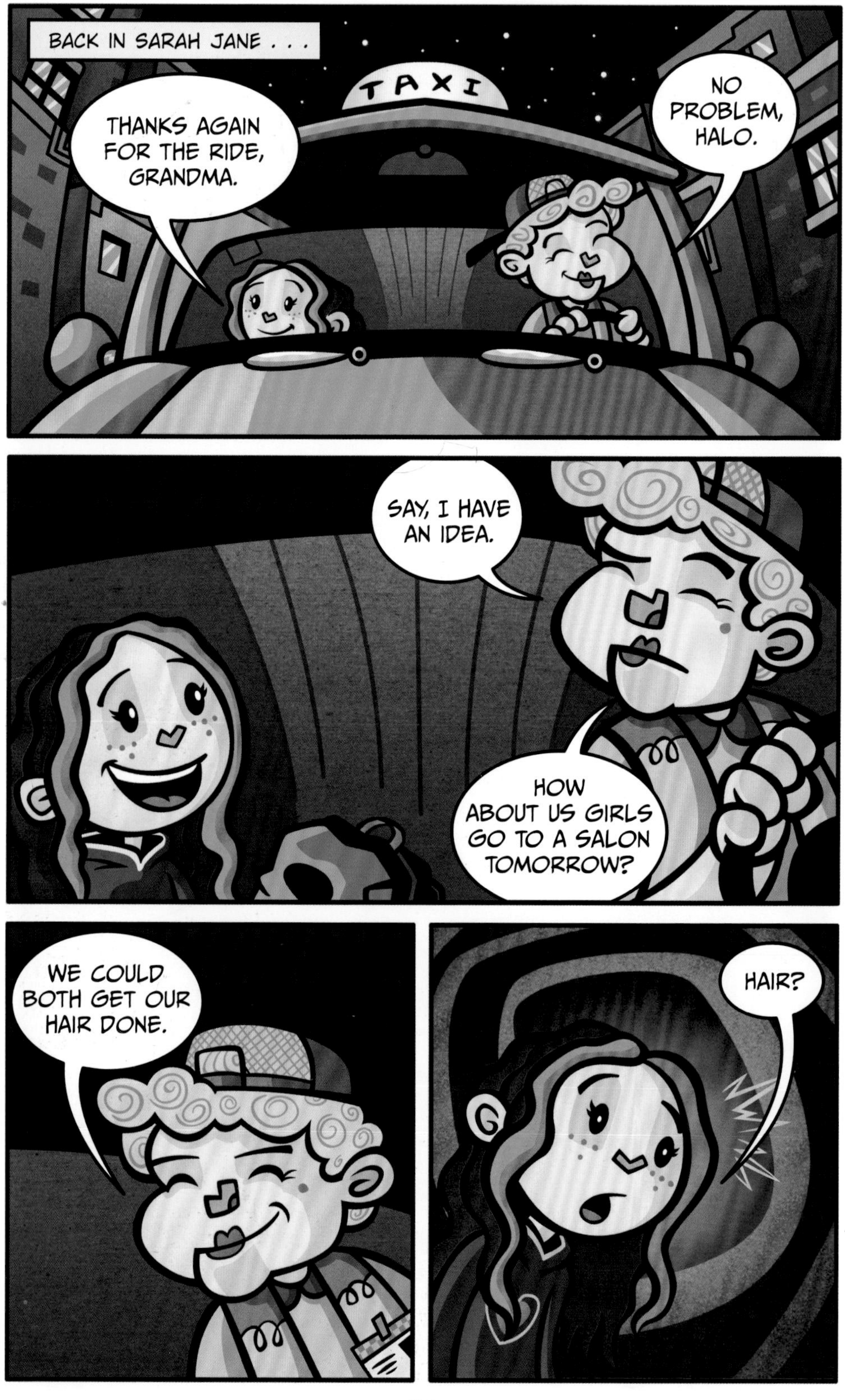
BACK IN SARAH JANE . . .
TAXI
THANKS AGAIN FOR THE RIDE, GRANDMA.
NO PROBLEM, HALO.
SAY, I HAVE AN IDEA.
HOW ABOUT US GIRLS GO TO A SALON TOMORROW?
WE COULD BOTH GET OUR HAIR DONE.
HAIR?

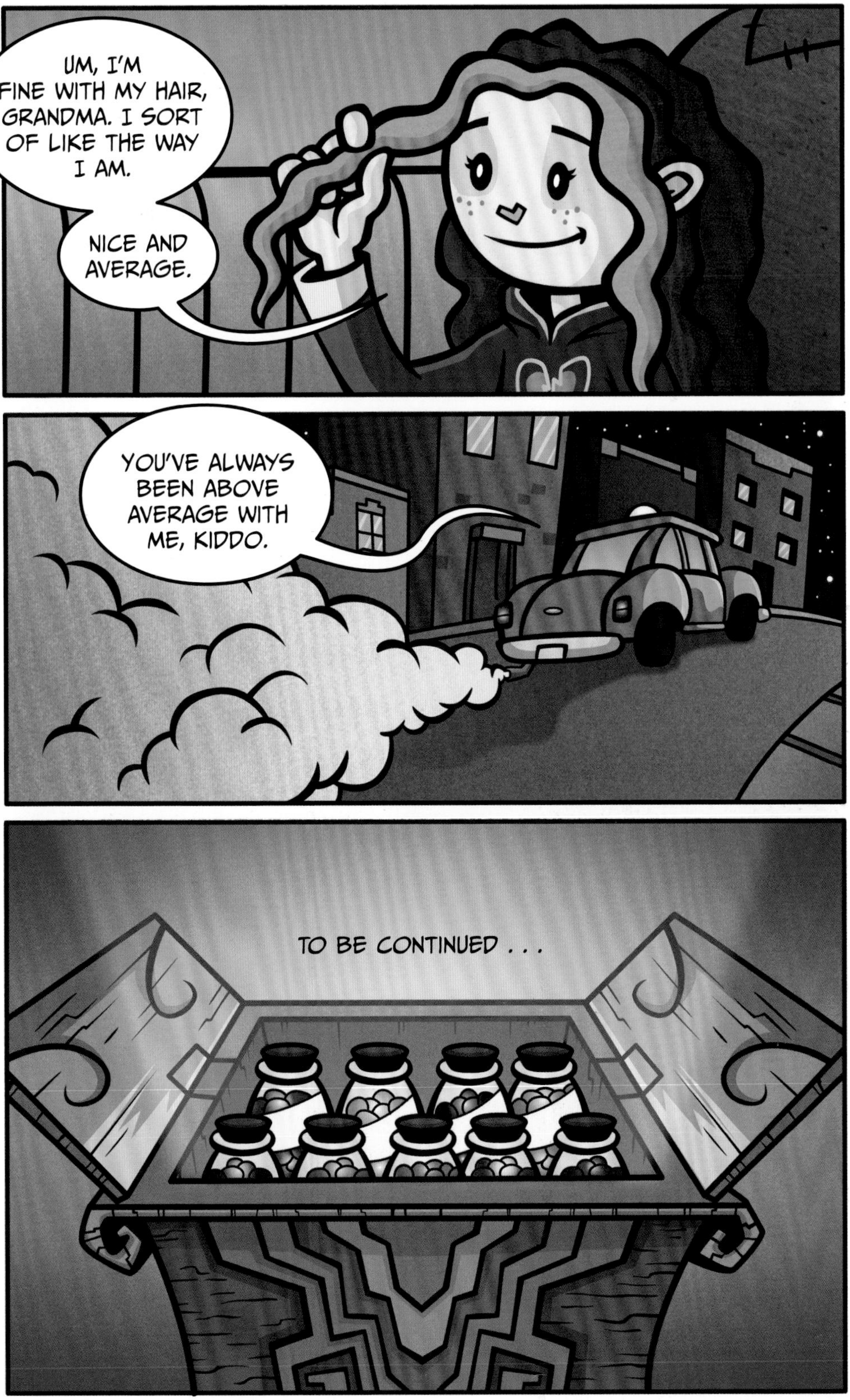
UM, I'M FINE WITH MY HAIR, GRANDMA. I SORT OF LIKE THE WAY I AM.
NICE AND AVERAGE.
YOU'VE ALWAYS BEEN ABOVE AVERAGE WITH ME, KIDDO.
TO BE CONTINUED . . .

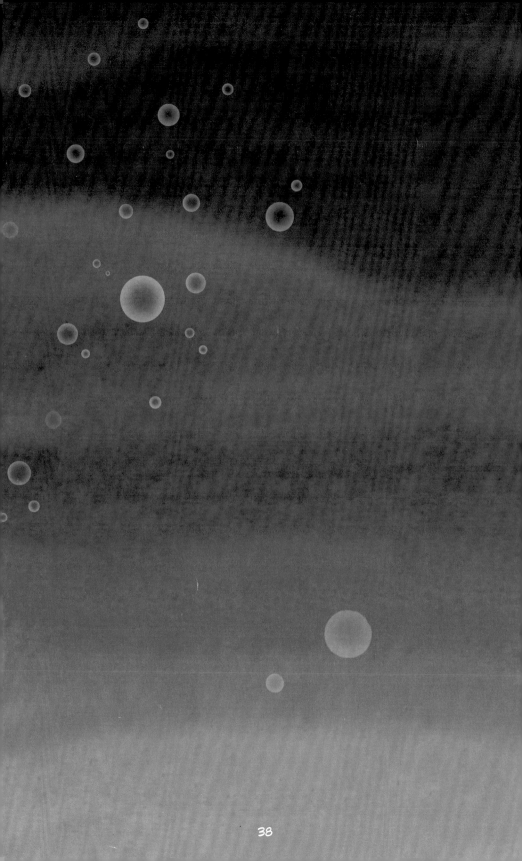

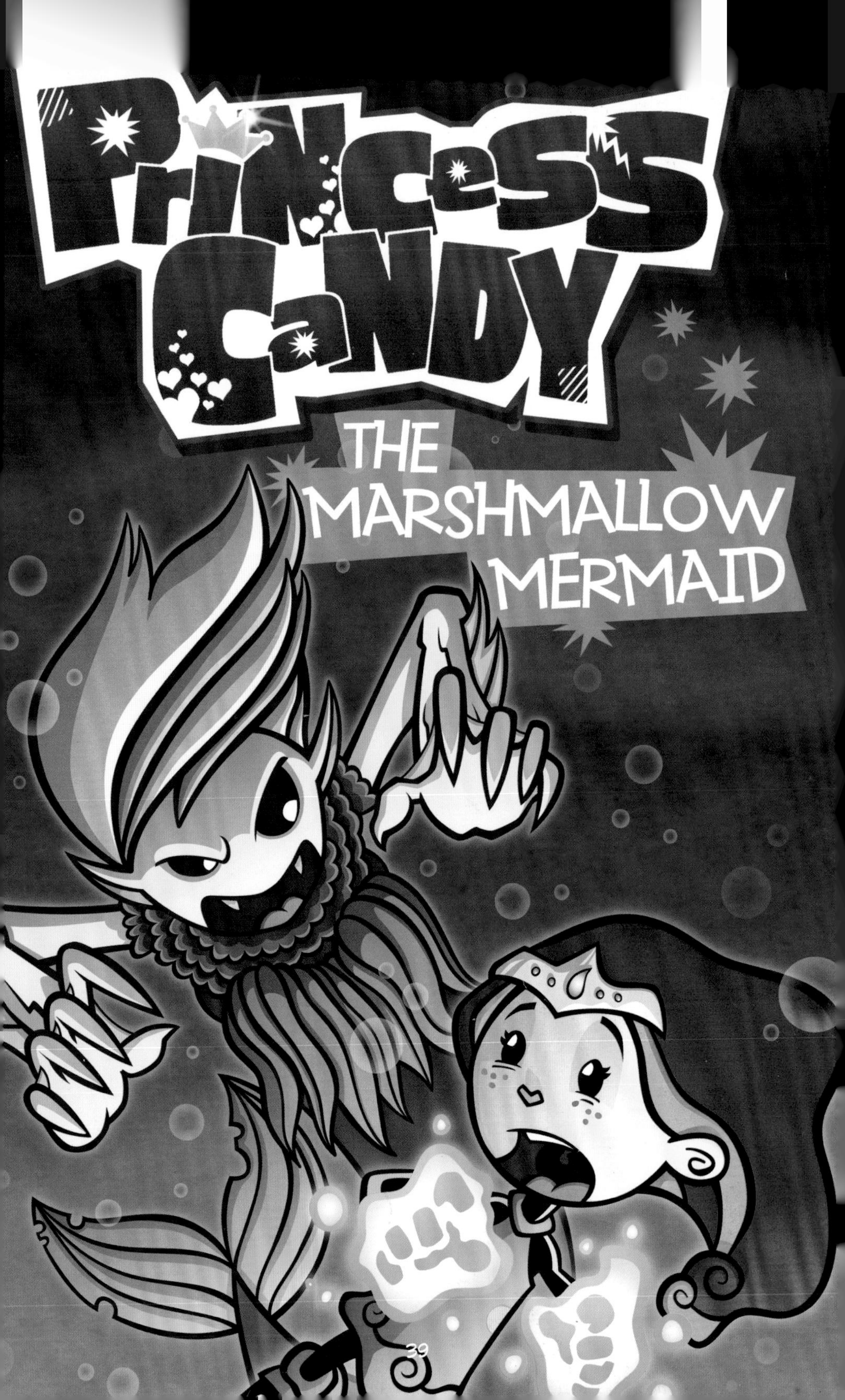
PRINCESS CANDY
THE MARSHMALLOW MERMAID

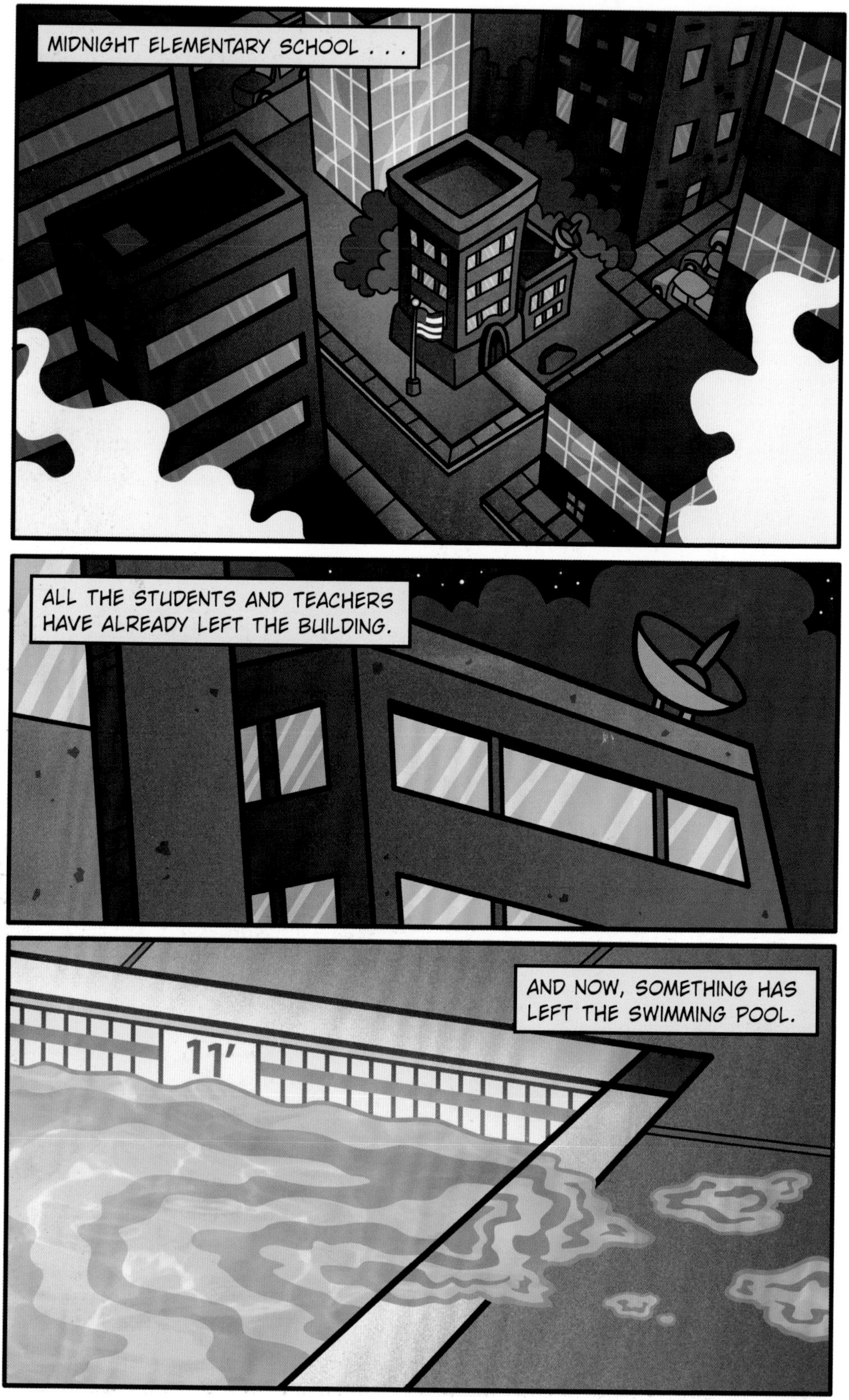
MIDNIGHT ELEMENTARY SCHOOL . . .
ALL THE STUDENTS AND TEACHERS HAVE ALREADY LEFT THE BUILDING.
AND NOW, SOMETHING HAS LEFT THE SWIMMING POOL.
11'

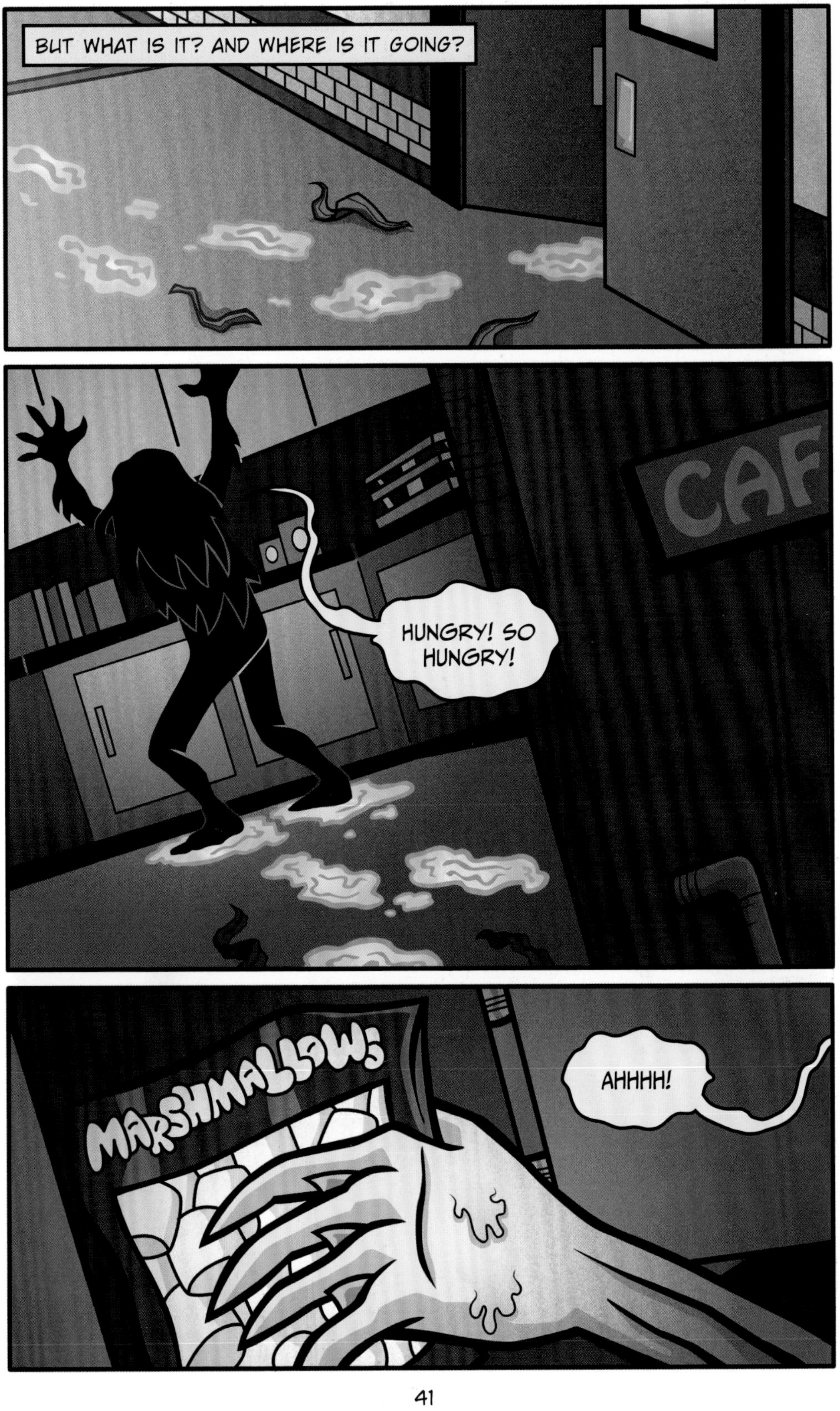
BUT WHAT IS IT? AND WHERE IS IT GOING?
HUNGRY! SO HUNGRY!
CAF
MARSHMALLOWS
MARSHMALLOWS
AHHHH!

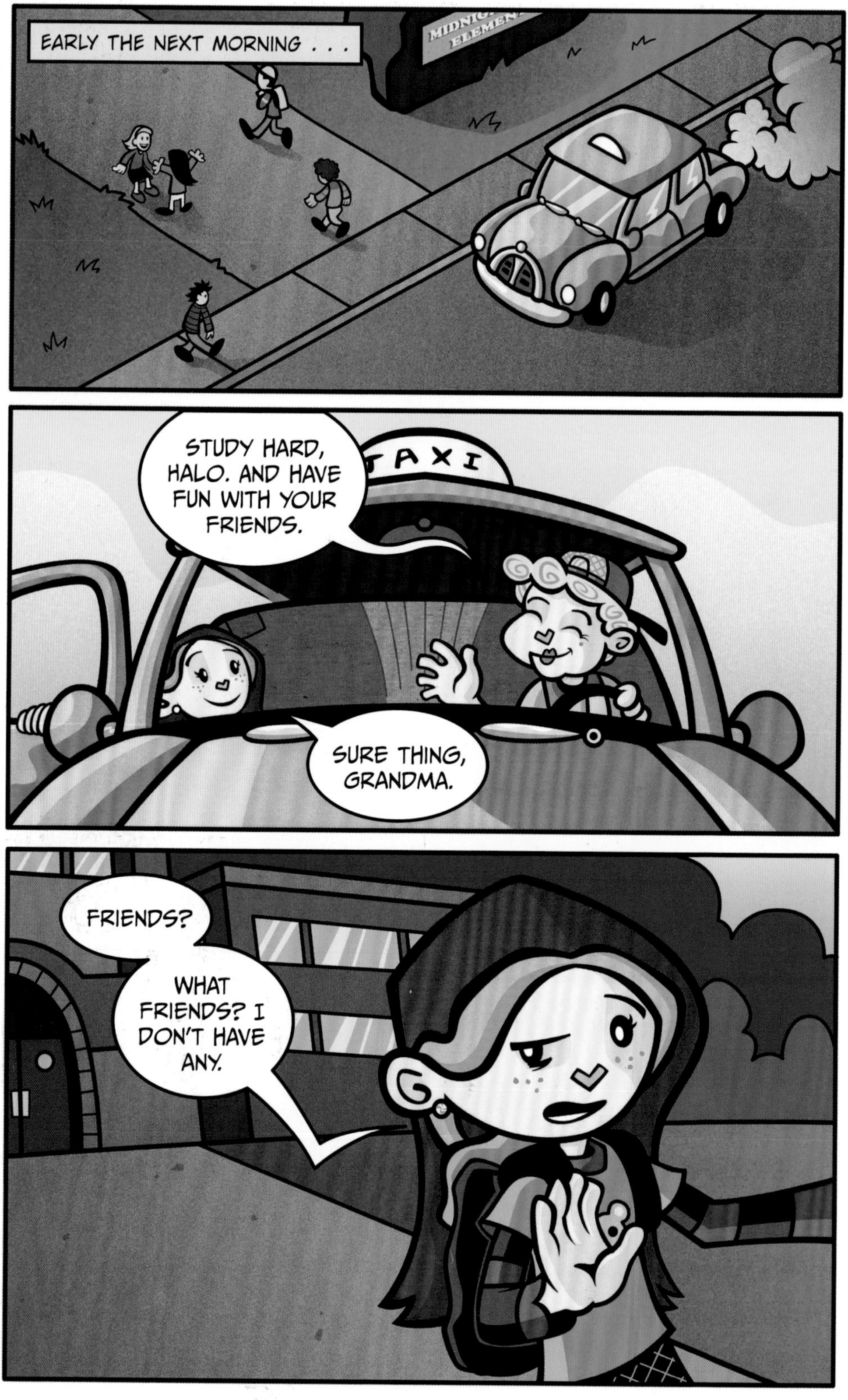
EARLY THE NEXT MORNING . . .
TAXI
STUDY HARD, HALO. AND HAVE FUN WITH YOUR FRIENDS.
SURE THING, GRANDMA.
FRIENDS?
WHAT FRIENDS? I DON'T HAVE ANY.

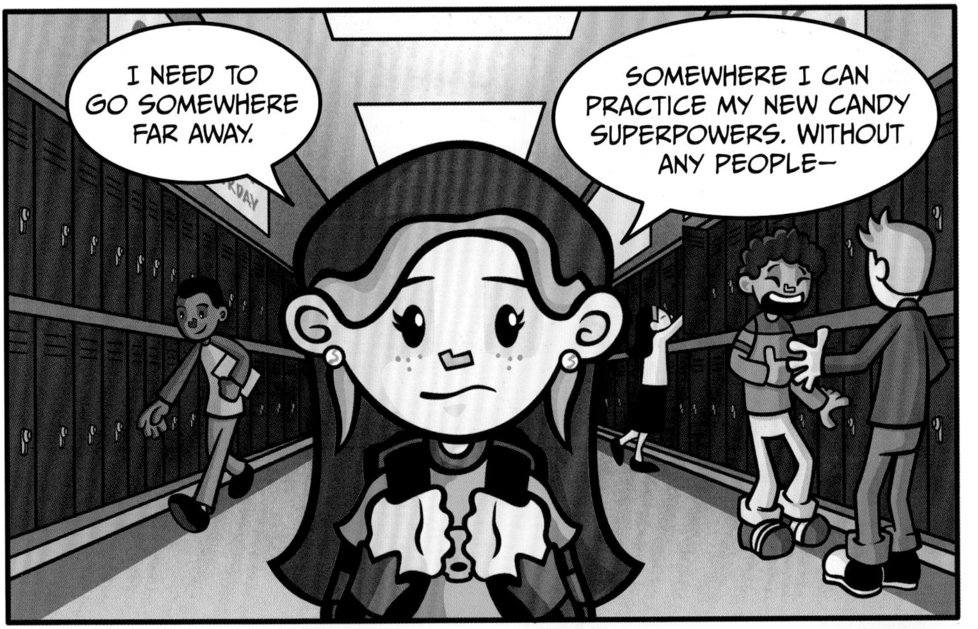
I NEED TO GO SOMEWHERE FAR AWAY.
SOMEWHERE I CAN PRACTICE MY NEW CANDY SUPERPOWERS. WITHOUT ANY PEOPLE—

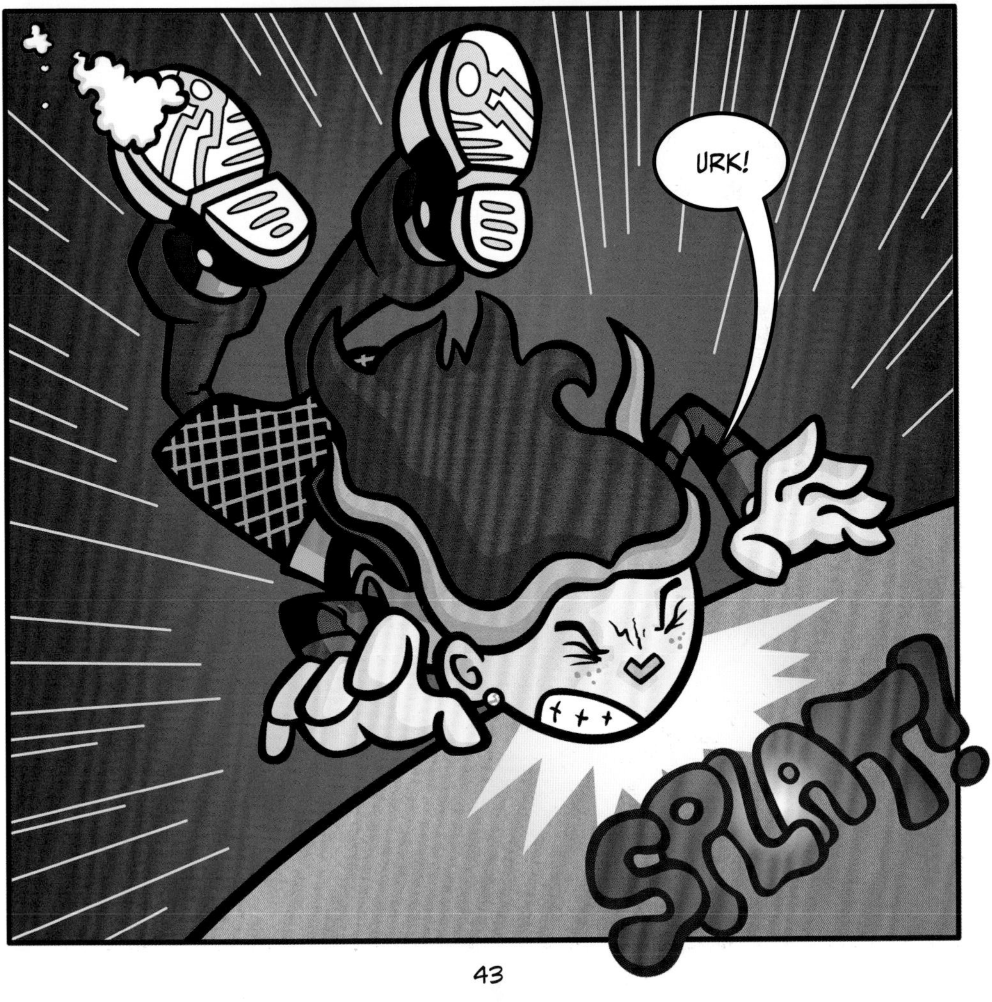
URK!
SPLAT!

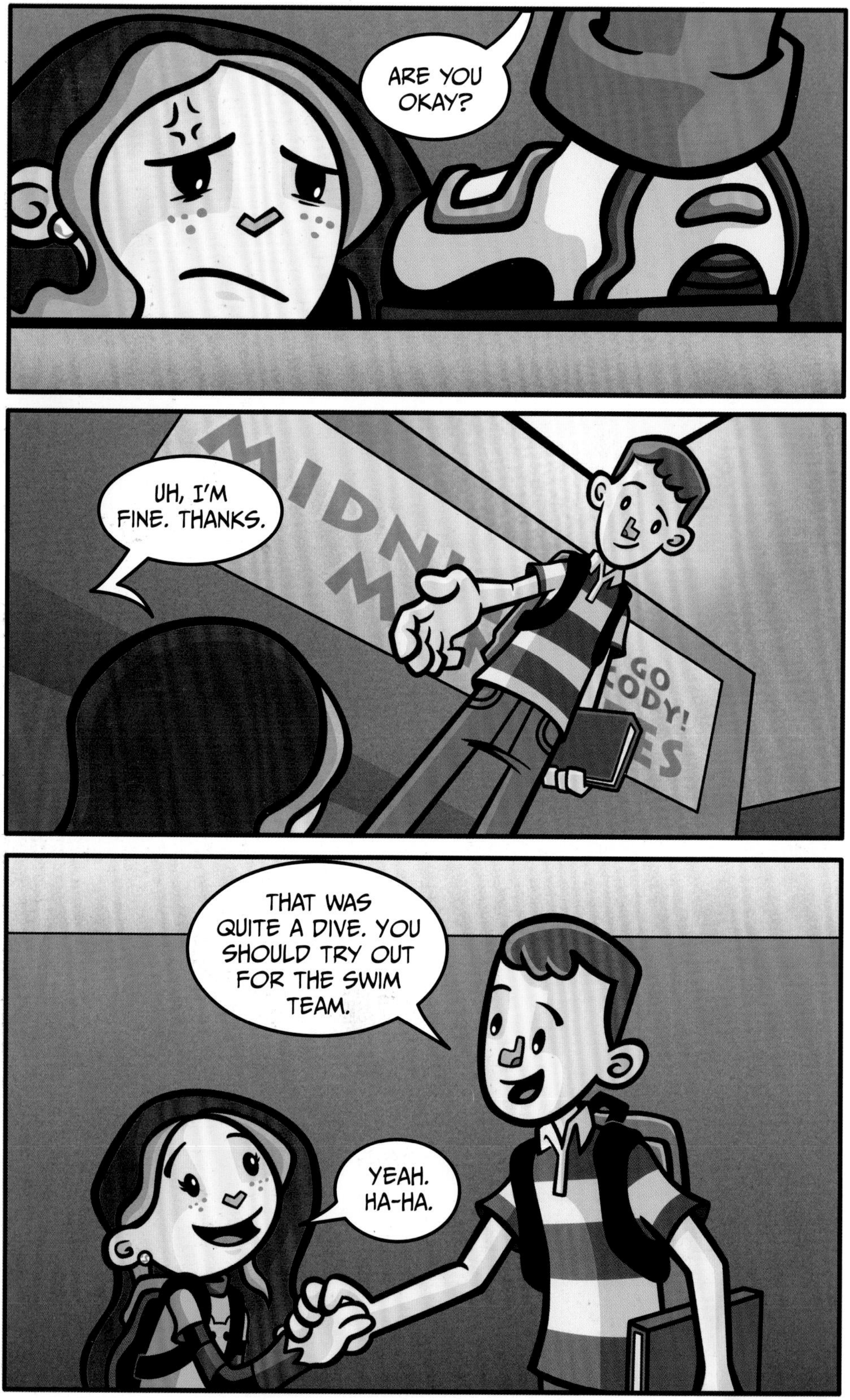
ARE YOU OKAY?
MIDNI M
UH, I'M FINE. THANKS.
GO CODY!
THAT WAS QUITE A DIVE. YOU SHOULD TRY OUT FOR THE SWIM TEAM.
YEAH. HA-HA.

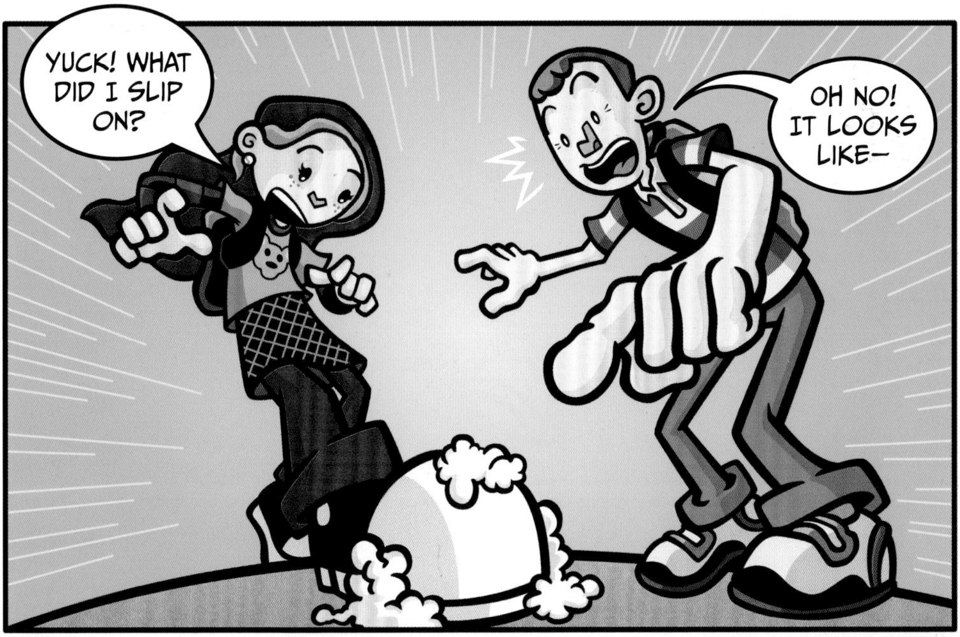
YUCK! WHAT DID I SLIP ON?
OH NO! IT LOOKS LIKE—

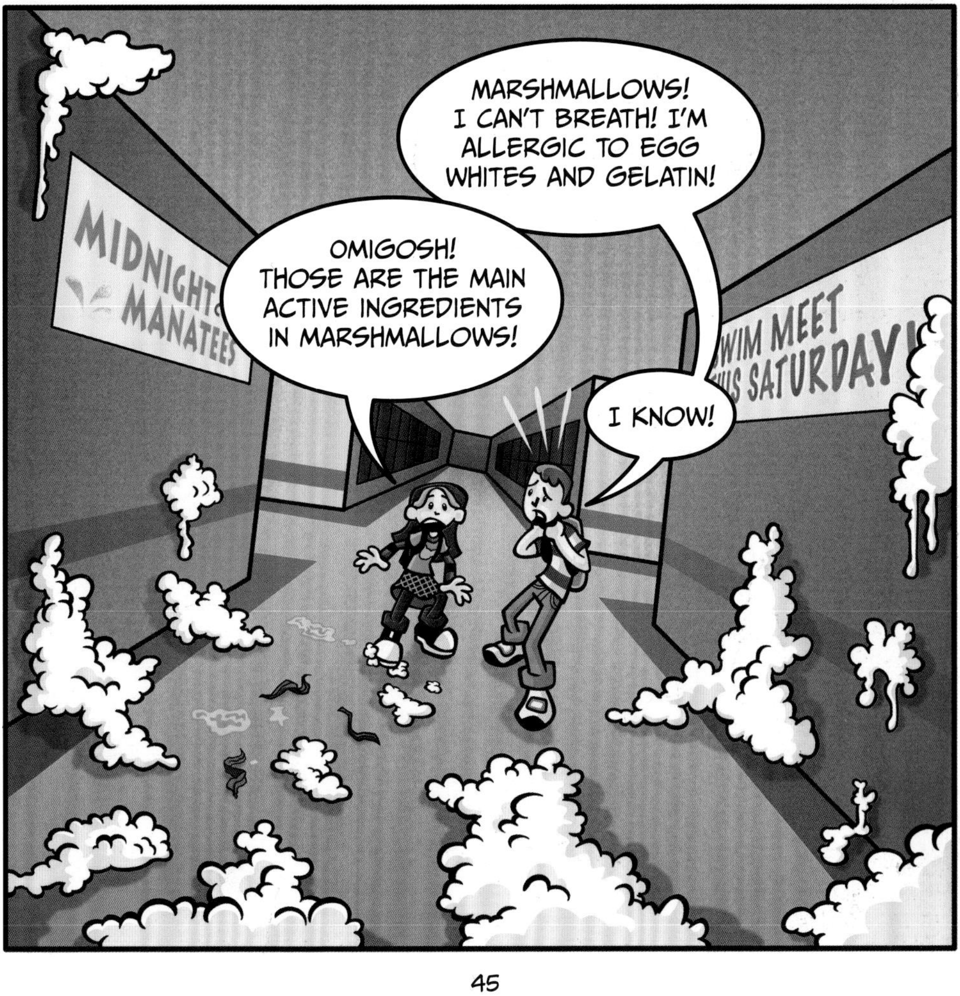
MARSHMALLOWS! I CAN'T BREATH! I'M ALLERGIC TO EGG WHITES AND GELATIN!
OMIGOSH! THOSE ARE THE MAIN ACTIVE INGREDIENTS IN MARSHMALLOWS!
I KNOW!
MIDNIGHT MANATEES

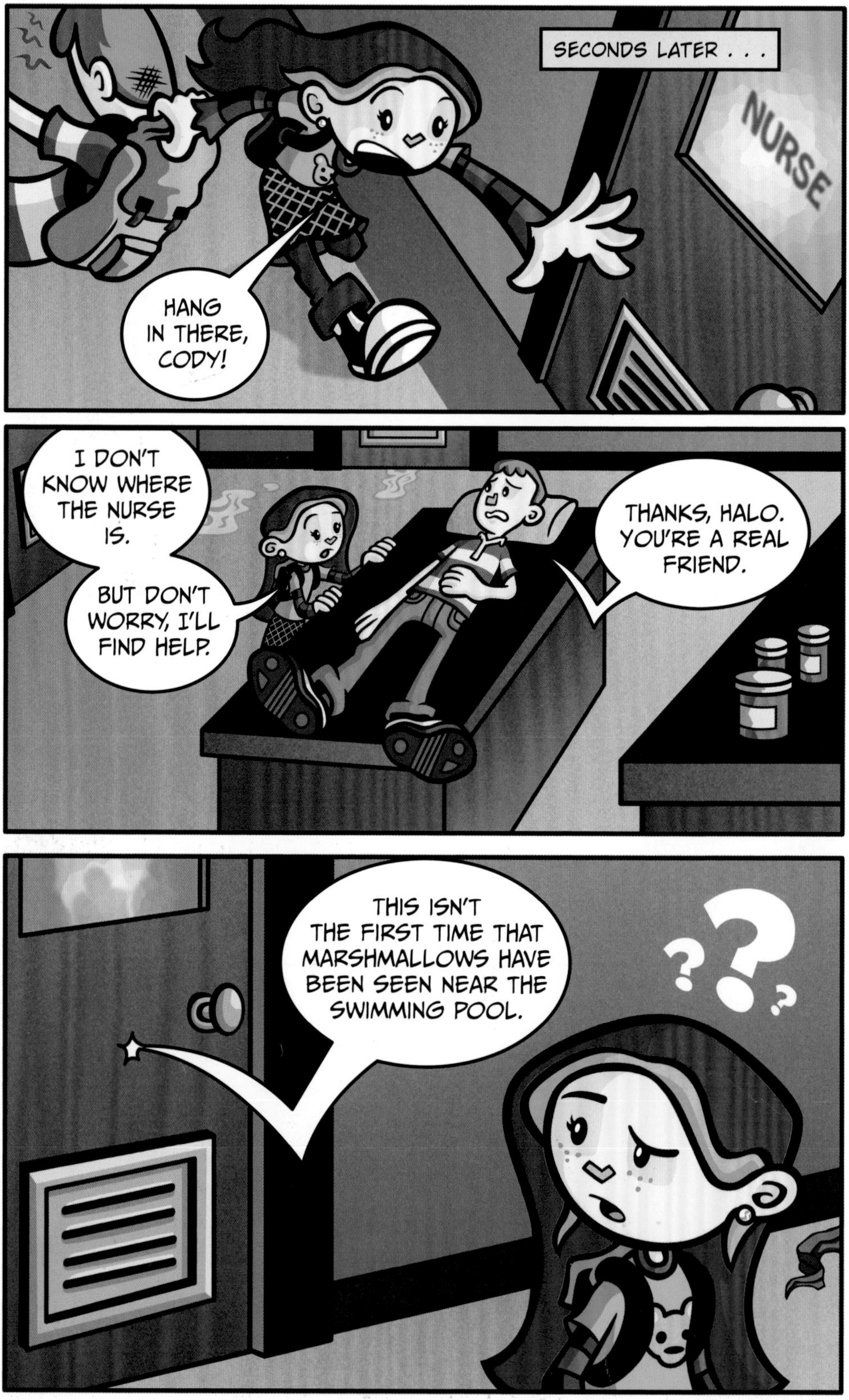
SECONDS LATER . . .
NURSE
HANG IN THERE, CODY!
I DON'T KNOW WHERE THE NURSE IS.
BUT DON'T WORRY, I'LL FIND HELP.
THANKS, HALO. YOU'RE A REAL FRIEND.
THIS ISN'T THE FIRST TIME THAT MARSHMALLOWS HAVE BEEN SEEN NEAR THE SWIMMING POOL.
? ? ?

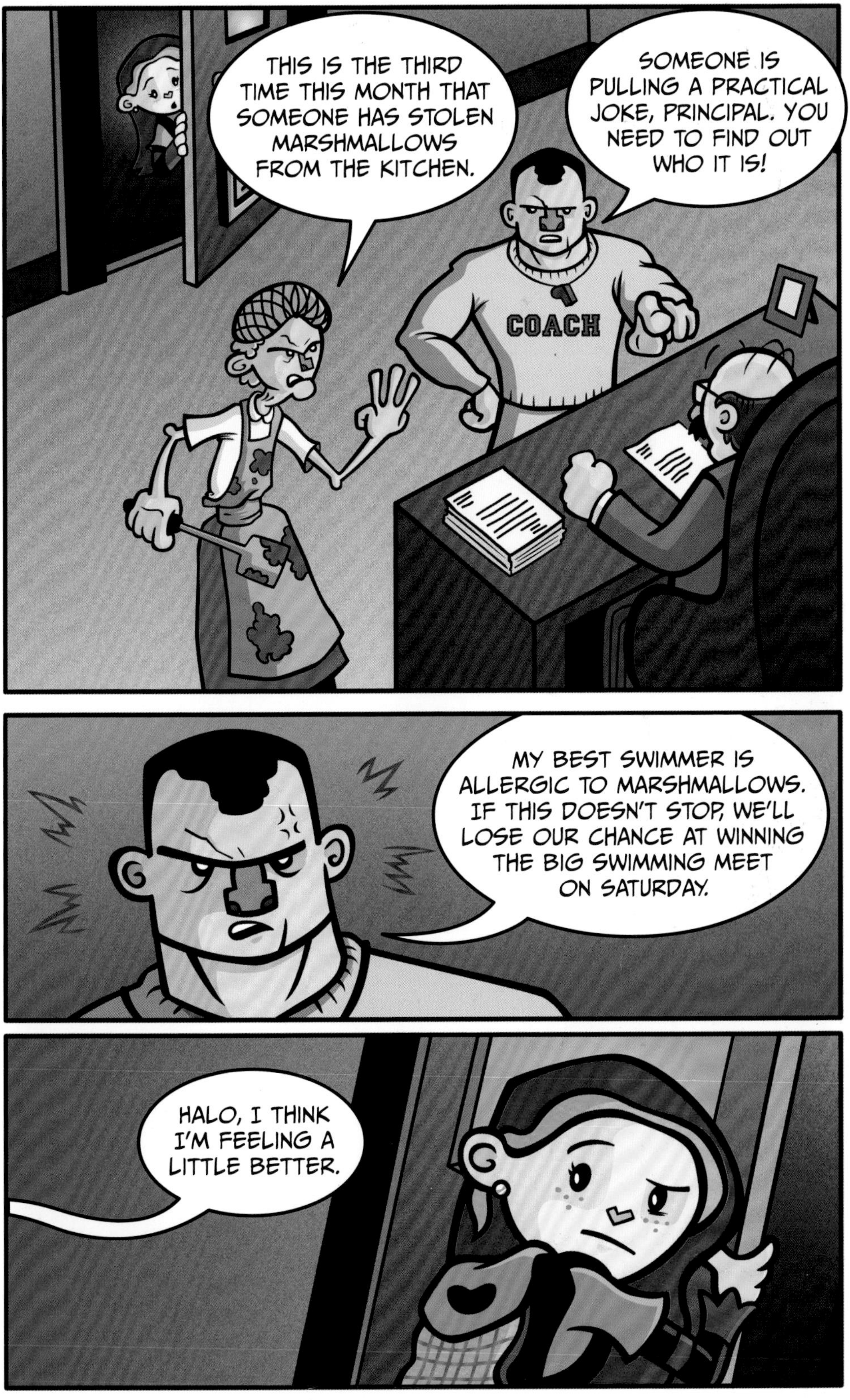
THIS IS THE THIRD TIME THIS MONTH THAT SOMEONE HAS STOLEN MARSHMALLOWS FROM THE KITCHEN.
SOMEONE IS PULLING A PRACTICAL JOKE, PRINCIPAL. YOU NEED TO FIND OUT WHO IT IS!
COACH
MY BEST SWIMMER IS ALLERGIC TO MARSHMALLOWS. IF THIS DOESN'T STOP, WE'LL LOSE OUR CHANCE AT WINNING THE BIG SWIMMING MEET ON SATURDAY.
HALO, I THINK I'M FEELING A LITTLE BETTER.

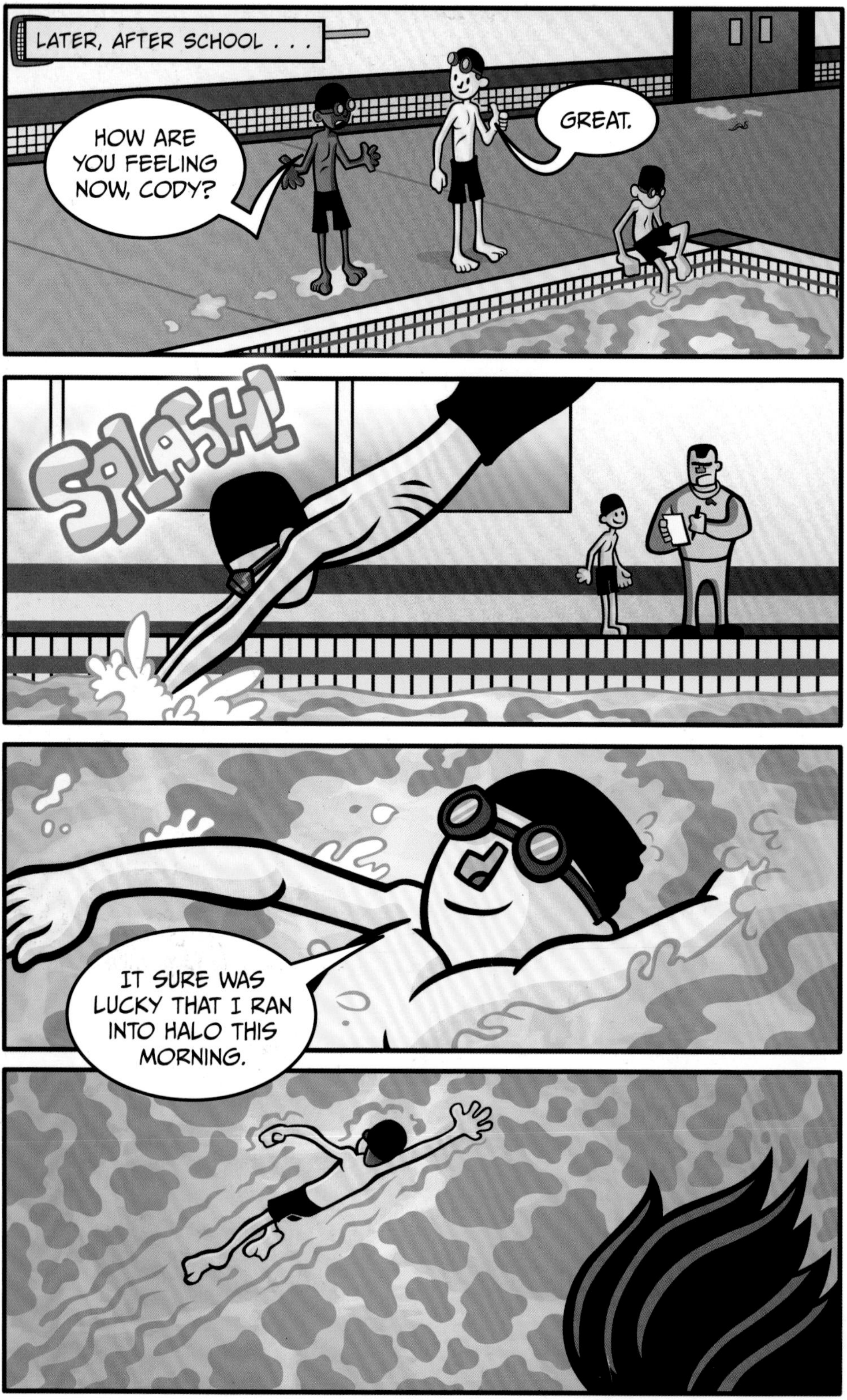
LATER, AFTER SCHOOL . . .
HOW ARE YOU FEELING NOW, CODY?
GREAT.
SPLASH!
IT SURE WAS LUCKY THAT I RAN INTO HALO THIS MORNING.

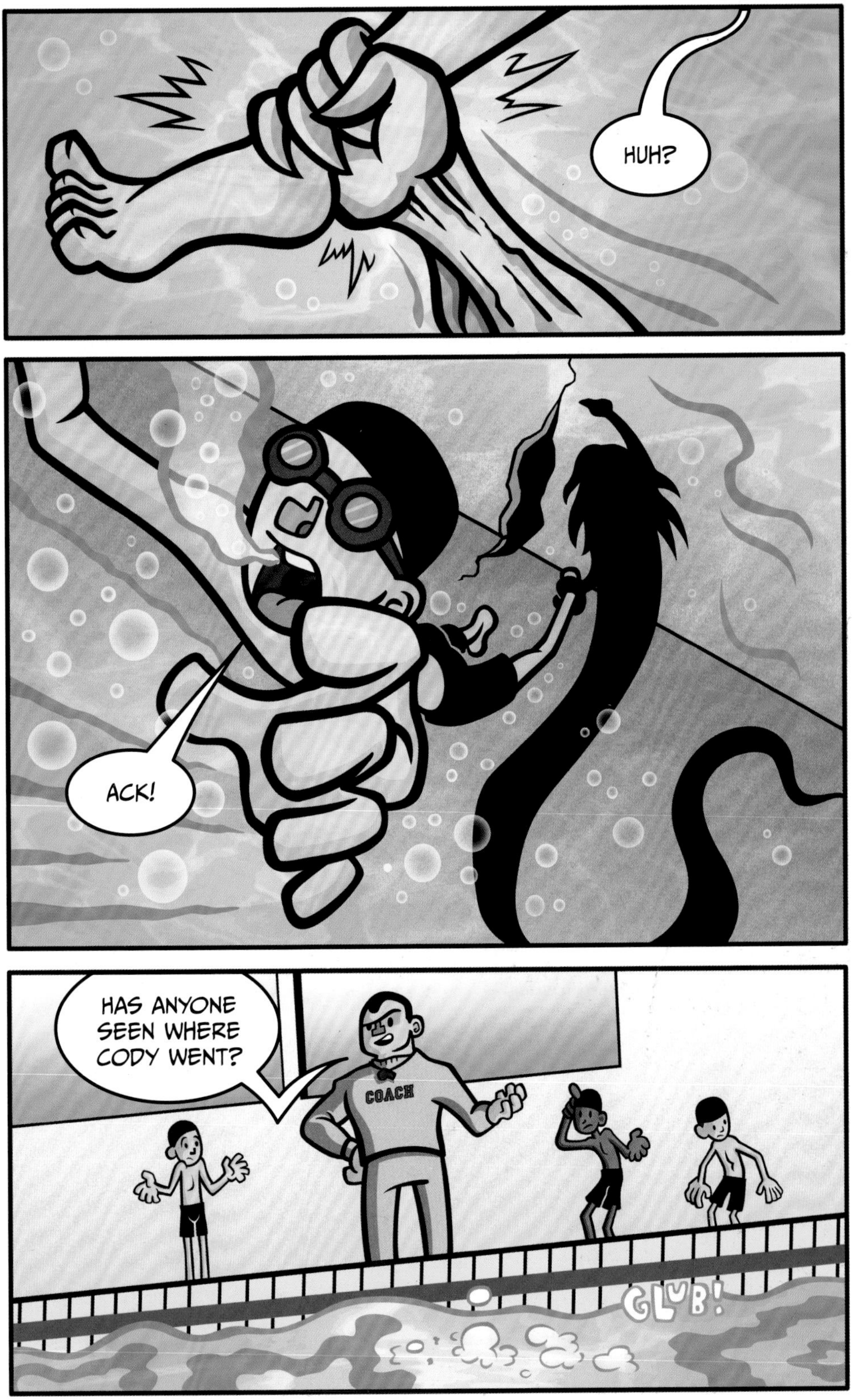
HUH?
ACK!
HAS ANYONE SEEN WHERE CODY WENT?
COACH
GLUB!

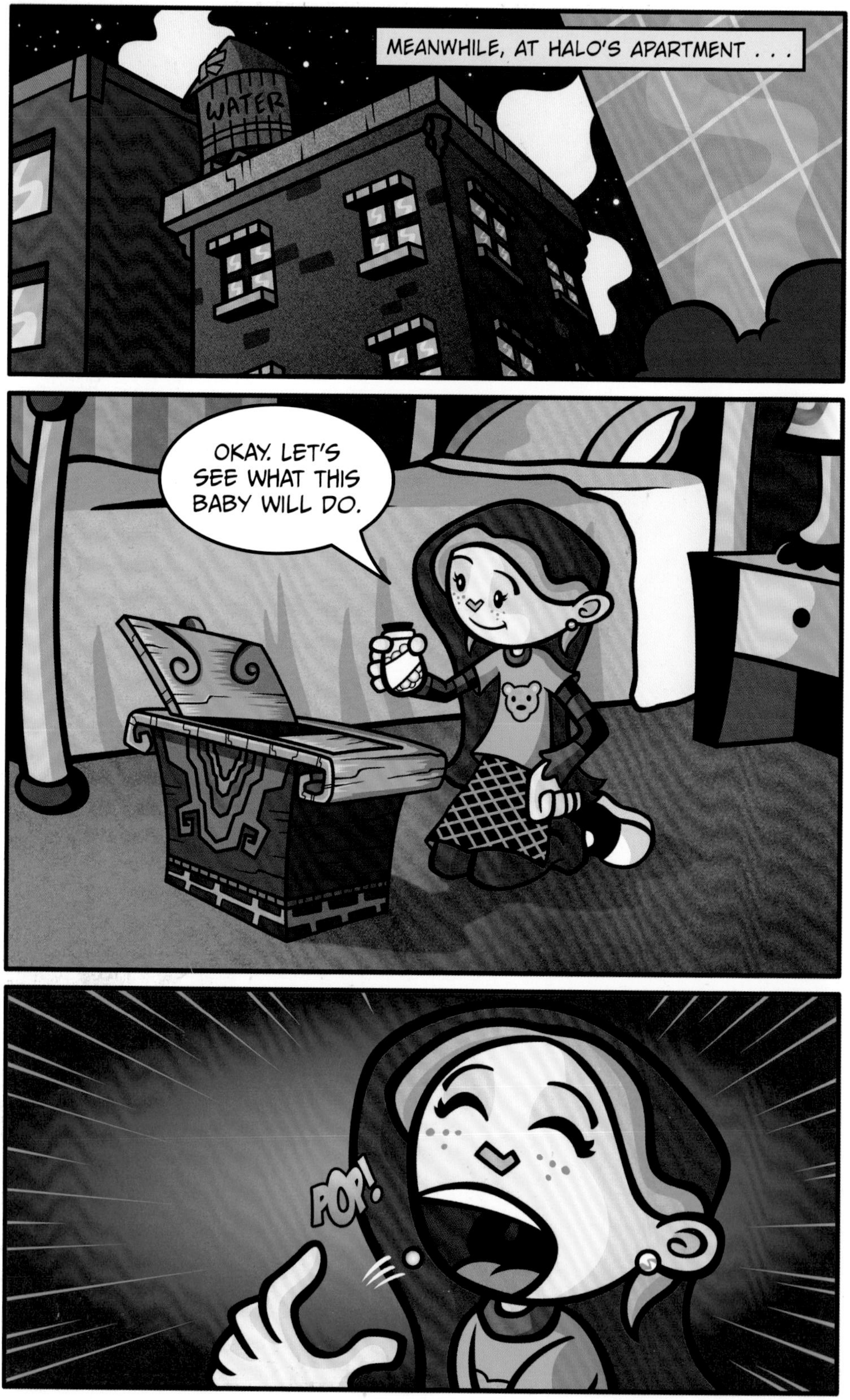
MEANWHILE, AT HALO'S APARTMENT . . .
WATER
OKAY. LET'S SEE WHAT THIS BABY WILL DO.
POP!

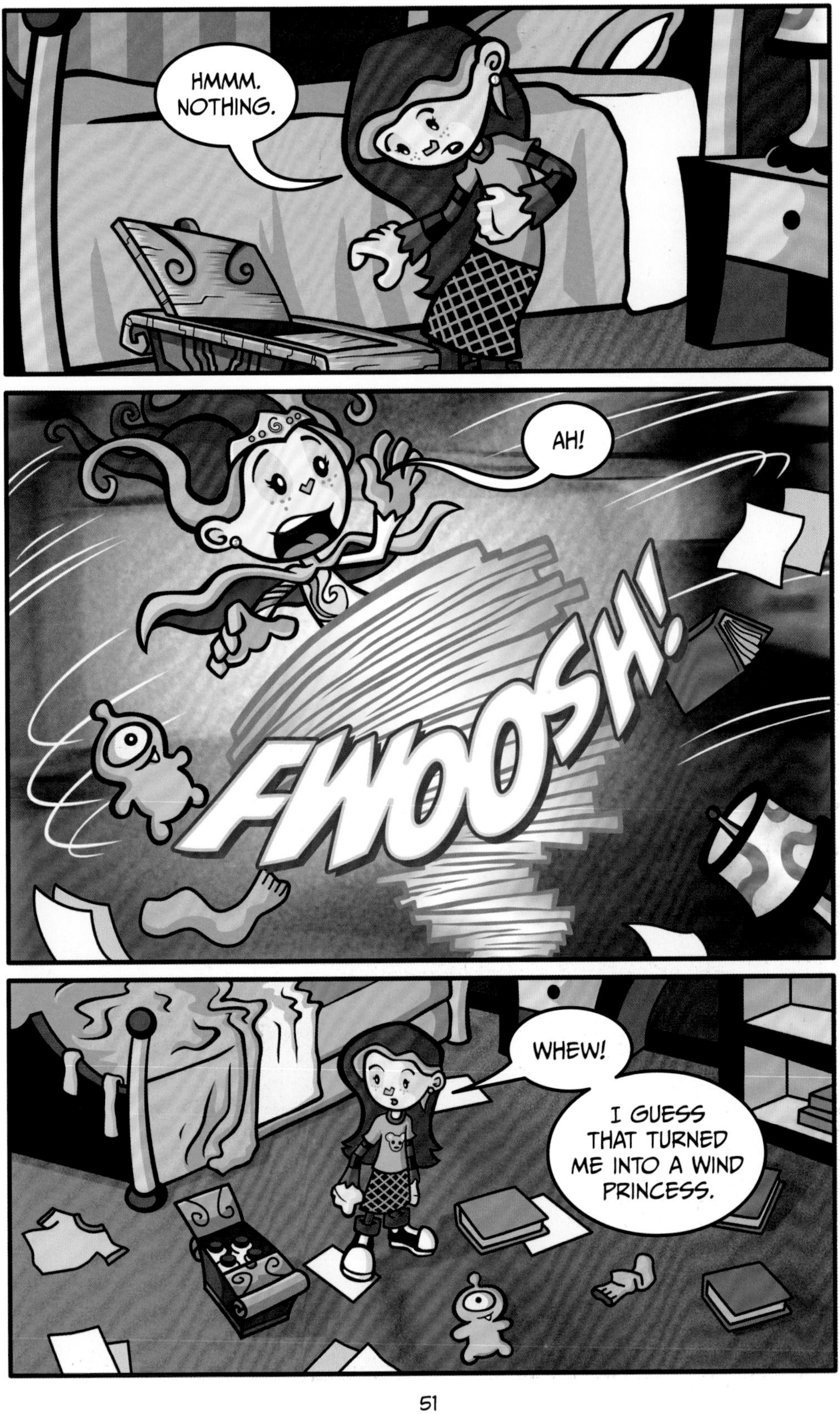
HMMM. NOTHING.
AH!
FWOOSH!
WHEW!
I GUESS THAT TURNED ME INTO A WIND PRINCESS.

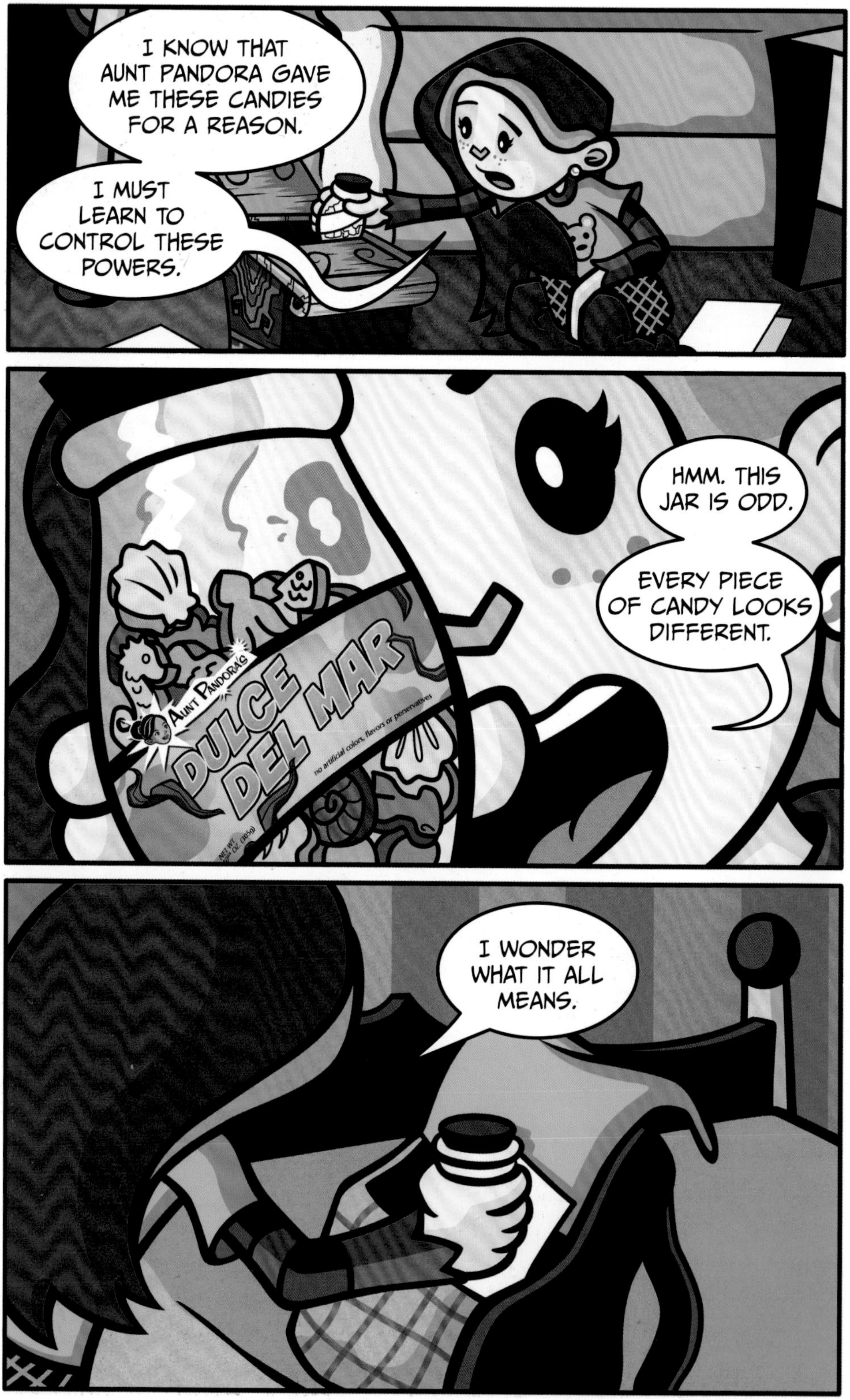
I KNOW THAT AUNT PANDORA GAVE ME THESE CANDIES FOR A REASON.
I MUST LEARN TO CONTROL THESE POWERS.
AUNT PANDORA'S
DULCE DEL MAR
HMM. THIS JAR IS ODD.
EVERY PIECE OF CANDY LOOKS DIFFERENT.
I WONDER WHAT IT ALL MEANS.

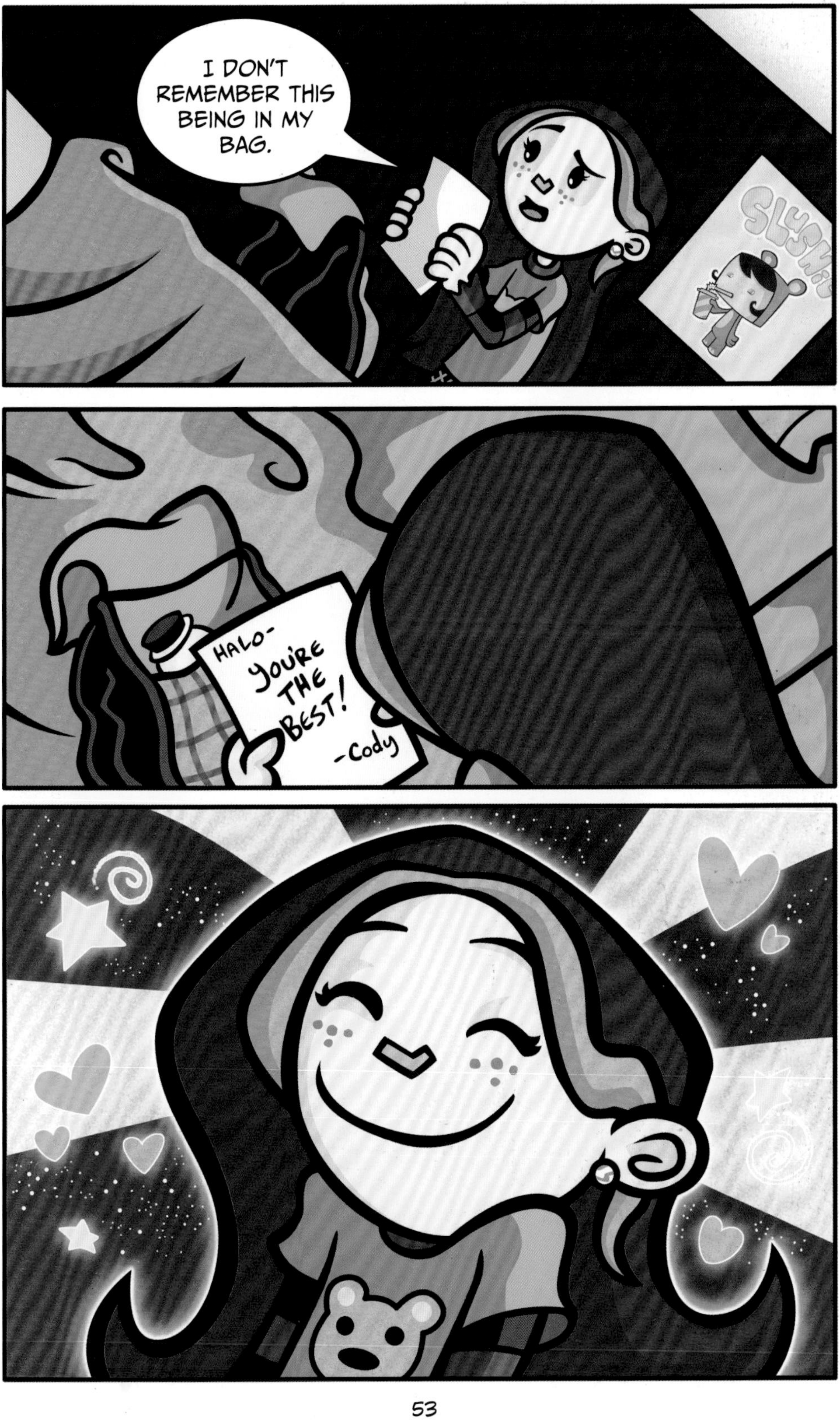
I DON'T REMEMBER THIS BEING IN MY BAG.
HALO-
YOU'RE THE BEST!
-Cody

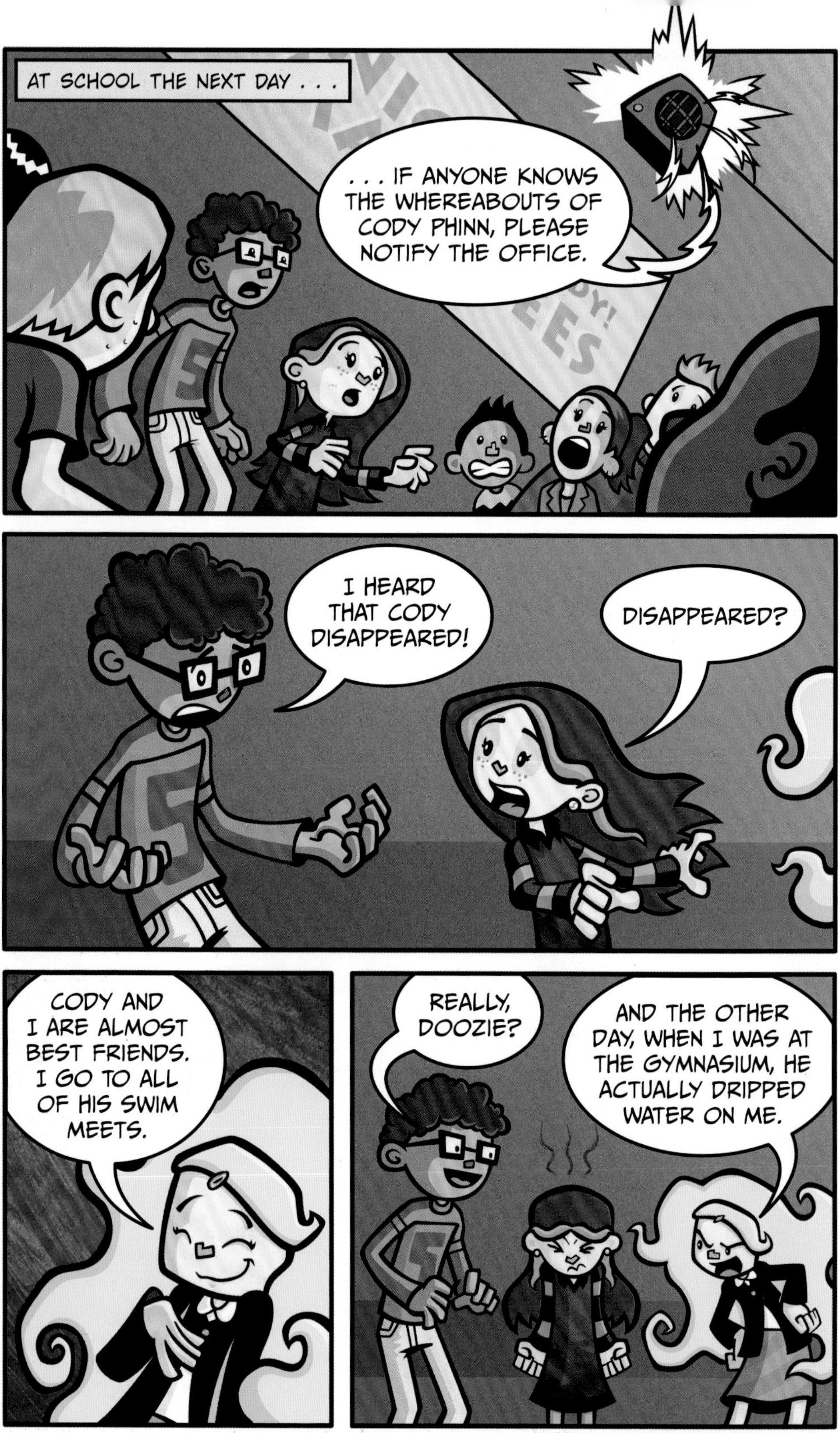
AT SCHOOL THE NEXT DAY . . .
. . . IF ANYONE KNOWS THE WHEREABOUTS OF CODY PHINN, PLEASE NOTIFY THE OFFICE.
I HEARD THAT CODY DISAPPEARED!
DISAPPEARED?
CODY AND I ARE ALMOST BEST FRIENDS. I GO TO ALL OF HIS SWIM MEETS.
REALLY, DOOZIE?
AND THE OTHER DAY, WHEN I WAS AT THE GYMNASIUM, HE ACTUALLY DRIPPED WATER ON ME.

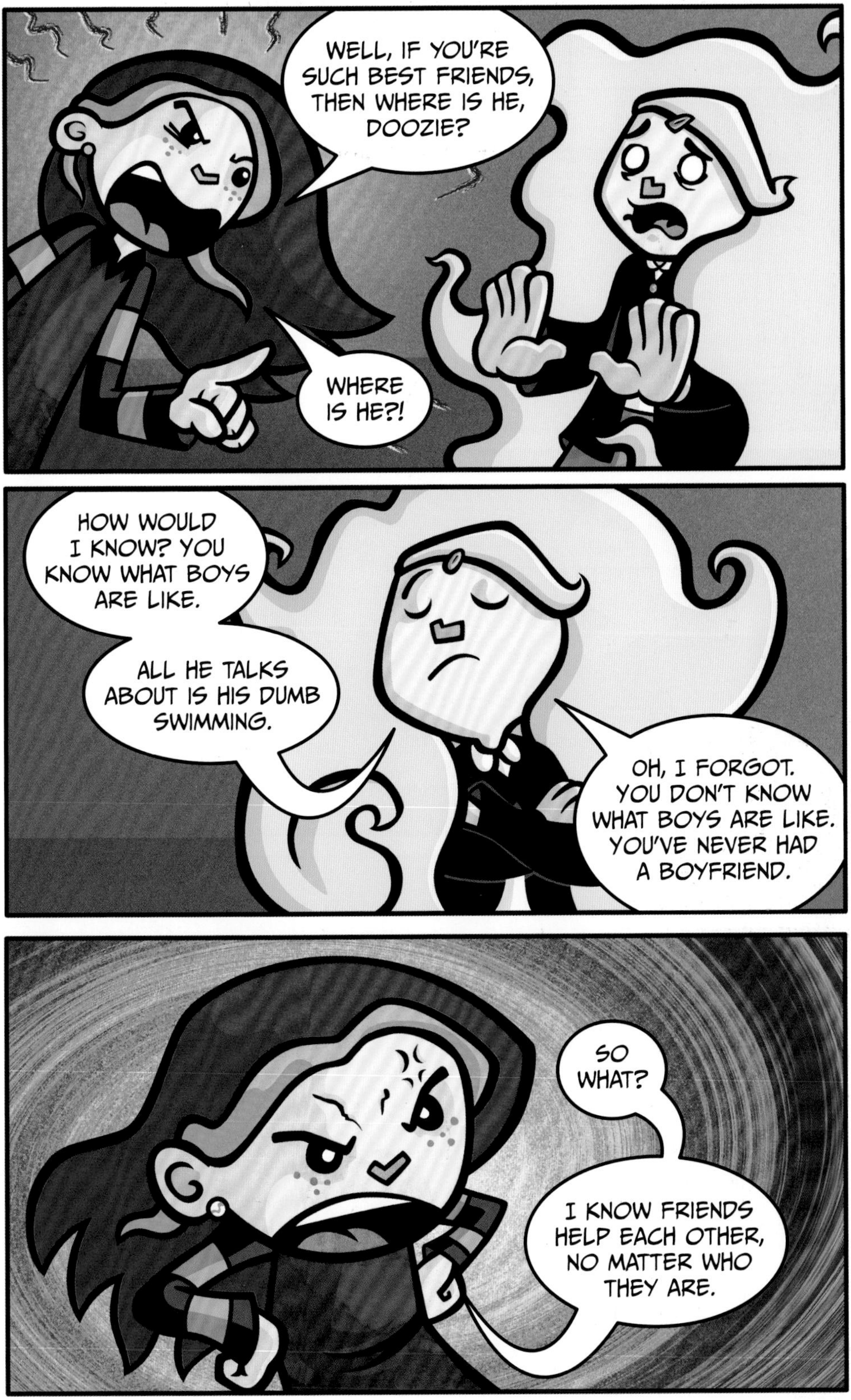
WELL, IF YOU'RE SUCH BEST FRIENDS, THEN WHERE IS HE, DOOZIE?
WHERE IS HE?!
HOW WOULD I KNOW? YOU KNOW WHAT BOYS ARE LIKE.
ALL HE TALKS ABOUT IS HIS DUMB SWIMMING.
OH, I FORGOT. YOU DON'T KNOW WHAT BOYS ARE LIKE. YOU'VE NEVER HAD A BOYFRIEND.
SO WHAT?
I KNOW FRIENDS HELP EACH OTHER, NO MATTER WHO THEY ARE.

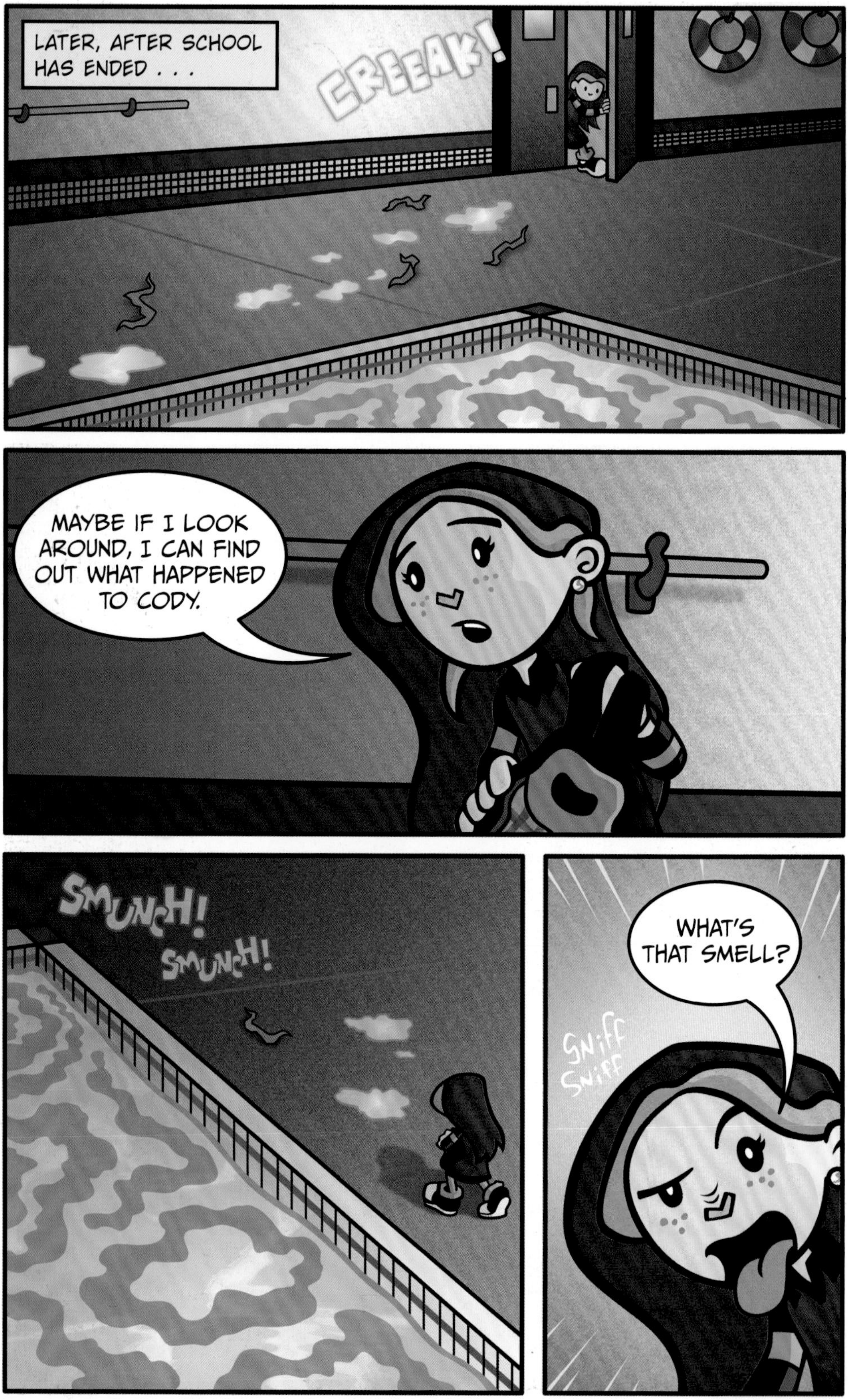
LATER, AFTER SCHOOL HAS ENDED . . .
CREEAK!
MAYBE IF I LOOK AROUND, I CAN FIND OUT WHAT HAPPENED TO CODY.
SMUNCH!
SMUNCH!
Sniff
Sniff
WHAT'S THAT SMELL?

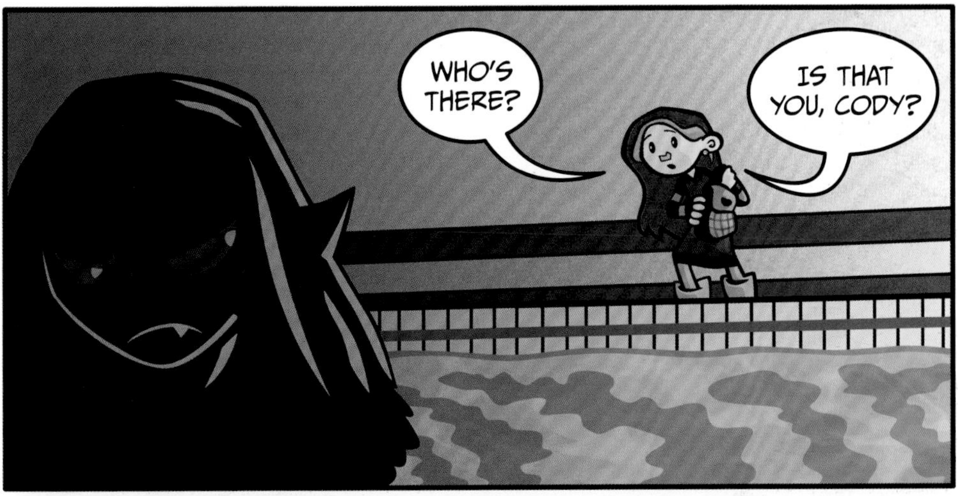
WHO'S THERE?
IS THAT YOU, CODY?

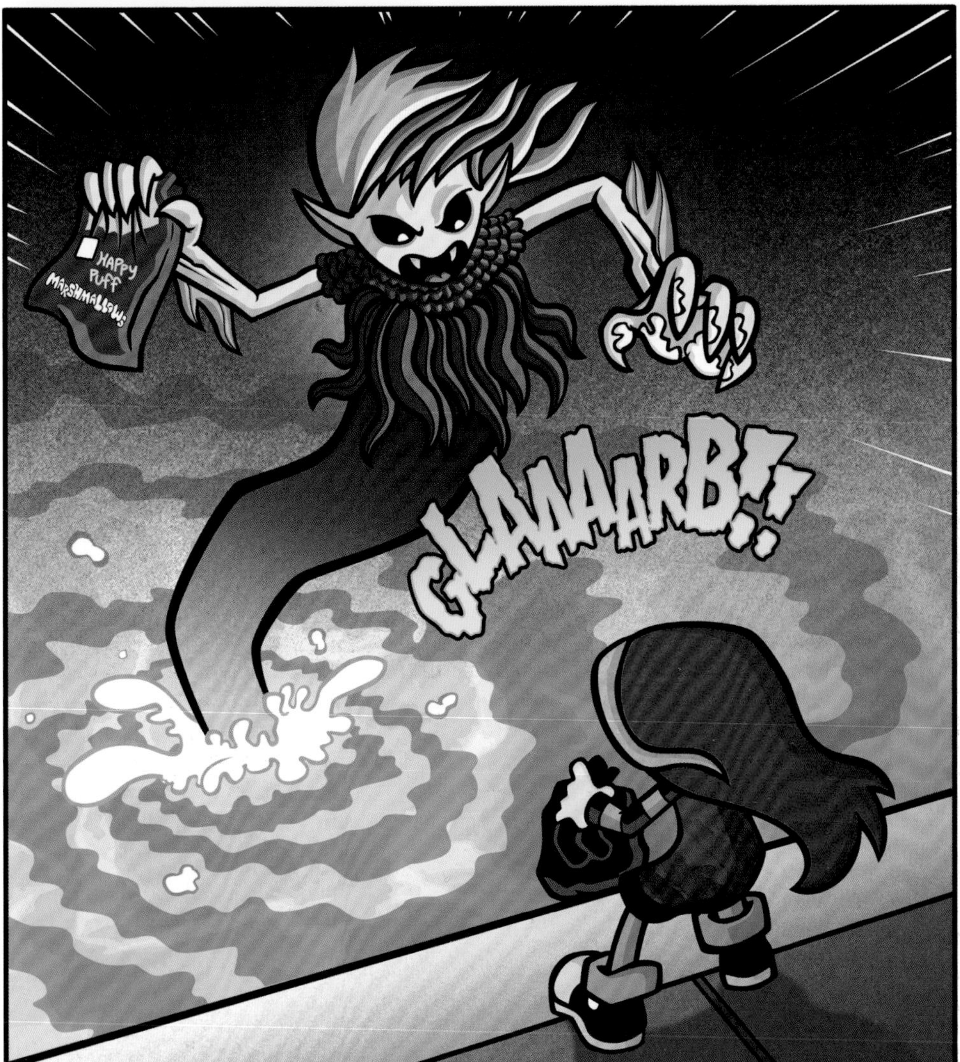
HAPPY PUFF MARSHMALLOWS
GLAAAARB!!

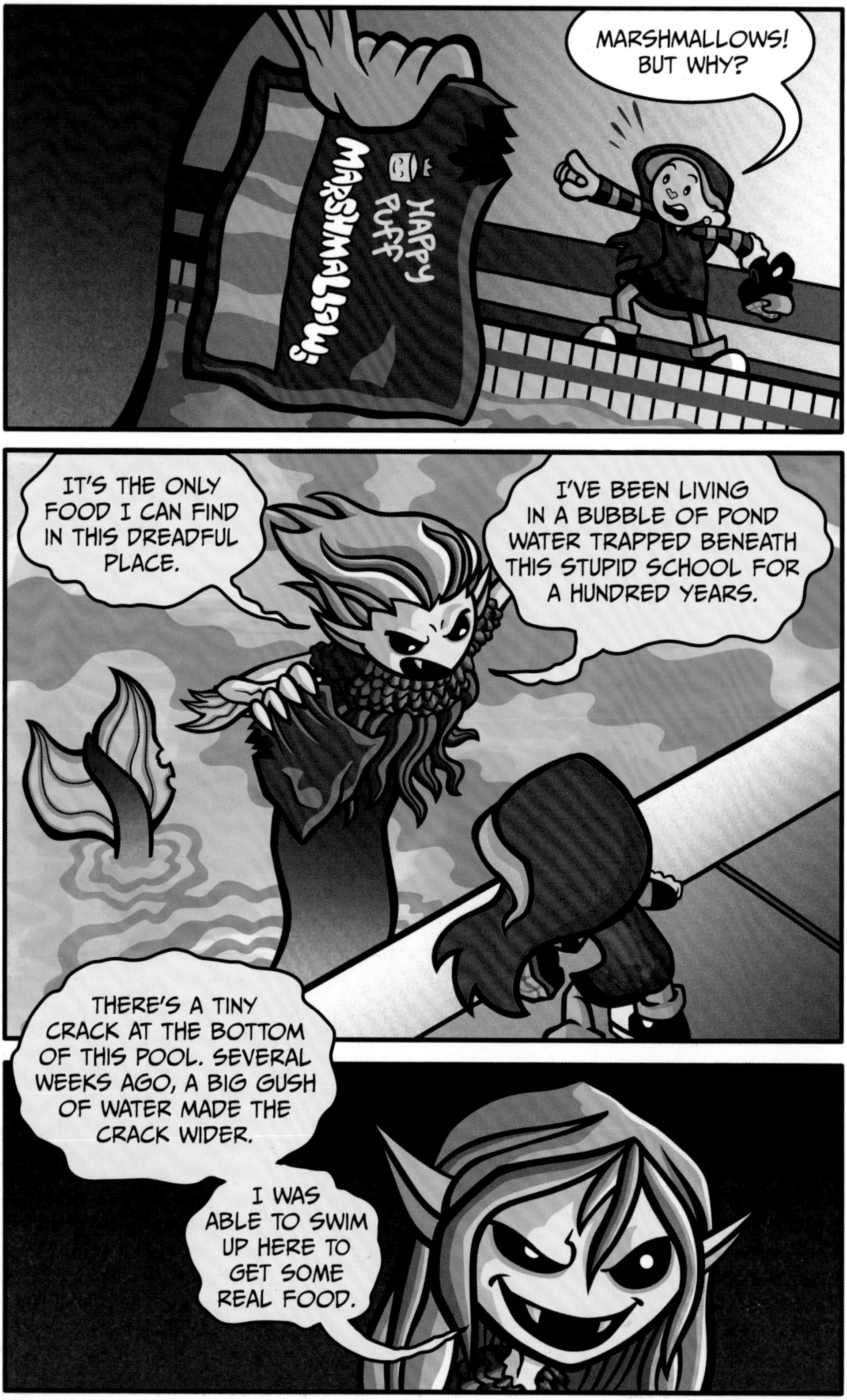

MARSHMALLOWS! BUT WHY?
HAPPY PUFF MARSHMALLOWS!
IT'S THE ONLY FOOD I CAN FIND IN THIS DREADFUL PLACE.
I'VE BEEN LIVING IN A BUBBLE OF POND WATER TRAPPED BENEATH THIS STUPID SCHOOL FOR A HUNDRED YEARS.
THERE'S A TINY CRACK AT THE BOTTOM OF THIS POOL. SEVERAL WEEKS AGO, A BIG GUSH OF WATER MADE THE CRACK WIDER.
I WAS ABLE TO SWIM UP HERE TO GET SOME REAL FOOD.

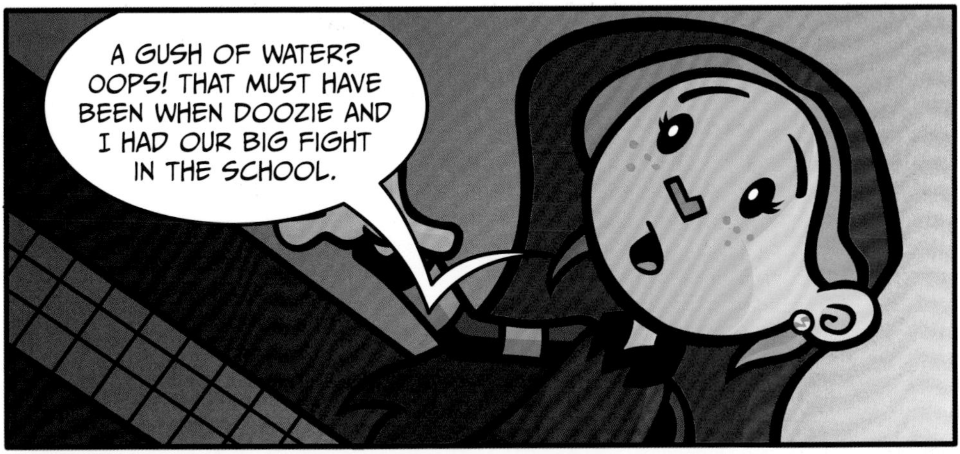
A GUSH OF WATER? OOPS! THAT MUST HAVE BEEN WHEN DOOZIE AND I HAD OUR BIG FIGHT IN THE SCHOOL.

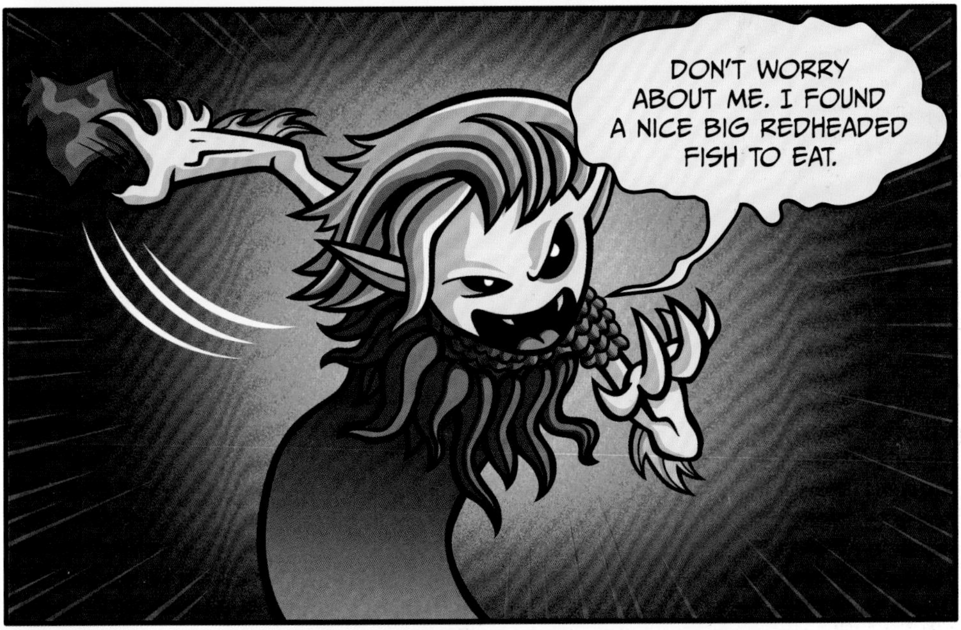
DON'T WORRY ABOUT ME. I FOUND A NICE BIG REDHEADED FISH TO EAT.

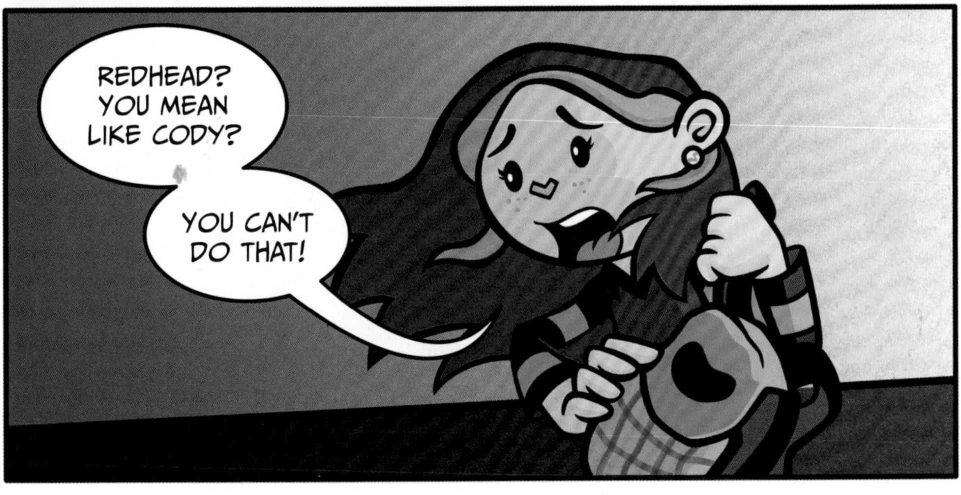
REDHEAD? YOU MEAN LIKE CODY?
YOU CAN'T DO THAT!

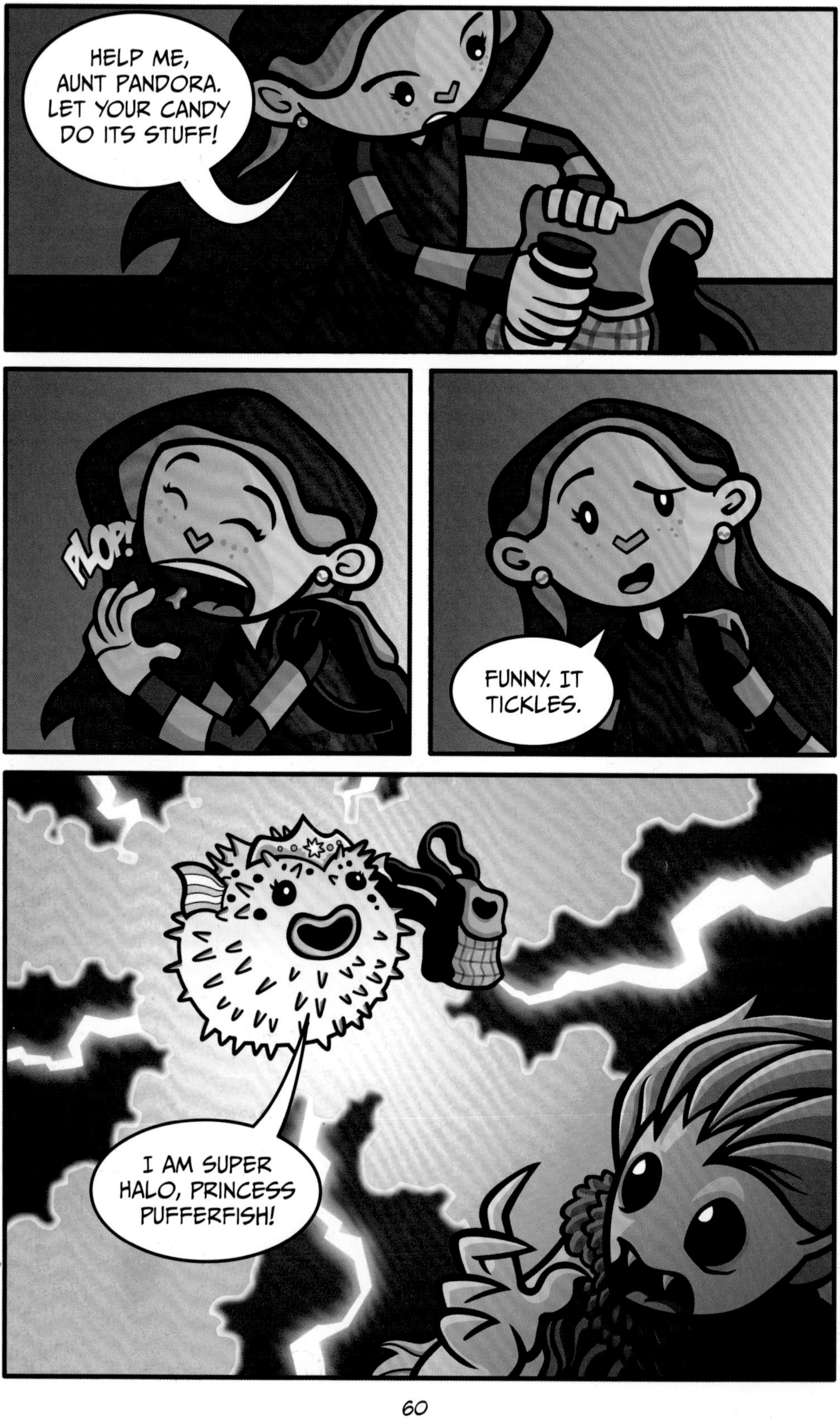
HELP ME, AUNT PANDORA. LET YOUR CANDY DO ITS STUFF!
PLOP!
FUNNY. IT TICKLES.
I AM SUPER HALO, PRINCESS PUFFERFISH!

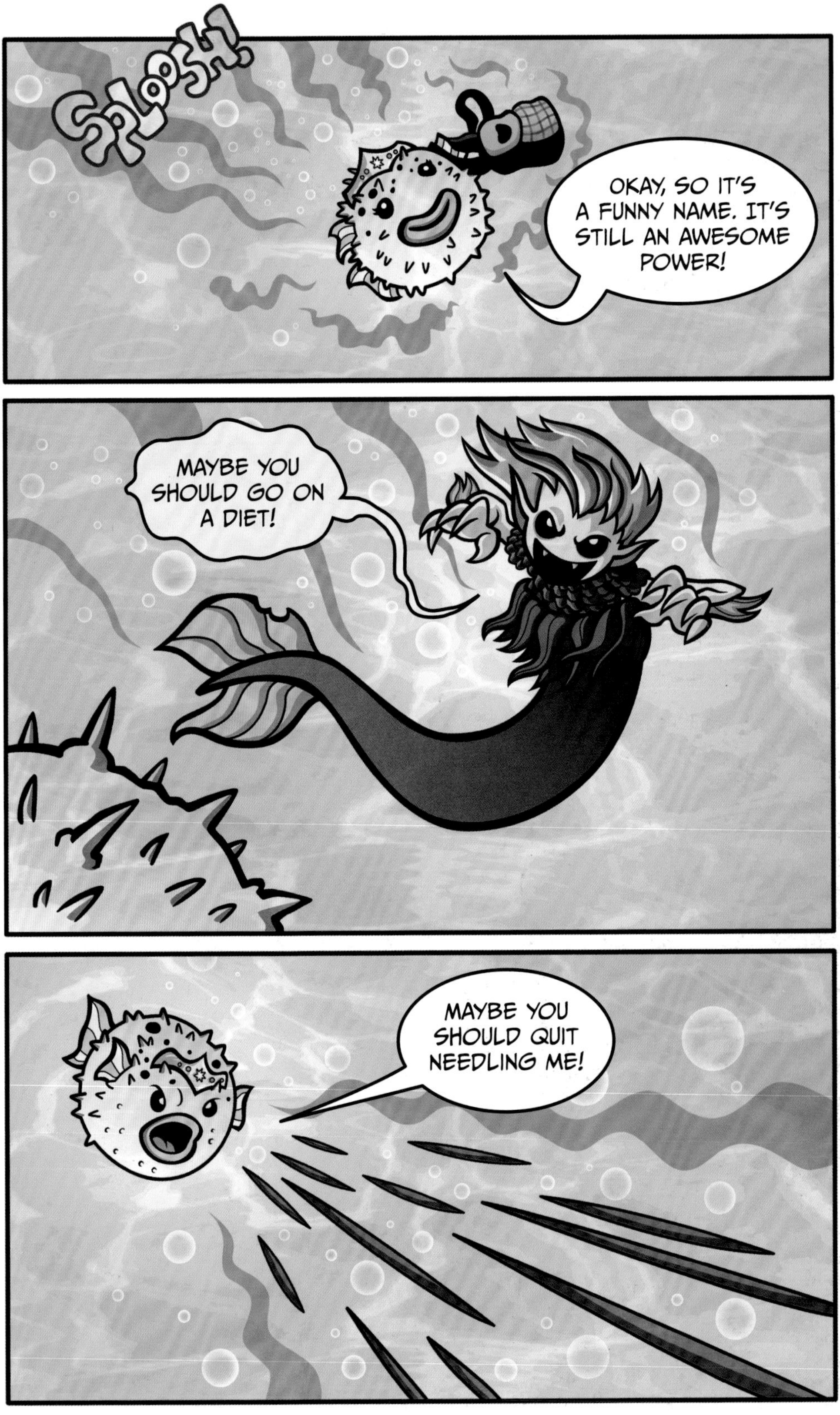
SPLOOSH!
OKAY, SO IT'S A FUNNY NAME. IT'S STILL AN AWESOME POWER!
MAYBE YOU SHOULD GO ON A DIET!
MAYBE YOU SHOULD QUIT NEEDLING ME!

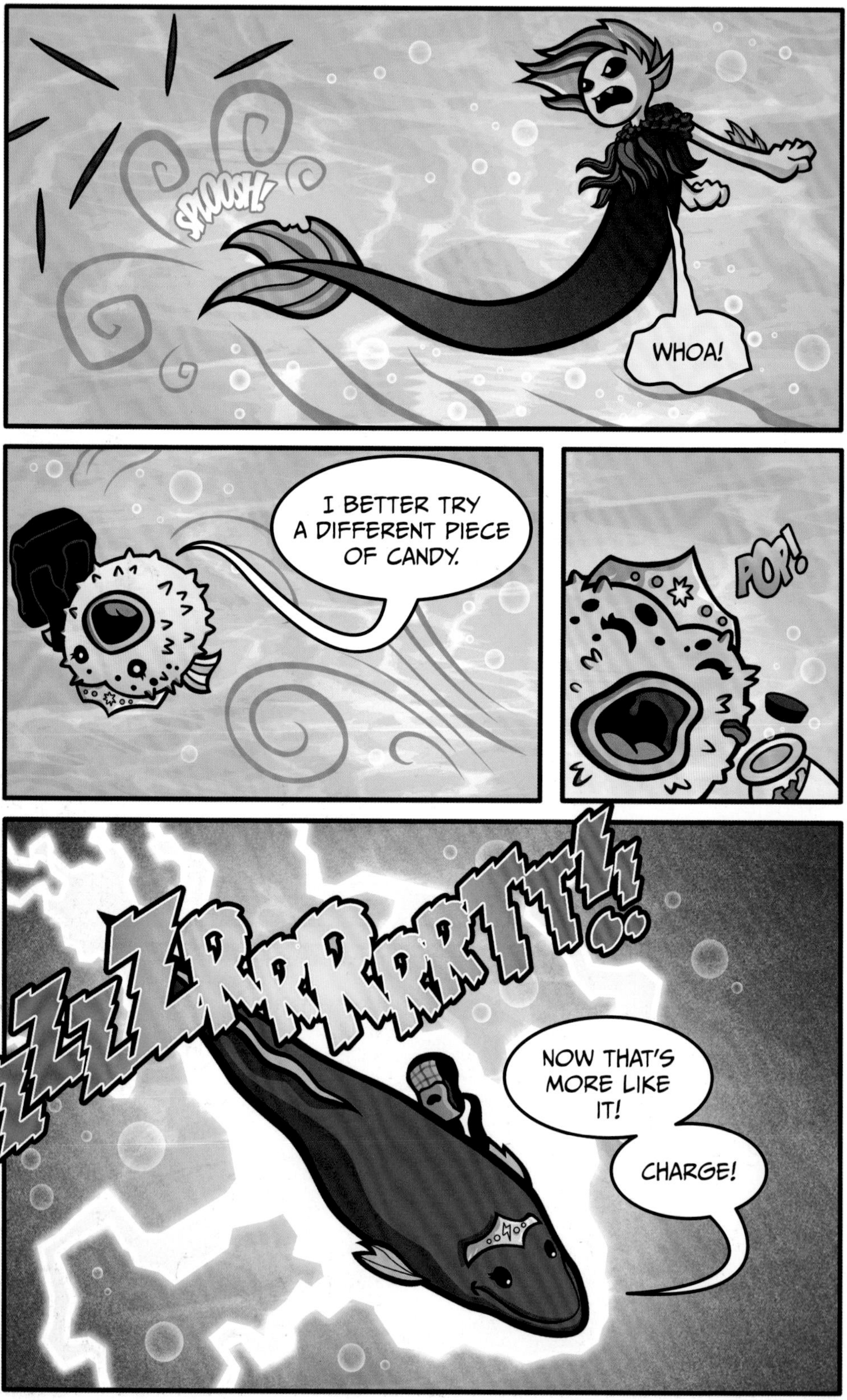
SPLOOSH!
WHOA!
I BETTER TRY A DIFFERENT PIECE OF CANDY.
POP!
ZZZZRRRRRRTTT!!
NOW THAT'S MORE LIKE IT!
CHARGE!

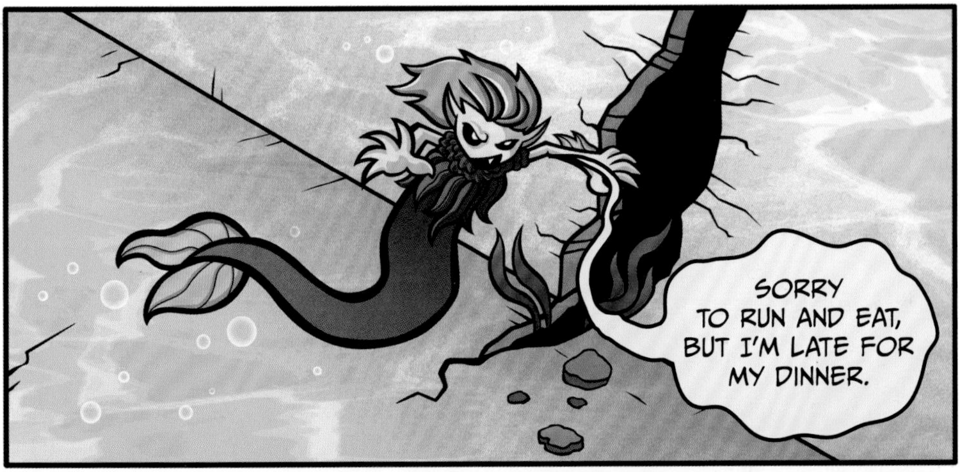
SORRY TO RUN AND EAT, BUT I'M LATE FOR MY DINNER.

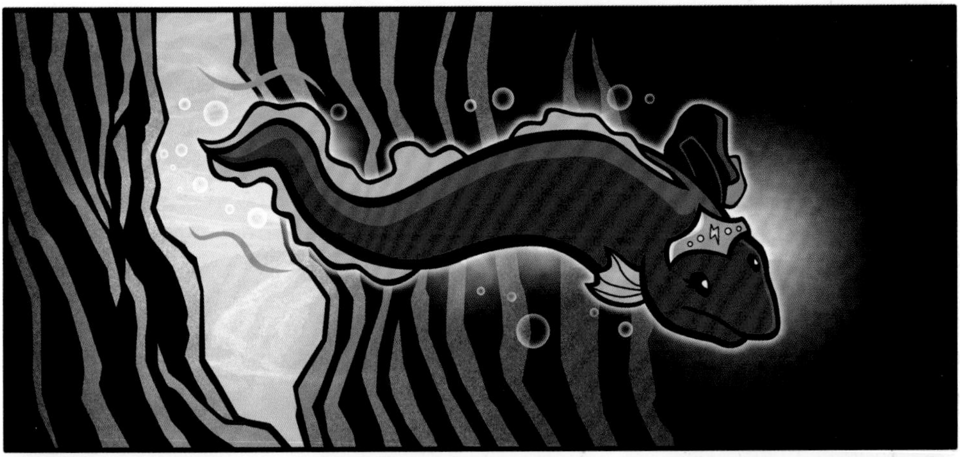

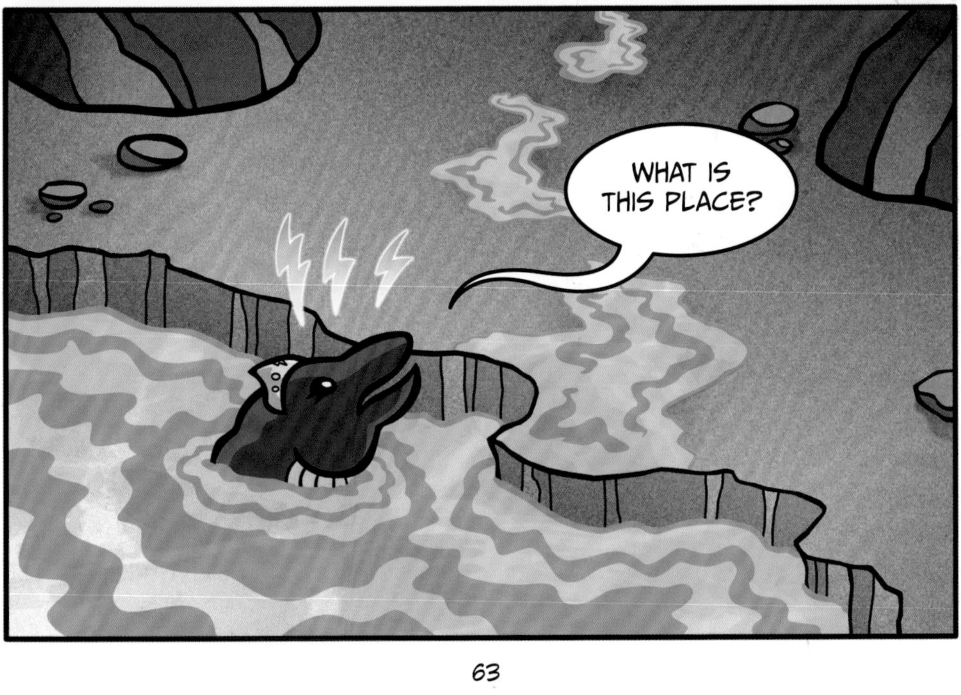
WHAT IS THIS PLACE?

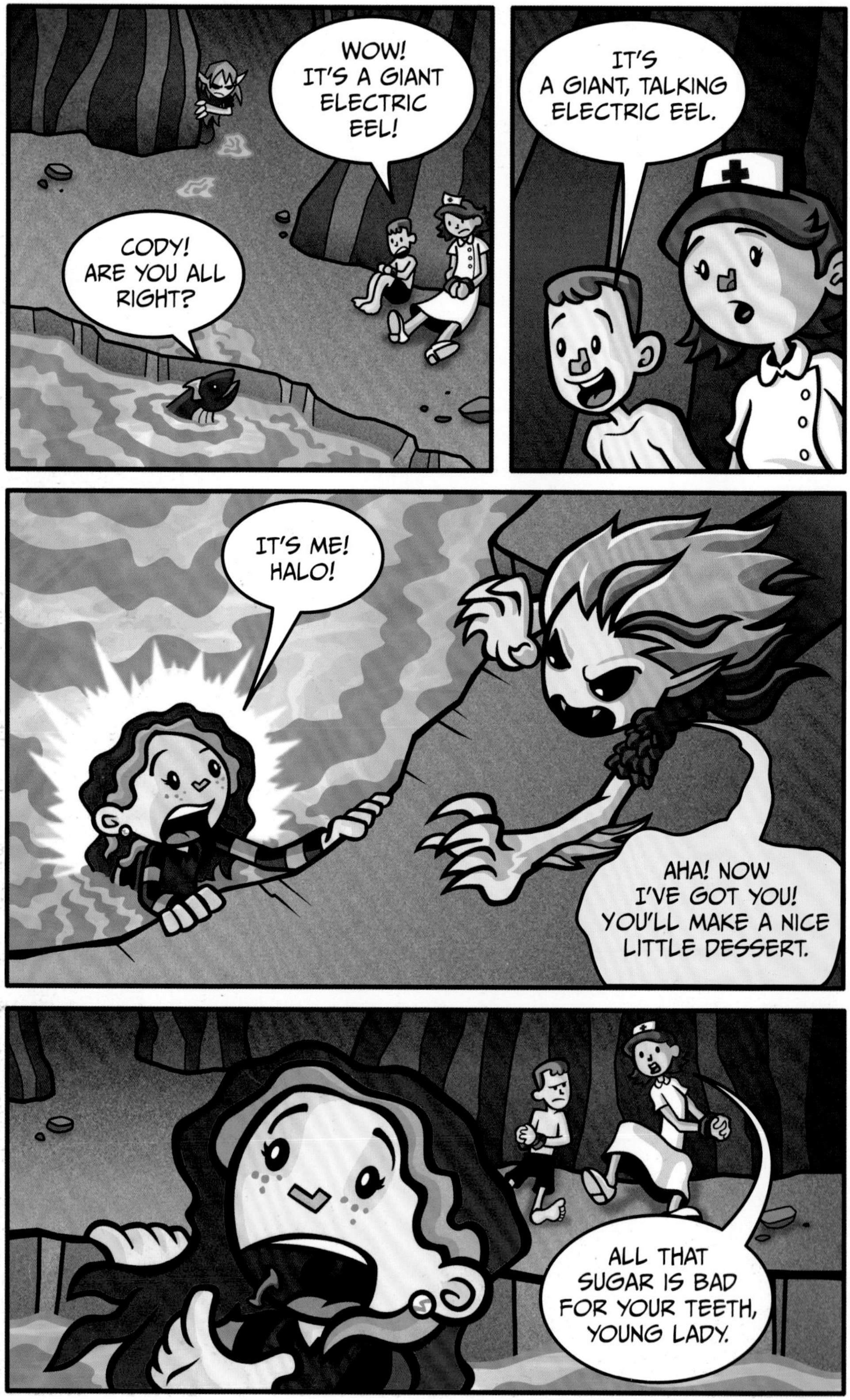
WOW! IT'S A GIANT ELECTRIC EEL!
CODY! ARE YOU ALL RIGHT?
IT'S A GIANT, TALKING ELECTRIC EEL.
IT'S ME! HALO!
AHA! NOW I'VE GOT YOU! YOU'LL MAKE A NICE LITTLE DESSERT.
ALL THAT SUGAR IS BAD FOR YOUR TEETH, YOUNG LADY.

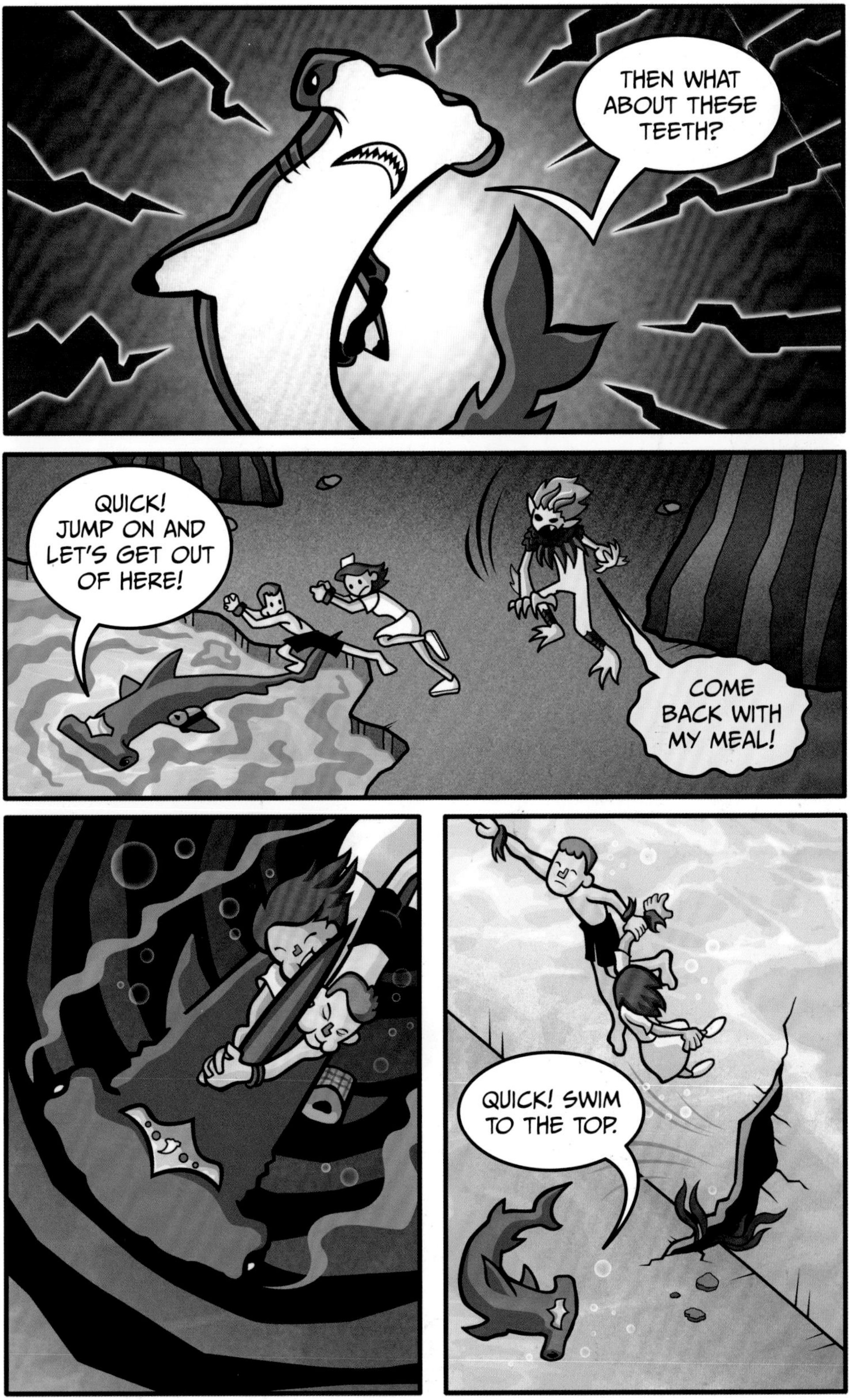
THEN WHAT ABOUT THESE TEETH?
QUICK! JUMP ON AND LET'S GET OUT OF HERE!
COME BACK WITH MY MEAL!
QUICK! SWIM TO THE TOP.

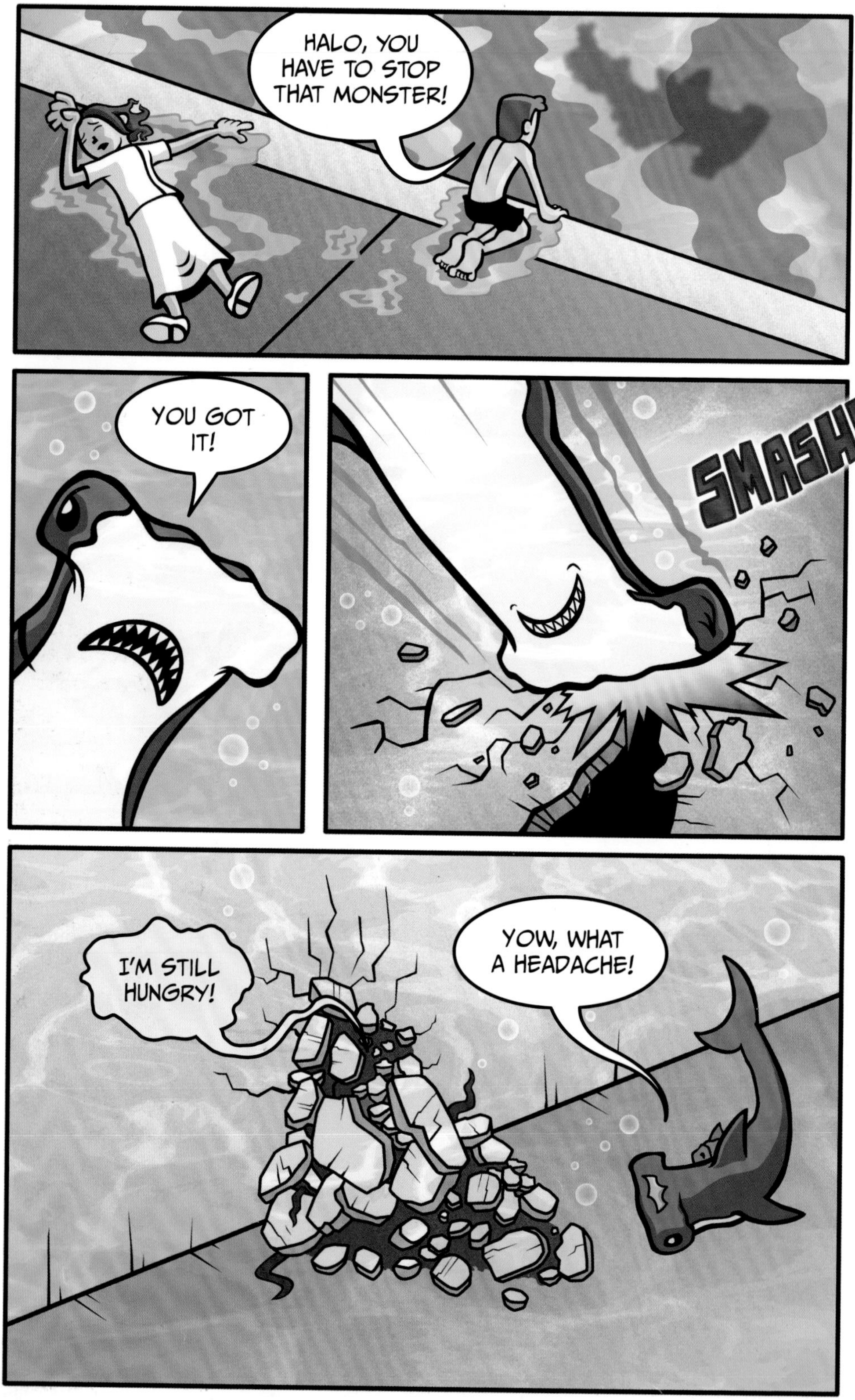
HALO, YOU HAVE TO STOP THAT MONSTER!
YOU GOT IT!
SMASH!
I'M STILL HUNGRY!
YOW, WHAT A HEADACHE!

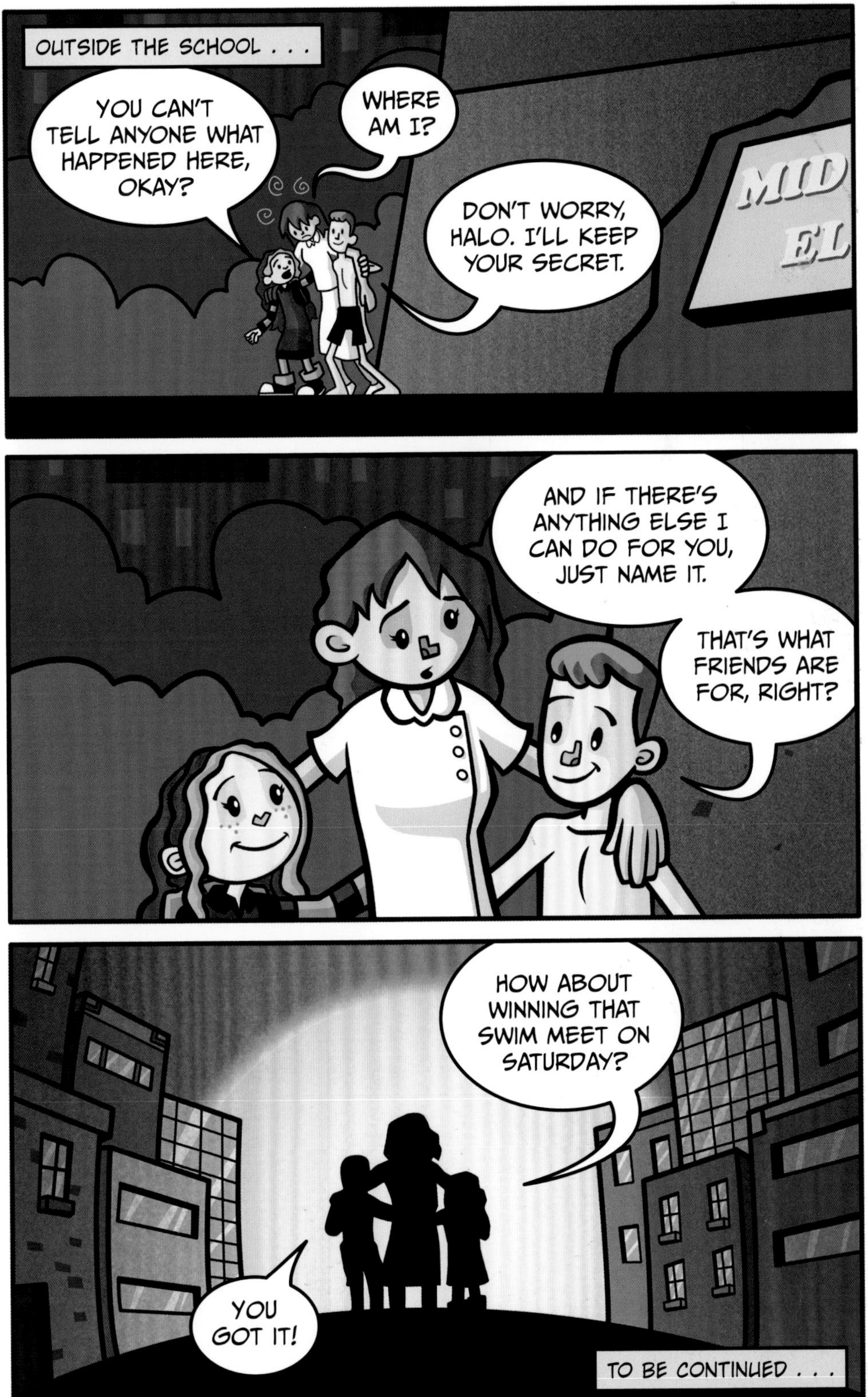
OUTSIDE THE SCHOOL . . .
YOU CAN'T TELL ANYONE WHAT HAPPENED HERE, OKAY?
WHERE AM I?
DON'T WORRY, HALO. I'LL KEEP YOUR SECRET.
AND IF THERE'S ANYTHING ELSE I CAN DO FOR YOU, JUST NAME IT.
THAT'S WHAT FRIENDS ARE FOR, RIGHT?
HOW ABOUT WINNING THAT SWIM MEET ON SATURDAY?
YOU GOT IT!
TO BE CONTINUED . . .

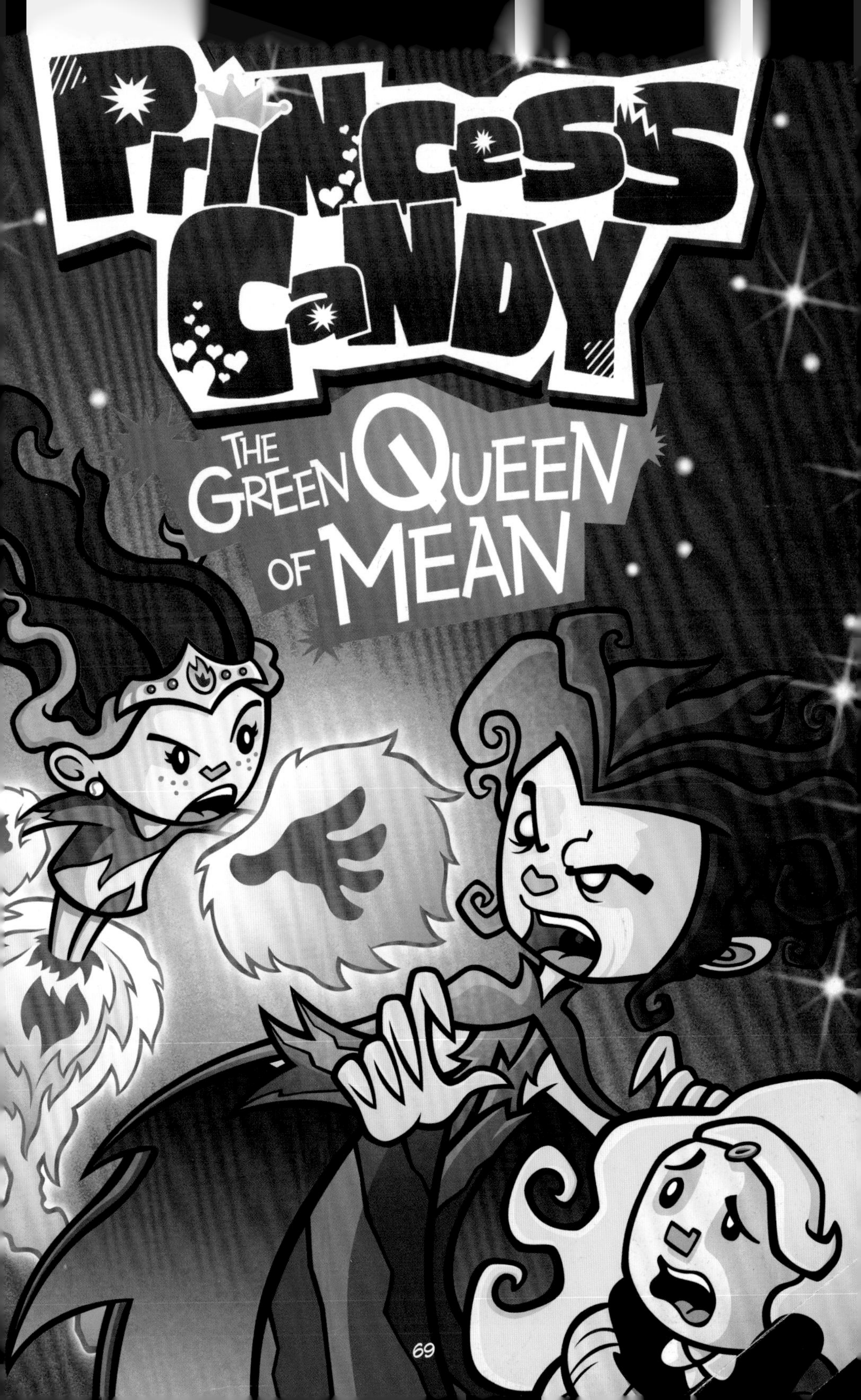
PRINCESS CANDY
THE GREEN QUEEN OF MEAN

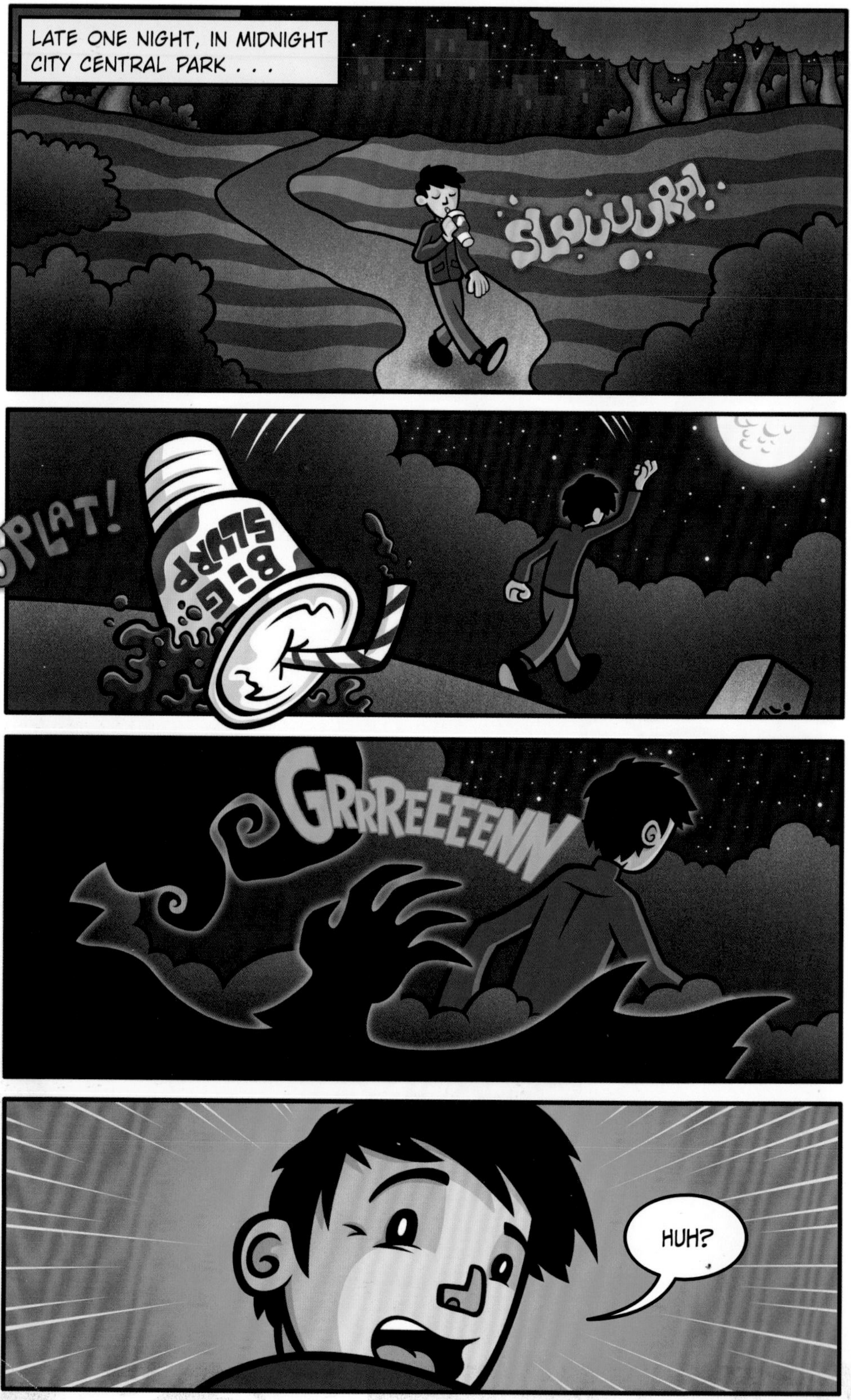
LATE ONE NIGHT, IN MIDNIGHT CITY CENTRAL PARK . . .
SLUUUURP!
SPLAT!
BIG SLURP
GRRREEEENN
HUH?

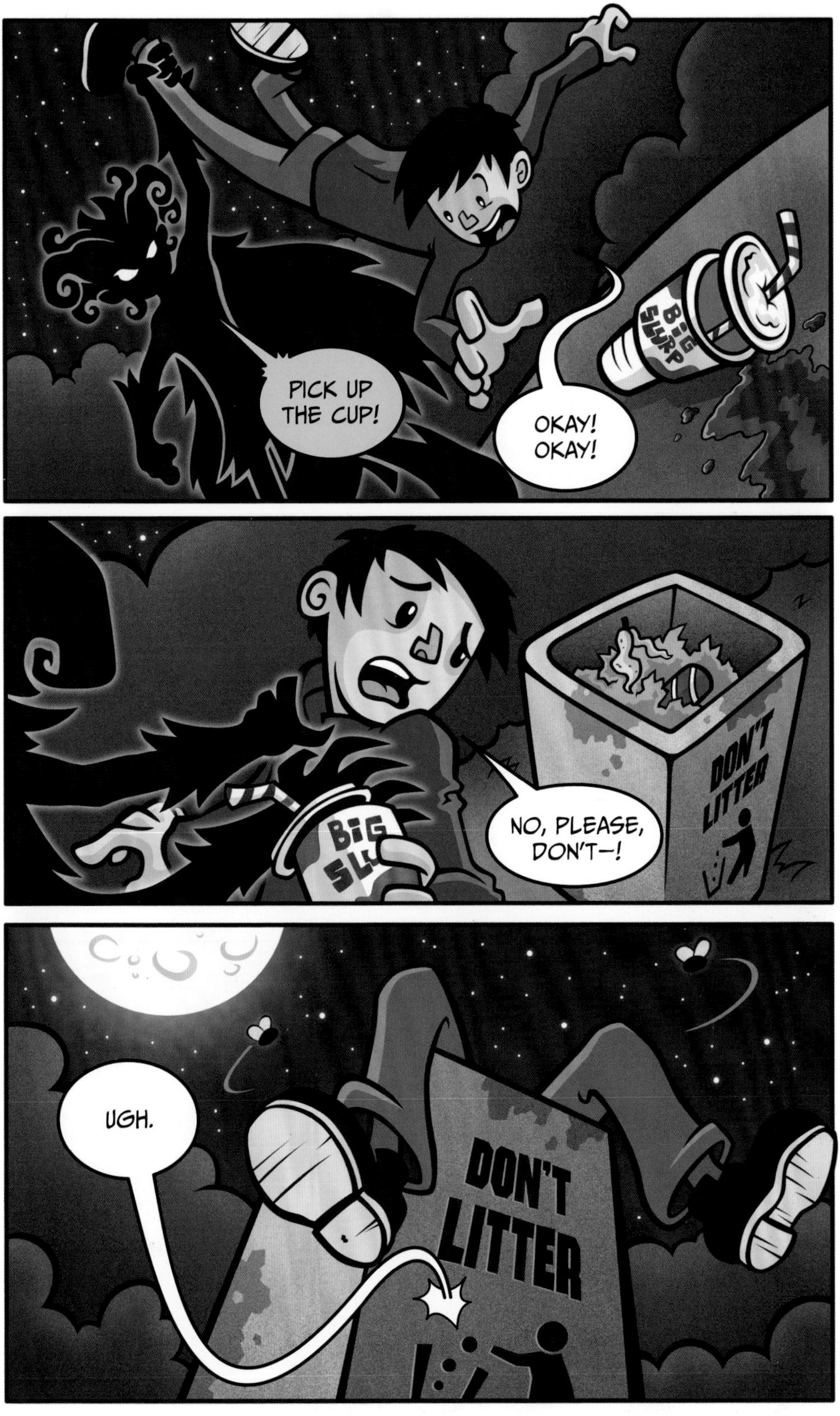

BIG SLURP
PICK UP THE CUP!
OKAY! OKAY!
NO, PLEASE, DON'T—!
DON'T LITTER
UGH.
DON'T LITTER

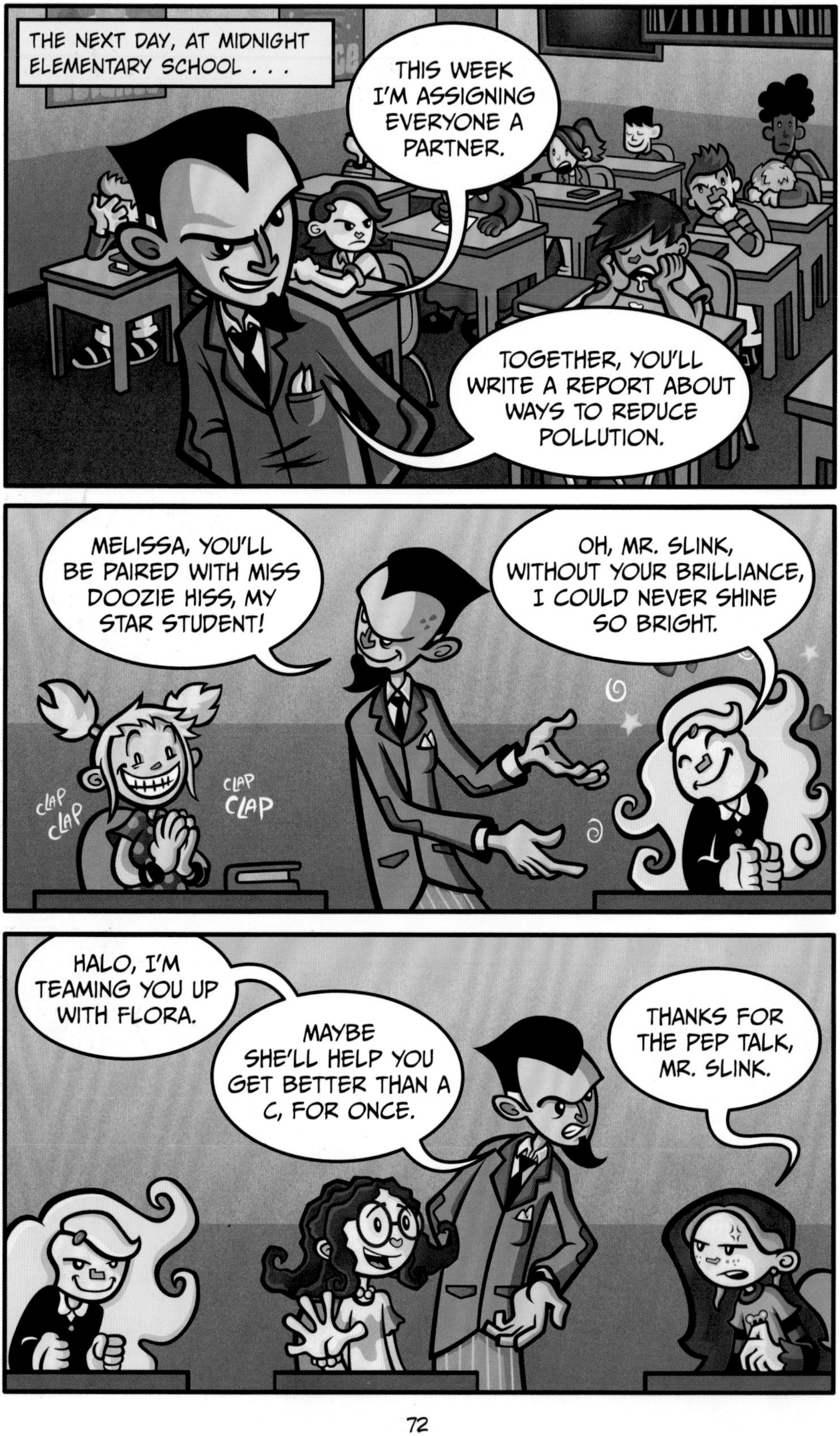

THE NEXT DAY, AT MIDNIGHT ELEMENTARY SCHOOL . . .
THIS WEEK I'M ASSIGNING EVERYONE A PARTNER.
TOGETHER, YOU'LL WRITE A REPORT ABOUT WAYS TO REDUCE POLLUTION.
MELISSA, YOU'LL BE PAIRED WITH MISS DOOZIE HISS, MY STAR STUDENT!
OH, MR. SLINK, WITHOUT YOUR BRILLIANCE, I COULD NEVER SHINE SO BRIGHT.
CLAP CLAP
CLAP CLAP
HALO, I'M TEAMING YOU UP WITH FLORA.
MAYBE SHE'LL HELP YOU GET BETTER THAN A C, FOR ONCE.
THANKS FOR THE PEP TALK, MR. SLINK.

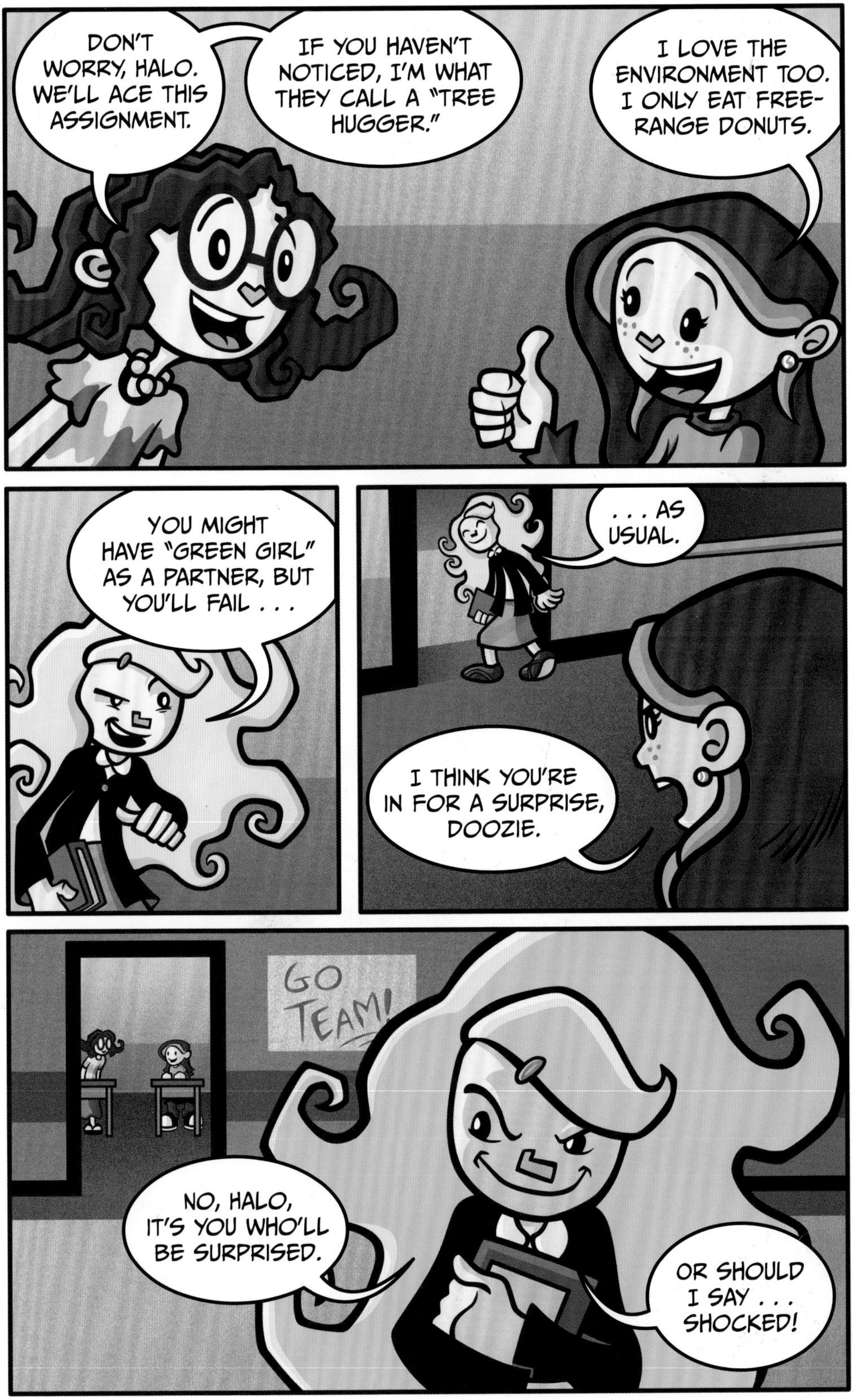
DON'T WORRY, HALO. WE'LL ACE THIS ASSIGNMENT.
IF YOU HAVEN'T NOTICED, I'M WHAT THEY CALL A "TREE HUGGER."
I LOVE THE ENVIRONMENT TOO. I ONLY EAT FREE-RANGE DONUTS.
YOU MIGHT HAVE "GREEN GIRL" AS A PARTNER, BUT YOU'LL FAIL . . .
. . . AS USUAL.
I THINK YOU'RE IN FOR A SURPRISE, DOOZIE.
GO TEAM!
NO, HALO, IT'S YOU WHO'LL BE SURPRISED.
OR SHOULD I SAY . . . SHOCKED!

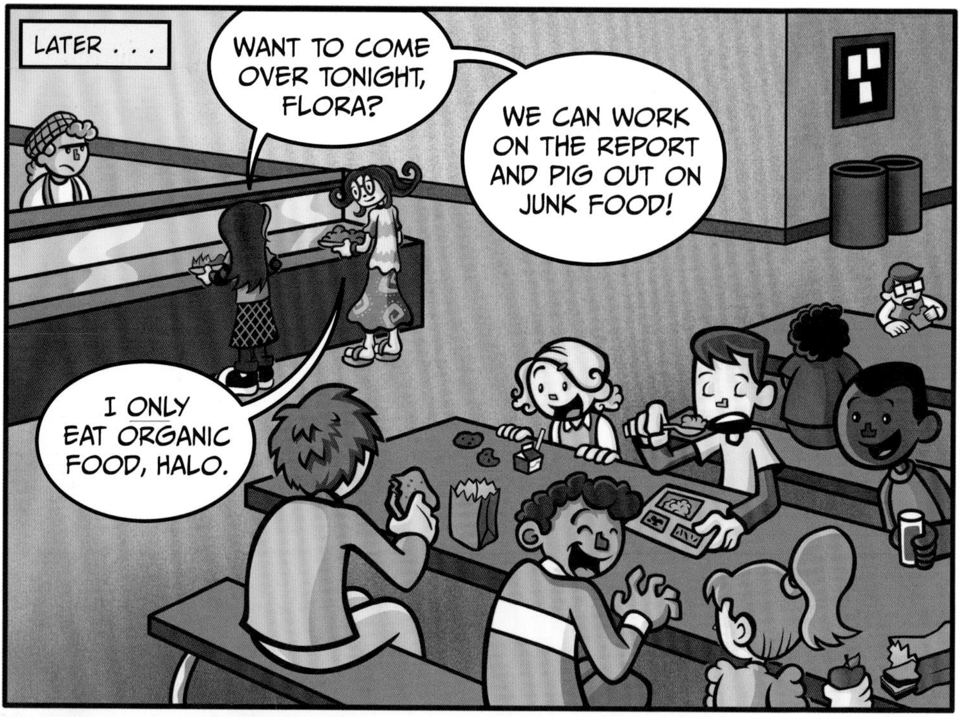
LATER . . .
WANT TO COME OVER TONIGHT, FLORA?
WE CAN WORK ON THE REPORT AND PIG OUT ON JUNK FOOD!
I ONLY EAT ORGANIC FOOD, HALO.

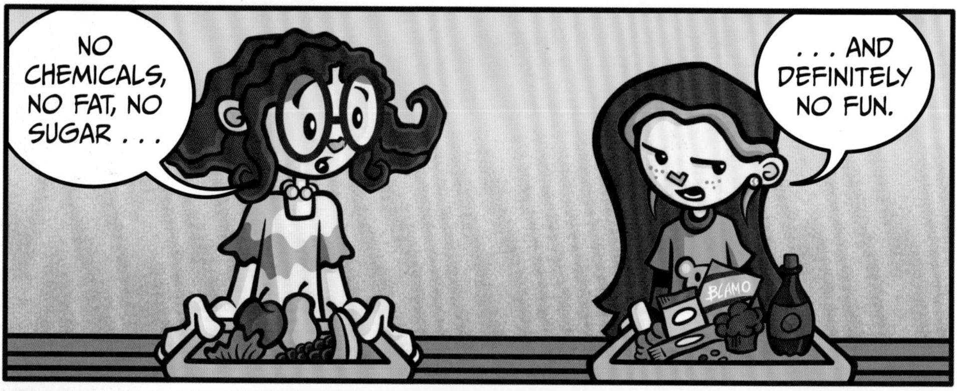
NO CHEMICALS, NO FAT, NO SUGAR . . .
. . . AND DEFINITELY NO FUN.
BLAMO

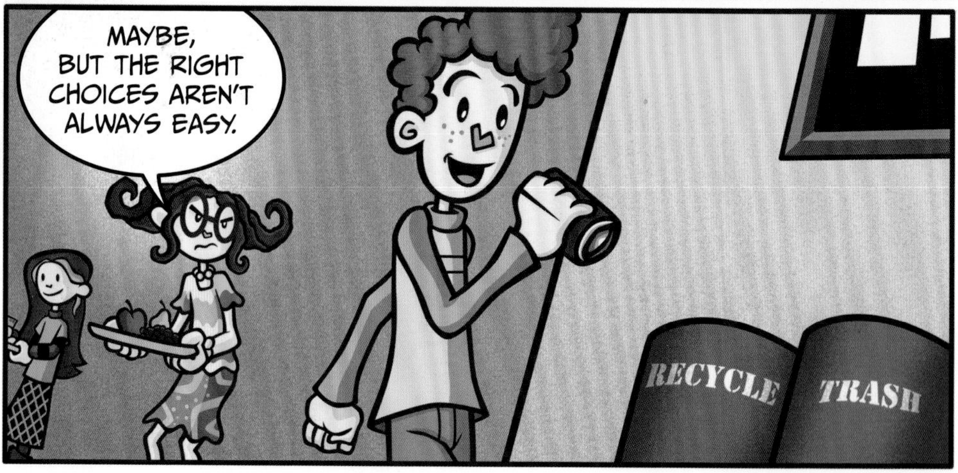
MAYBE, BUT THE RIGHT CHOICES AREN'T ALWAYS EASY.
RECYCLE
TRASH

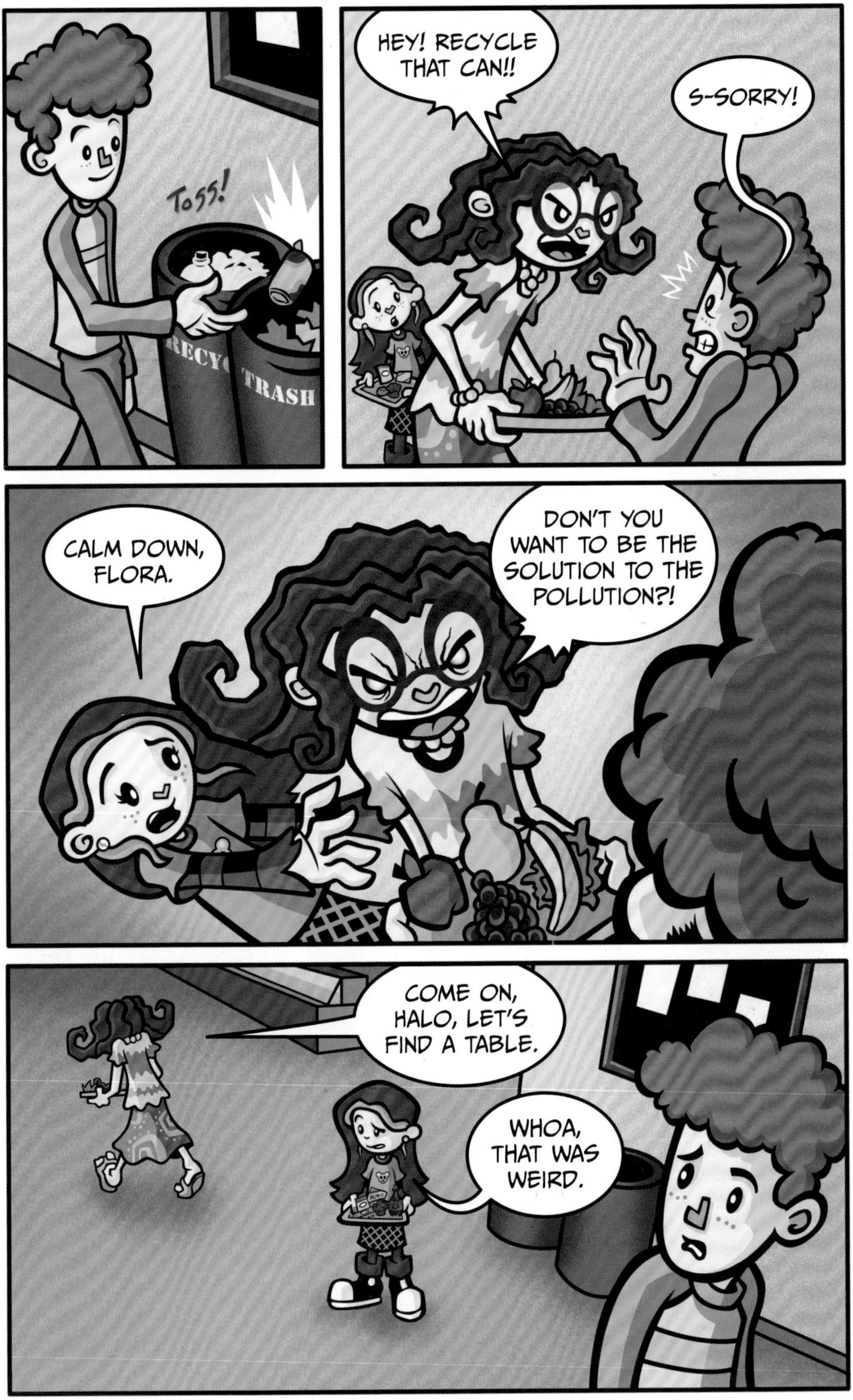
TOSS!
RECYC
TRASH
HEY! RECYCLE THAT CAN!!
S-SORRY!
CALM DOWN, FLORA.
DON'T YOU WANT TO BE THE SOLUTION TO THE POLLUTION?!
COME ON, HALO, LET'S FIND A TABLE.
WHOA, THAT WAS WEIRD.

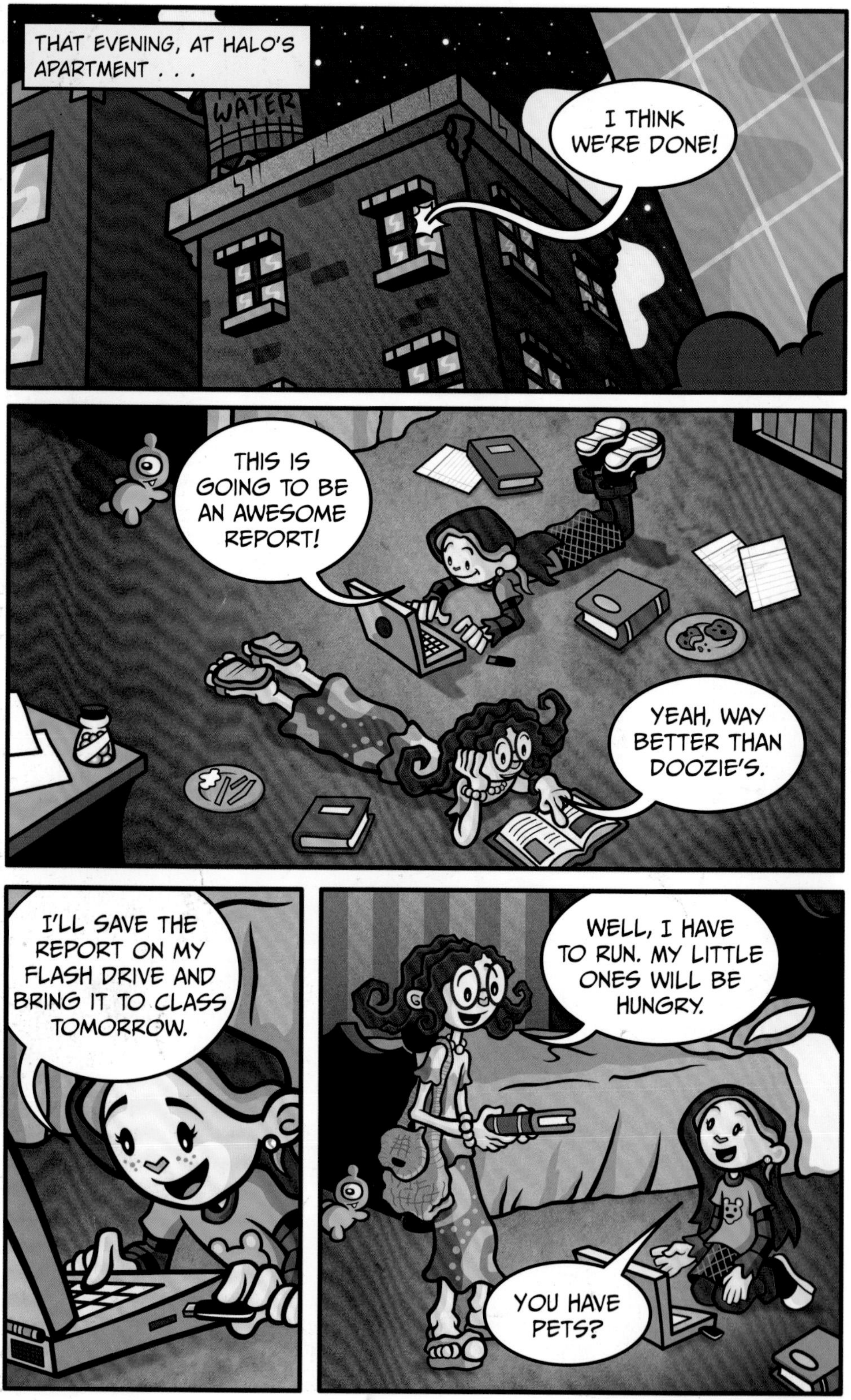
THAT EVENING, AT HALO'S APARTMENT . . .
WATER
I THINK WE'RE DONE!
THIS IS GOING TO BE AN AWESOME REPORT!
YEAH, WAY BETTER THAN DOOZIE'S.
I'LL SAVE THE REPORT ON MY FLASH DRIVE AND BRING IT TO CLASS TOMORROW.
WELL, I HAVE TO RUN. MY LITTLE ONES WILL BE HUNGRY.
YOU HAVE PETS?

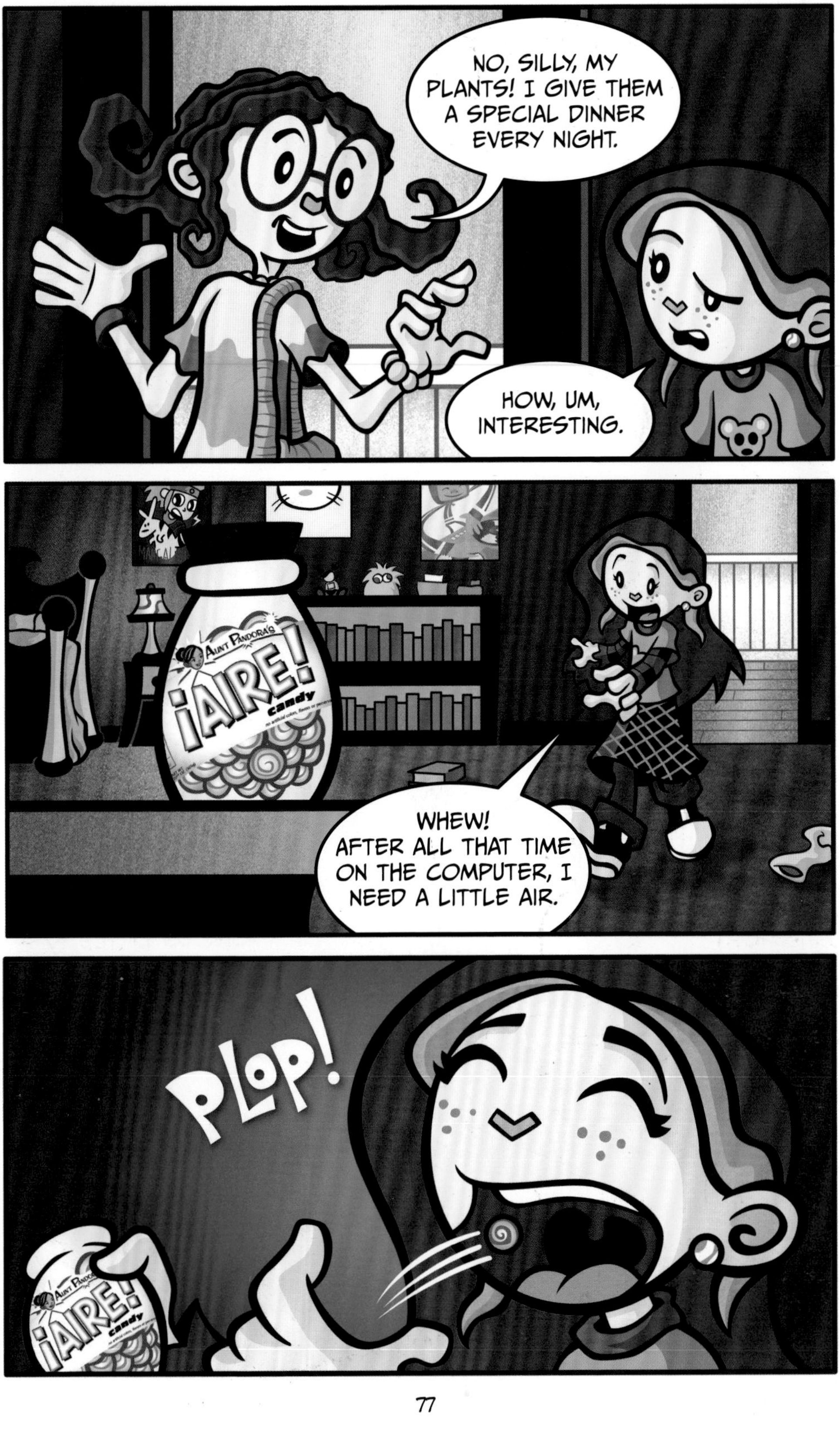
NO, SILLY, MY PLANTS! I GIVE THEM A SPECIAL DINNER EVERY NIGHT.
HOW, UM, INTERESTING.
AUNT PANDORA'S
¡AIRE!
candy
WHEW! AFTER ALL THAT TIME ON THE COMPUTER, I NEED A LITTLE AIR.
PLOP!

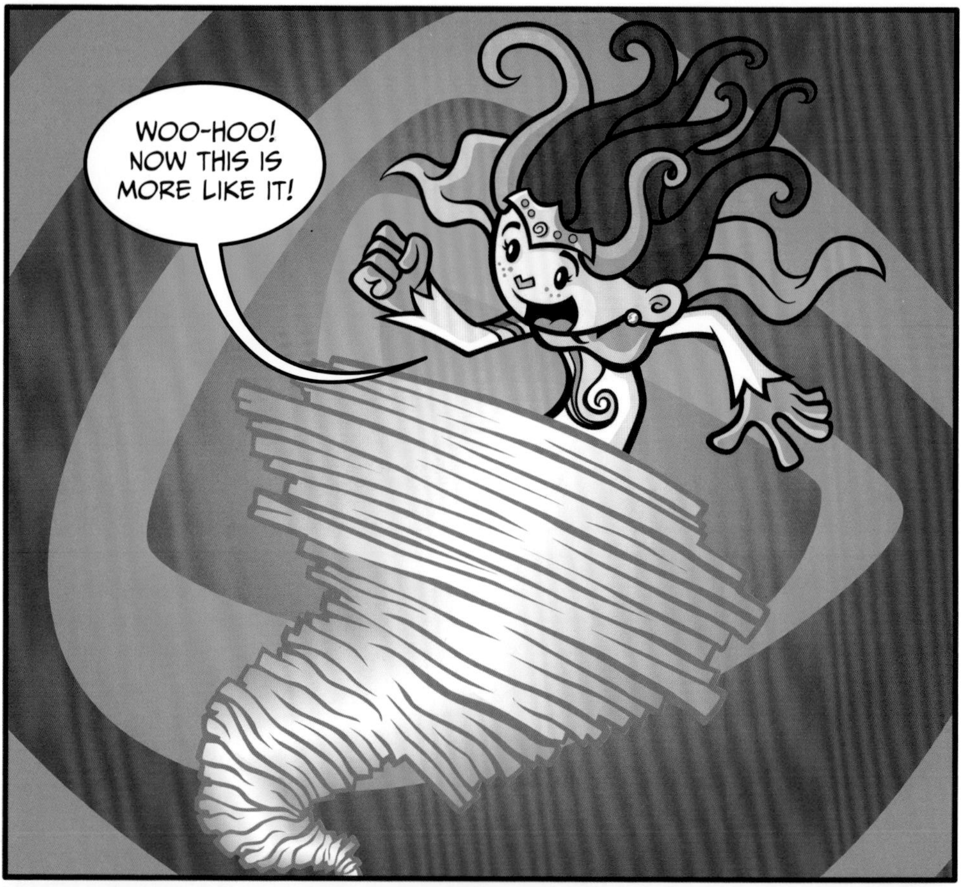
WOO-HOO! NOW THIS IS MORE LIKE IT!

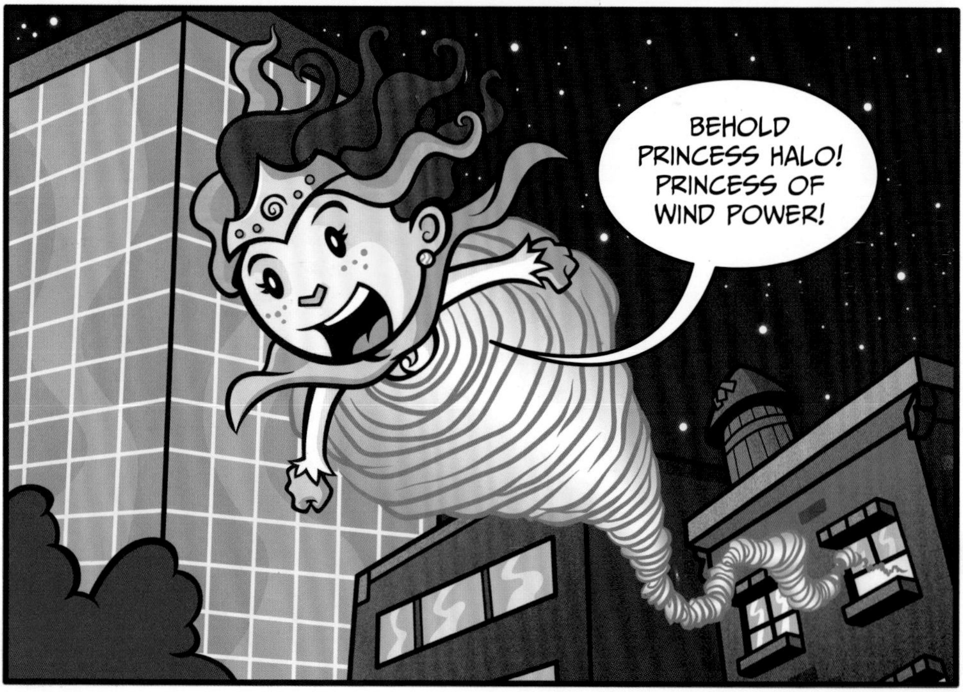
BEHOLD PRINCESS HALO! PRINCESS OF WIND POWER!

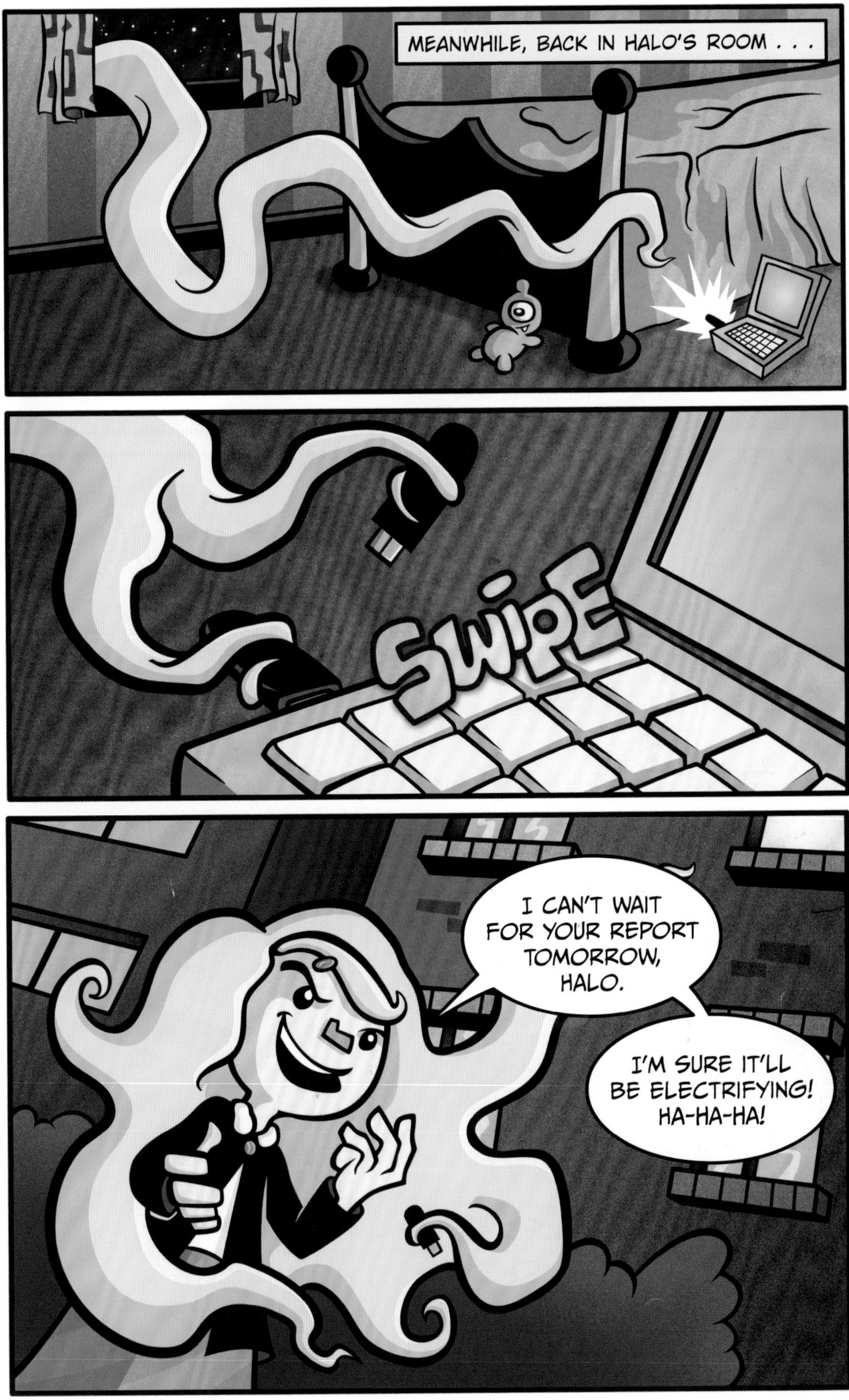
MEANWHILE, BACK IN HALO'S ROOM . . .
SWIPE
I CAN'T WAIT FOR YOUR REPORT TOMORROW, HALO.
I'M SURE IT'LL BE ELECTRIFYING! HA-HA-HA!

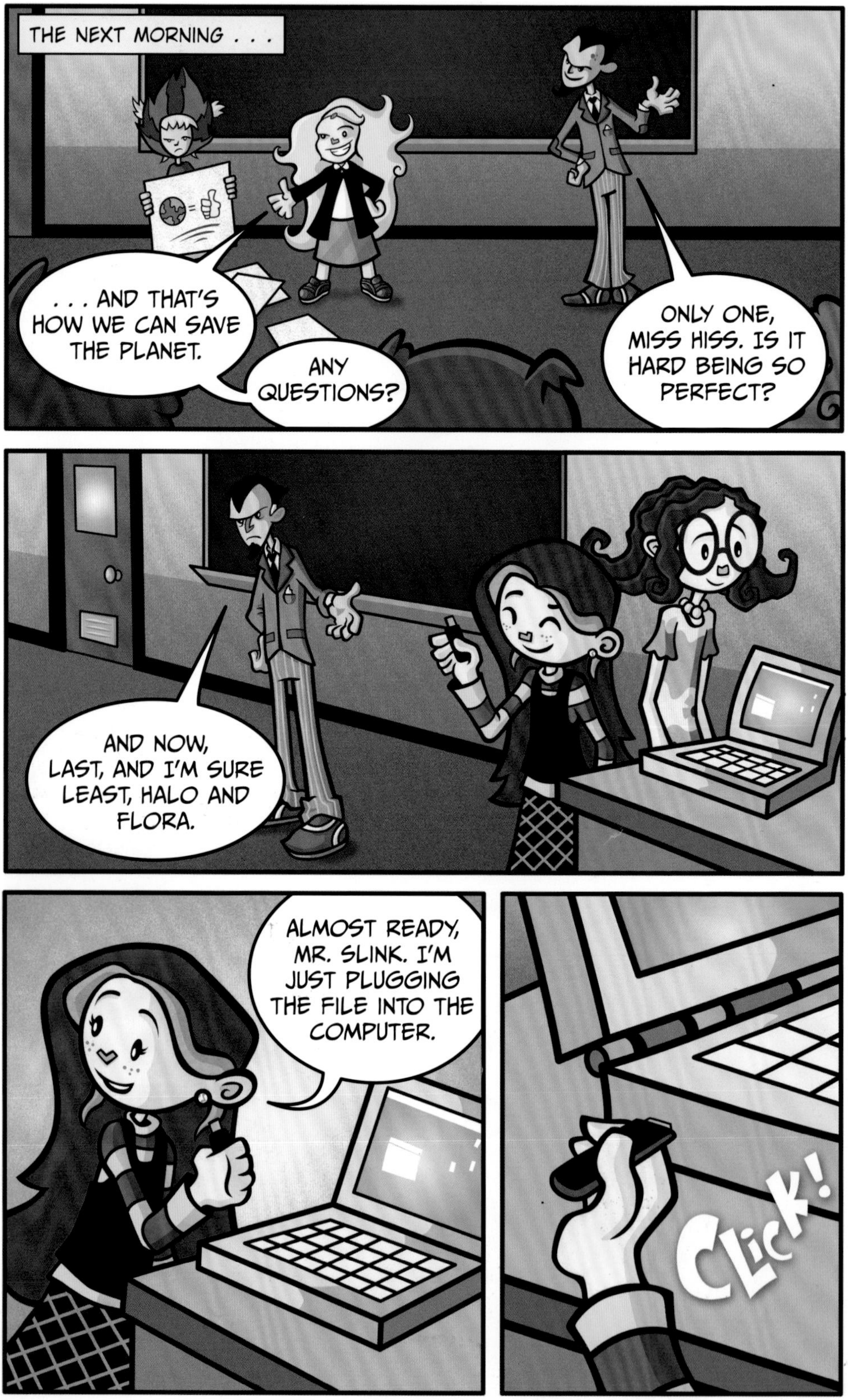
THE NEXT MORNING . . .
. . . AND THAT'S HOW WE CAN SAVE THE PLANET.
ANY QUESTIONS?
ONLY ONE, MISS HISS. IS IT HARD BEING SO PERFECT?
AND NOW, LAST, AND I'M SURE LEAST, HALO AND FLORA.
ALMOST READY, MR. SLINK. I'M JUST PLUGGING THE FILE INTO THE COMPUTER.
CLICK!

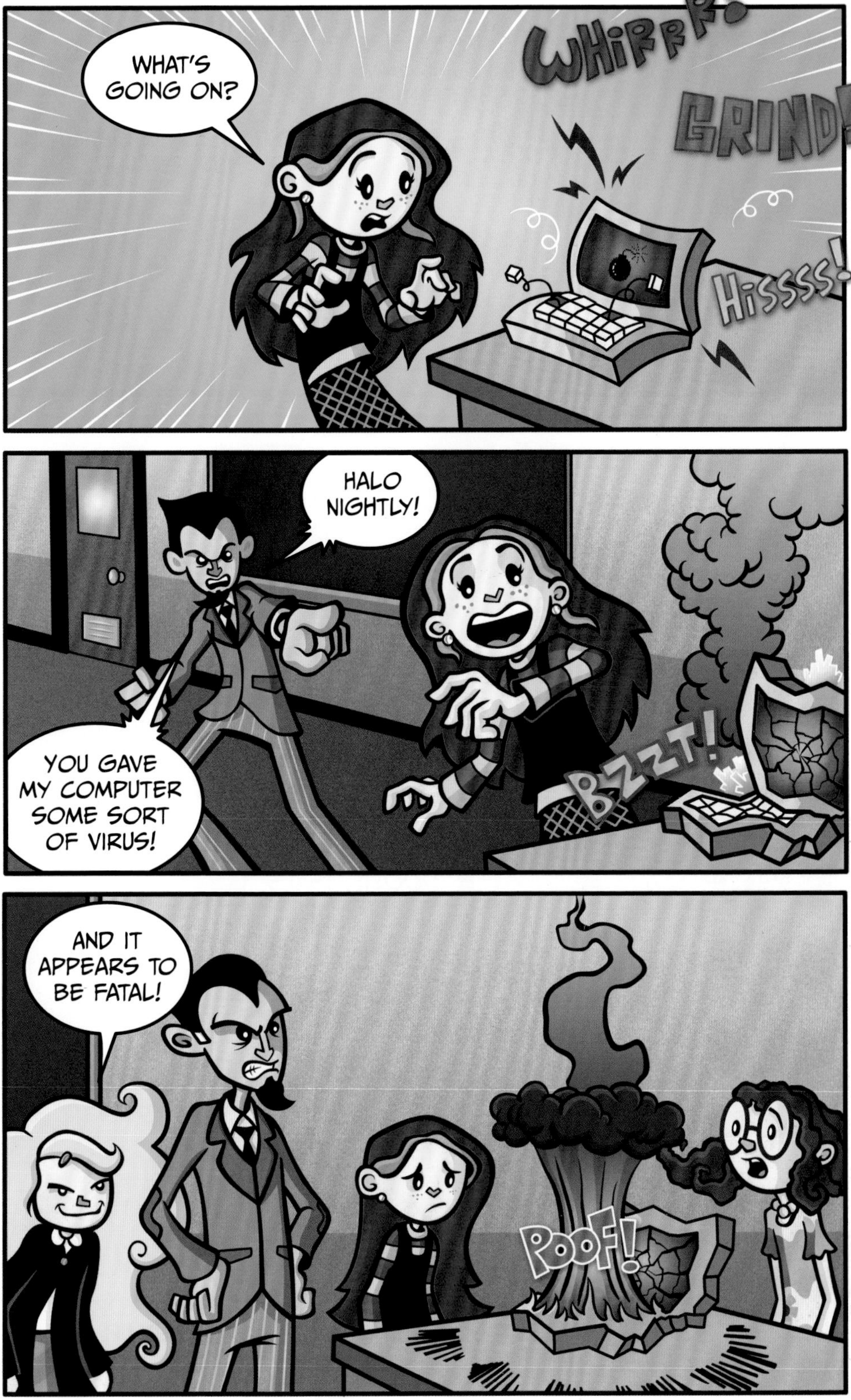
WHAT'S GOING ON?
WHIRRR!
GRIND!
HISSSSS!
HALO NIGHTLY!
YOU GAVE MY COMPUTER SOME SORT OF VIRUS!
BZZZT!
AND IT APPEARS TO BE FATAL!
POOF!

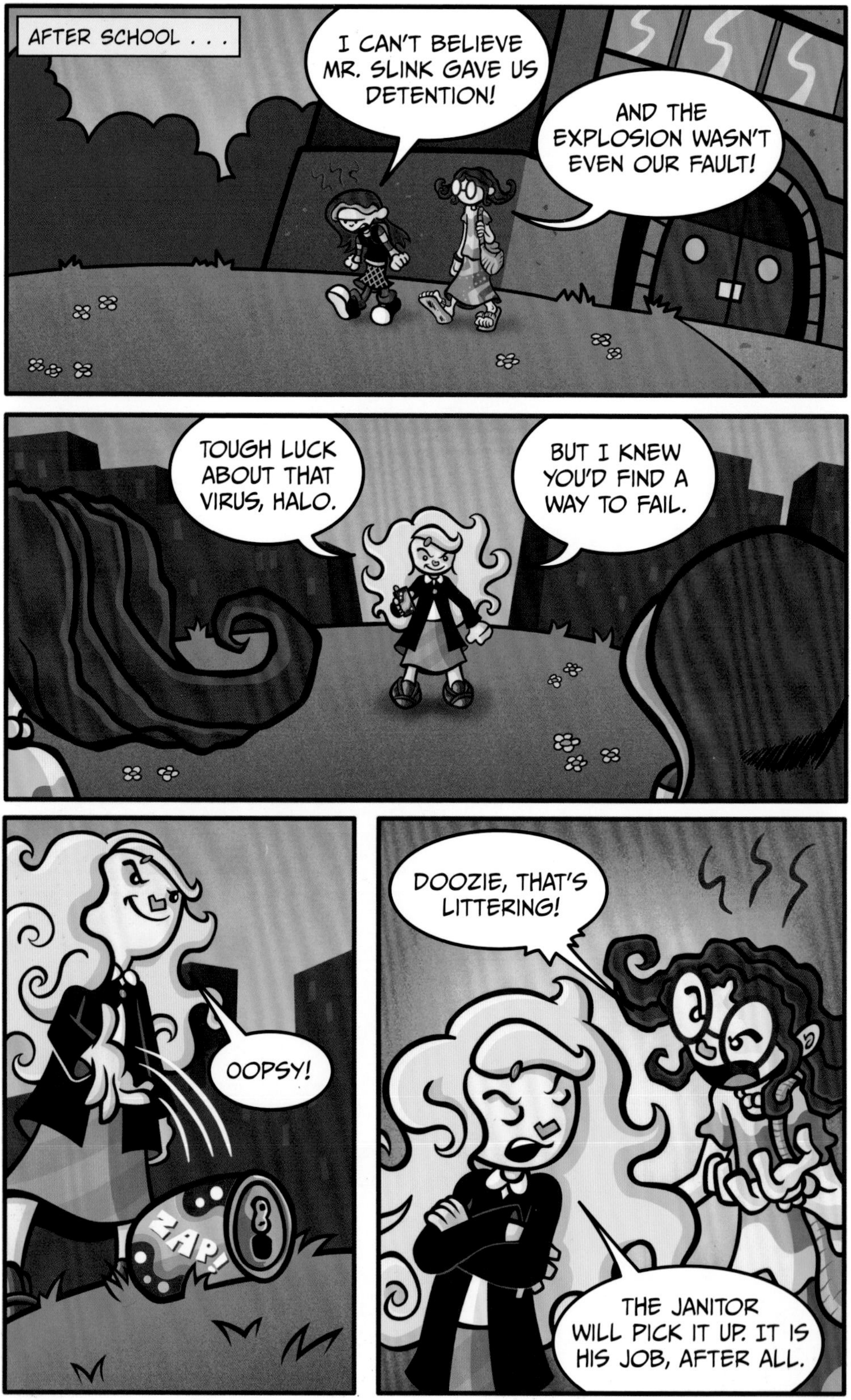
AFTER SCHOOL . . .
I CAN'T BELIEVE MR. SLINK GAVE US DETENTION!
AND THE EXPLOSION WASN'T EVEN OUR FAULT!
TOUGH LUCK ABOUT THAT VIRUS, HALO.
BUT I KNEW YOU'D FIND A WAY TO FAIL.
OOPSY!
ZAP!
DOOZIE, THAT'S LITTERING!
THE JANITOR WILL PICK IT UP. IT IS HIS JOB, AFTER ALL.

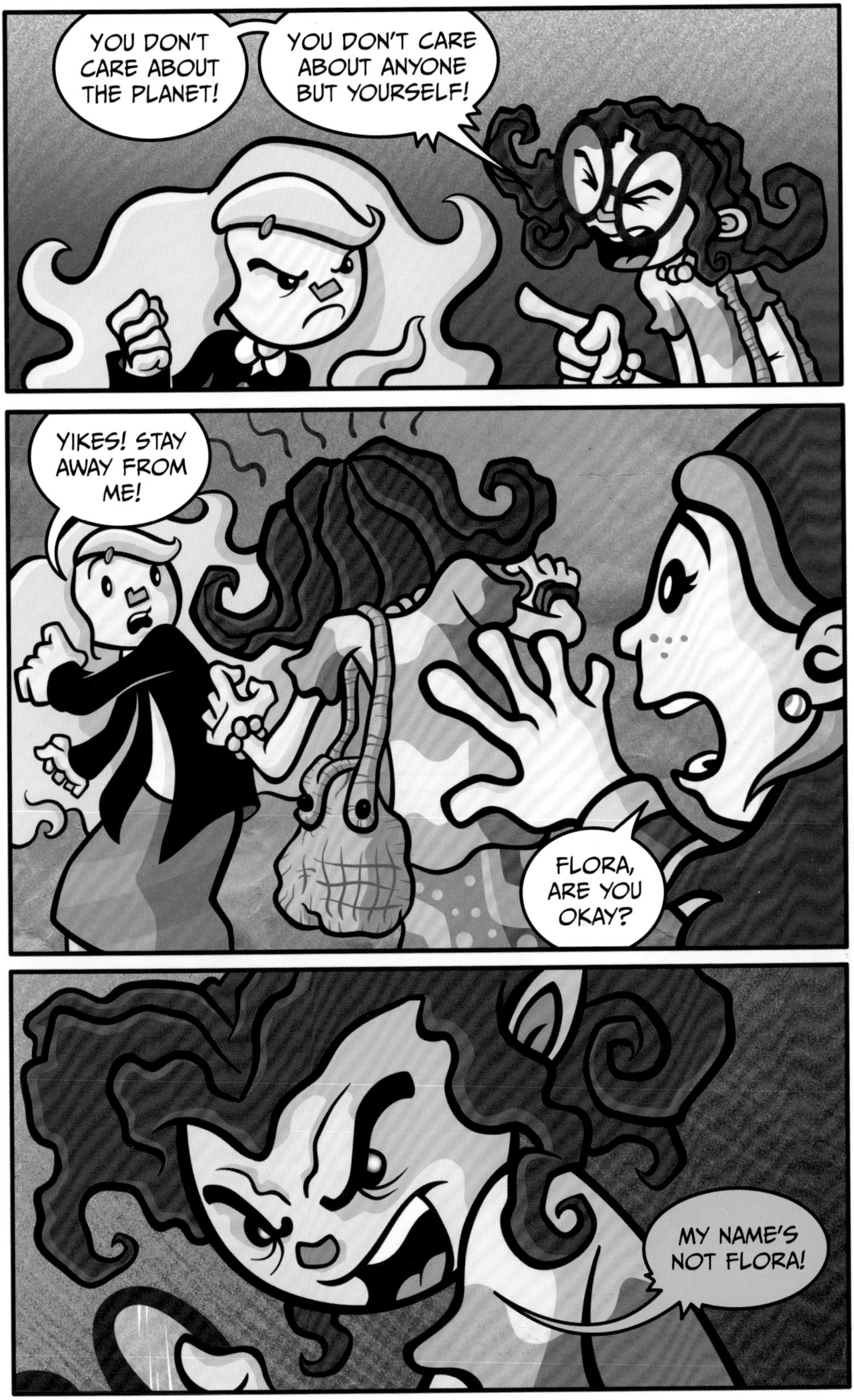
YOU DON'T CARE ABOUT THE PLANET!
YOU DON'T CARE ABOUT ANYONE BUT YOURSELF!
YIKES! STAY AWAY FROM ME!
FLORA, ARE YOU OKAY?
MY NAME'S NOT FLORA!

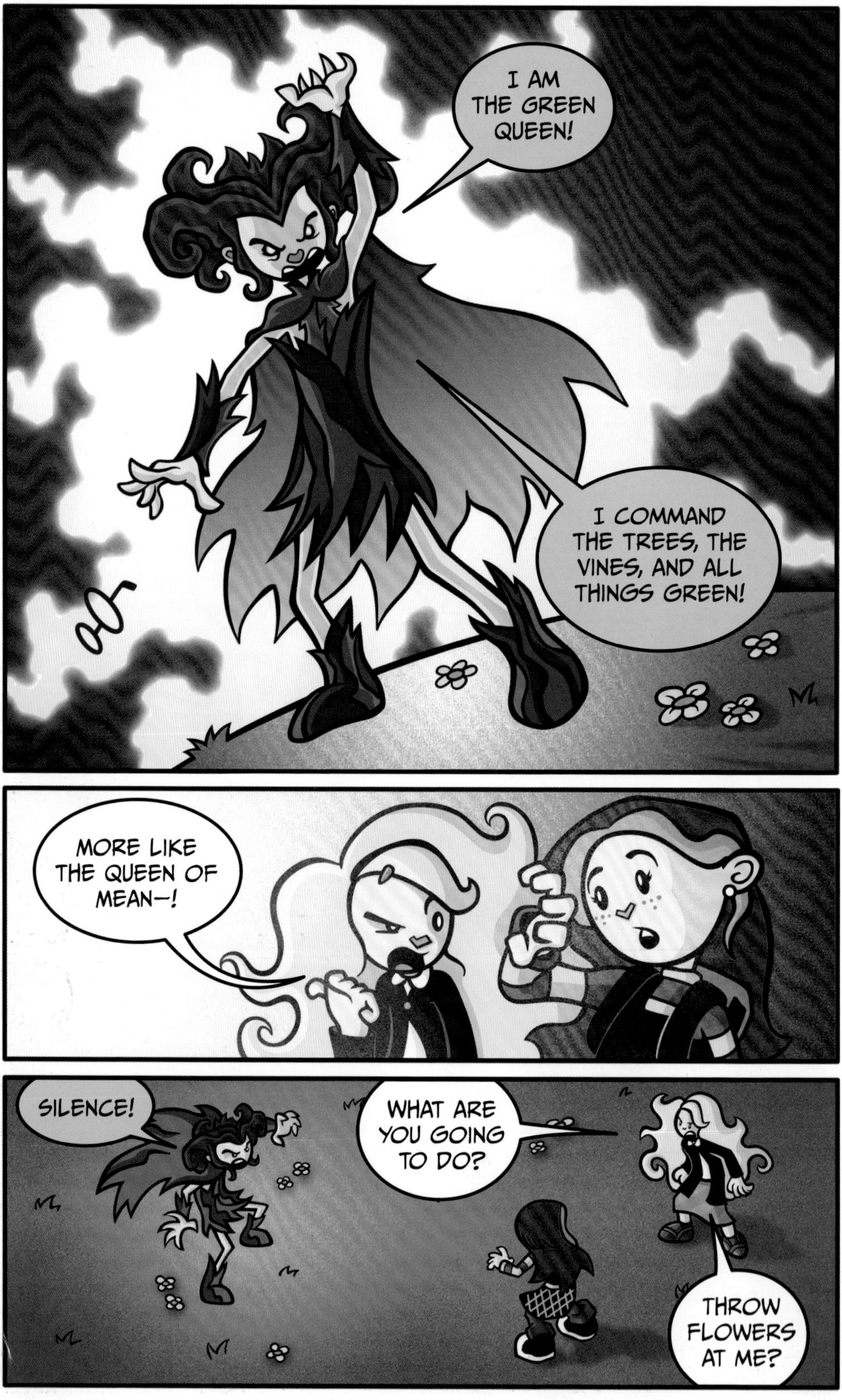
I AM THE GREEN QUEEN!
I COMMAND THE TREES, THE VINES, AND ALL THINGS GREEN!
MORE LIKE THE QUEEN OF MEAN—!
SILENCE!
WHAT ARE YOU GOING TO DO?
THROW FLOWERS AT ME?

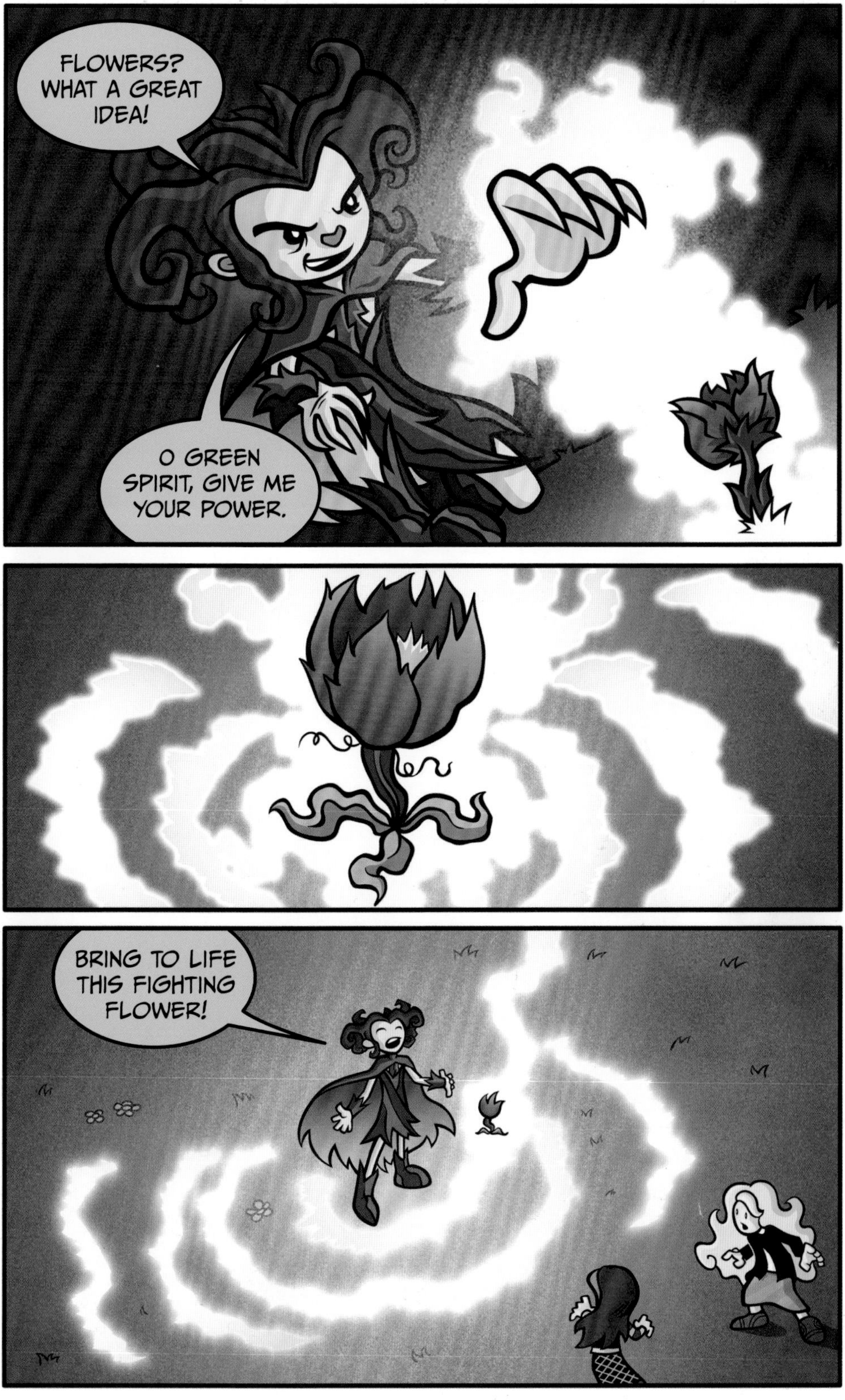
FLOWERS? WHAT A GREAT IDEA!
O GREEN SPIRIT, GIVE ME YOUR POWER.
BRING TO LIFE THIS FIGHTING FLOWER!

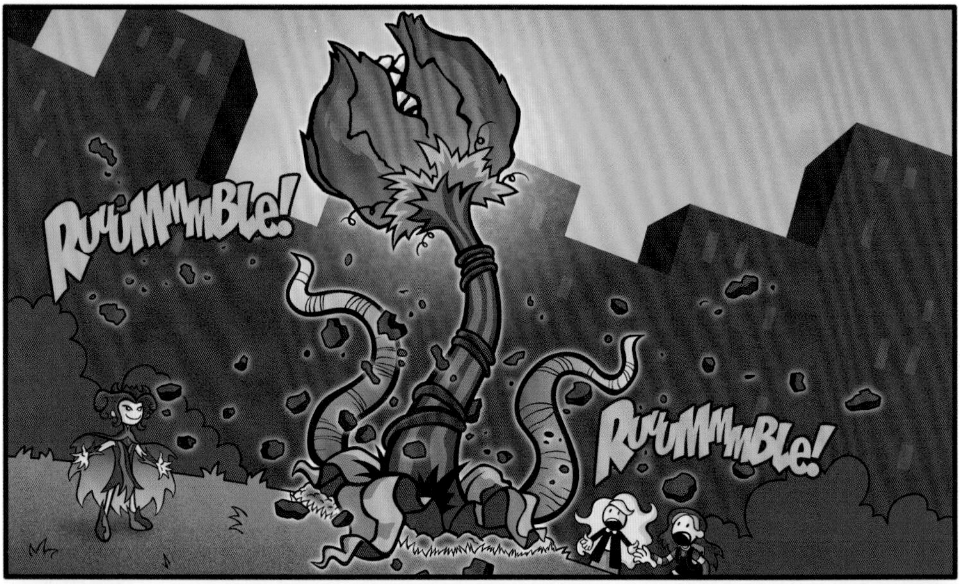
RUUMMMBLE!
RUUMMMBLE!

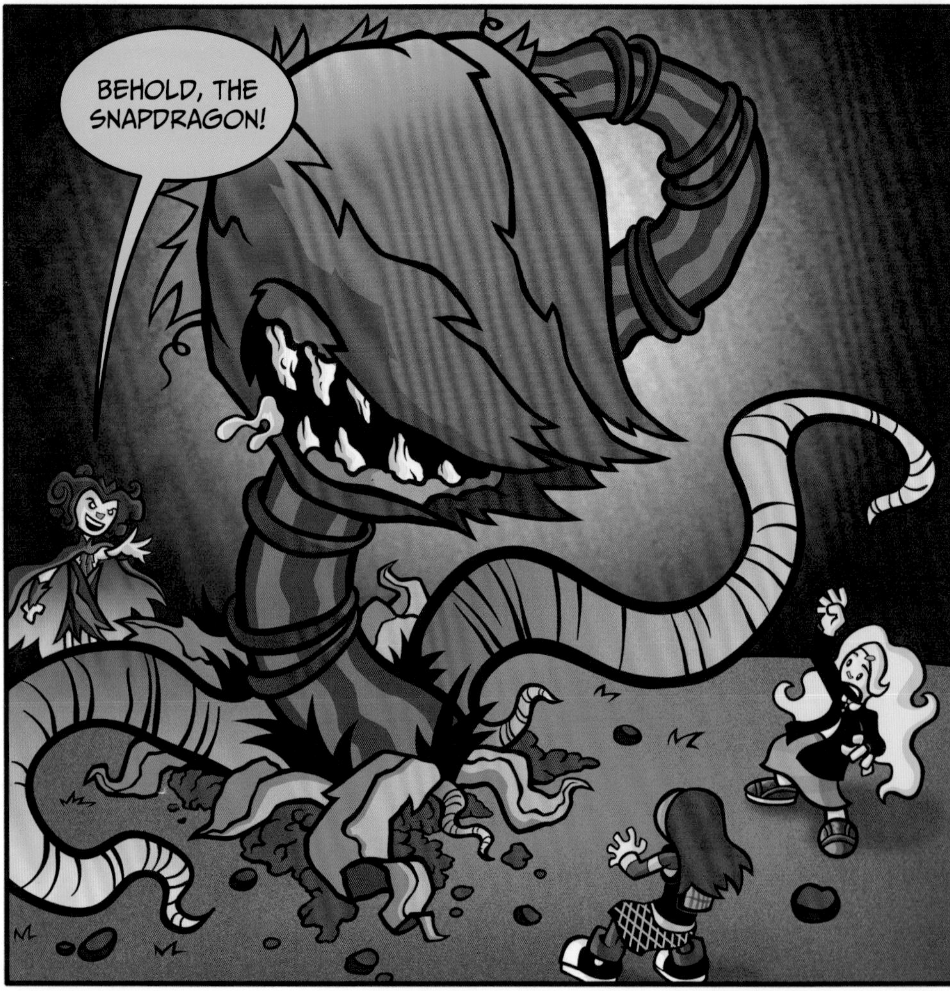
BEHOLD, THE SNAPDRAGON!

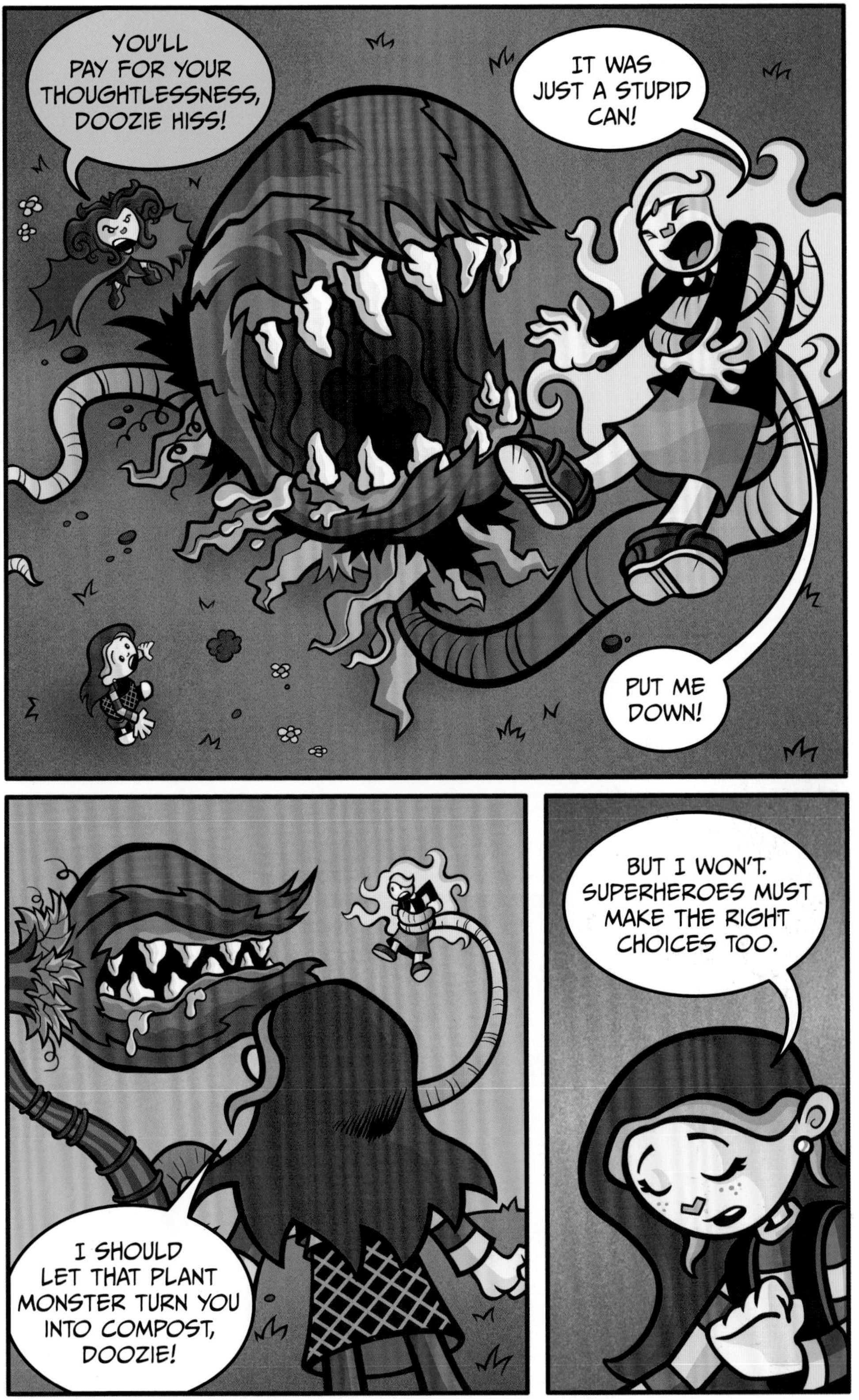
YOU'LL PAY FOR YOUR THOUGHTLESSNESS, DOOZIE HISS!
IT WAS JUST A STUPID CAN!
PUT ME DOWN!
I SHOULD LET THAT PLANT MONSTER TURN YOU INTO COMPOST, DOOZIE!
BUT I WON'T. SUPERHEROES MUST MAKE THE RIGHT CHOICES TOO.

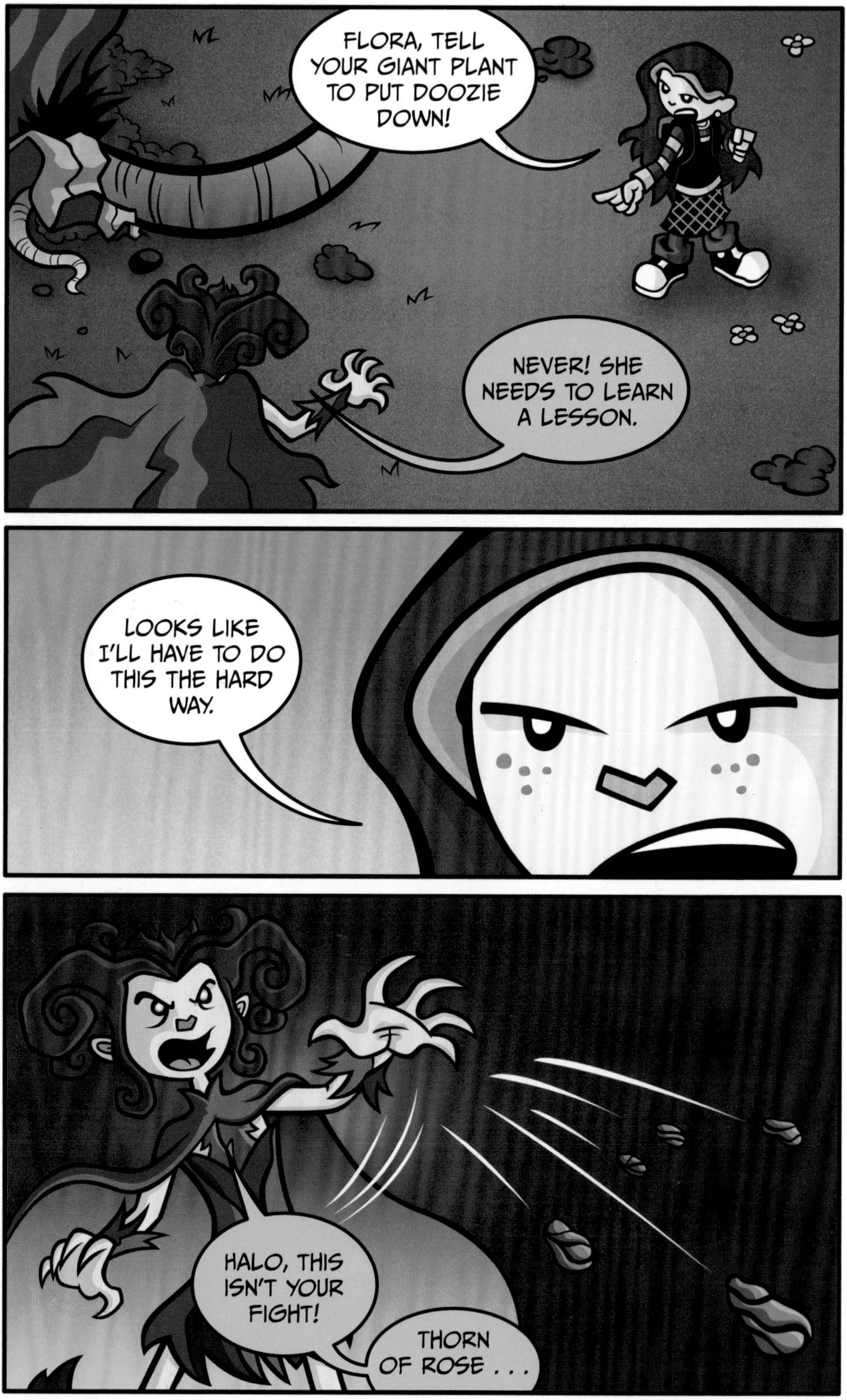
FLORA, TELL YOUR GIANT PLANT TO PUT DOOZIE DOWN!
NEVER! SHE NEEDS TO LEARN A LESSON.
LOOKS LIKE I'LL HAVE TO DO THIS THE HARD WAY.
HALO, THIS ISN'T YOUR FIGHT!
THORN OF ROSE . . .

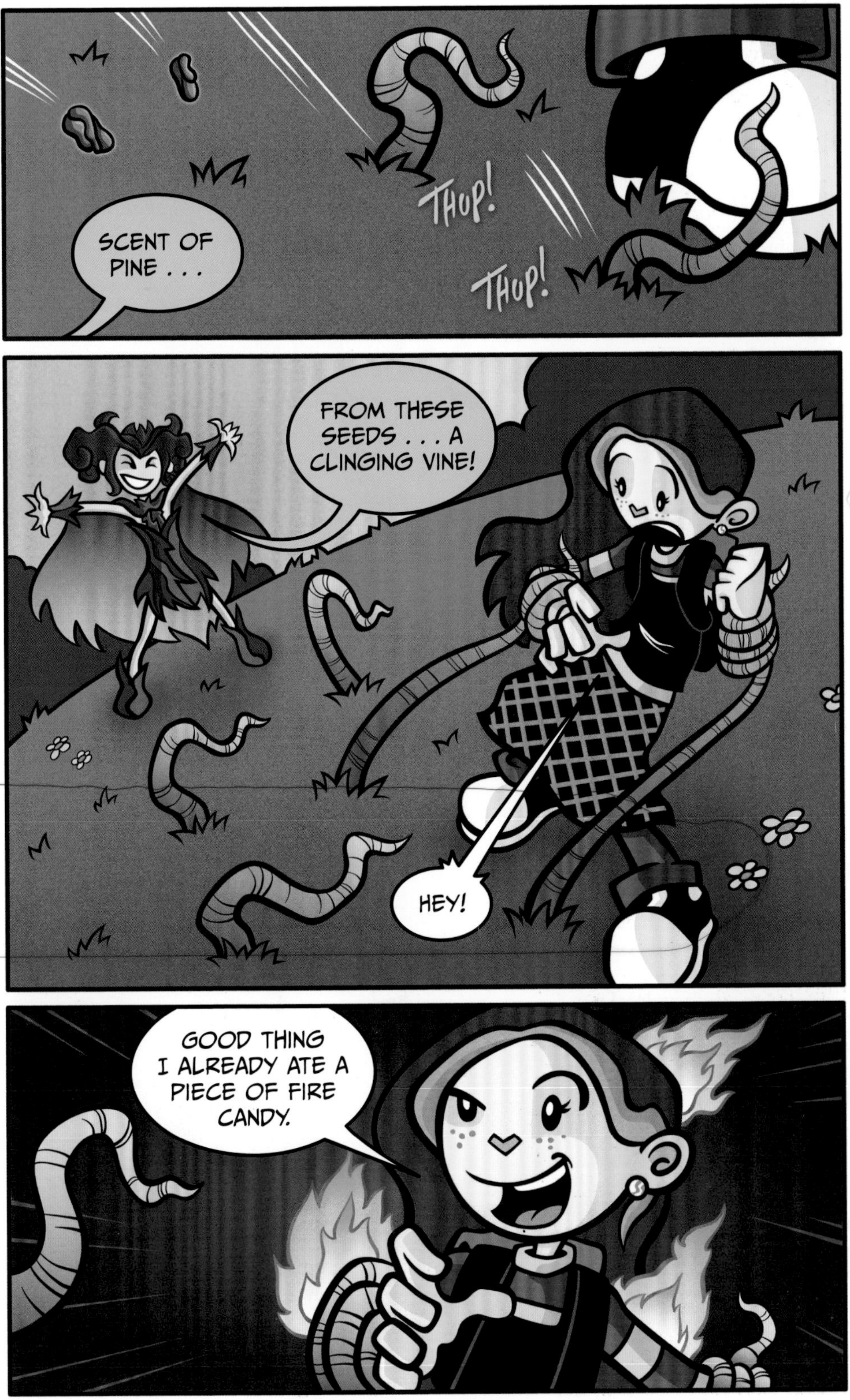
SCENT OF PINE . . .
THUP!
THUP!
FROM THESE SEEDS . . . A CLINGING VINE!
HEY!
GOOD THING I ALREADY ATE A PIECE OF FIRE CANDY.

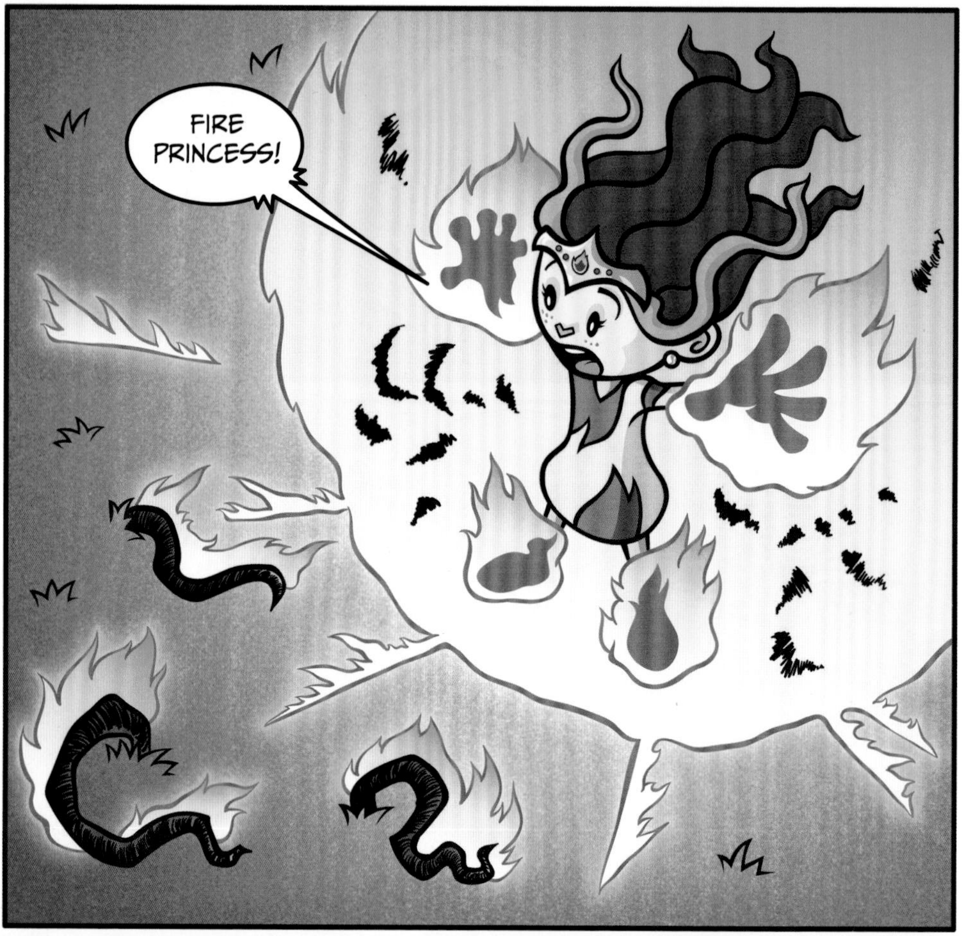
FIRE PRINCESS!

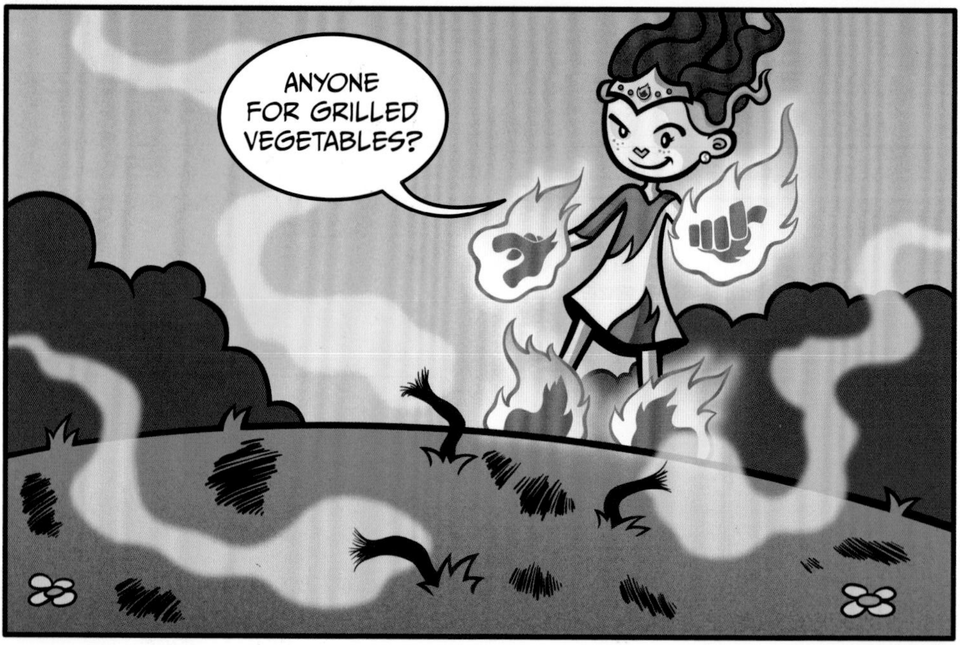
ANYONE FOR GRILLED VEGETABLES?

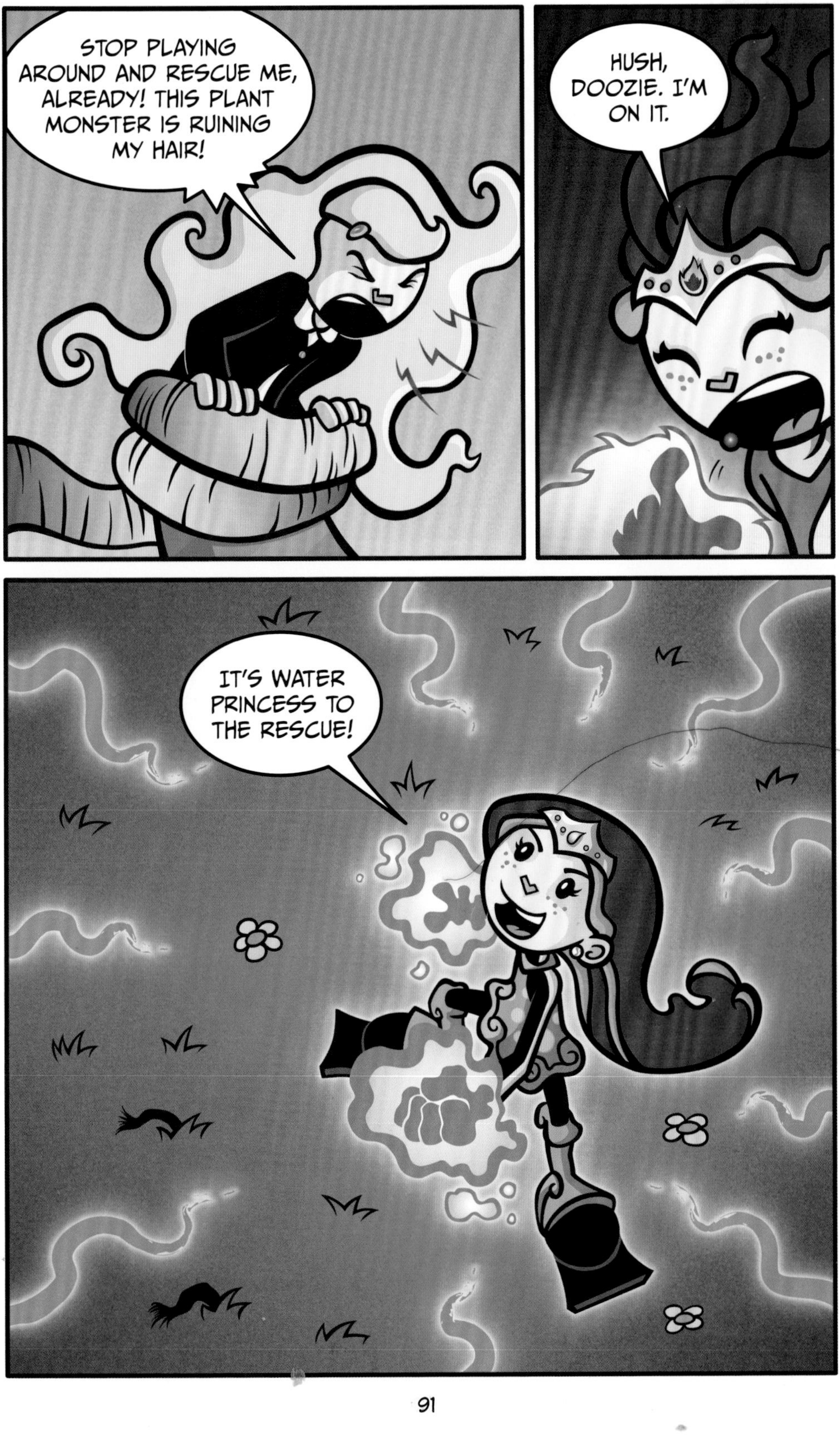
STOP PLAYING AROUND AND RESCUE ME, ALREADY! THIS PLANT MONSTER IS RUINING MY HAIR!
HUSH, DOOZIE. I'M ON IT.
IT'S WATER PRINCESS TO THE RESCUE!

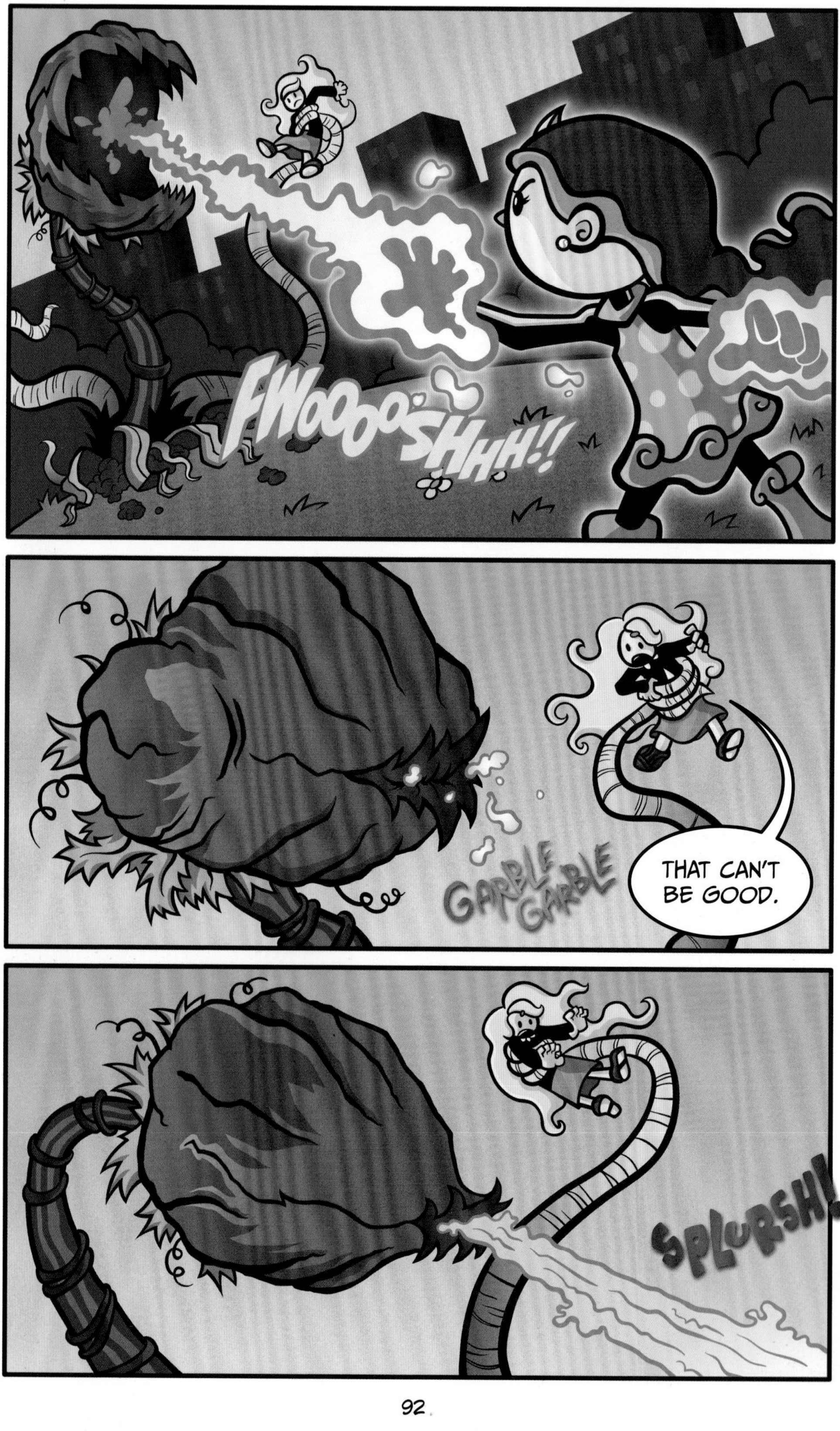
FWOOOOOSHHH!!
GARBLE GARBLE
THAT CAN'T BE GOOD.
SPLURSH!

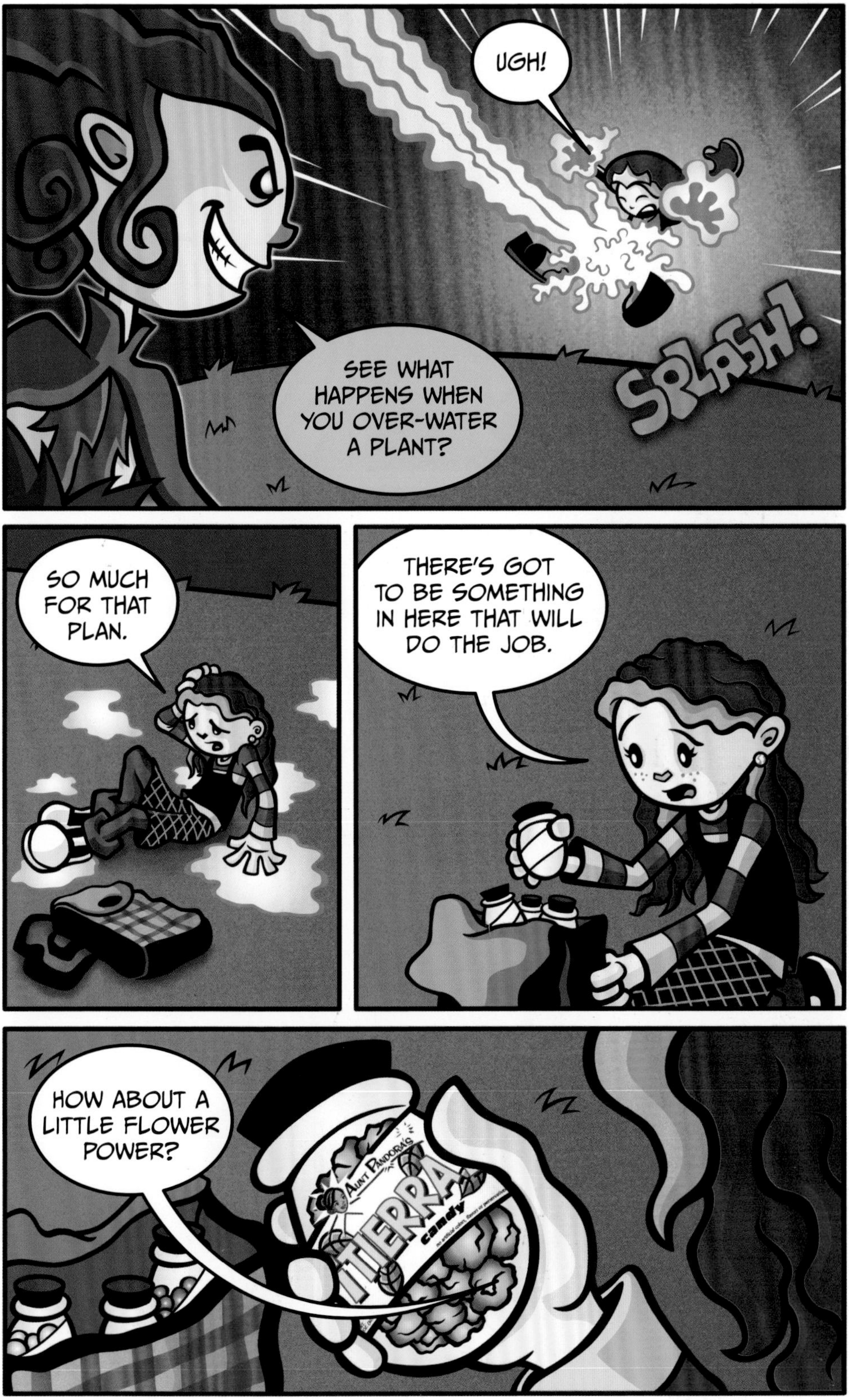
UGH!
SEE WHAT HAPPENS WHEN YOU OVER-WATER A PLANT?
SPLASH!
SO MUCH FOR THAT PLAN.
THERE'S GOT TO BE SOMETHING IN HERE THAT WILL DO THE JOB.
HOW ABOUT A LITTLE FLOWER POWER?
AUNT PANDORA'S
TIERRA
candy

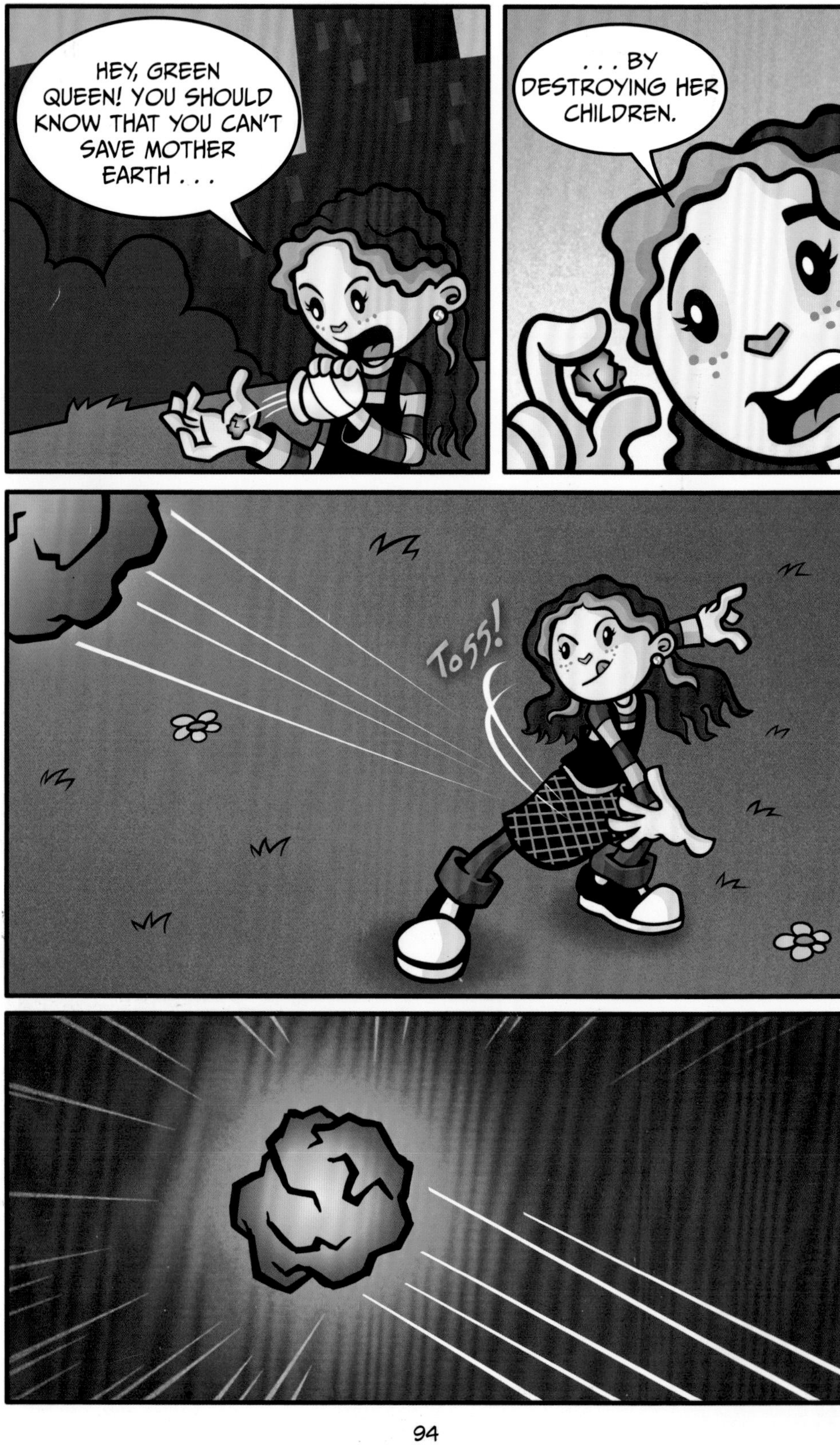
HEY, GREEN QUEEN! YOU SHOULD KNOW THAT YOU CAN'T SAVE MOTHER EARTH . . .
. . . BY DESTROYING HER CHILDREN.
TOSS!

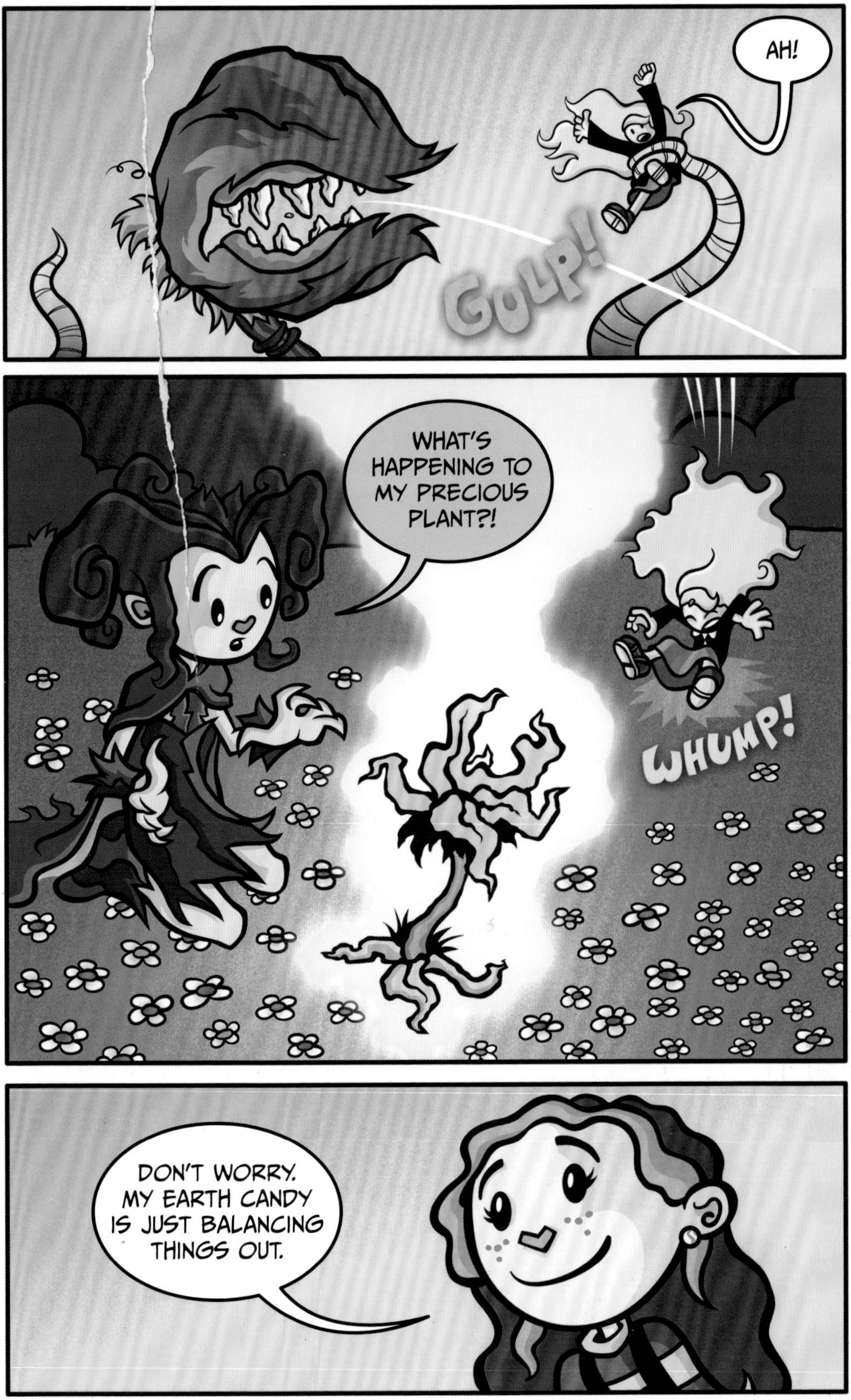
AH!
GULP!
WHAT'S HAPPENING TO MY PRECIOUS PLANT?!
WHUMP!
DON'T WORRY. MY EARTH CANDY IS JUST BALANCING THINGS OUT.

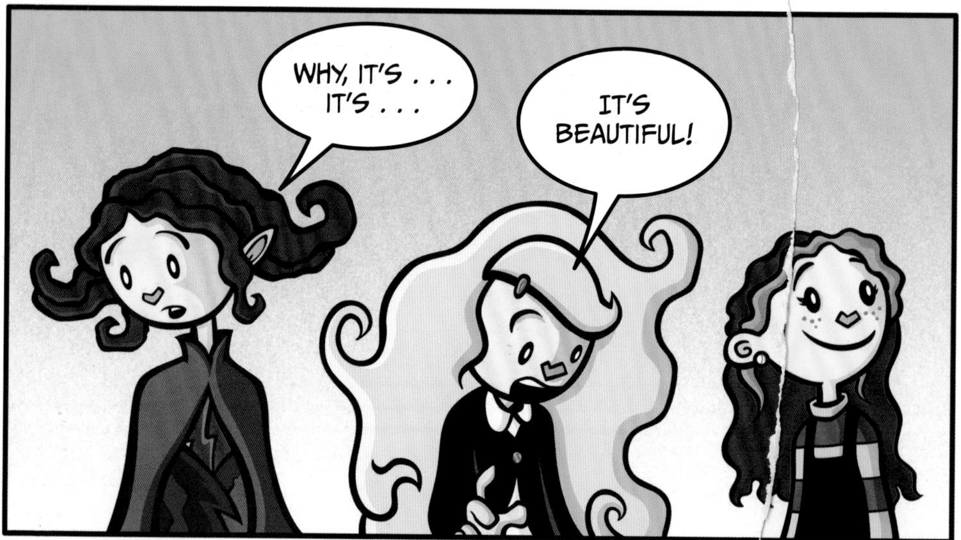
WHY, IT'S . . .
IT'S . . .
IT'S BEAUTIFUL!

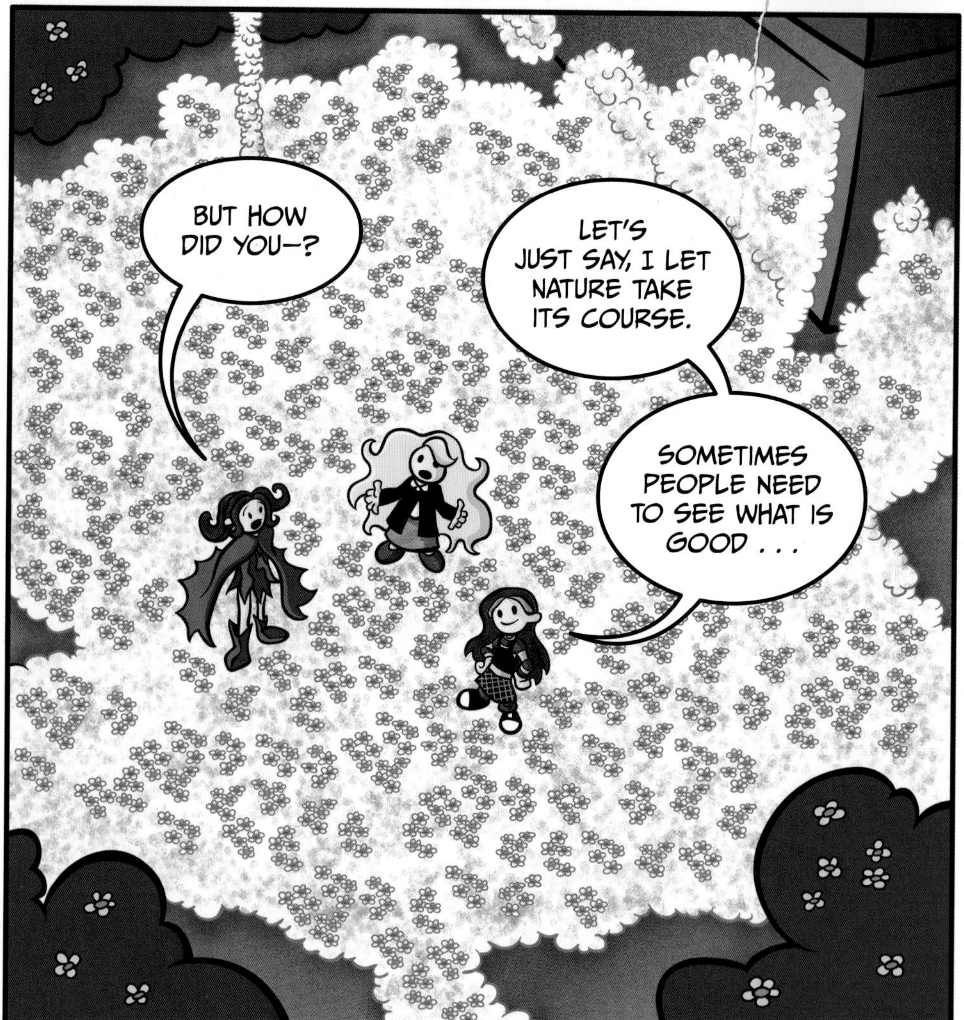
BUT HOW DID YOU–?
LET'S JUST SAY, I LET NATURE TAKE ITS COURSE.
SOMETIMES PEOPLE NEED TO SEE WHAT IS GOOD . . .

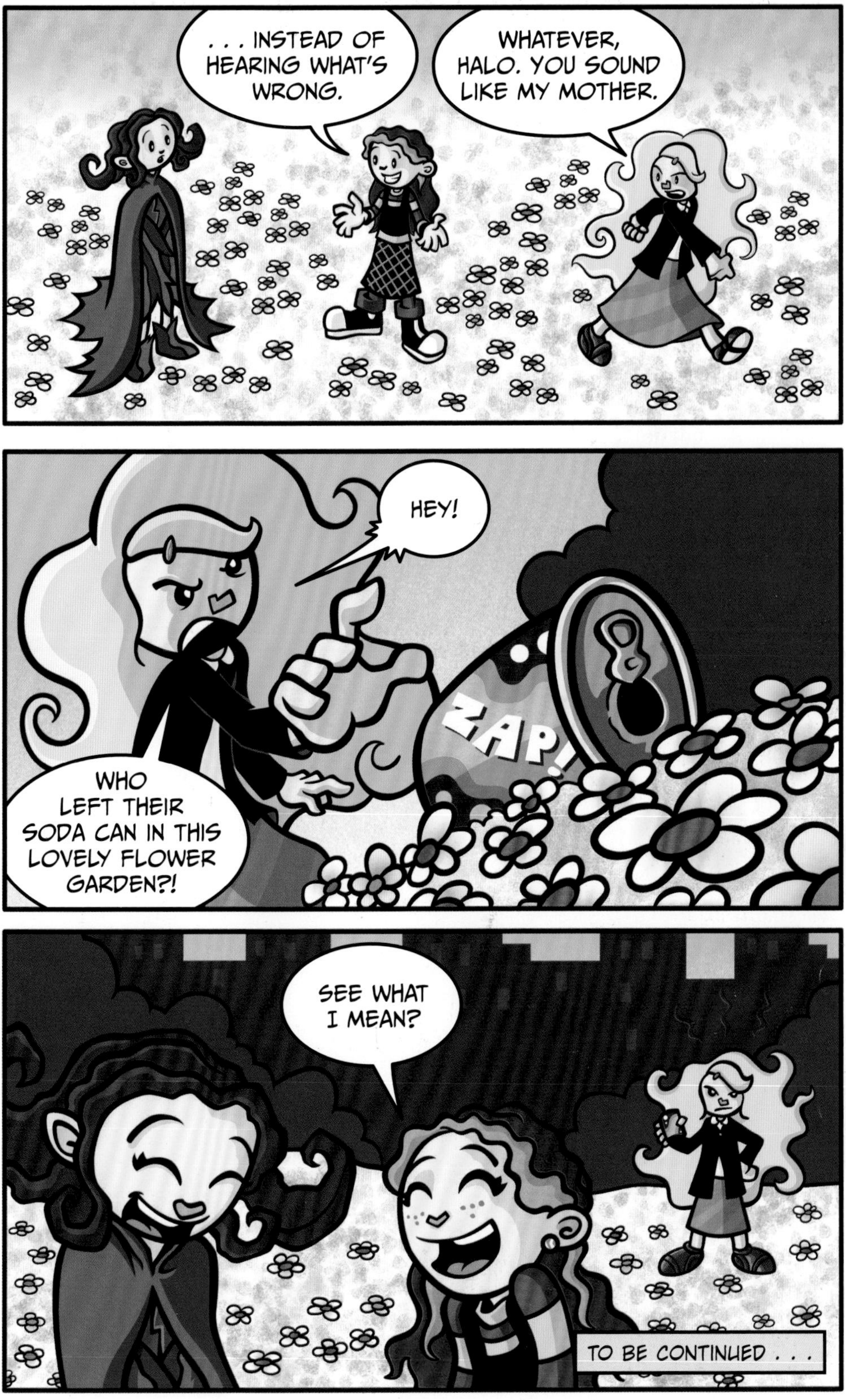

. . . INSTEAD OF HEARING WHAT'S WRONG.
WHATEVER, HALO. YOU SOUND LIKE MY MOTHER.
HEY!
ZAP!
WHO LEFT THEIR SODA CAN IN THIS LOVELY FLOWER GARDEN?!
SEE WHAT I MEAN?
TO BE CONTINUED . . .

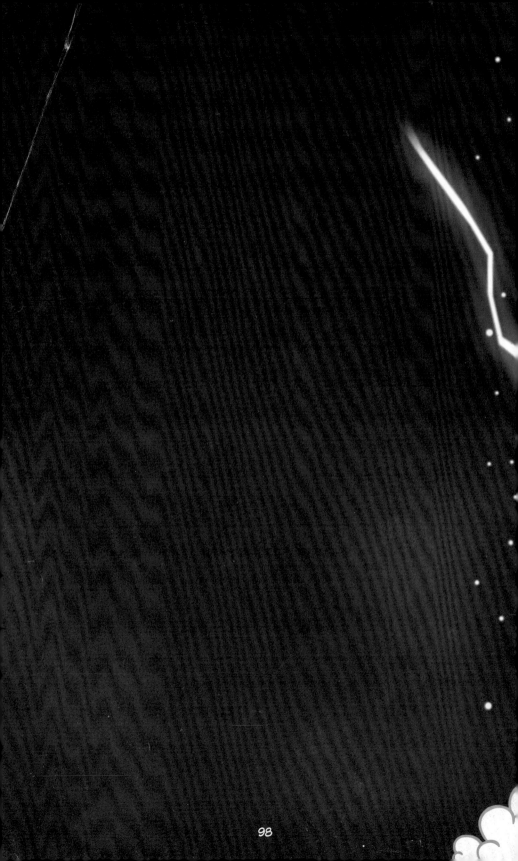

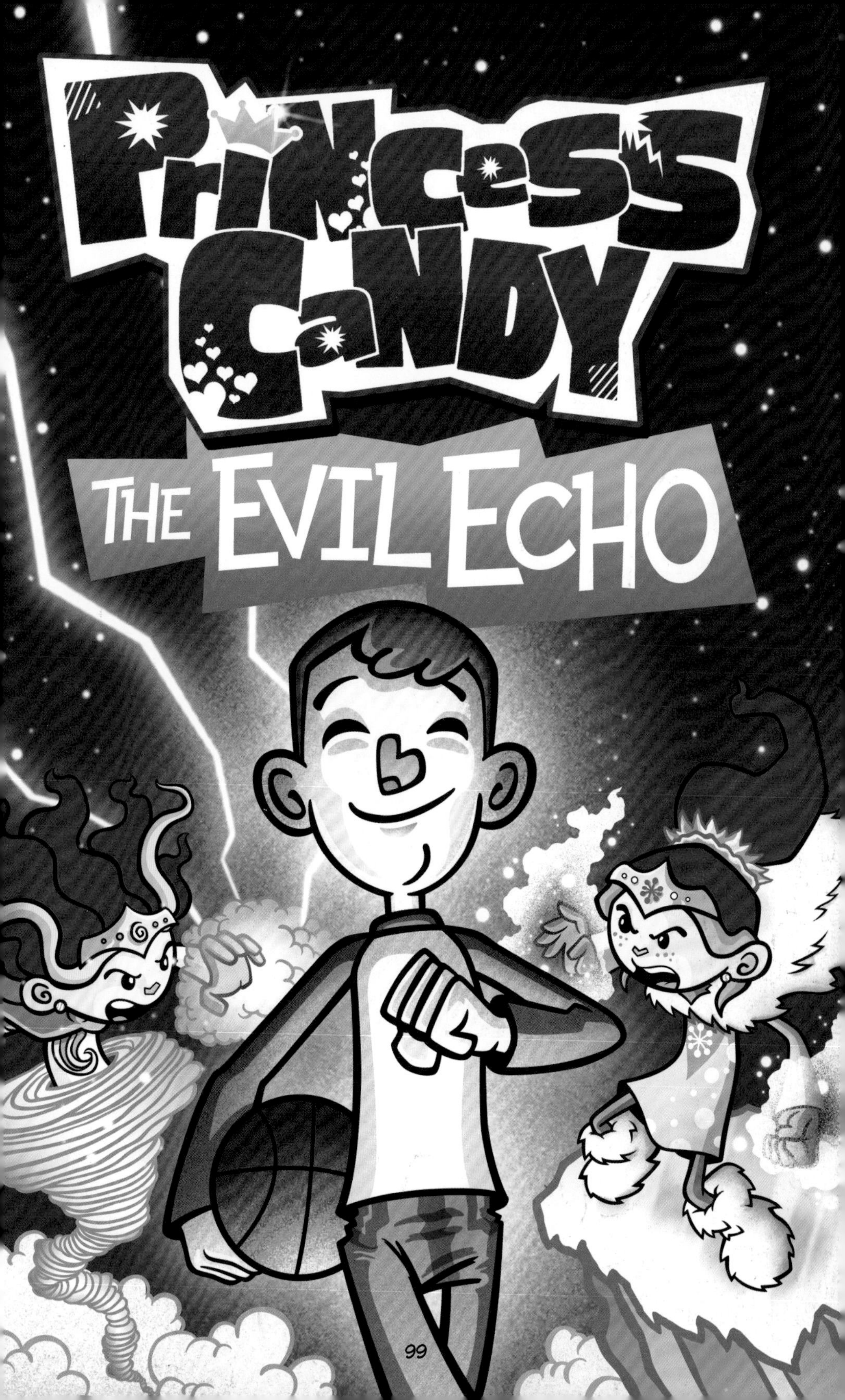
PRINCESS CANDY
THE EVIL ECHO

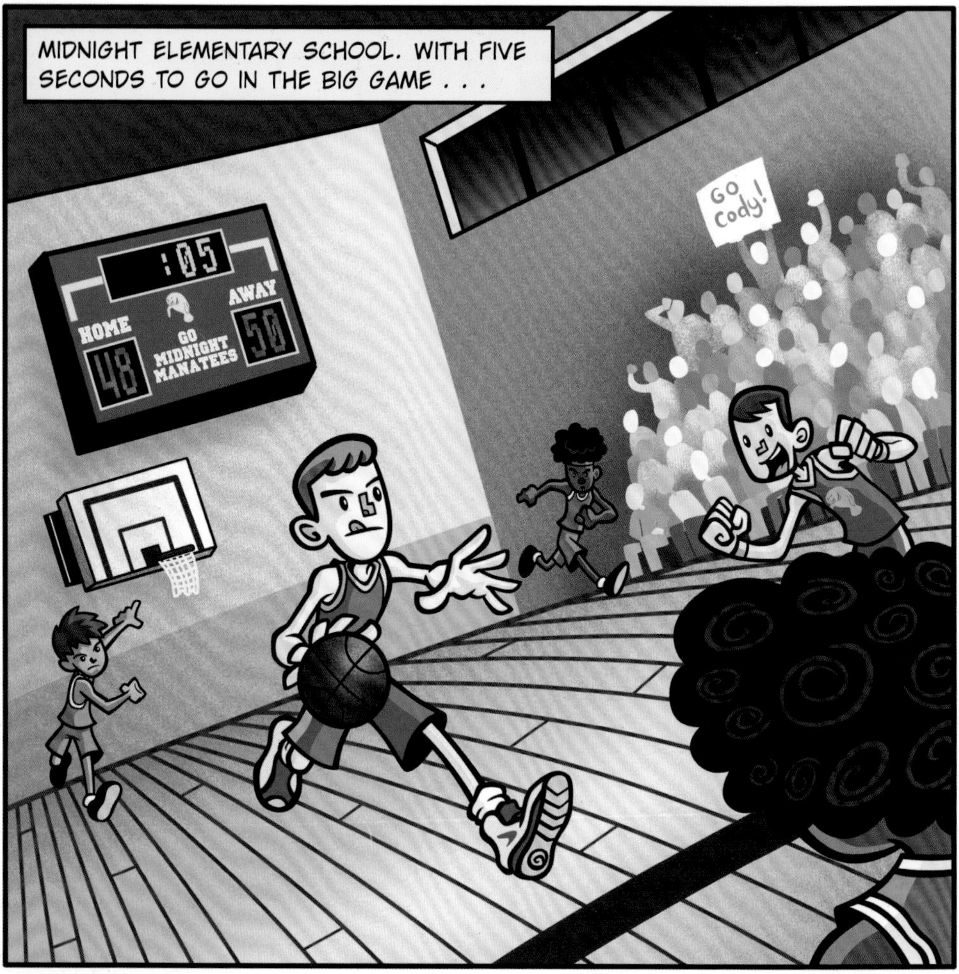
MIDNIGHT ELEMENTARY SCHOOL. WITH FIVE SECONDS TO GO IN THE BIG GAME . . .
:05
HOME
48
GO MIDNIGHT MANATEES
AWAY
50
GO cody!

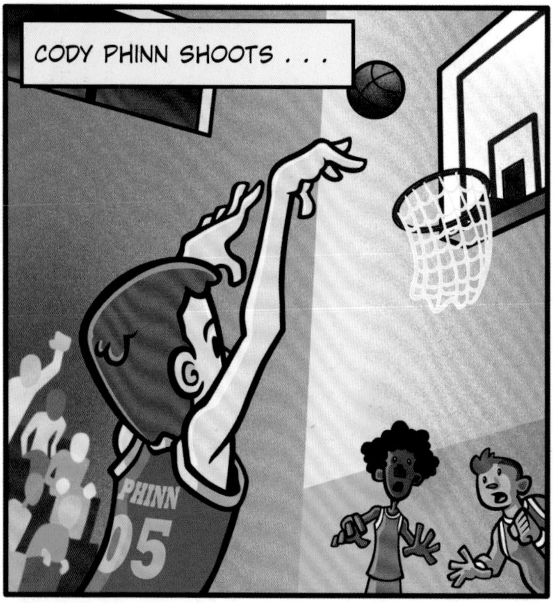
CODY PHINN SHOOTS . . .
PHINN
05

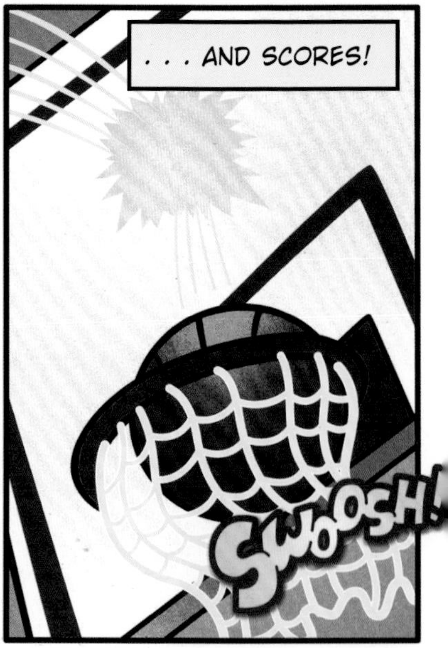
. . . AND SCORES!
SWOOSH!

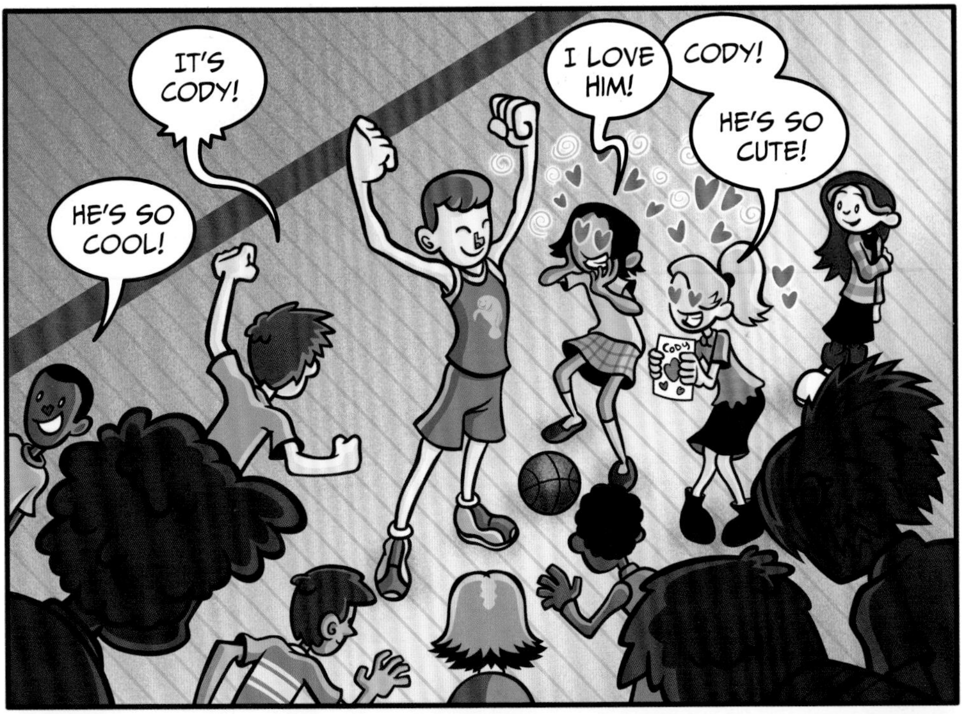
IT'S CODY!
HE'S SO COOL!
I LOVE HIM!
CODY!
HE'S SO CUTE!

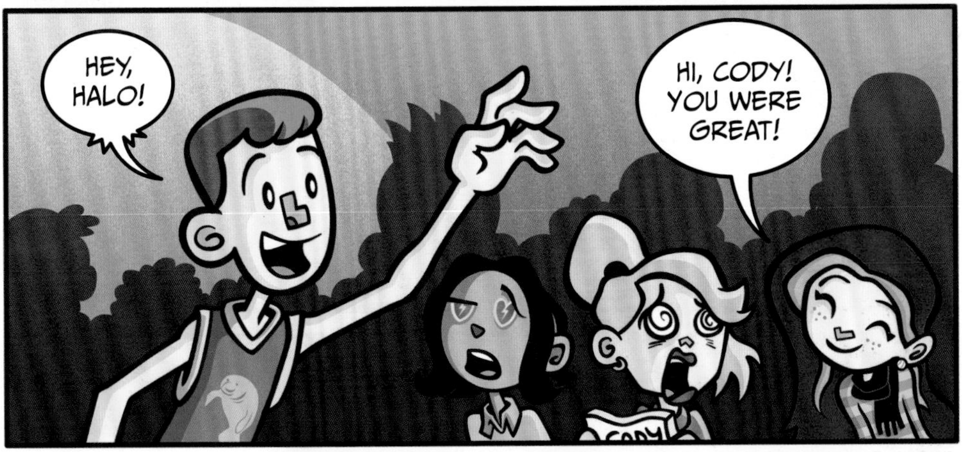
HEY, HALO!
HI, CODY! YOU WERE GREAT!

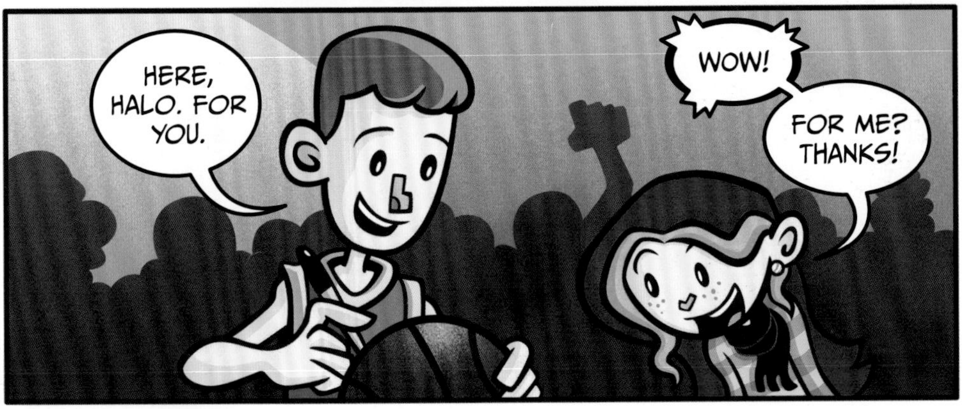
HERE, HALO. FOR YOU.
WOW!
FOR ME? THANKS!

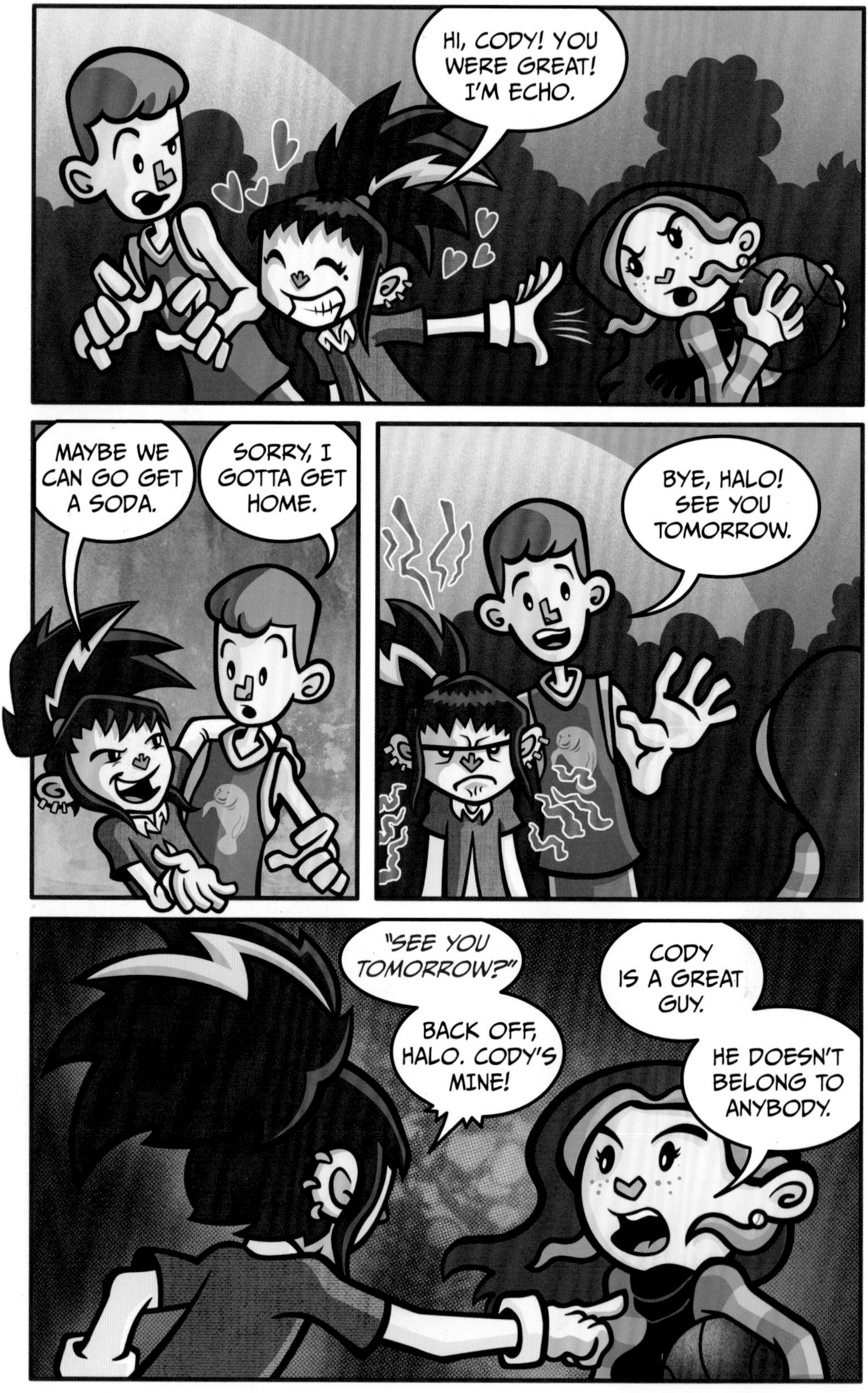
HI, CODY! YOU WERE GREAT! I'M ECHO.
MAYBE WE CAN GO GET A SODA.
SORRY, I GOTTA GET HOME.
BYE, HALO! SEE YOU TOMORROW.
"SEE YOU TOMORROW?"
BACK OFF, HALO. CODY'S MINE!
CODY IS A GREAT GUY.
HE DOESN'T BELONG TO ANYBODY.

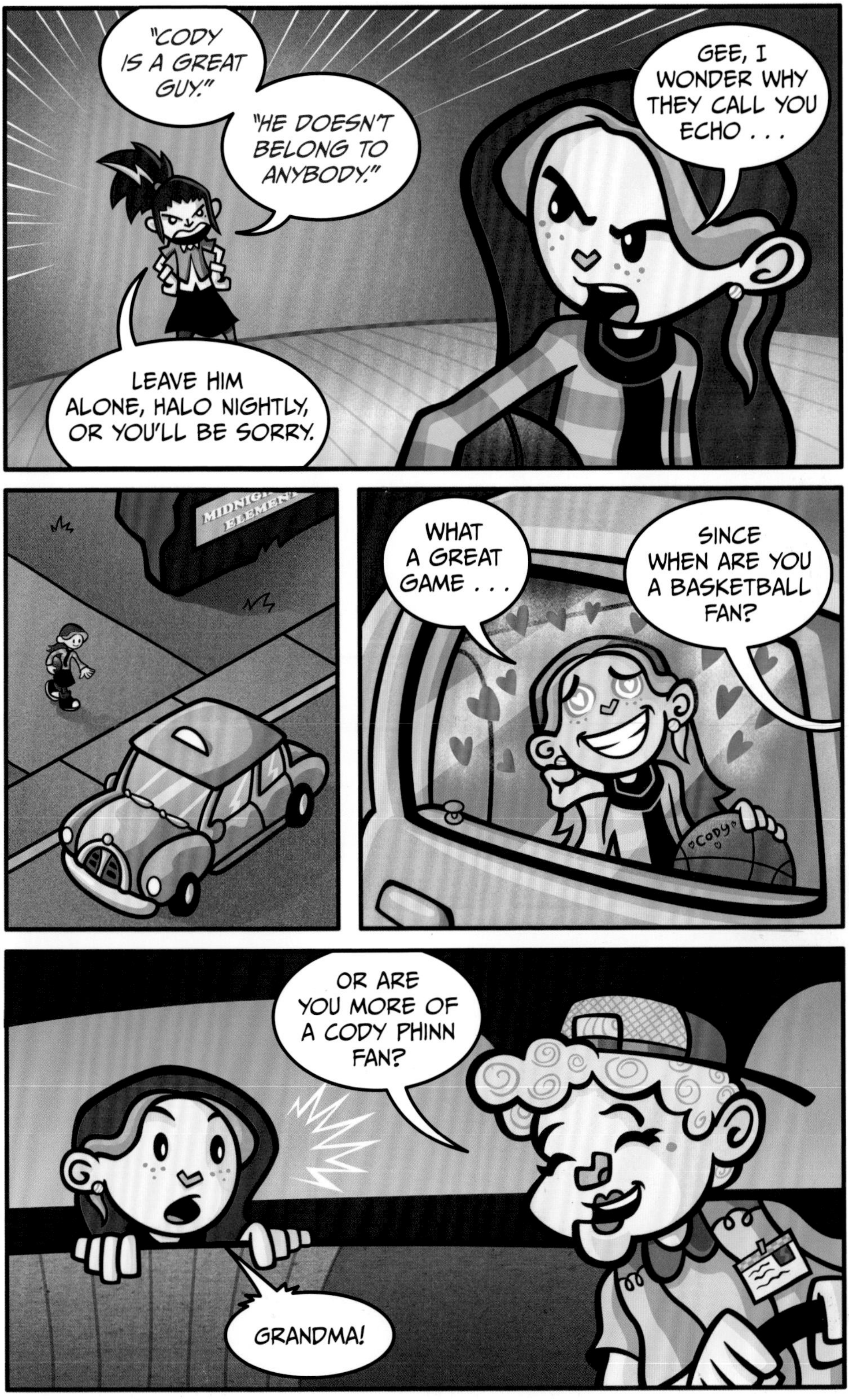
"CODY IS A GREAT GUY."
"HE DOESN'T BELONG TO ANYBODY."
LEAVE HIM ALONE, HALO NIGHTLY, OR YOU'LL BE SORRY.
GEE, I WONDER WHY THEY CALL YOU ECHO . . .
WHAT A GREAT GAME . . .
SINCE WHEN ARE YOU A BASKETBALL FAN?
CODY
OR ARE YOU MORE OF A CODY PHINN FAN?
GRANDMA!

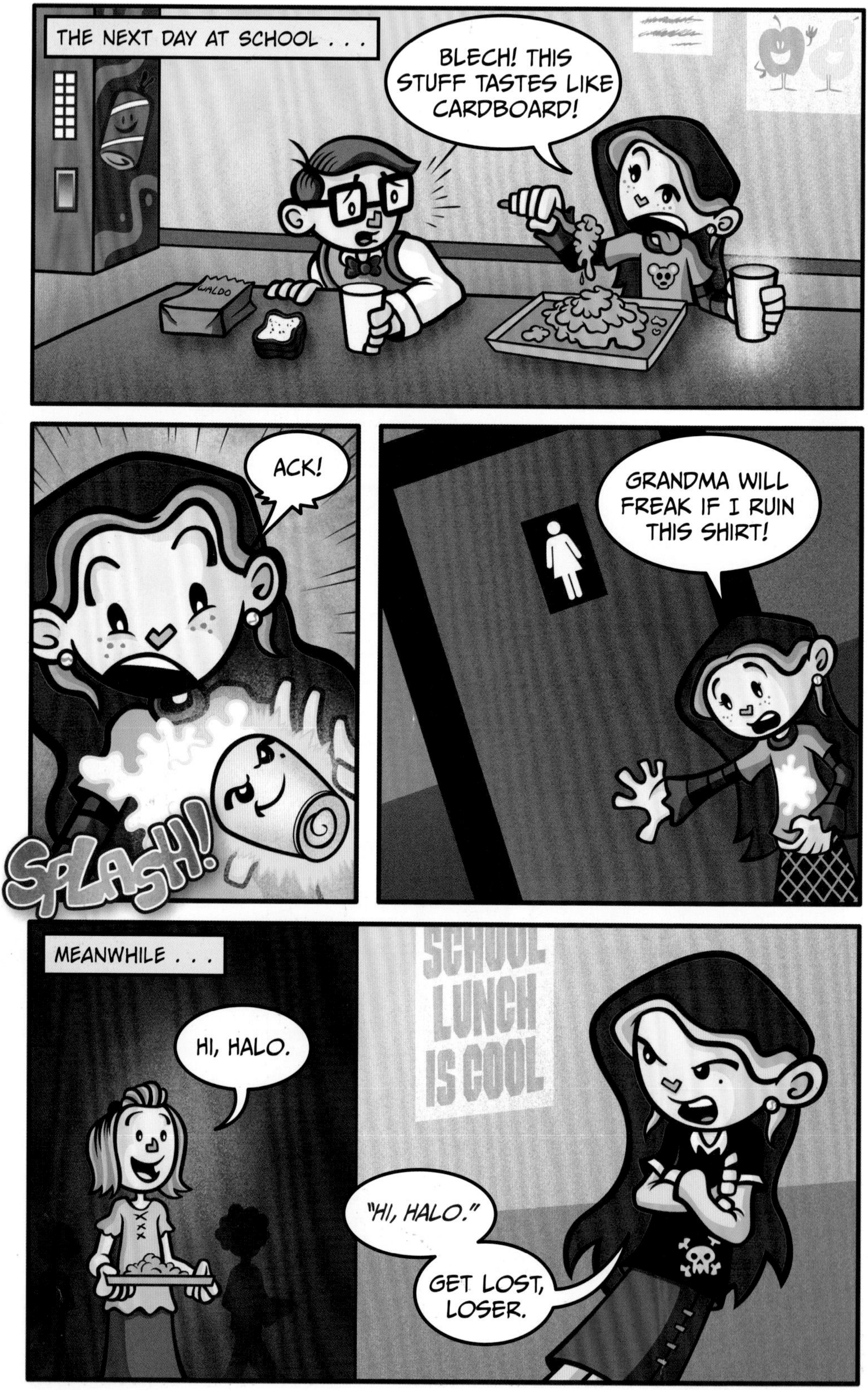
THE NEXT DAY AT SCHOOL . . .
BLECH! THIS STUFF TASTES LIKE CARDBOARD!
WALDO
ACK!
SPLASH!
GRANDMA WILL FREAK IF I RUIN THIS SHIRT!
MEANWHILE . . .
SCHOOL LUNCH IS COOL
HI, HALO.
"HI, HALO."
GET LOST, LOSER.

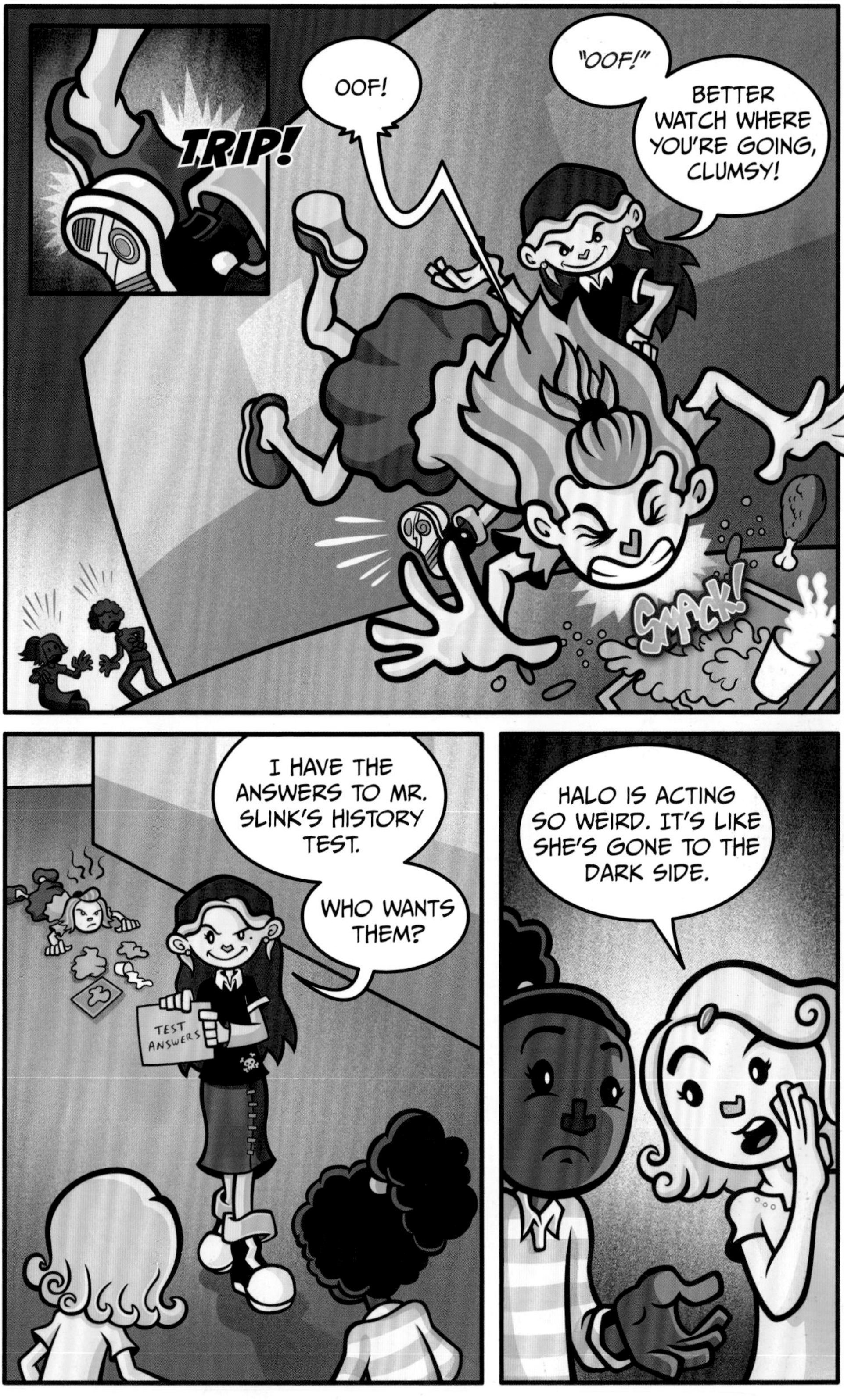
TRIP!
OOF!
"OOF!"
BETTER WATCH WHERE YOU'RE GOING, CLUMSY!
SMACK!
I HAVE THE ANSWERS TO MR. SLINK'S HISTORY TEST.
WHO WANTS THEM?
TEST ANSWERS
HALO IS ACTING SO WEIRD. IT'S LIKE SHE'S GONE TO THE DARK SIDE.

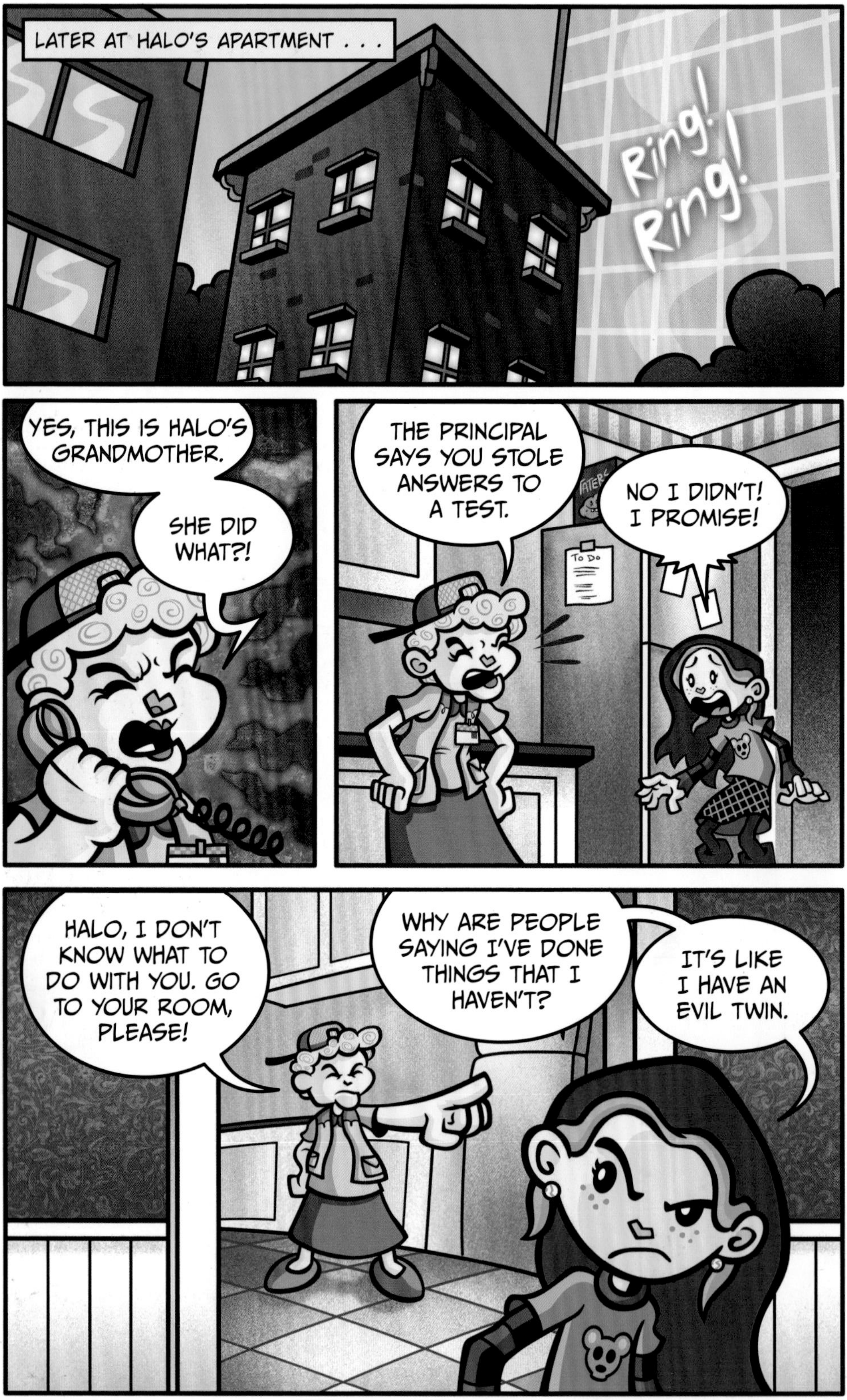

LATER AT HALO'S APARTMENT . . .
Ring! Ring!
YES, THIS IS HALO'S GRANDMOTHER.
SHE DID WHAT?!
THE PRINCIPAL SAYS YOU STOLE ANSWERS TO A TEST.
NO I DIDN'T! I PROMISE!
TO DO
HALO, I DON'T KNOW WHAT TO DO WITH YOU. GO TO YOUR ROOM, PLEASE!
WHY ARE PEOPLE SAYING I'VE DONE THINGS THAT I HAVEN'T?
IT'S LIKE I HAVE AN EVIL TWIN.

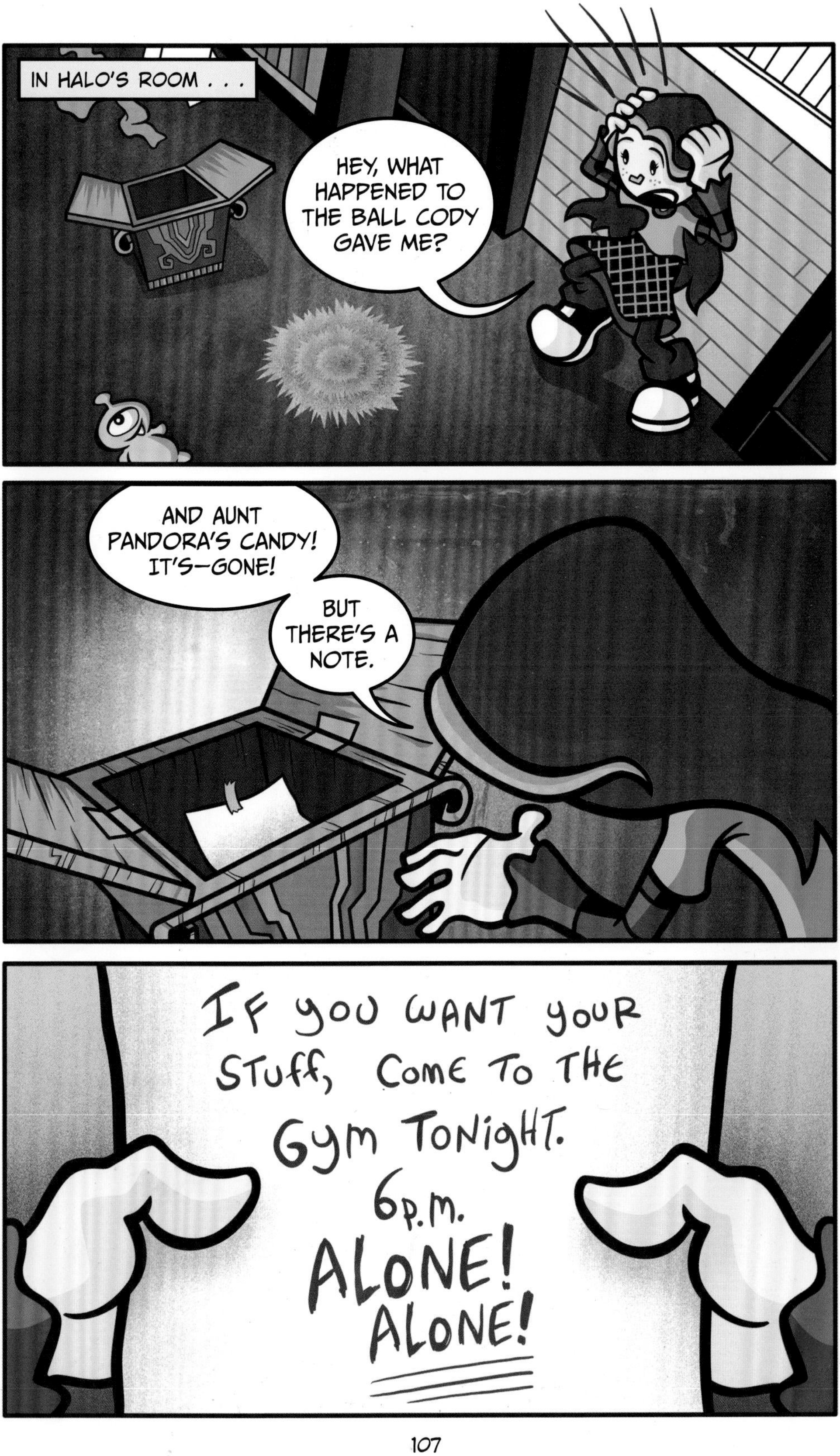
IN HALO'S ROOM . . .
HEY, WHAT HAPPENED TO THE BALL CODY GAVE ME?
AND AUNT PANDORA'S CANDY! IT'S—GONE!
BUT THERE'S A NOTE.
IF YOU WANT YOUR STUFF, COME TO THE GYM TONIGHT. 6 P.M. ALONE! ALONE!

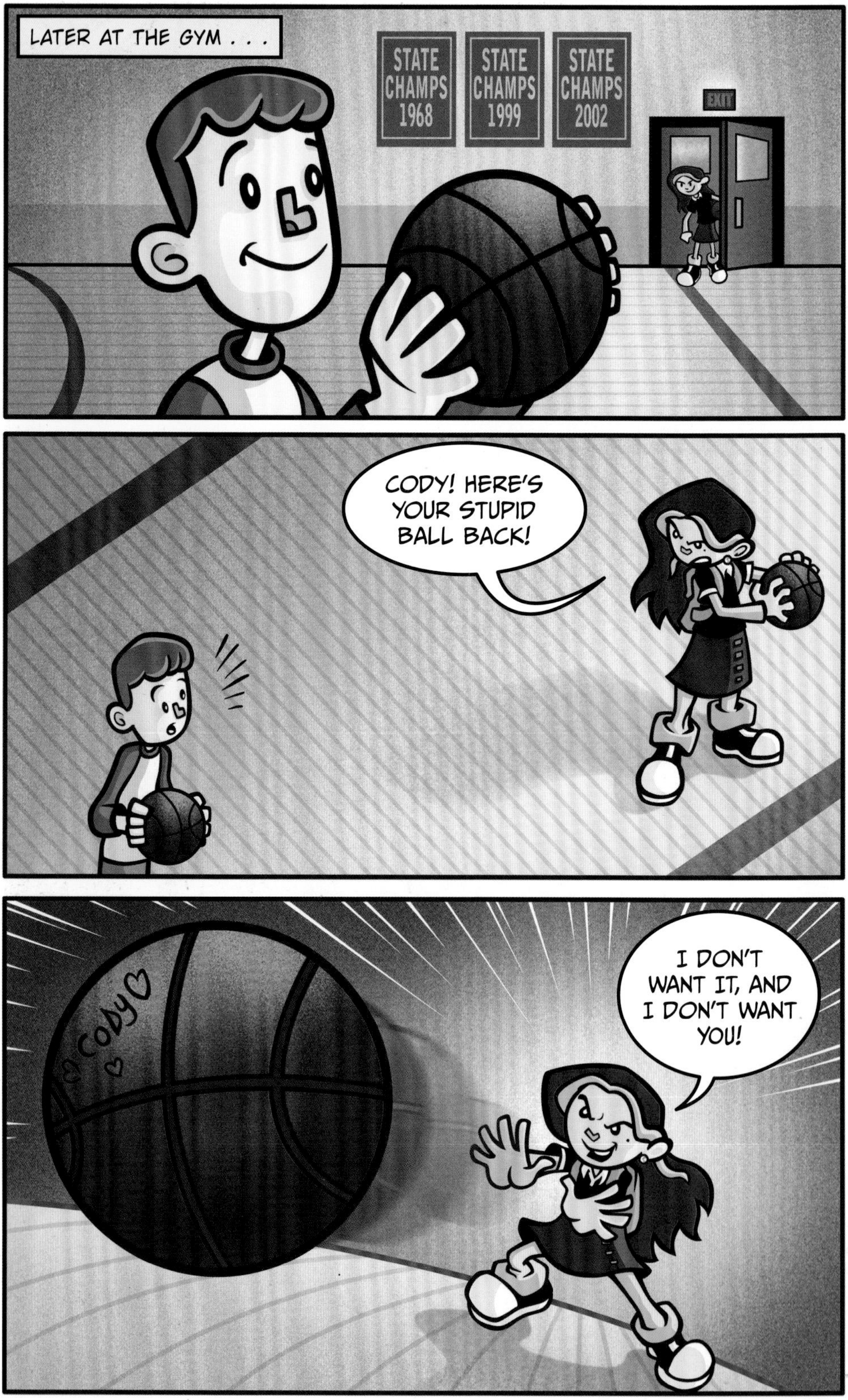
LATER AT THE GYM . . .
STATE CHAMPS 1968
STATE CHAMPS 1999
STATE CHAMPS 2002
EXIT
CODY! HERE'S YOUR STUPID BALL BACK!
CODY
I DON'T WANT IT, AND I DON'T WANT YOU!

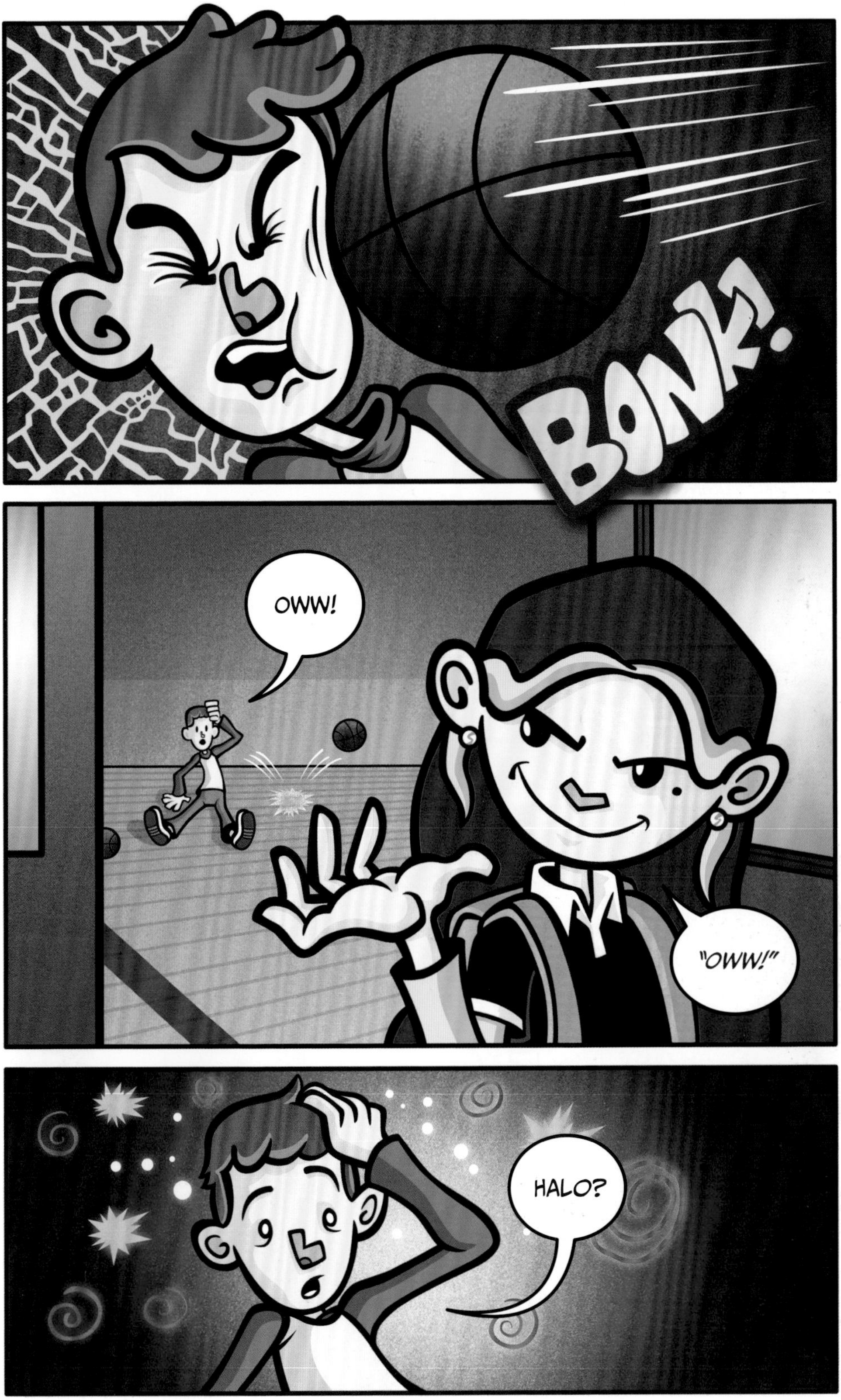
BONK!
OWW!
"OWW!"
HALO?

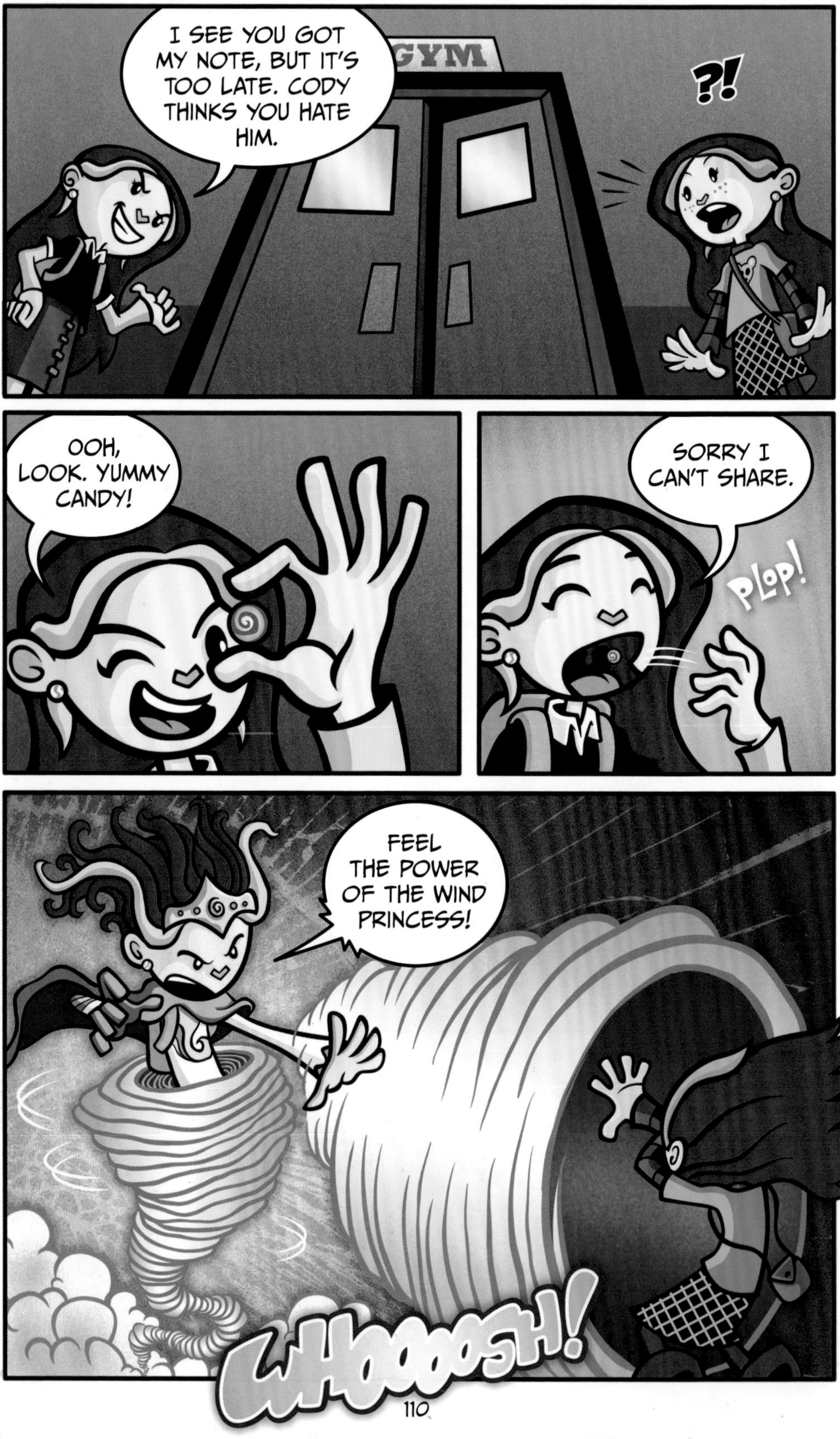

I SEE YOU GOT MY NOTE, BUT IT'S TOO LATE. CODY THINKS YOU HATE HIM.
GYM
?!
OOH, LOOK. YUMMY CANDY!
SORRY I CAN'T SHARE.
PLOP!
FEEL THE POWER OF THE WIND PRINCESS!
WHOOOOSH!

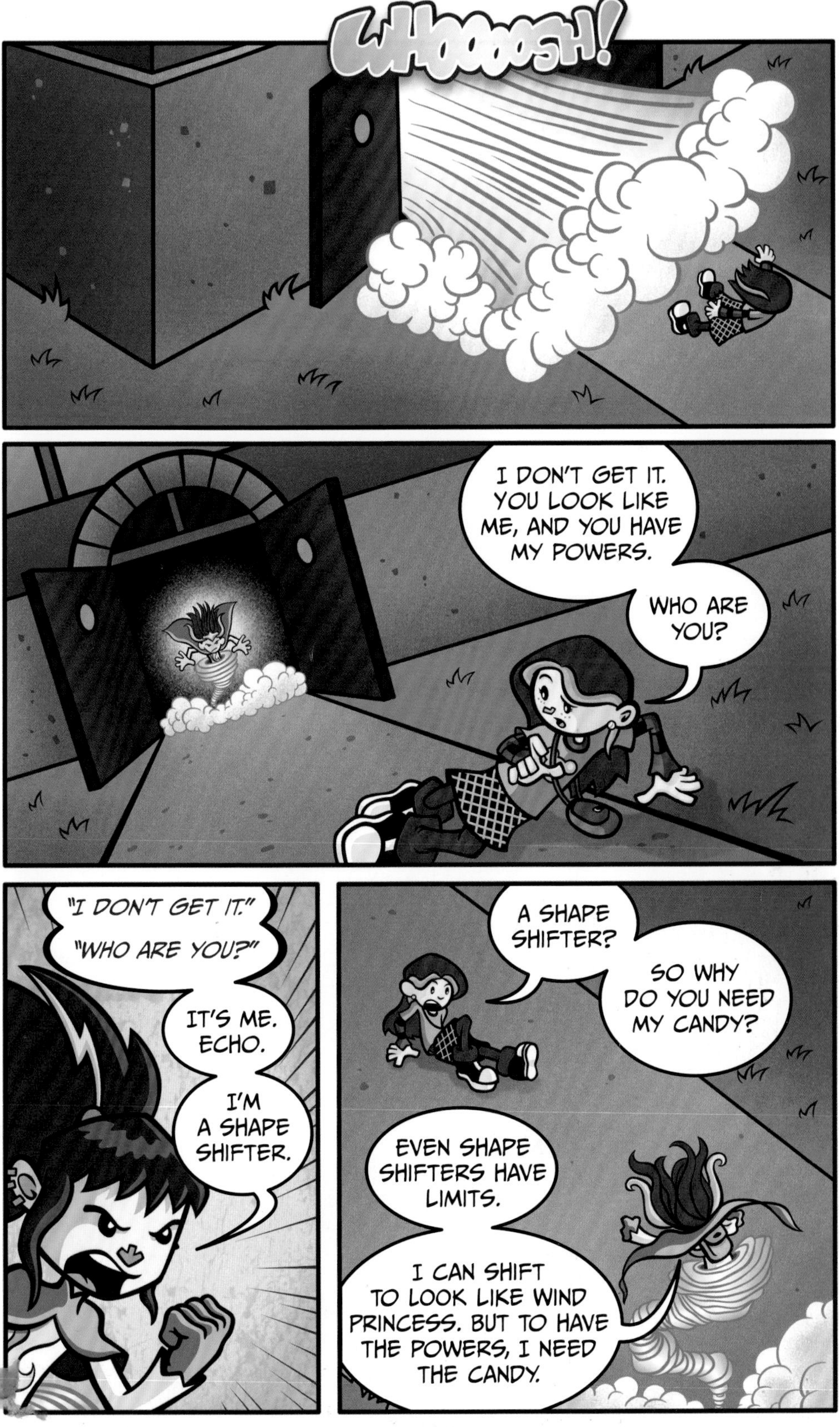
WHOOOOOSH!
I DON'T GET IT. YOU LOOK LIKE ME, AND YOU HAVE MY POWERS.
WHO ARE YOU?
"I DON'T GET IT."
"WHO ARE YOU?"
IT'S ME. ECHO.
I'M A SHAPE SHIFTER.
A SHAPE SHIFTER?
SO WHY DO YOU NEED MY CANDY?
EVEN SHAPE SHIFTERS HAVE LIMITS.
I CAN SHIFT TO LOOK LIKE WIND PRINCESS. BUT TO HAVE THE POWERS, I NEED THE CANDY.

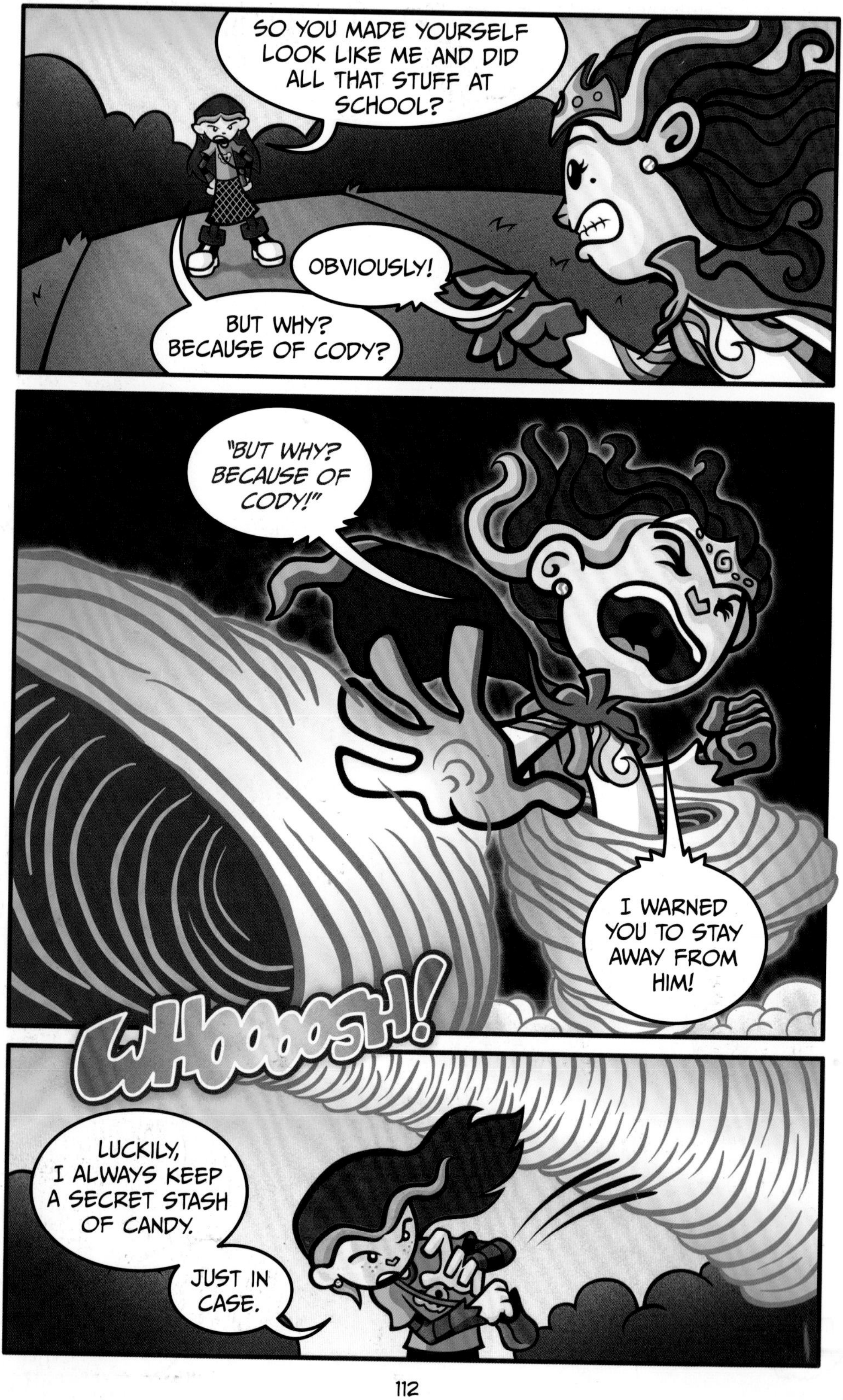
SO YOU MADE YOURSELF LOOK LIKE ME AND DID ALL THAT STUFF AT SCHOOL?
OBVIOUSLY!
BUT WHY? BECAUSE OF CODY?
"BUT WHY? BECAUSE OF CODY!"
I WARNED YOU TO STAY AWAY FROM HIM!
WHOOOOSH!
LUCKILY, I ALWAYS KEEP A SECRET STASH OF CANDY.
JUST IN CASE.

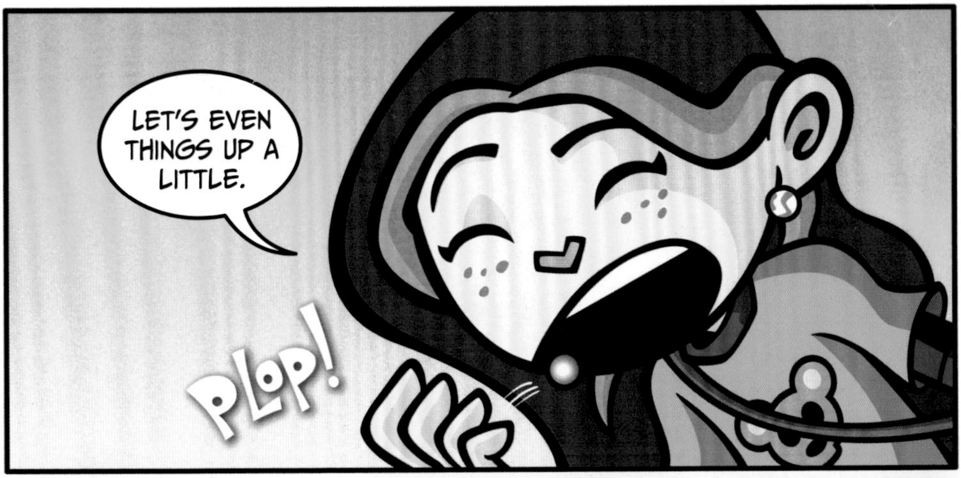
LET'S EVEN THINGS UP A LITTLE.
PLOP!

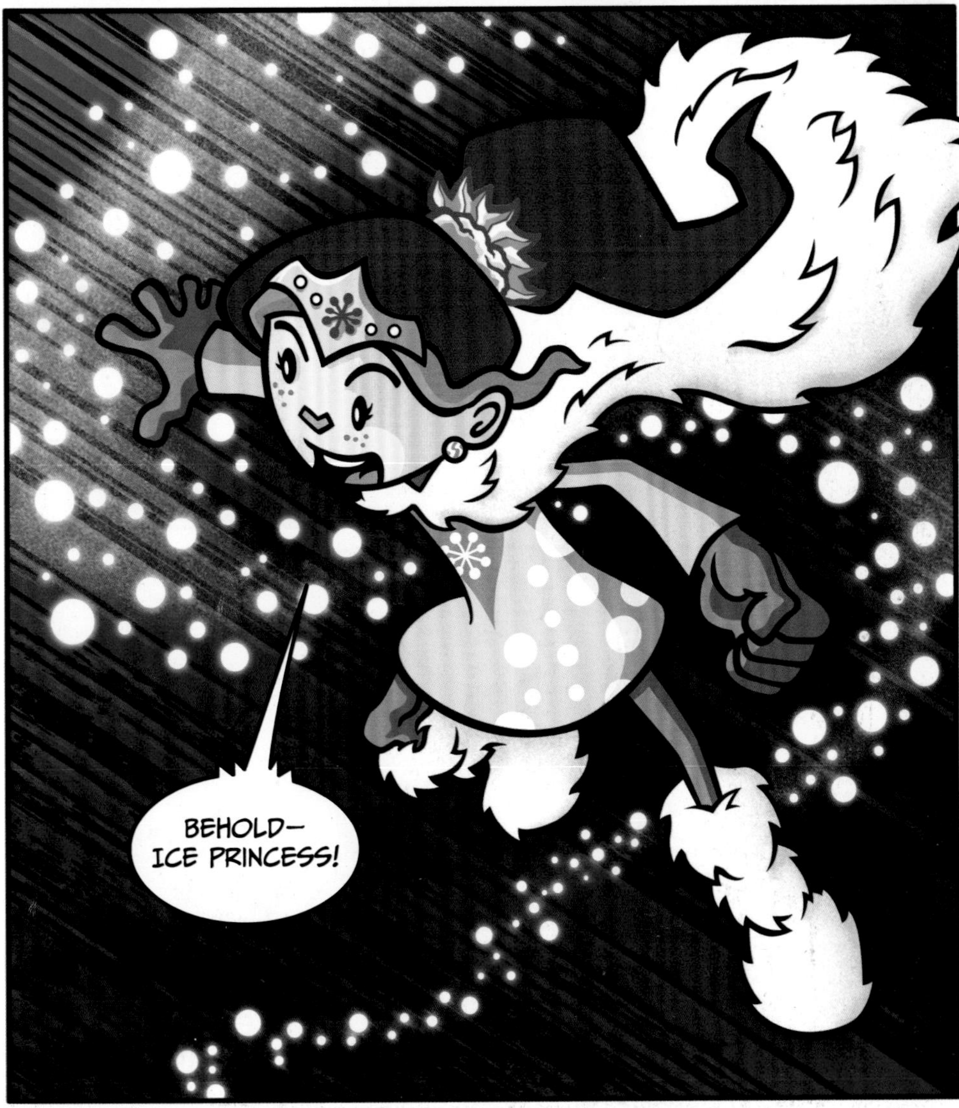
BEHOLD— ICE PRINCESS!

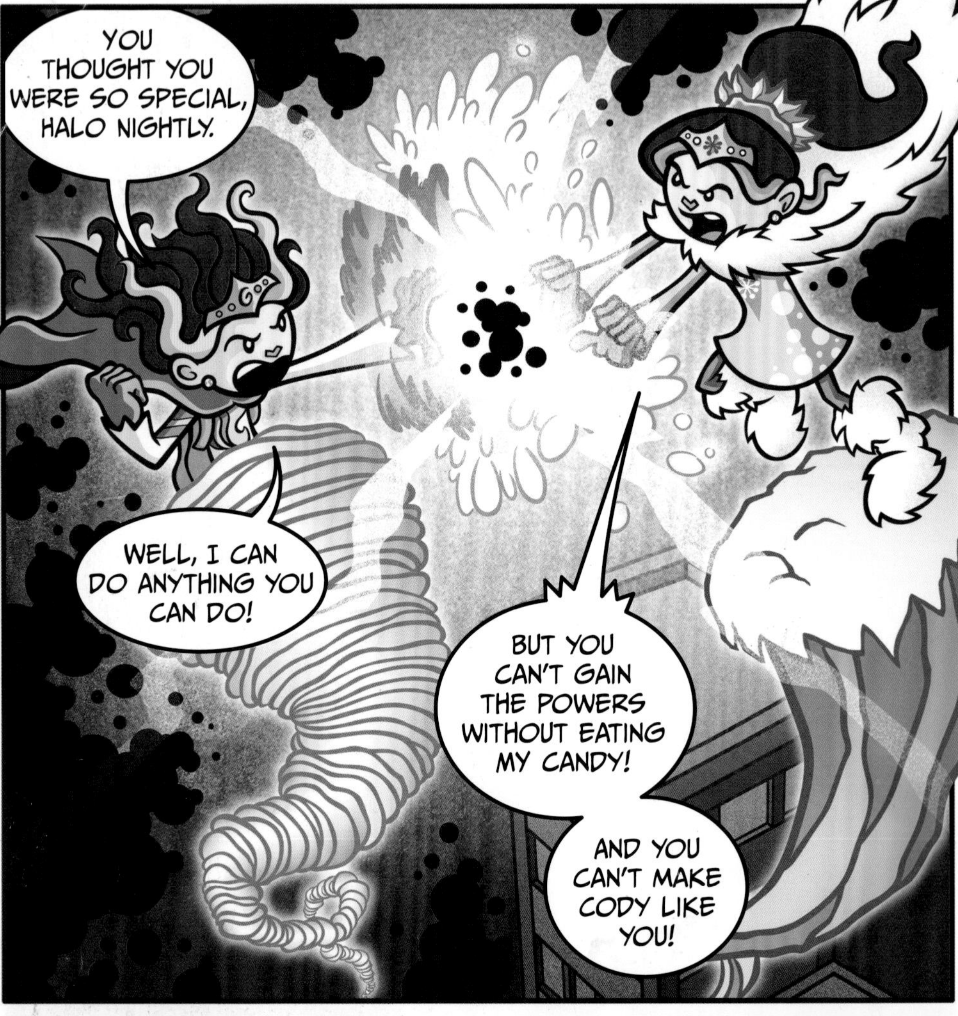
YOU THOUGHT YOU WERE SO SPECIAL, HALO NIGHTLY.
WELL, I CAN DO ANYTHING YOU CAN DO!
BUT YOU CAN'T GAIN THE POWERS WITHOUT EATING MY CANDY!
AND YOU CAN'T MAKE CODY LIKE YOU!

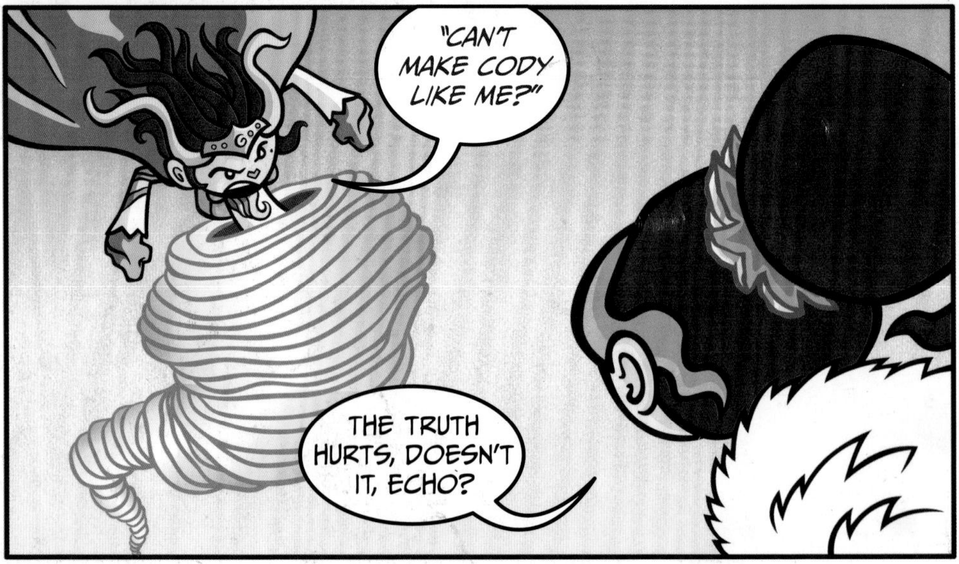
"CAN'T MAKE CODY LIKE ME?"
THE TRUTH HURTS, DOESN'T IT, ECHO?

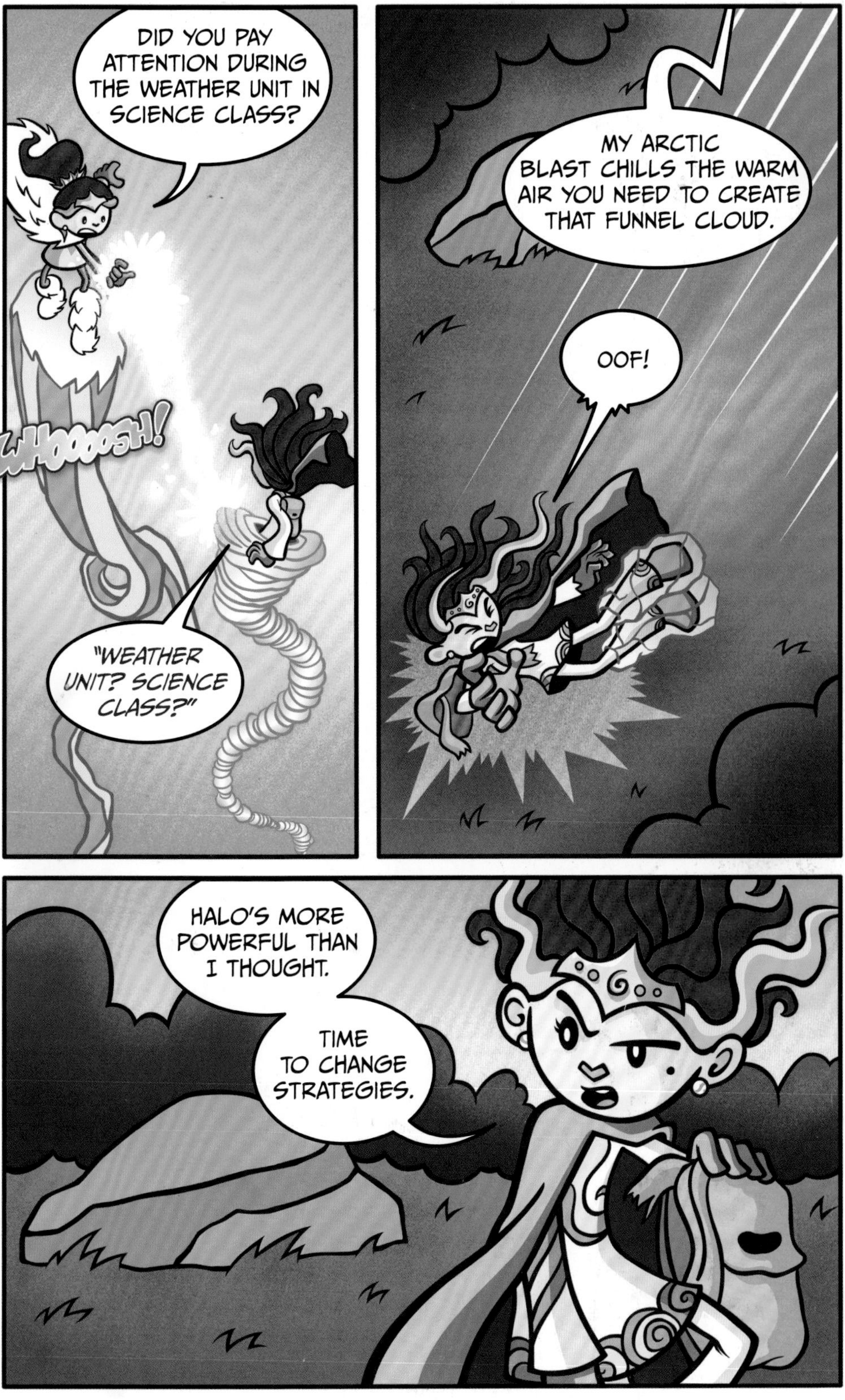
DID YOU PAY ATTENTION DURING THE WEATHER UNIT IN SCIENCE CLASS?
WHOOOOOSH!
"WEATHER UNIT? SCIENCE CLASS?"
MY ARCTIC BLAST CHILLS THE WARM AIR YOU NEED TO CREATE THAT FUNNEL CLOUD.
OOF!
HALO'S MORE POWERFUL THAN I THOUGHT.
TIME TO CHANGE STRATEGIES.

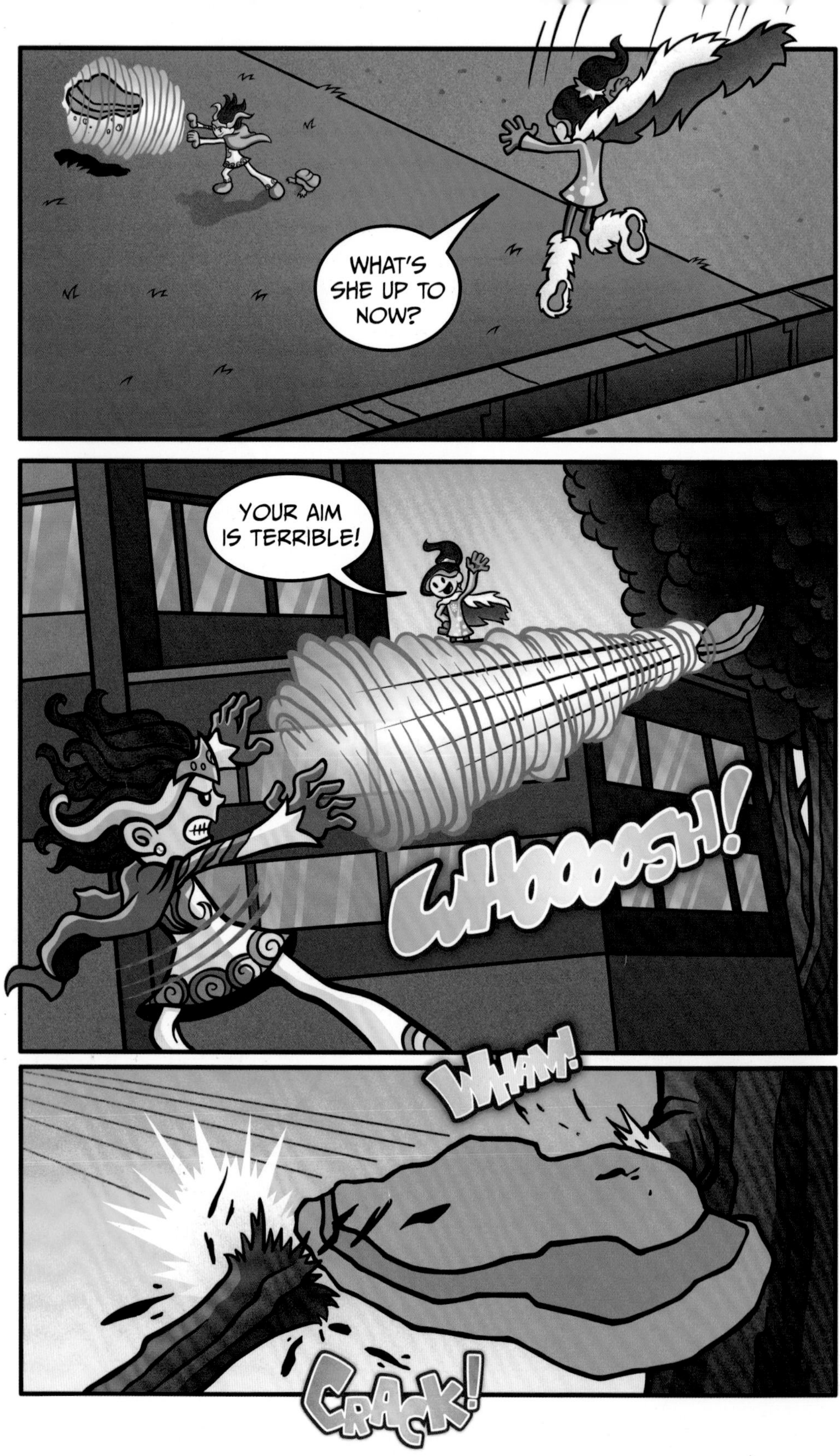
WHAT'S SHE UP TO NOW?
YOUR AIM IS TERRIBLE!
WHOOOOSH!
WHAM!
CRACK!

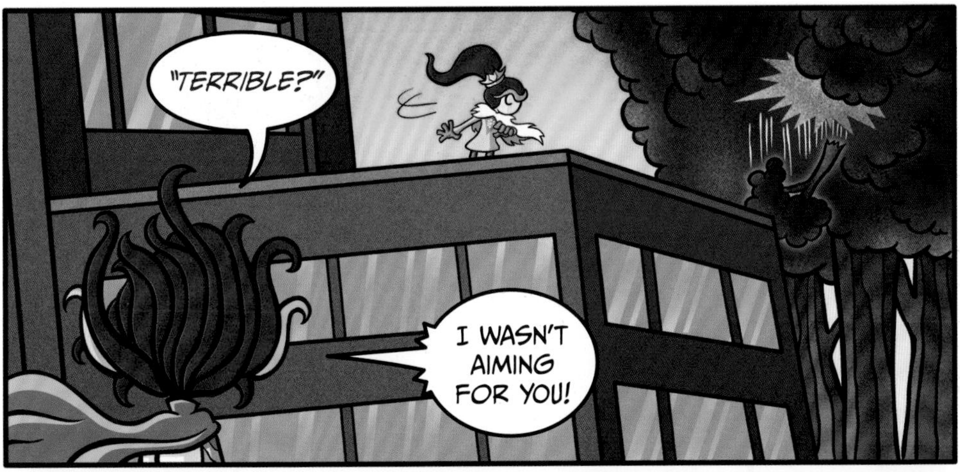
"TERRIBLE?"
I WASN'T AIMING FOR YOU!

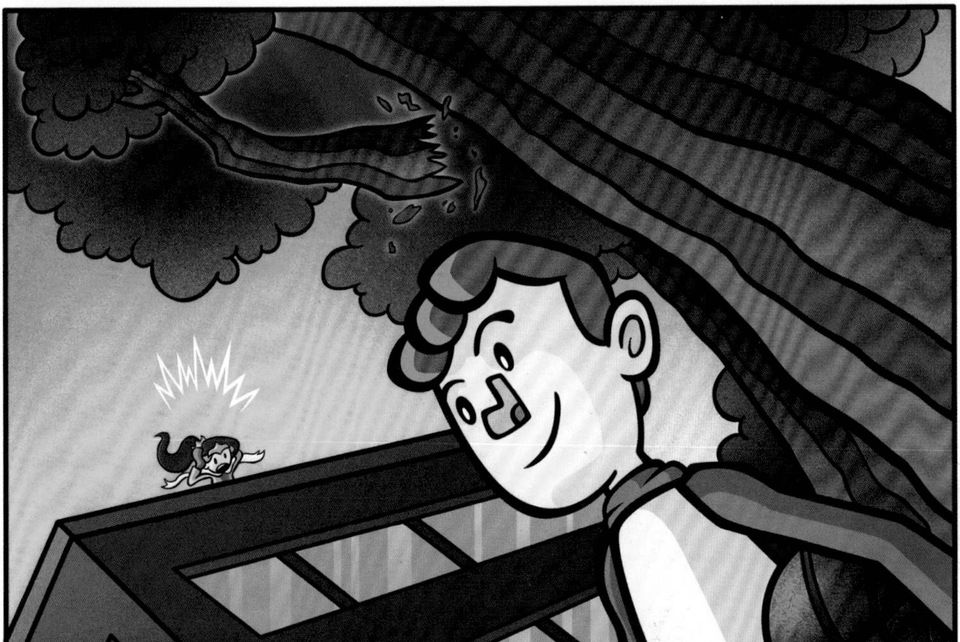

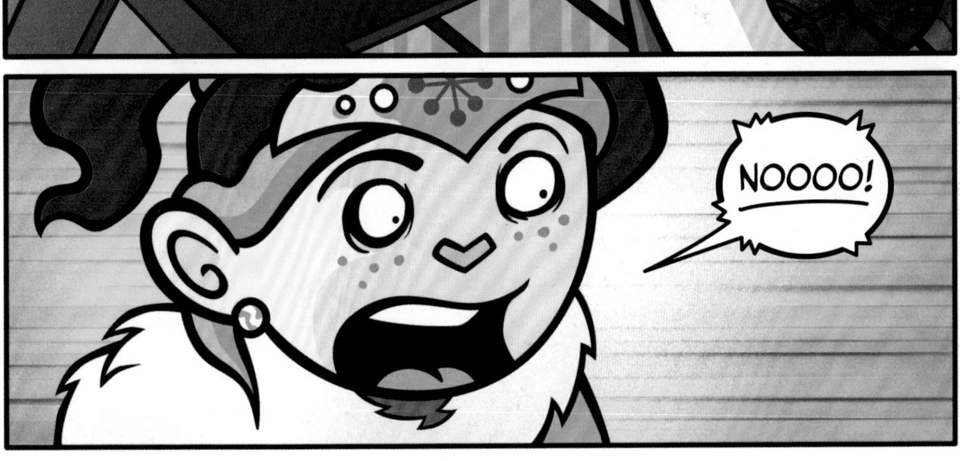
NOOOO!

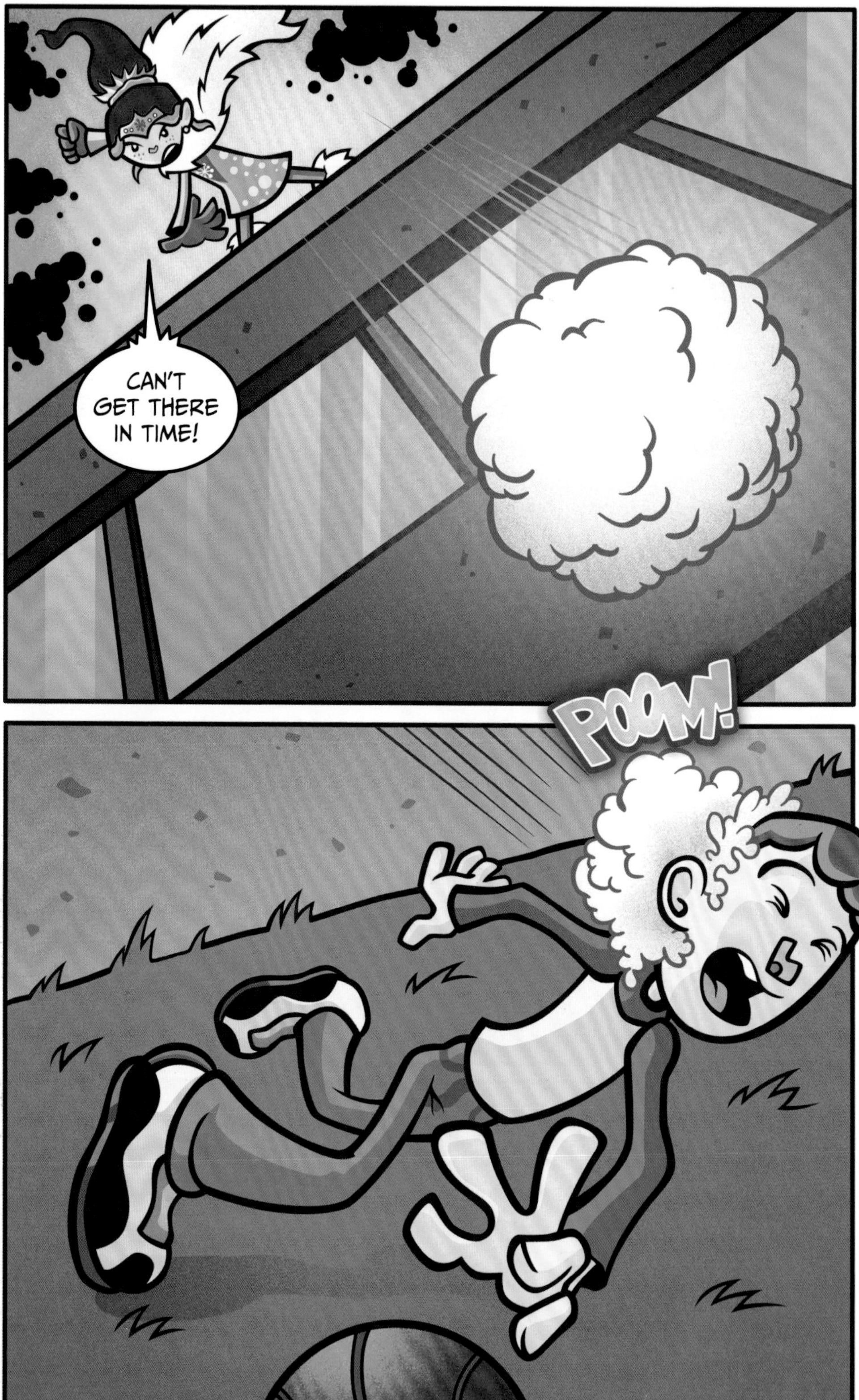
CAN'T GET THERE IN TIME!
POOM!

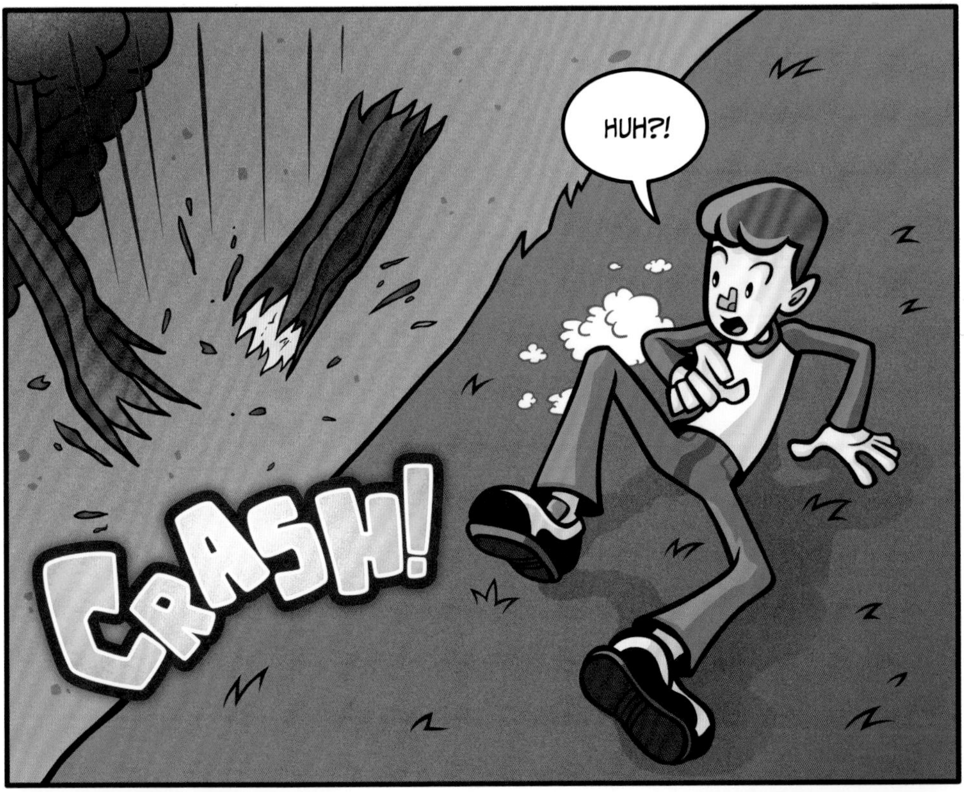
HUH?!
CRASH!

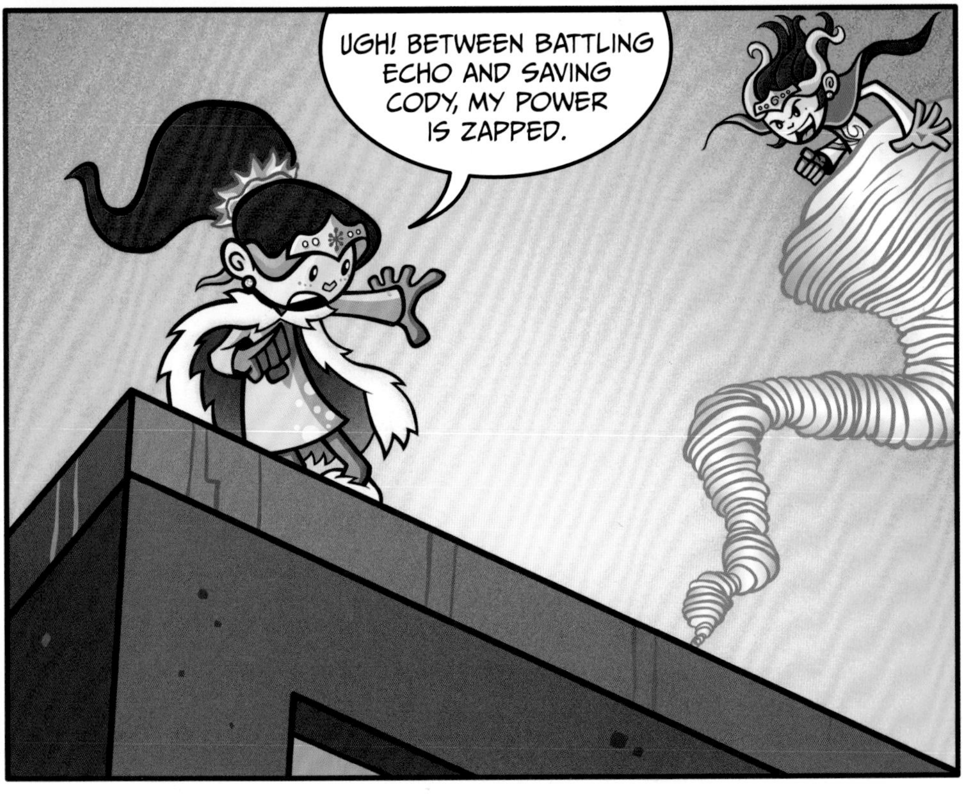
UGH! BETWEEN BATTLING ECHO AND SAVING CODY, MY POWER IS ZAPPED.

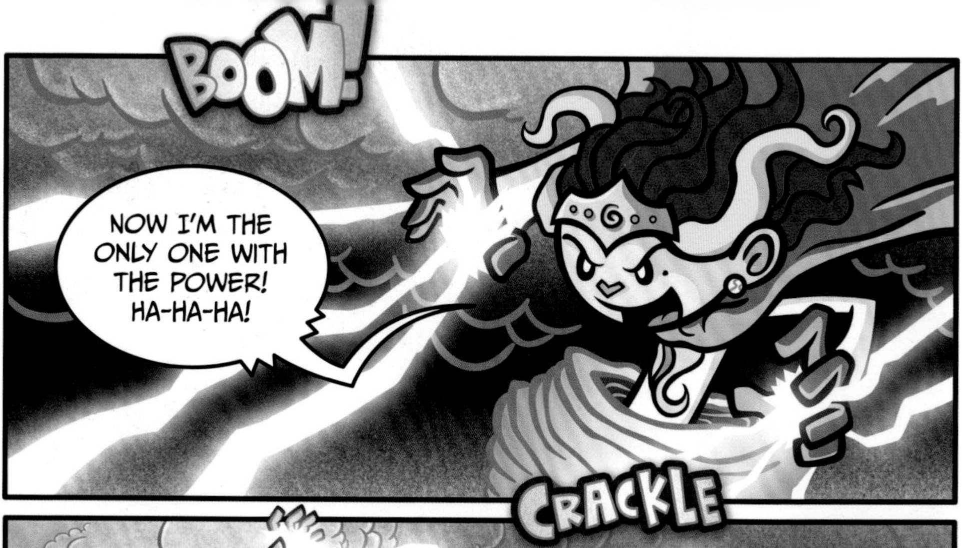
BOOM!
NOW I'M THE ONLY ONE WITH THE POWER! HA-HA-HA!
CRACKLE

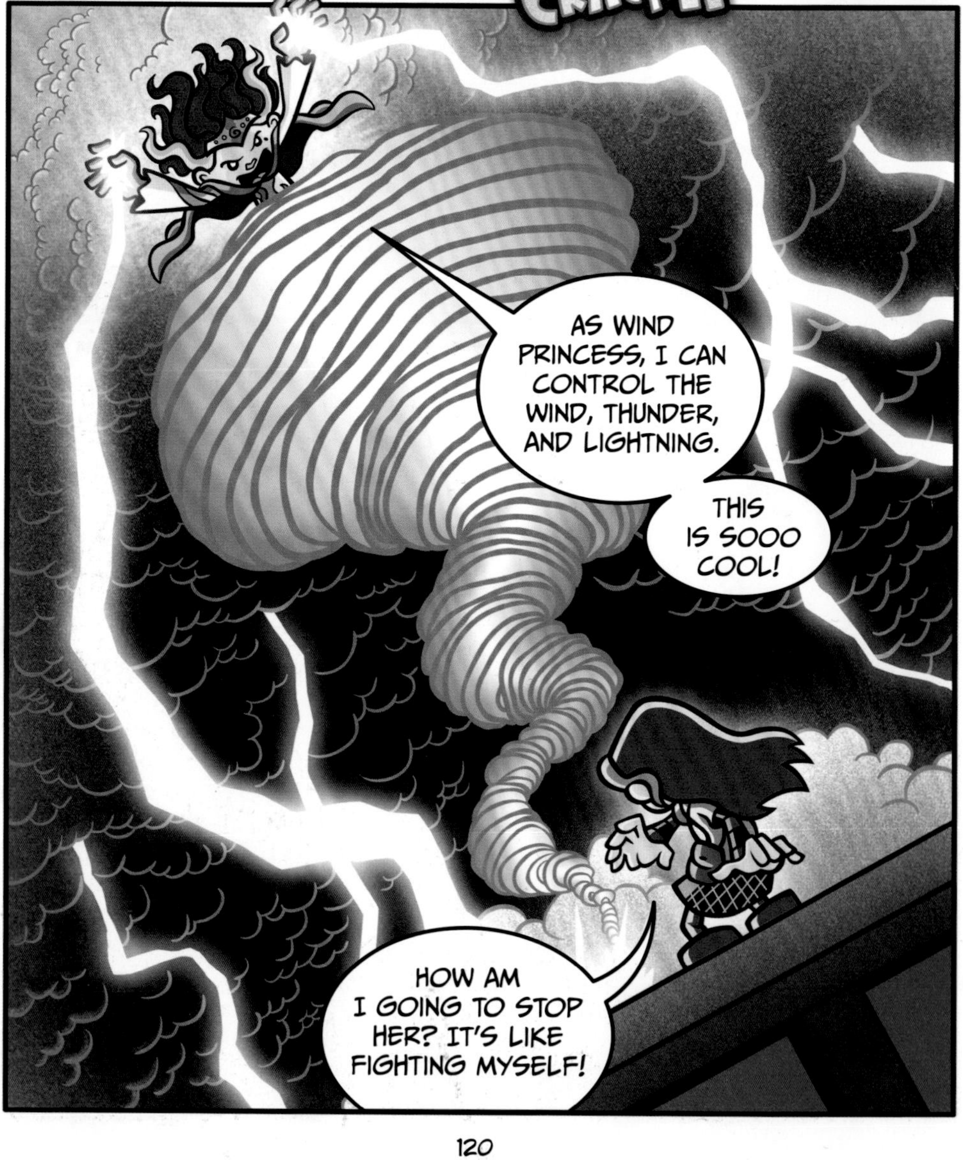
AS WIND PRINCESS, I CAN CONTROL THE WIND, THUNDER, AND LIGHTNING.
THIS IS SOOO COOL!
HOW AM I GOING TO STOP HER? IT'S LIKE FIGHTING MYSELF!

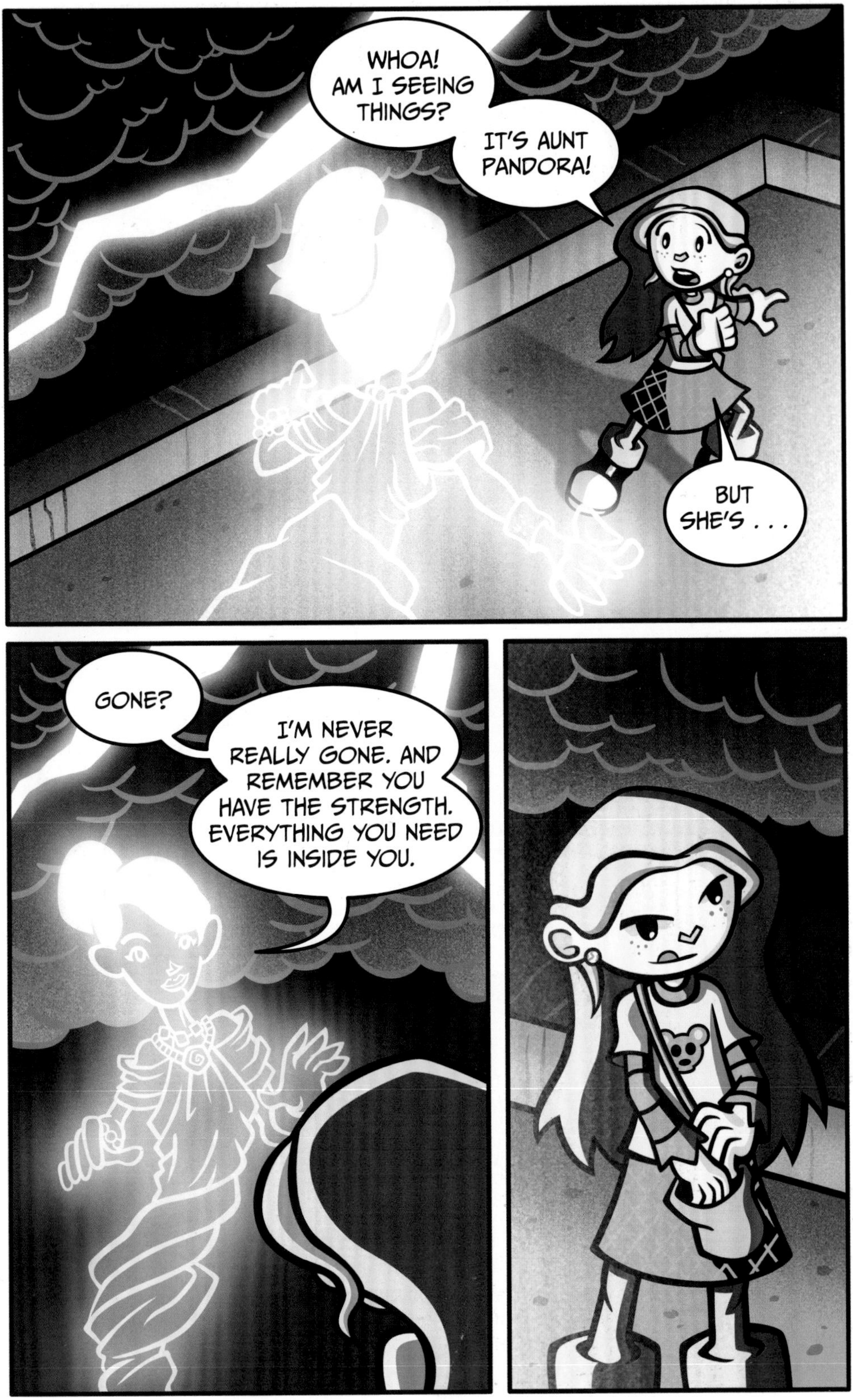
WHOA! AM I SEEING THINGS?
IT'S AUNT PANDORA!
BUT SHE'S . . .
GONE?
I'M NEVER REALLY GONE. AND REMEMBER YOU HAVE THE STRENGTH. EVERYTHING YOU NEED IS INSIDE YOU.

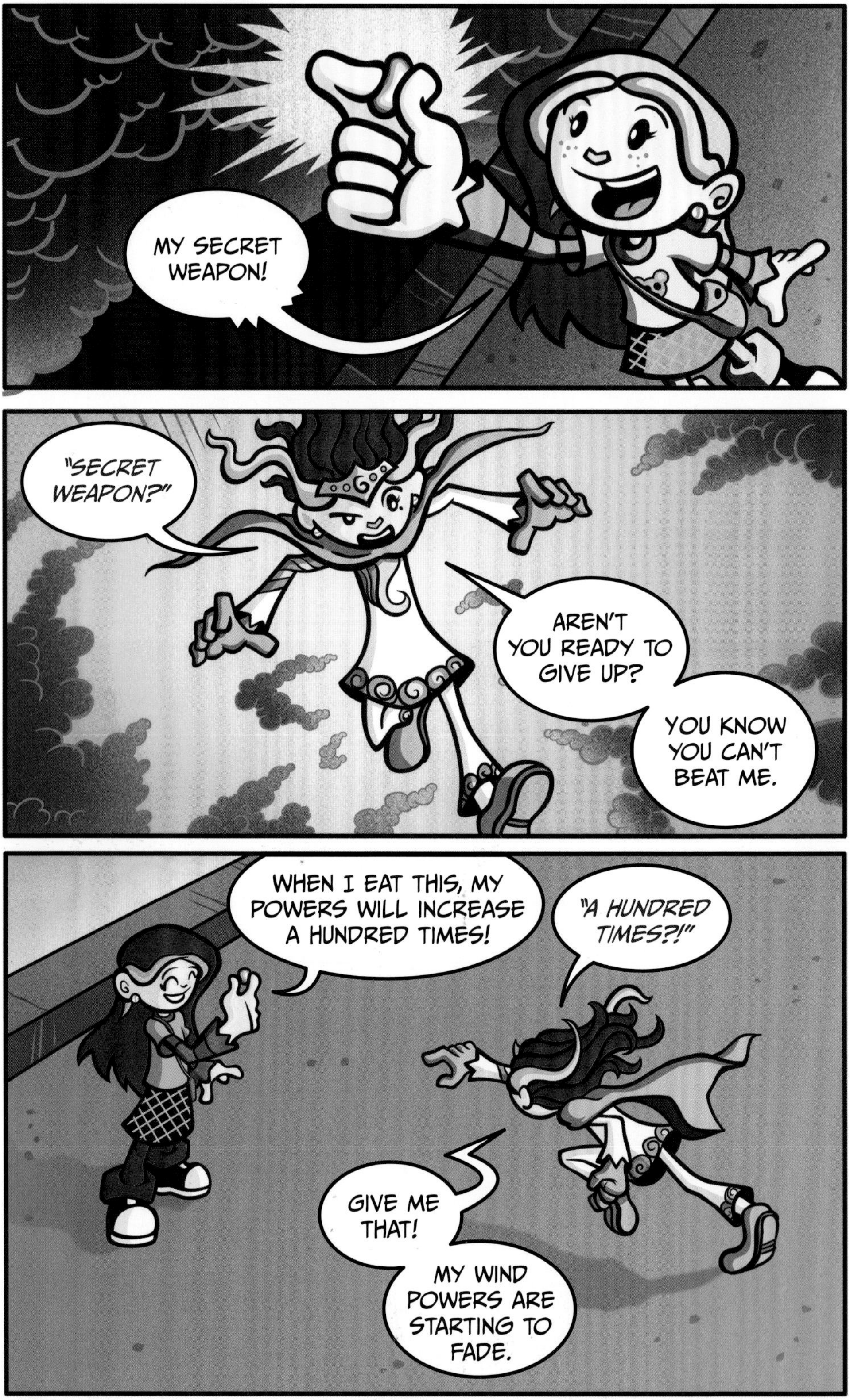
MY SECRET WEAPON!
"SECRET WEAPON?"
AREN'T YOU READY TO GIVE UP?
YOU KNOW YOU CAN'T BEAT ME.
WHEN I EAT THIS, MY POWERS WILL INCREASE A HUNDRED TIMES!
"A HUNDRED TIMES?!"
GIVE ME THAT!
MY WIND POWERS ARE STARTING TO FADE.

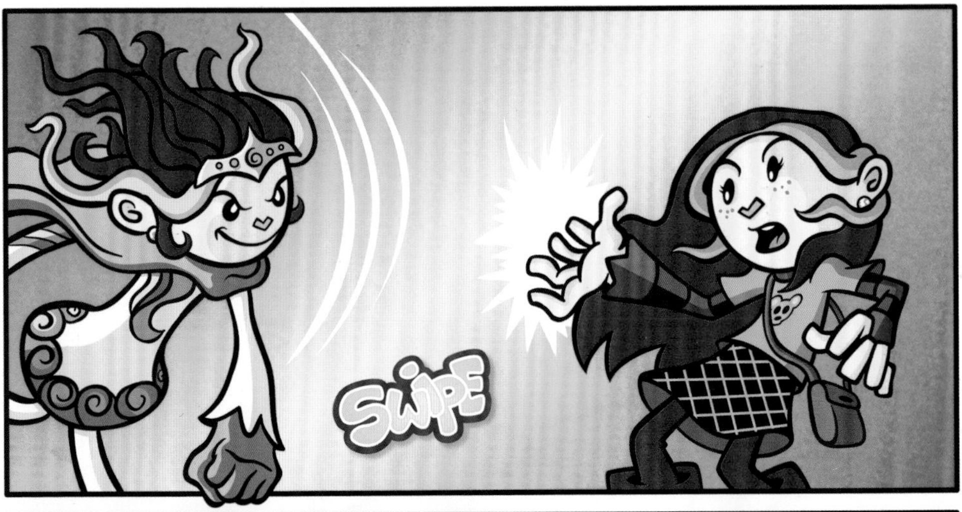
SWIPE

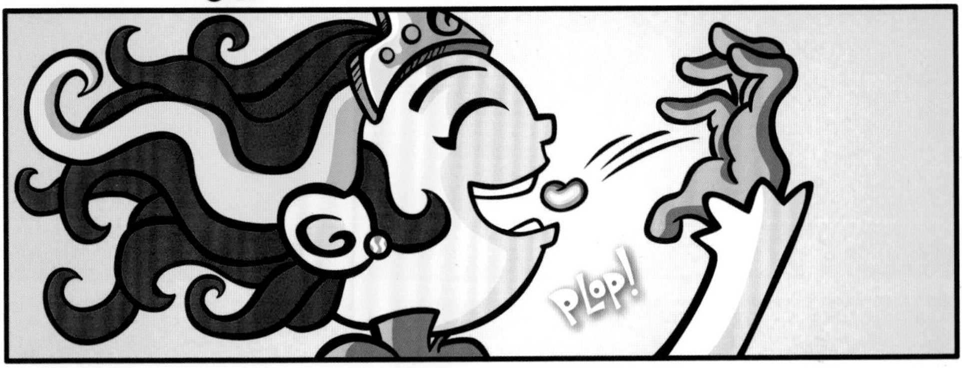
PLOP!

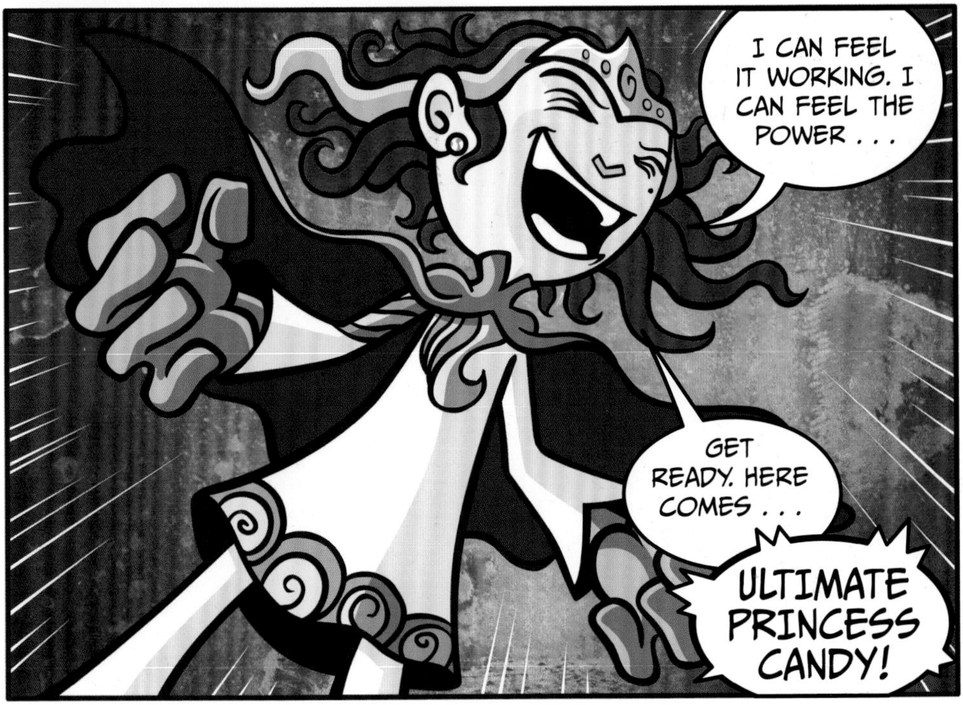
I CAN FEEL IT WORKING. I CAN FEEL THE POWER . . .
GET READY. HERE COMES . . .
ULTIMATE PRINCESS CANDY!

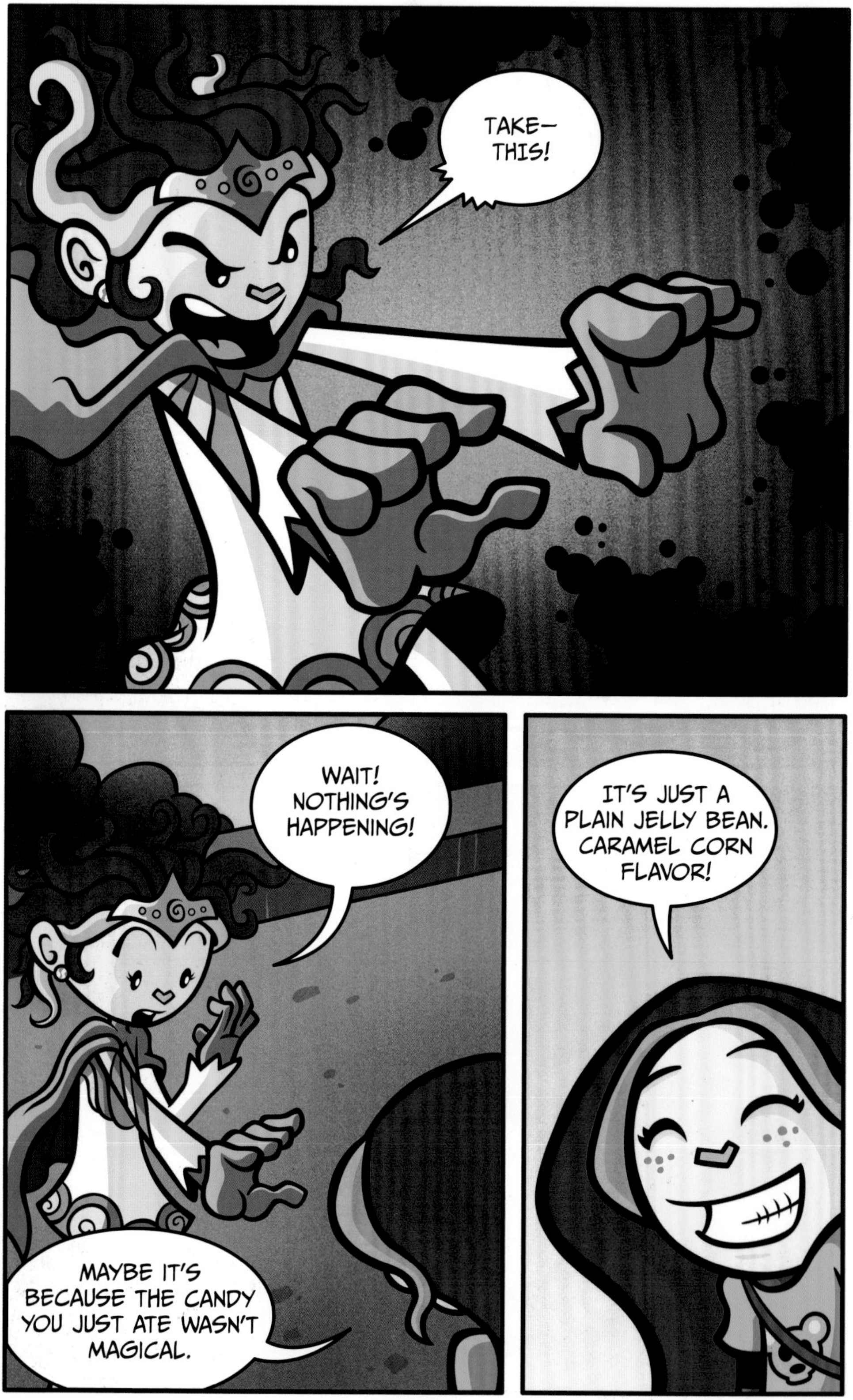
TAKE—
THIS!
WAIT!
NOTHING'S
HAPPENING!
MAYBE IT'S
BECAUSE THE CANDY
YOU JUST ATE WASN'T
MAGICAL.
IT'S JUST A
PLAIN JELLY BEAN.
CARAMEL CORN
FLAVOR!

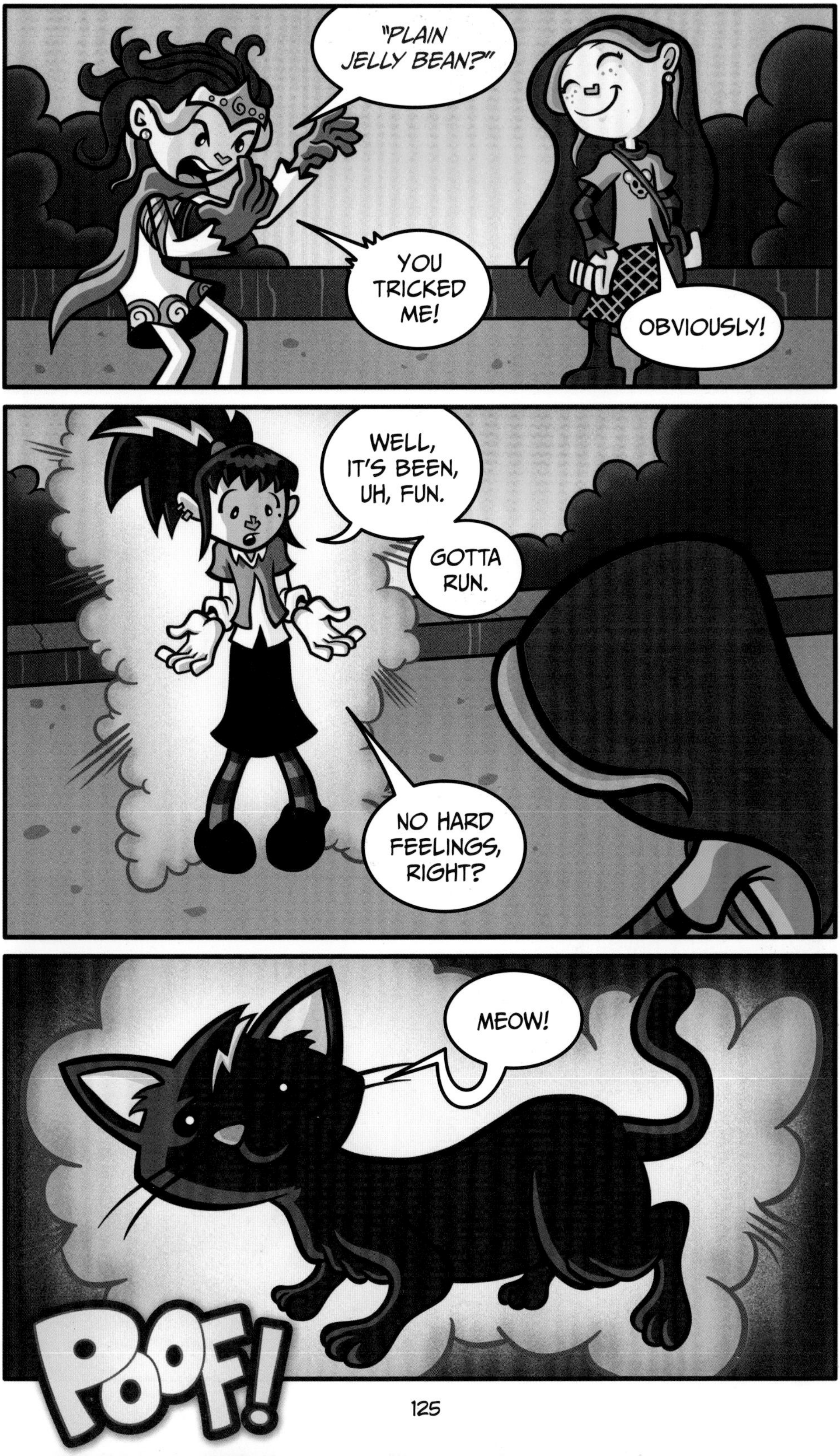
"PLAIN
JELLY BEAN?"
YOU TRICKED ME!
OBVIOUSLY!
WELL, IT'S BEEN, UH, FUN.
GOTTA RUN.
NO HARD FEELINGS, RIGHT?
MEOW!
POOF!

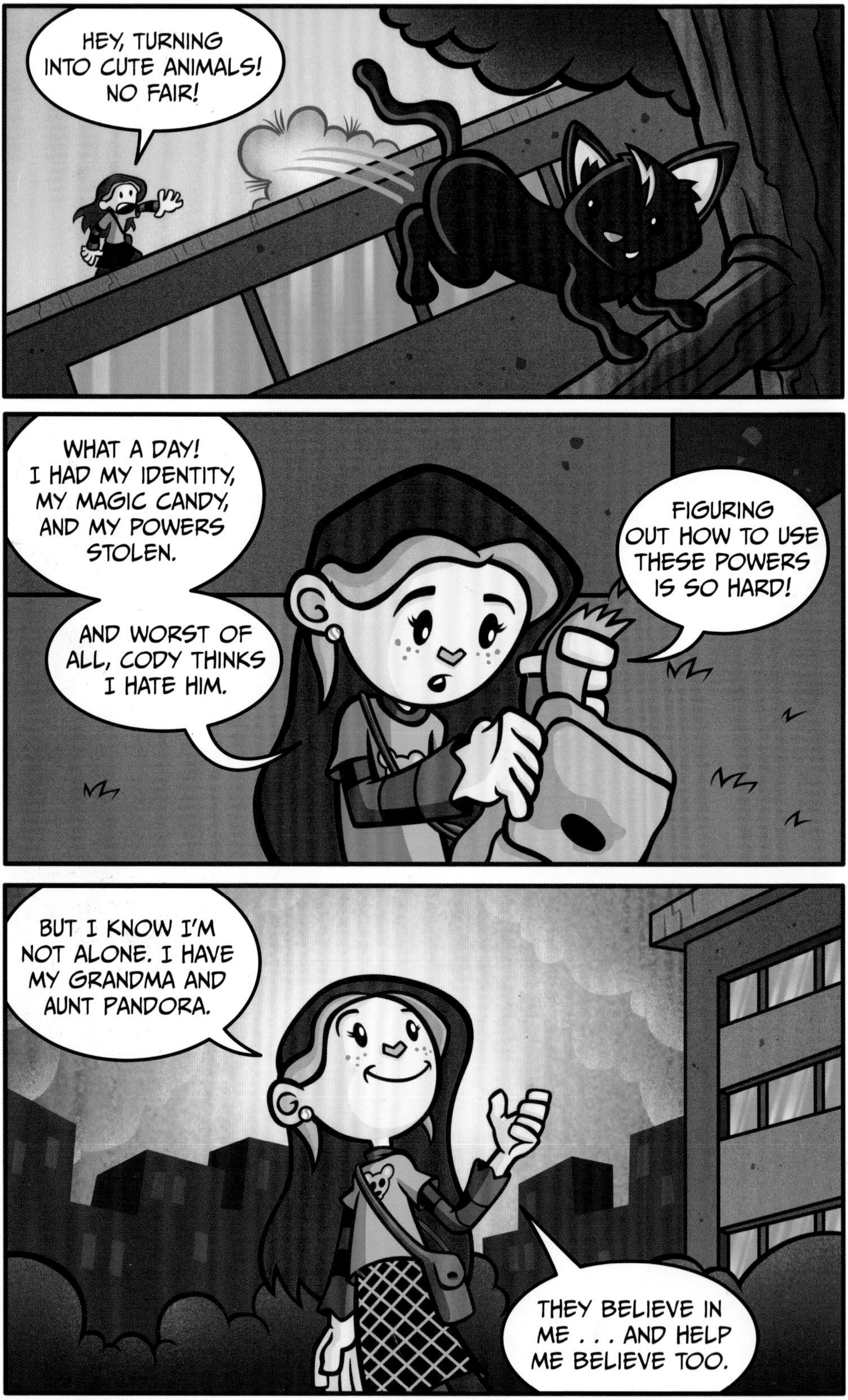
HEY, TURNING INTO CUTE ANIMALS! NO FAIR!
WHAT A DAY! I HAD MY IDENTITY, MY MAGIC CANDY, AND MY POWERS STOLEN.
AND WORST OF ALL, CODY THINKS I HATE HIM.
FIGURING OUT HOW TO USE THESE POWERS IS SO HARD!
BUT I KNOW I'M NOT ALONE. I HAVE MY GRANDMA AND AUNT PANDORA.
THEY BELIEVE IN ME . . . AND HELP ME BELIEVE TOO.

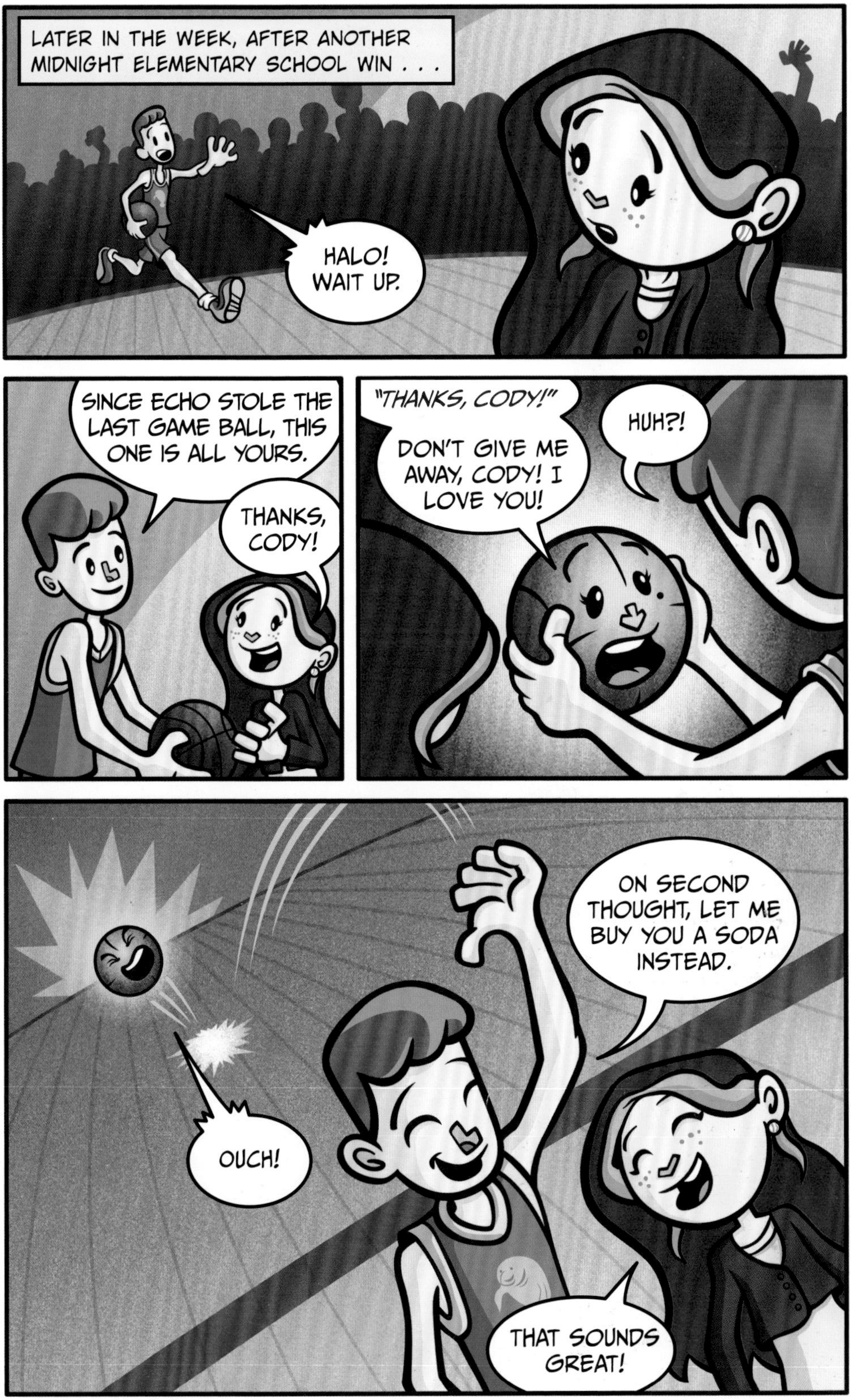
LATER IN THE WEEK, AFTER ANOTHER MIDNIGHT ELEMENTARY SCHOOL WIN . . .
HALO! WAIT UP.
SINCE ECHO STOLE THE LAST GAME BALL, THIS ONE IS ALL YOURS.
THANKS, CODY!
"THANKS, CODY!"
DON'T GIVE ME AWAY, CODY! I LOVE YOU!
HUH?!
ON SECOND THOUGHT, LET ME BUY YOU A SODA INSTEAD.
OUCH!
THAT SOUNDS GREAT!

PRINCESS CANDY

SOUR-VILLAINS

DOOZIE HISS

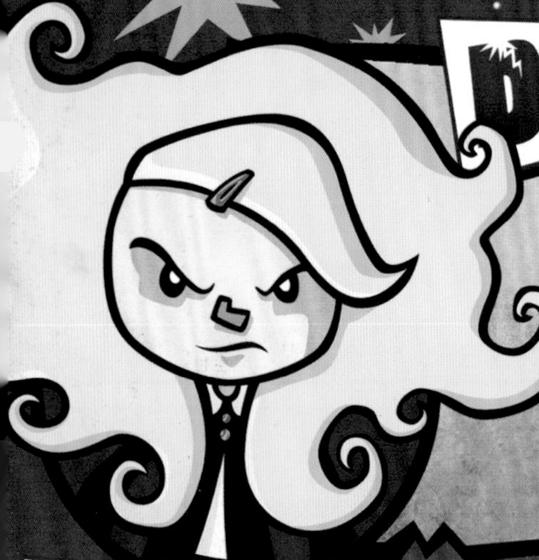

ON THE MORNING OF HER THIRD-GRADE CLASS PHOTO, MEDUSA AWOKE TO A HORRENDOUS HAIR DAY. HER MOTHER, A GENETIC SCIENTIST, CREATED A HIGH-TECH HAIR GEL TO TAME THE UNRULY DO. BUT AFTER HER FATHER APPLIED THE PRODUCT, MEDUSA'S HAIR TURNED DEADLY. WITH HER LIZARD LOCKS, SHE HAD BECOME THE EVIL AND ANNOYING DOOZIE HISS.

MARSHMALLOW MERMAID

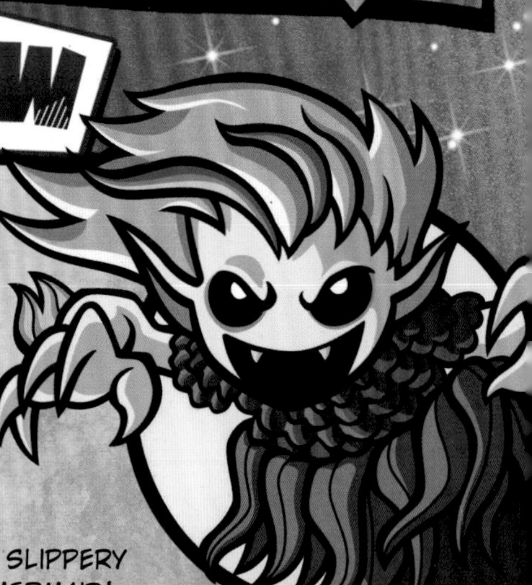

WHILE PREPARING FOR THE 1889 POND SWIMMING CHAMPIONSHIPS, YOUNG MILDRED BARNACLE WENT MISSING. YEARS LATER, WORKERS DRAINED THE POND AND BUILT MIDNIGHT ELEMENTARY IN ITS PLACE. THEN ONE DAY, MILDRED EMERGED FROM HER WATERY GRAVE. SHE HAD BECOME THE SLIPPERY AND SWEET-TOOTHED MARSHMALLOW MERMAID!

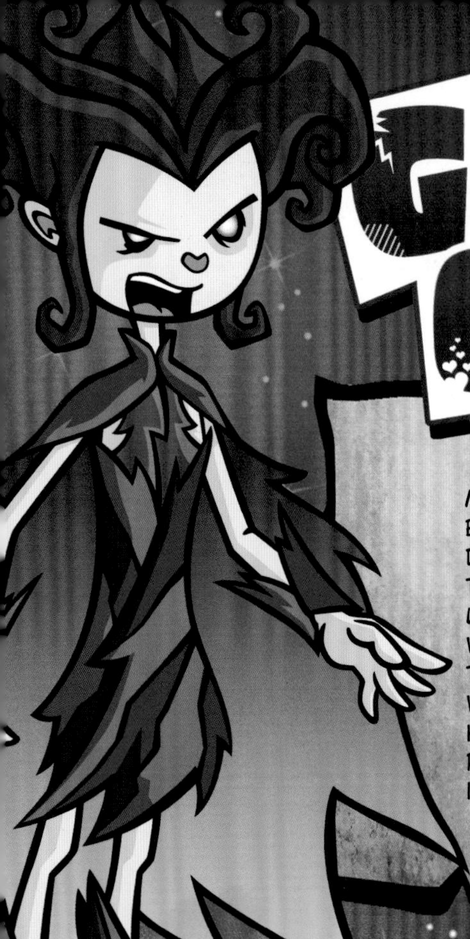

Green Queen

MOST GARDENERS WEED THEIR GARDENS, BUT FLORA FAWN HAS A COMPLETELY DIFFERENT KIND OF WEEDING TO DO. THIS TREE HUGGER IS TRYING TO CLEAN UP MOTHER EARTH, BUT NOT EVERYONE WANTS TO LISTEN TO HER HELPFUL TIPS FOR SAVING THE PLANET. ANYONE WHO DOESN'T HEED THIS HIGH-SPIRITED HIPPIE'S WARNINGS FACES FLORA'S RECYCLING RAGE, TRANSFORMING HER INTO THE FEROCIOUS GREEN QUEEN!

Evil Echo

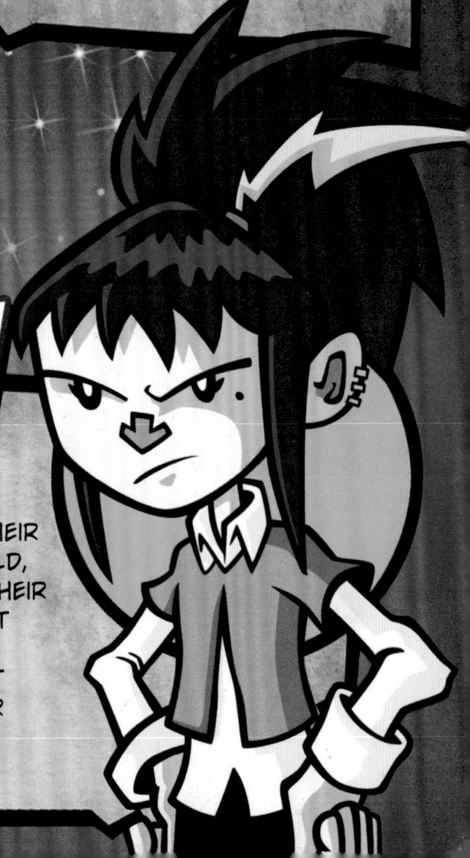

KELLY AND KELLI REPEATER HAD ALWAYS DREAMED OF HAVING TWINS. SO WHEN THEIR DAUGHTER ECHO WAS BORN AN ONLY CHILD, THEY WERE SHATTERED. TO COPE WITH THEIR DISAPPOINTMENT, THE REPEATERS TAUGHT ECHO TO REPEAT PHRASES. THEN ONE DAY, ECHO DISCOVERED SHE COULD SHIFT SHAPES, TRANSFORMING INTO ANYONE OR ANYTHING SHE CHOOSES.

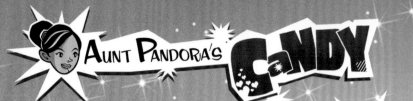

AUNT PANDORA'S CANDY

AUNT PANDORA'S BIRTHDAY GIFT TO HALO IS A SPECIAL METAL BOX CONTAINING A COLLECTION OF JARS. SOON HALO LEARNS THAT EACH JAR HOLDS A CANDY THAT GIVES HER A SPECIFIC SUPERPOWER. HERE ARE A FEW OF HALO'S FAVORITES!

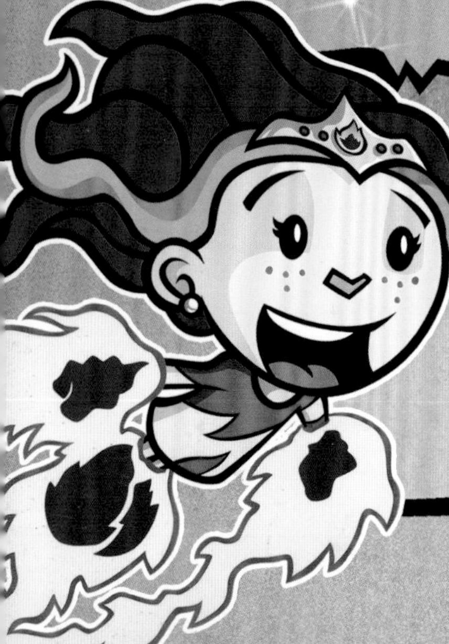

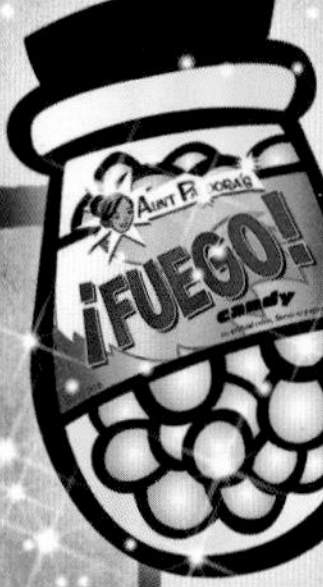
AUNT PANDORA'S
¡FUEGO!
candy

FUEGO CANDIES GIVE HALO THE POWER OF FIRE. WITH JUST ONE OF THESE SWEET, YELLOW TREATS, HALO LIGHTS UP THE NIGHT. SHE CAN BREATHE FIRE, LAUNCH FIREBALLS AT HER ENEMIES, AND ROCKET ACROSS THE SKY!

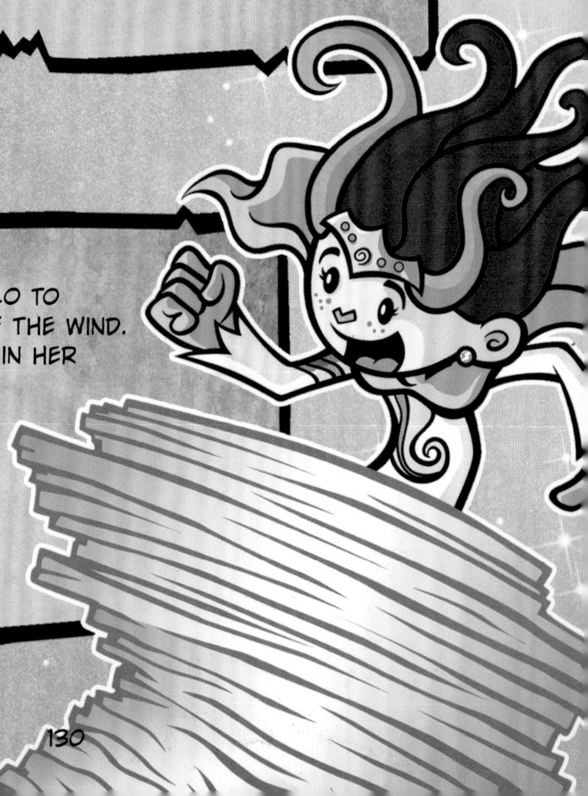

AIRE CANDIES ALLOW HALO TO HARNESS THE POWER OF THE WIND. BY SIMPLY POPPING ONE IN HER MOUTH, SHE CAN TRAVEL BY TWISTER, BLAST HER FOES WITH AN AIR CANNON, AND EVEN CALL FORTH THE AWESOME POWER OF THUNDER AND LIGHTNING!

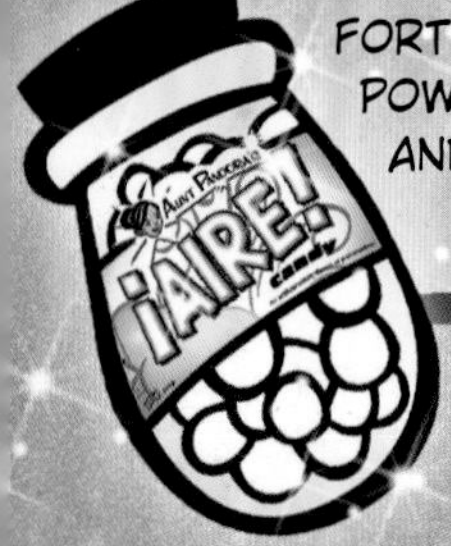
AUNT PANDORA'S
¡AIRE!
candy

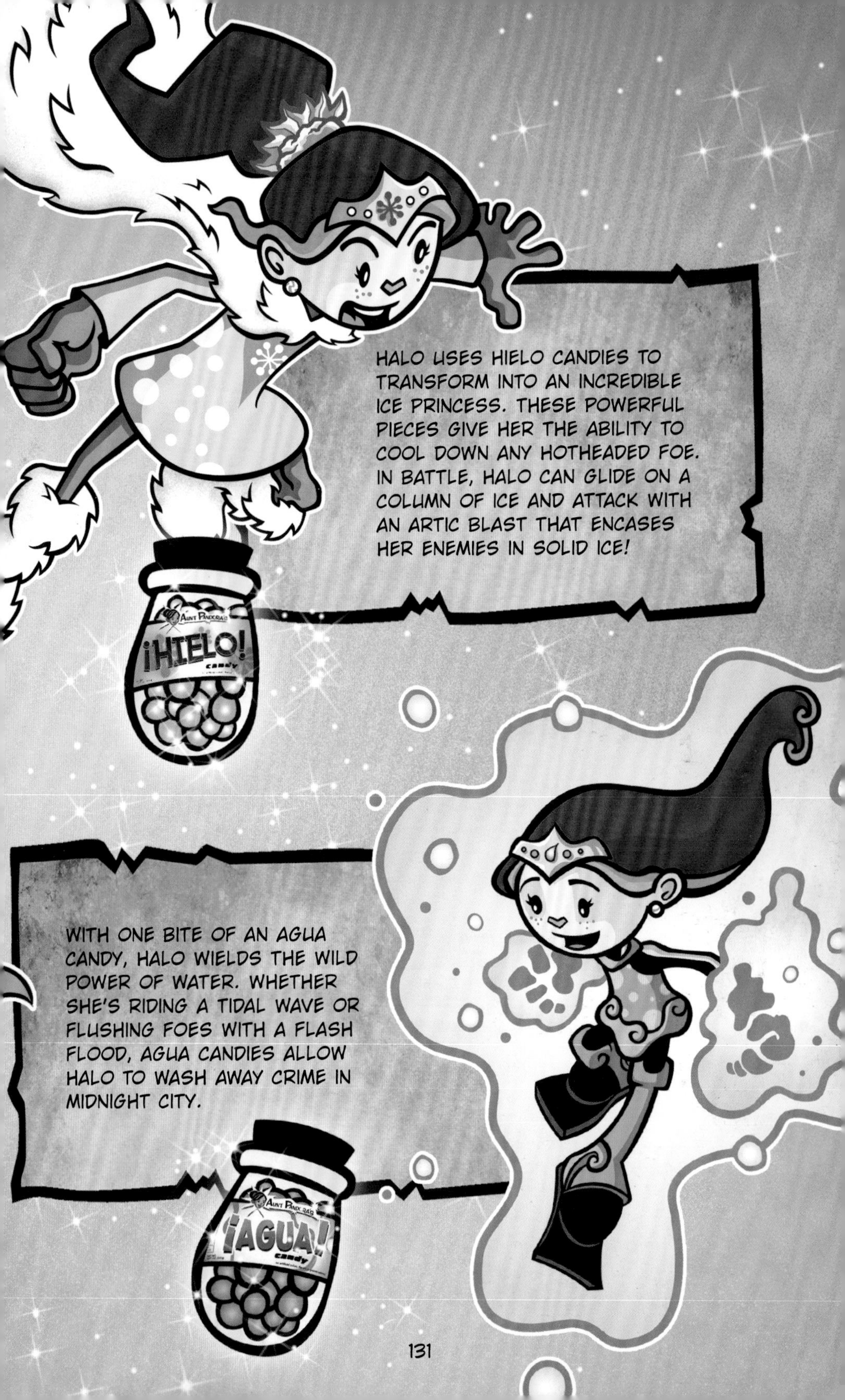
HALO USES HIELO CANDIES TO TRANSFORM INTO AN INCREDIBLE ICE PRINCESS. THESE POWERFUL PIECES GIVE HER THE ABILITY TO COOL DOWN ANY HOTHEADED FOE. IN BATTLE, HALO CAN GLIDE ON A COLUMN OF ICE AND ATTACK WITH AN ARTIC BLAST THAT ENCASES HER ENEMIES IN SOLID ICE!
¡HIELO!
candy
WITH ONE BITE OF AN AGUA CANDY, HALO WIELDS THE WILD POWER OF WATER. WHETHER SHE'S RIDING A TIDAL WAVE OR FLUSHING FOES WITH A FLASH FLOOD, AGUA CANDIES ALLOW HALO TO WASH AWAY CRIME IN MIDNIGHT CITY.
¡AGUA!
candy

CREATORS

About The Authors

MICHAEL DAHL HAS WRITTEN MORE THAN 200 BOOKS FOR CHILDREN AND YOUNG ADULTS. HE IS THE CREATOR OF PRINCESS CANDY AND AUTHOR OF "SUGAR HERO" AND "THE MARSHMALLOW MERMAID," THE FIRST TWO STORIES OF THIS BOOK.

SCOTT NICKEL IS A HUMOR WRITER, CARTOONIST, AND A LIFELONG FAN OF COMICS, HUMOR MAGAZINES, AND MONSTERS. IN ADDITION TO HIS DAY JOB AT PAWS, INC. (JIM DAVIS' GARFIELD STUDIO), SCOTT PRODUCES THE ONLINE SYNDICATED COMIC STRIP EEK!, CREATES HUMOROUS GREETING CARDS, WRITES CHILDREN'S BOOKS, AND DRAWS GAG CARTOONS FOR NATIONAL MAGAZINES. SCOTT WAS NOMINATED FOR A NATIONAL CARTOONIST SOCIETY DIVISIONAL AWARD FOR GREETING CARDS IN 2016 AND 2018. HE LIVES IN INDIANA WITH HIS WIFE, SON, AND CATS (PRINCESS FRISKAMINA VON FRISKY IS HIS FAVORITE).

About The Illustrator

JEFF CROWTHER HAS BEEN DRAWING COMICS FOR AS LONG AS HE CAN REMEMBER. SINCE GRADUATING FROM COLLEGE, JEFF HAS WORKED ON A VARIETY OF ILLUSTRATIONS FOR CLIENTS INCLUDING DISNEY, *ADVENTURES MAGAZINE*, AND *BOYS' LIFE MAGAZINE*. HE ALSO WROTE AND ILLUSTRATED A WEBCOMIC SKETCHBOOK AND HAS SELF-PUBLISHED SEVERAL MINI-COMICS. JEFF LIVES IN BOARDMAN, OHIO, WITH HIS WIFE, ELIZABETH, AND THEIR CHILDREN, JONAS AND NOELLE.

Q&A WITH MICHAEL DAHL

Capstone: Can you tell us a little about where the idea for Princess Candy came from?

Dahl: I had been re-reading Alice in Wonderland, and there's a part where Alice drinks a potion that makes her shrink. Then she eats a piece of cake and she grows as big as a giant. That started me thinking about eating something that can change you or give you superpowers.

Capstone: What has been your favorite part of this character to tackle?

Dahl: I love coming up with transformations for Halo/Princess Candy. What can she change into next? I have so many ideas: a rhino, a mirror, a fly, a water tower, an asteroid . . . I try to think of something cool, but that could also get her into trouble.

Capstone: What's your favorite part about working in comics?

Dahl: Seeing what the illustrator will come up with! I would never have thought of giving Halo magenta hair. But I love it. I'm lucky to work with such a funny and imaginative artist as Jeff Crowther.

Capstone: What was the first comic you remember reading?

Dahl: A small store down the block had new comics every week, and one of the first I bought by myself was a Superboy comic. I was in 2nd grade.

Capstone: Tell us why everyone should read comic books.

Dahl: Whenever I finish reading a comic, it feels as if I've just watched a fantastic movie or been INSIDE the story. The artwork adds so much to the words. Reading a comic can put you in other countries, other worlds, other galaxies. And you never have to leave your house!

Glossary

active ingredients (AK-tiv in-GREE-dee-uhnts)—the main items that something is made from

allergic (uh-LUR-jik)—if you are allergic to something, it can cause a reaction, such as a rash, sneezing, or sickness

agua (AH-kwah)—a Spanish word meaning "water"

charcoal (CHAR-kole)—a form of carbon made from partially burned wood, often used as barbecue fuel

compost (KOM-pohst)—dead organic matter used to fertilize soil

environment (en-VYE-ruhn-muhnt)—the natural world of the land, sea, and air

fatal (FAY-tuhl)—causing death, or deadly

fuego (FWAY-go)—a Spanish word meaning "fire"

funnel cloud (FUHN-uhl KLOUD)—a cloud that is wide at the top and narrow at the bottom; funnel clouds often become tornadoes

gelatin (JEL-uh-tuhn)—a clear substance often used for making jelly or desserts

metropolis (meh-TRAH-poh-liss)—a large city

organic (or-GAN-ik)—using only natural products and no chemicals or pesticides

pressure (PRESH-ur)—a burden or strain

property (PROP-ur-tee)—anything that is owned by an individual

salon (sah-LAHN)—a stylish business or shop

strategies (STRAT-uh-jeez)—clever plans for winning a battle or achieving a goal

tree hugger (TREE HUH-guhr)—sometimes used as an insult against people who support protecting the environment

woozy (WOO-zee)—dizzy or mildly sick

SHARE YOUR IDEAS

1. Why do you think Aunt Pandora chose to give Halo the superpowered candy? What do you think she wanted Halo to do with it?

2. When she eats a piece of candy, Halo gains some amazing superpowers. If you could have just one superpower, what would it be? Explain.

3. If Doozie Hiss was captured by the Marshmallow Mermaid, do you think Halo would save her? Why or why not?

WRITE YOUR OWN STORIES

1. Think about your favorite candy. Now imagine that sweet treat could turn you into a superhero. Write about what you would do with your newfound powers.

2. Write your own Princess Candy comic. What kind of candy will Halo try next time? What super-villlain will she face? Use your imagination.

3. Imagine that one of Flora's plant creations is out of control, and only Halo can stop it. First, draw a picture of this new plant monster. Then, write a short story about how Halo overcomes her leafy foe!

SNEAK PEEK!

MONSTER AND ME

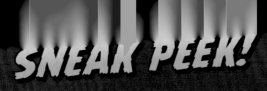

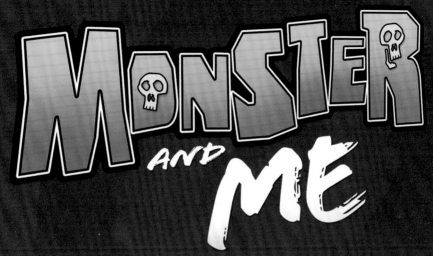

THE COMPLETE COMICS COLLECTION

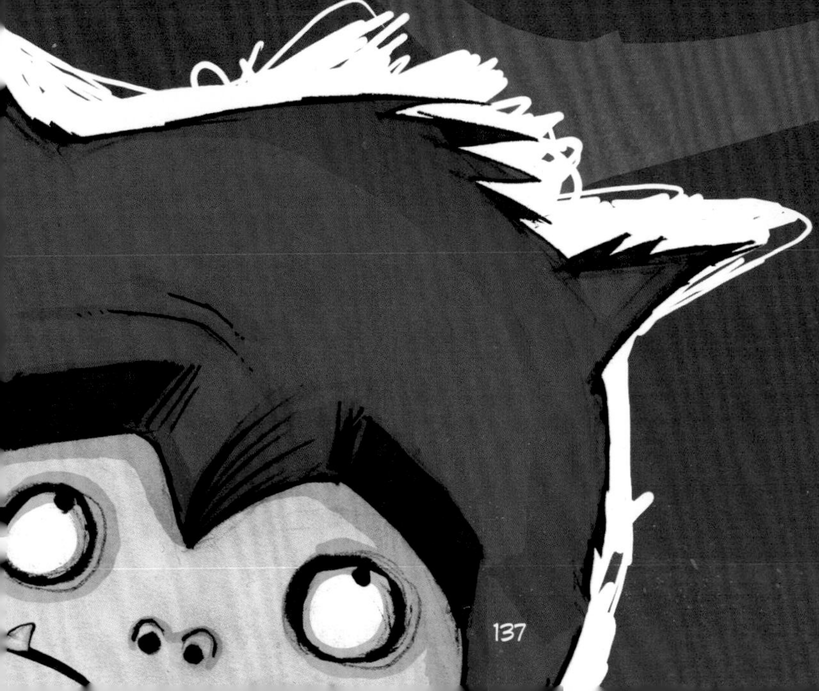

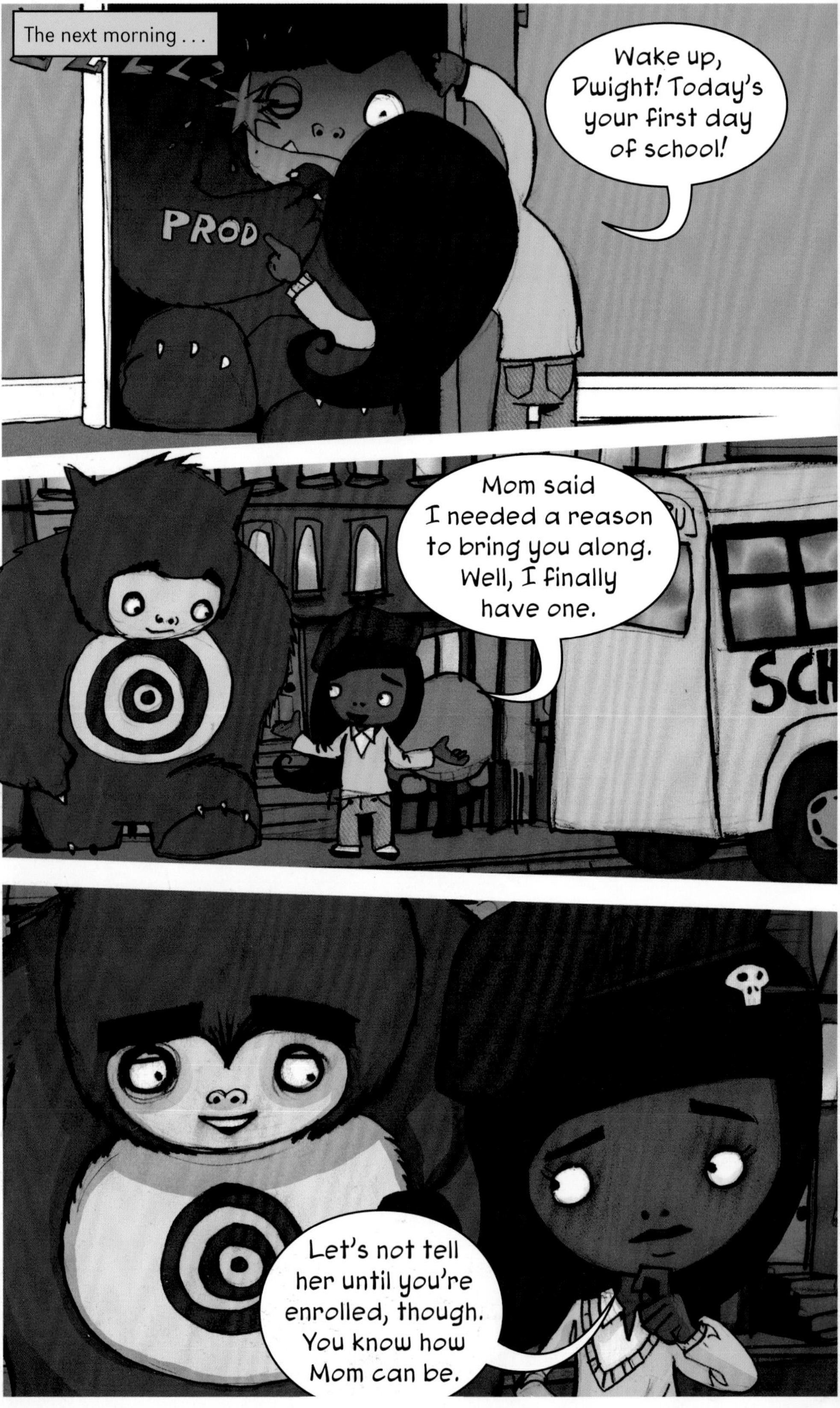
The next morning . . .
PROD
Wake up, Dwight! Today's your first day of school!
Mom said I needed a reason to bring you along. Well, I finally have one.
SCH
Let's not tell her until you're enrolled, though. You know how Mom can be.

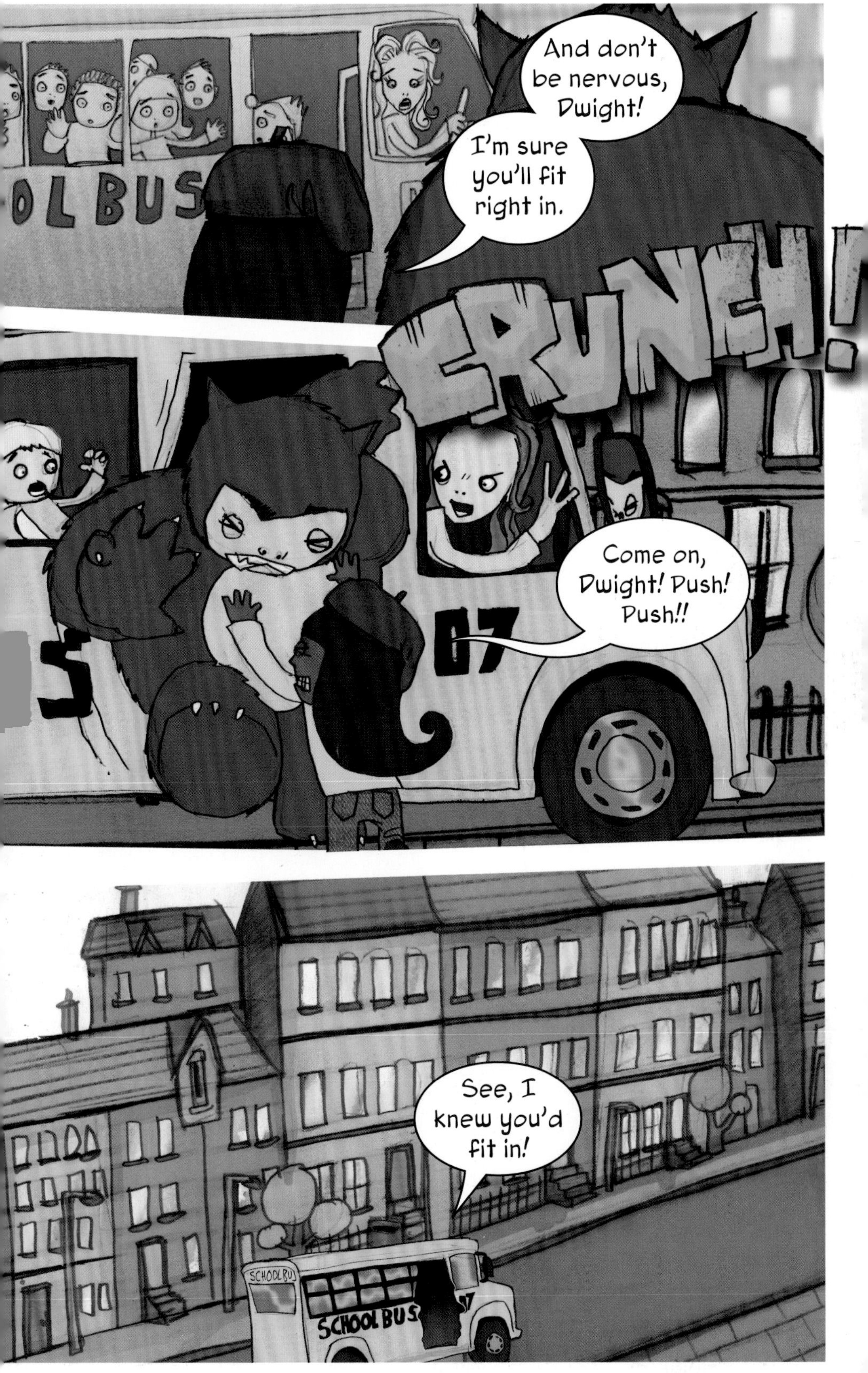
And don't be nervous, Dwight!
I'm sure you'll fit right in.
CRUNCH!
07
Come on, Dwight! Push! Push!!
See, I knew you'd fit in!
SCHOOLBUS
SCHOOL BUS

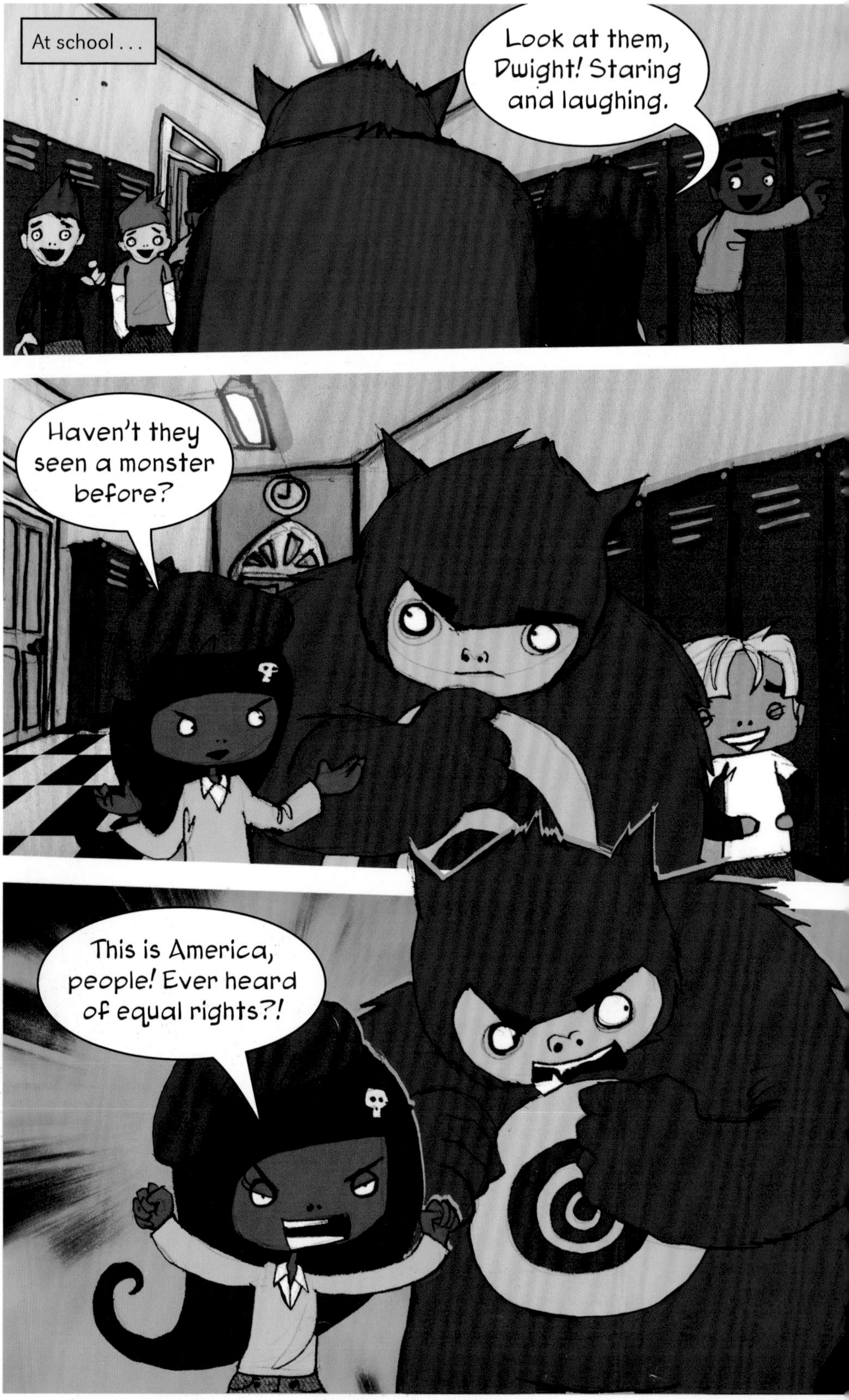
At school . . .
Look at them, Dwight! Staring and laughing.
Haven't they seen a monster before?
This is America, people! Ever heard of equal rights?!

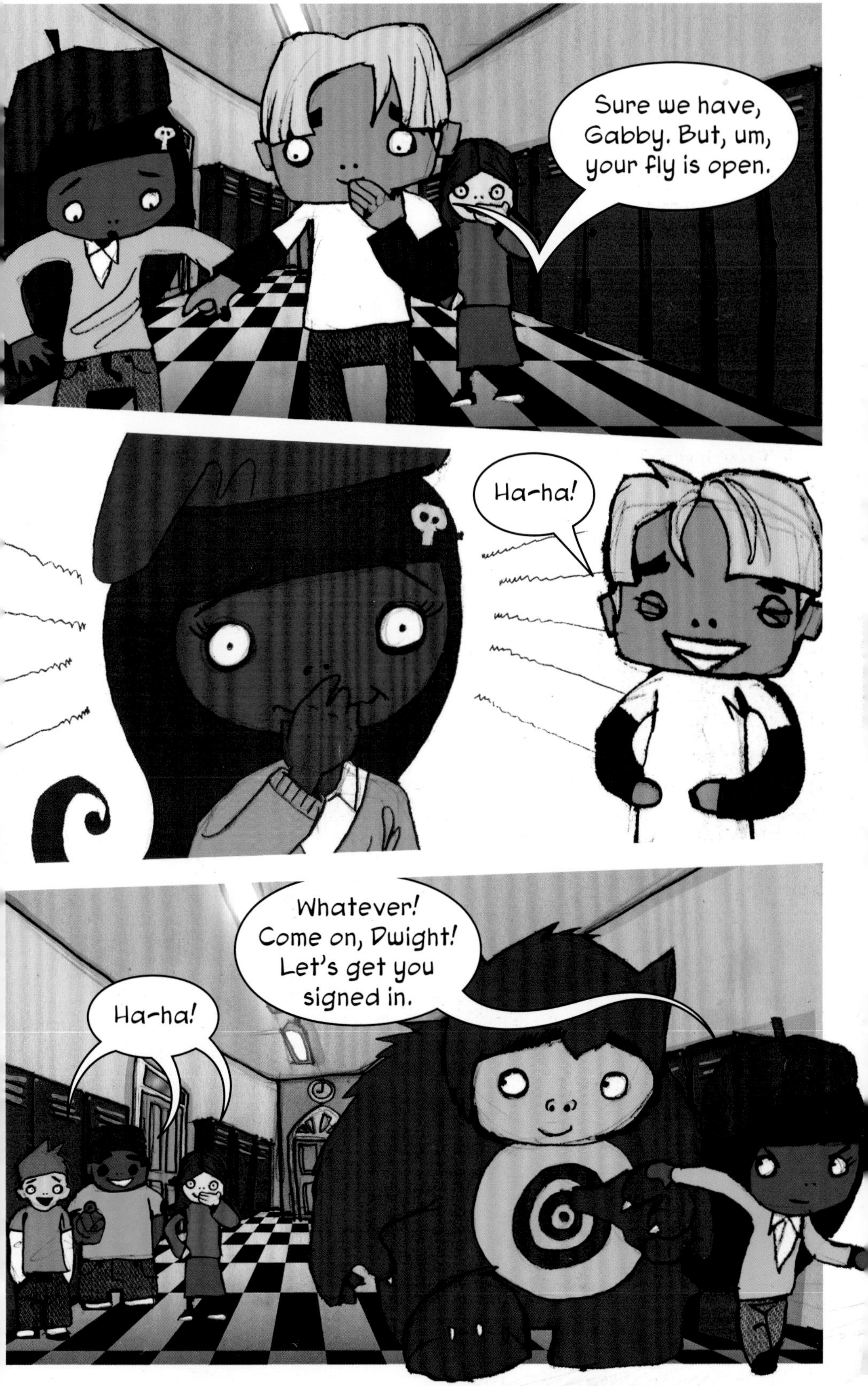
Sure we have, Gabby. But, um, your fly is open.
Ha-ha!
Whatever! Come on, Dwight! Let's get you signed in.
Ha-ha!

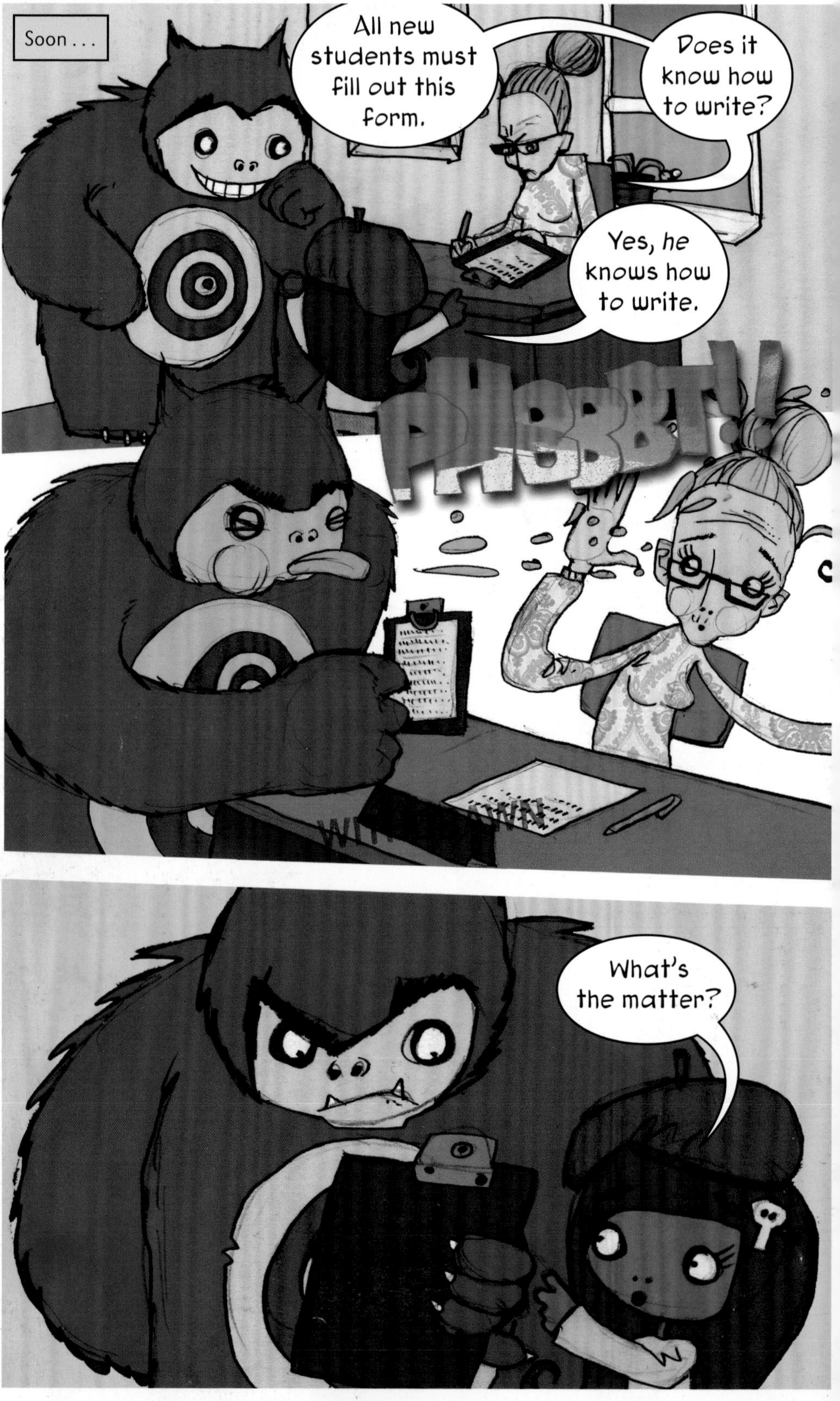
Soon . . .
All new students must fill out this form.
Does it know how to write?
Yes, he knows how to write.
PHBBBT!!
What's the matter?

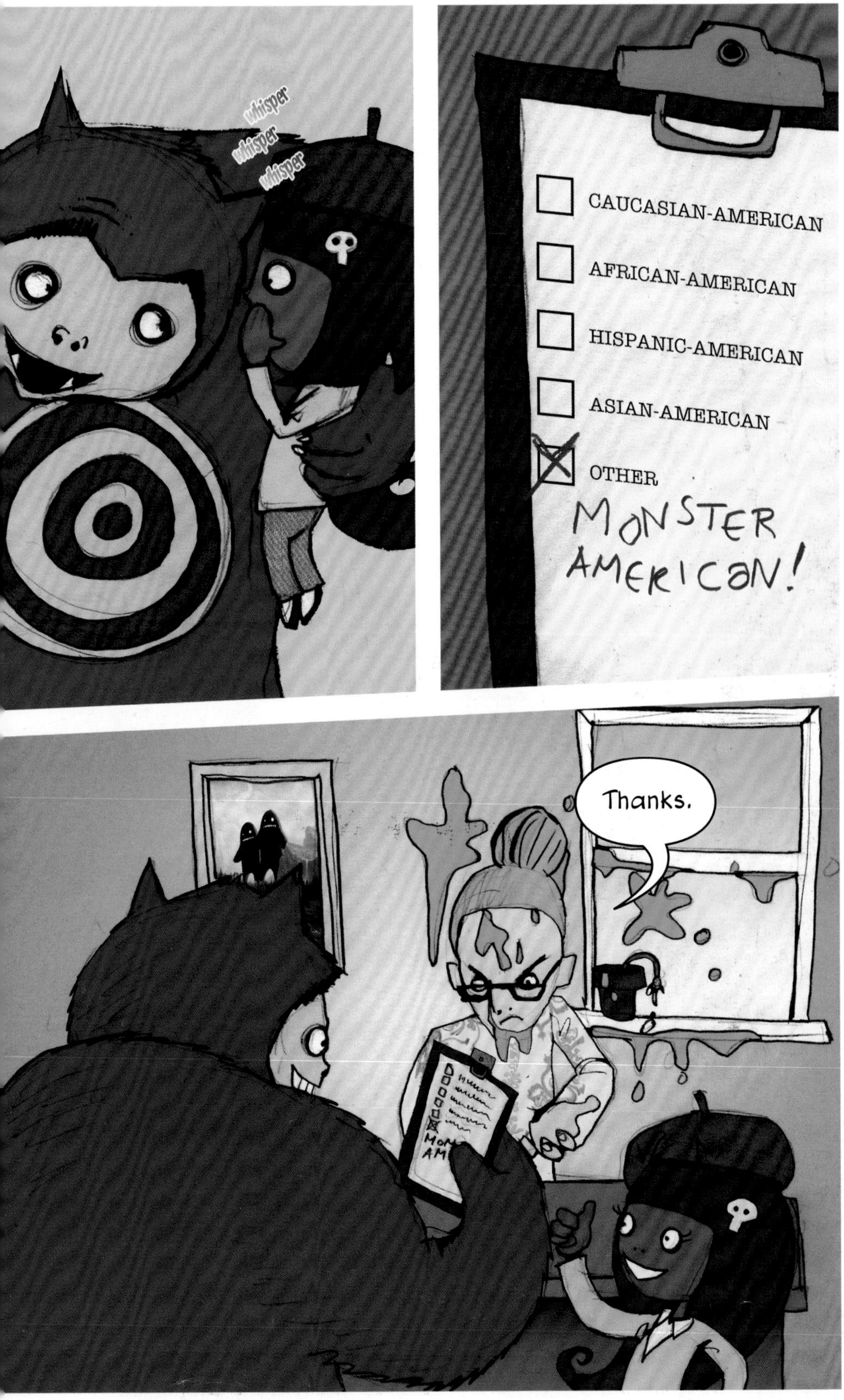
whisper
whisper
whisper
CAUCASIAN-AMERICAN
AFRICAN-AMERICAN
HISPANIC-AMERICAN
ASIAN-AMERICAN
OTHER
MONSTER AMERICAN!
Thanks.

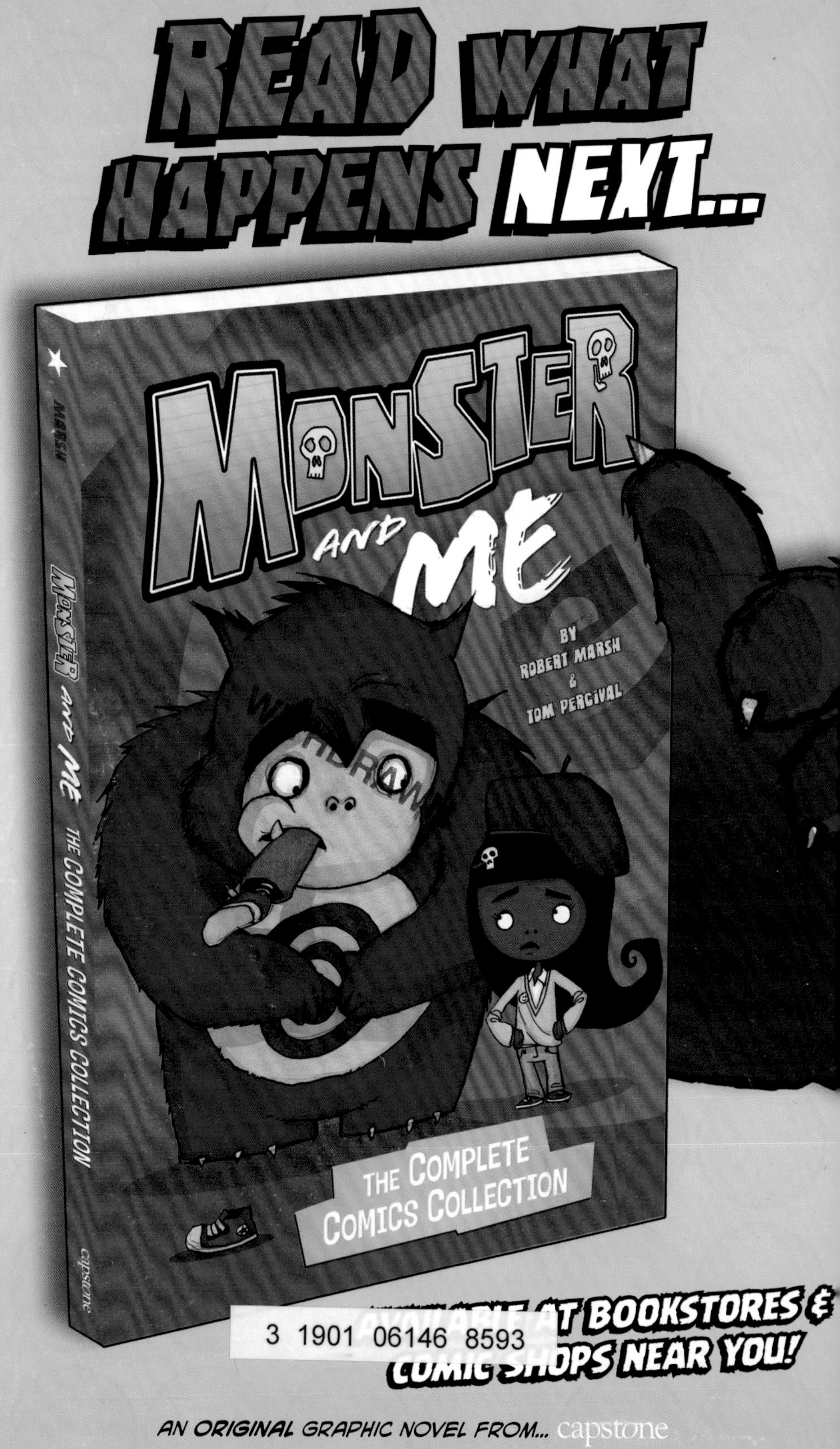
MARSH
MONSTER AND ME THE COMPLETE COMICS COLLECTION
capstone
MONSTER AND ME
BY
ROBERT MARSH
&
TOM PERCIVAL
THE COMPLETE COMICS COLLECTION